# LOOK NO FURTHER

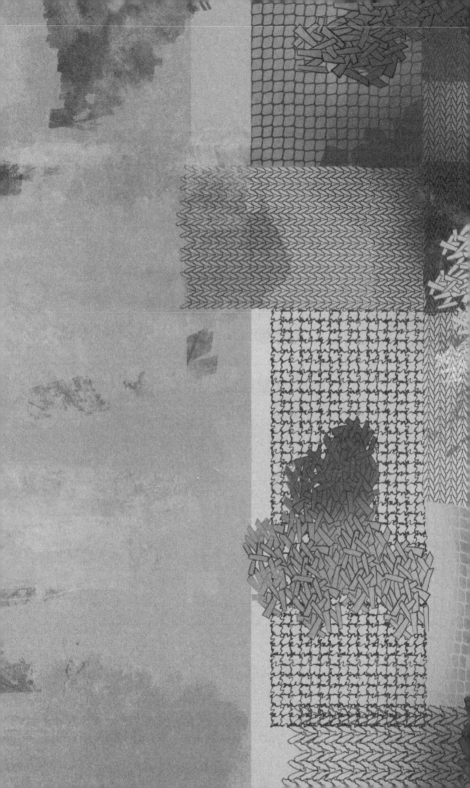

# LOOK NO FURTHER

RIOGHNACH ROBINSON
SIOFRA ROBINSON

AMULET BOOKS • NEW YORK

Cataloging-in-Publication Data has been applied for and may be obtained from the Library of Congress.

ISBN 978-1-4197-5740-2

Text © 2023 Abrams
Book design by Chelsea Hunter

Printed and bound in U.S.A.
10 9 8 7 6 5 4 3 2 1

Amulet Books are available at special discounts when purchased in quantity for premiums and promotions as well as fundraising or educational use. Special editions can also be created to specification. For details, contact specialsales@abramsbooks.com or the address below.

Amulet Books® is a registered trademark of Harry N. Abrams, Inc.

**ABRAMS** The Art of Books
195 Broadway, New York, NY 10007
abramsbooks.com

*To Ah Mah, with our love.*
*And to Ah Kong. We miss you.*

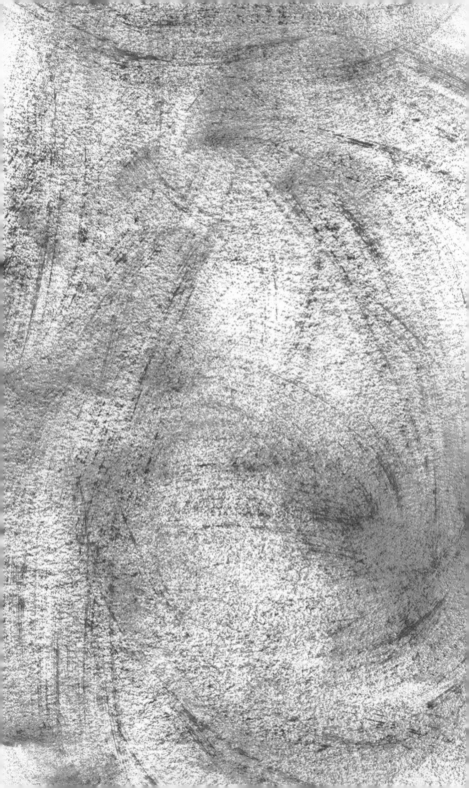

# Chapter 1

## NIKO CASTADI

This rejection envelope is bigger than I expected it to be.

I weigh it in my hands, eyeing the *Ogilvy Summer Art Institute* logo on the front, the small metal seal on the back. Actually, the envelope could be described as more of a packet. It's like there might be a folder in here with documents inside. Documents that aren't just the sentence "No, and also who do you think you're kidding," phrased in a fancier way.

I tear the envelope open. My mouth grows dry.

No way.

"Niko, honey?" calls a voice from upstairs. "Did you remember to take out the trash?" My mom emerges on the second-floor landing, her long blonde hair held in one fist as she prepares to tie it back in a ponytail. She stops at the top of the steps when she sees my face. "Niko? What's going on?"

I hold up the folder, which has a huge, orange CONGRATULATIONS! printed diagonally across an abstract background.

"I got into the Ogilvy summer thing," I tell her blankly. "They took me off the waitlist."

My mom lets out a small shriek and drops her scrunchie. "Phil! Phil, come here!"

My dad barges out from his office, his gray eyes wide in panic, like he thinks the house is under siege or something, and my mom starts exclaiming, and it's all washing over me in wave after wave of disbelief. I don't get it. Did my parents bribe someone to get me off the waitlist? My GPA is hovering in the mid-2s, and the application was such a rush job. Three days before the submission deadline, I still hadn't written a word for either of the essay questions.

In my defense, the prompts were terrible. The first was, "Why do you wish to enroll in the Ogilvy Summer Art Institute?" In the end, I made up a generic page about wanting to broaden my artistic horizons, since I've lived my whole life in a tiny California tourist town. But my honest answer would have gone something like this:

Dear Admissions Committee:

To tell you the truth, my parents are forcing me to apply because they think your summer program will turn my college prospects around. Having seen my grades, you'll probably agree this is both naïve and sad. Please reject me now so that we can all get used to the feeling of rejection early on! Thanks!

Niko

It's not that I don't want to go to Ogilvy. Art is the only subject at school I like anymore, the only one I've gotten an A in since freshman year. But I've looked through the Ogilvy website. With the number of times that they use the words "elite" and "high-achieving," I thought it was obvious this wasn't going to work out.

The second essay question was even worse: "What makes you unique?"

I mean, come on. Where do application writers get these god-awful questions? You want me to look at my entire life and describe, in under five hundred words, what makes me an individual person? You want me to know, psychically, what I've got that every other person in the stack doesn't?

I don't think I'm unique. There, I said it. The thing we're apparently not allowed to admit on applications. I think I'm mostly the same as other people, and I've got no interest in sitting down and thinking about how I might be different. Is that supposed to feel good? Separating myself out from everyone around me?

If they'd asked, "What makes you similar to other people?"—now that I could answer. Like everyone who's grown up in Landry Beach, I'm mostly sick of the town but would fight to the death to defend Egghead, that breakfast place on the corner of Seventh and Shiloh. Like everyone at school, I fill out basketball brackets in March and talk shit about my friends' choices, and when one of us predicts a freak upset, we gloat about it for months. Like both of my best friends, I want to go to CSU Monterey Bay. None of us know what we want to major in. We've got that in common, too.

I *do* have some interests besides art. I've been surfing forever, and for a year or so, I've been pretty into weightlifting, too. I like the way my arms feel heavy when they're sore. I've put on a decent amount of muscle in the last year, and I like looking at myself and feeling like I've got control over what I'm seeing.

But who puts this stuff into applications? I'm not making the Olympic surfing team anytime soon, and admissions officers don't let people into programs for being excited about their hobbies. Having interests doesn't make me unique. It makes me normal.

The Ogilvy people must have seen something unique in my application, though, because here it is. *Congratulations. How to prepare for your transformative five-week Ogilvy experience.*

Still, I know the truth: that I squeaked in off the waitlist. Looking down at the welcome letter, all I can see is a promise that everybody at camp is going to be an artistic genius. And then there'll be me.

My parents are chattering excitedly now, talking about booking flights to New York and how I have to start packing soon. I nod, try to smile. I should be excited. Instead my stomach is churning, a feeling I know too well from surfing—that spinning, directionless feeling of being underwater.

"Now," Devin calls. I pop up on my board, and the moment my feet hit resin, I can feel the whole Pacific Ocean rolling under me, pushing and pulling under six-foot-three of board.

The wave roars, lifting the three of us. Swell's up at a head and a half, and the wind is nice and low, so the waves have been decent, no unexpected shifting or crumbling.

I stabilize myself, arms out and crooked. There's swearing from my left. That'll be Grayson getting tugged out to the corner—didn't get out fast enough. He always has trouble catching lefts.

But Devin and I slip down onto the face no problem. Foam hisses at my side and back. Salt air washes into my mouth so I can taste it.

Ten feet away, Devin's steady in a low crouch, his board holding at the bottom. I'm hanging in the steepest section, seawater flecking my bare back, the wave peeling beautifully to my side. The hollow of the wave is gorgeous, steady and supportive, the roll of thousands of pounds of water somehow easy to balance under the soles of my feet.

Ahead, some kids on the golden strip of beach are pointing at us, and I glimpse the tropical green of Hailey's towel and the relaxed incline of her body. The June sunshine is full but not too bright. For the first time since the Ogilvy letter arrived, I feel relaxed.

Devin lets out a whoop as the wave runs itself out, leaving us both in the shallows. "Next one?" he calls, a wide smile on his sunburned face.

"Might be the last one in the set," I say, squinting back at the ocean. The tide's coming down, and we've gotten lucky the last twenty minutes.

"Hey, wait up, assholes," Grayson calls as he paddles toward us.

"Nothing to wait for," Devin calls back, kicking a splash of water at Grayson. "We're heading in."

Sticky with salt and sweat, we slope up the beach. Devin's board slips off his shoulder, and he gropes to replace it, his lanky limbs all over the place. Grayson, who has twice Devin's muscle, laughs and shoves Devin's board out of place again, and soon they're getting into a fake tussle. As usual, they're starting to make idiots out of themselves as we approach Hailey and her friends.

I don't blame the guys. Even now, after a month of us dating, it's unreal to me that Hailey Maxwell towed her friends across town just because I told her I'd be surfing today. I still think about her like that sometimes, with the full name, *Hailey Maxwell*, like she's still an impossible crush instead of my girlfriend.

To be fair, she's full-name Hailey-Maxwell to everyone else at Landry High. Back in the first month of freshman year, our class of three hundred somehow magically decided which dozen kids everyone was going to admire, envy, and gossip about for the next four years. Hailey topped the list.

So, this February, when Mr. Elliott rotated our seating chart in English and seated me next to her, I already knew way too much about her. I knew which law firm her dad owned. I'd heard about her ex-boyfriends—both captains of varsity sports named John, a weird enough coincidence that the entire school joked about it. And I'd watched Hailey pulling up to school in the morning dozens of times. It's always this whole production. Every day at 8:15, she and Gigi Pace and Kelsey Whitney slide out of Kelsey's Tesla in unison, beautiful and laughing and holding lattes, their perfect hair shining around their shoulders. They are the girls who define the phrase "out of your league."

When Hailey started talking to me before English, I told myself it was nothing. Then she started taking a longer way to Precalc so we could keep talking after class. That was harder to ignore. Soon there were arm touches, and eye contact, and other things I thought about obsessively at home while failing to focus on algebra.

By April, we were doodling on the edges of each other's notes, and on the last day of school before spring break, we walked down the hall from class in silence, then stopped at the spot where we usually split ways. Hailey shook back her hair and said, "So?"

"So what?" I said.

She reached out and tugged one of the straps dangling from my backpack. "So, Elliott's going to rotate the seats after we get back. I won't get to read any more of your essays."

I laughed. "Yeah, how are you going to survive?"

She raised her eyebrows. Hailey can get away with that sort of stuff, raising her eyebrows instead of responding, like it's your job to entertain her. The thing is, it feels good even for her to do that—to want more from you.

"I could text you essays about how the surfing's going," I said, casually as I could.

"Do that," she said, handing me her phone.

Now, as we stop beside the girls, Hailey levers herself up on her forearms and lifts her sunglasses onto her golden hair. Her eyes are the kind of blue you hear songs about, the kind that get compared to oceans or skies. "Do I know you?" she asks.

"Mm . . . I don't think so. Kind of weird that you're lying on my towel."

It's the right answer. She and her friends laugh. Around Hailey's group of friends, there's always a right answer, and you can always tell when you give the wrong one—one that isn't cool or clever or careless enough.

Devin and Grayson complain about that, but I don't have a problem with it. It's like a game. No reason to mind, if you know how to win.

"How were the waves?" asks Kelsey with an ironic edge. She says most things with an ironic edge and never sounds curious about anything. It's more like she lobs questions at people to see how they'll embarrass themselves.

"Waves were great," I tell her. "Why, you want to get out there?"

"Oh, yeah. I've been super excited to drown lately," says Kelsey to Gigi, squeezing seawater out of her dark hair. Gigi laughs. This seems to be Gigi's main interaction with her friends: laughing and agreeing. Hailey says she's shy.

"We're about to head out," says Grayson in the voice he always uses around girls. It's deeper, slower, self-consciously manly. It sort of gives me secondhand embarrassment, but I never say anything about it. Grayson is five-foot-four. Things are tough out there for short guys.

As the girls pack their tote bags, I scan the beach. Everyone in Landry Beach complains about summer because of the tourists. The towels are a dozen rows deep today, and the shallows are ninety-five percent toddler. But secretly I love the whole cycle, the way the crowds pour in at the start of summer, the easily impressed kids and parents who'll clap for anyone halfway decent at surfing. I love the closing-time atmosphere in early fall, when the vacationers trickle out and leave the beaches trampled and peaceful, the hot dog and snack stands wheeling away until it's just the sand and sea again.

Ogilvy means five weeks away from all this. Five weeks of long distance with Hailey, too, and it's not like we have some year-long relationship to bank on. I had plans to impress her this summer, especially on the trip we were all going to take weekend after next.

Hailey hoists her bag onto her shoulder, straight-backed as a ballet dancer, and glances my way. "What's up, Niko?"

"Nothing." As we wind between sunbathers toward the parking lot, I hike my board higher. "But just so y'all know, I'm not going to be in town next month after all, so I can't do Pismo Beach."

Devin and Grayson stop arguing about whether a chunkier board does better on hollow waves. "Why?" Devin says. "Where are you going?"

I shrug and explain the surprise Ogilvy acceptance in as few words as I can.

"Niko!" Hailey exclaims. "Why didn't you text me? That's amazing!" She drops her tote bag on the dunes and flings her arms around me, pressing a kiss to my cheek. She smells like sunscreen and lemon. I relax against her for a moment.

As she pulls away, Devin says, "Bro, I knew this would happen." He shoves me with a grin. "I knew they'd let you in."

"What? No, you didn't. Why?"

We approach the edge of the lot and Grayson's SUV, sand scraping between our flip-flops and the surfacing asphalt. "You know," Devin says. He makes a jittery little gesture at my face. "You'll go great on their admissions pamphlets."

The others laugh. I tilt my chin dramatically, saying, "Oh, yeah, my modeling career's about to take off"—pretending that's what he meant.

I don't focus on the heated prickle under my skin.

"Wait, wait," says Grayson, looking confused. "Seriously, Niko, why'd they let you in? I thought it was a crazy overachiever camp."

"It is."

Hailey gives me a playful smile. "Oh, so it'll be a hundred other Asians. But like, legit Asians."

The prickling under my skin intensifies. My smile starts to feel strange on my face, but I keep it in place. "Yeah, that's probably where the admissions people got confused."

The others laugh again. As we load our boards onto the rack and tie them down, I run my hand through my hair, suddenly wondering if it's still got any volume in it. The back of my neck is hot, although I applied enough sunscreen to ward off a burn for the next year. "I mean," I say, "it's not like it's a math camp or something, though. I think it'll be cool."

Hailey says, "No, of course, it'll be amazing! I'm just teasing."

She kisses me before we climb into the car. When her lips slip against mine, some of the heat leaches out of my body. I reach up and tug her hair out of its bun so it falls in salt-damp waves down her back, and she smiles into our kiss.

"Get a room," Grayson says, rolling down the driver's window. I give him the finger before breaking away from Hailey.

As we shut the car doors, Hailey launches into a story about how much she loved New York when she visited last summer. Kelsey, who went with her, chimes in occasionally from the back, sounding less ironic than usual. Gigi makes wistful noises.

I try to relax back against the SUV's middle seat as Grayson takes us out onto the road. I'm breathing steadily. But the prickling under my skin is still there.

It feels hypocritical to get annoyed about the Asian jokes, since Hailey and my friends aren't the only ones who make them. I do it, too, playing around that I'm a ninja on the waves, pretending to have some great understanding of the food at Lee's Chinese. Still, school stuff feels touchy. People make so many jokes about nerdy Asian kids. In comparison to all that, it's always felt weirdly good to be a slacker at school and more into sports. I guess the logic there is, maybe I'm an idiot, but at least I'm not a stereotype.

Anyway, I get bored of all this getting brought up. Sometimes I think, *OK, I get it, I look Chinese*. I don't know why people have to talk about it so much.

When I look over at Hailey, I soften right away. Her cheeks are burned, and she gives me that half-smile, the one that makes me feel like I'm the only one who gets to know her secrets. This is Hailey. She texts me memes from across the classroom like she can't even wait until the end of the period to talk to me. She snuck out to the beach with me at three in the morning. She gets me.

"Bro," says Devin.

I startle and look up to the passenger seat. "What?"

He's tying back his long hair, which looks like it's on fire in the sunset. "I said, when do you fly out?"

"The camp's in Manhattan, right, babe?" Hailey adds, cracking a tin of breath mints.

"Oh. Yeah. And I head over next Saturday. Gone for five weeks."

Devin whistles. "That's fucking cool, man. You've got to paint me something when you're there."

I find myself laughing. "Dev, I'm not a painter. They're not going to teach me how to paint from scratch."

"He didn't say it had to be a *good* painting," drawls Kelsey from the back.

Hailey cracks a smile and offers me the breath mints tin, and I see it's filled with the weed gummies her sister sometimes gets her. "Here, take like six of these and suddenly you'll be the next Dalí."

"Yes," Grayson half-yells, turning the car onto my street. "Get high as balls and make me the world's worst painting of Devin. I can hang it up in my bathroom. He can be the guardian of the toilet."

Hailey's friends don't usually get my friends' jokes, but even they start laughing now, and as we joke about what the terrible painting should look like, the heated feeling under my skin melts away. I don't know why I keep getting in my feelings about the Asian stuff these days. No one's trying to be mean.

We pull into my driveway. I lean over to kiss Hailey on the forehead, then jog up to the garage. After loading my board onto its storage pegs, I head up the back steps, and when I emerge in the kitchen, my parents are dicing a spread of vegetables on the counter.

"*Hi* there, Mr. Big Fancy Artist," my mom says with an ear-to-ear smile.

"Did you remember sunscreen?" asks my dad.

"Always do," I say, heaving a boulder-sized bottle of SPF 50 out of my athletic bag. That's life when your parents are paranoid dermatologists. But they both look a decade younger than they are, so, it could be they're on to something. Every time my friends' parents meet up with mine, they're all, *Celia, Phil, you* have *to tell us your secrets!* with a lot of eyebrow-wiggling, like they think the secret is plastic surgery.

"Niko, I am so excited," Mom says in that ringing, brassy voice that fills every corner of the room. "I can't stop thinking about how much you're going to get out of Ogilvy. Finally, something that's really going to motivate you." My dad nods so fervently that his glasses slip down his nose.

I give them a resigned smile. My parents have been waiting for me to show signs of motivation my whole life.

I don't feel like an unmotivated person. It's not like I spend all day lying around. But it's true that I'm not my parents, with their coffee-fueled work obsessions and their terminal degrees, or even my little siblings—Justin, who's twelve and has already blazed through Algebra II, or Anastasia, who's in fourth grade and reading *Great Expectations*. When my parents stress out about my siblings, it's because they're "too advanced" and "not being challenged." Those are Castadi family problems, the kind my parents understand. They're also so far from my experience at school that sometimes I feel like a different species.

I seriously doubt Ogilvy is going to change that. But with how much this camp thing is going to cost, I don't want to seem ungrateful. I say, "I'm excited, too. New York's going to be awesome."

"I want to go to New York," Anastasia announces from the breakfast bar, smoothing down the tutu she's wearing over a pair of wide-leg jeans. "Mom, why can't I go?"

"You're nine. You couldn't do anything interesting in New York," scoffs Justin, who's slumped at the dining table, circling answers in his vocabulary book. "If anyone else is going, it should be me."

I grin, knocking Justin's chair with my toe as I pass by. "Yeah, because being twelve makes such a massive difference, Turtle."

"Niko," Mom says sharply, her knife frozen mid-onion. "Uh-uh."

My dad continues cutting peppers. Anastasia's finger stops on her iPad game. She sneaks a glance at Justin, who isn't looking at any of us.

"Right," I say. "I forgot. Sorry, Justin."

"It's fine. I don't care," Justin mumbles.

Another uncomfortable pause. "I'm going to put my stuff upstairs," I announce over the hiss of onions hitting oil.

I head out of the kitchen fast. Soon I'm padding down the ivory-carpeted hall on the second floor, past Anastasia's bedroom door—

plastered with glossy photos of wolves—and past Justin's, which stands ajar to reveal his guitar lying on his black bedspread.

I measure out a breath, slowing at his door. I can't wait for things to get back to normal.

Back in April, my family found out that Justin had been bullying a kid at his middle school for most of the school year. Justin came home beat-up because the kid finally snapped and fought back, and ever since, he and my parents have been seeing a family counselor once a week. It's bizarre, looking at my little brother and thinking there's someone out there who could be described as his victim.

They haven't roped me into the counseling sessions yet, but a few weeks ago, my mom dragged me out to the grocery store like she sometimes does when she wants to talk with me in private. After parking the car, she said, "Sweetie, we've talked with Dr. Flynn, and we think it's best if you stop with the nicknames. The things you call Justin."

I felt a defensive twist in my stomach. "What? I don't call him anything bad."

"'Turtle' isn't the most flattering thing in the world."

"I call him Turtle because he used to be obsessed with turtles!"

"He's a younger sibling, Niko. It might be hard to understand. Embarrassing nicknames can create outsider feelings, so Dr. Flynn thinks it's best to take them off the table."

*Outsider feelings?* I almost repeated, incredulous. I hadn't wanted to say it. But it seemed so ridiculous and unfair, the idea that *I* could make *Justin* feel like an outsider in our family. Justin, budding math genius like our uncle, who always gets gushed over at Christmas by our grandparents, because "Phil, he looks more like you every year!" Justin, who's never had to deal with people thinking he's an exchange student or friend of the family when we're out in public.

"Justin didn't mess with that kid for six months because I called him some stupid nickname," I muttered.

Mom squeezed my shoulder. "Honey, I know. I said it all during the counseling session. And no one thinks this is your fault, OK?"

"Good."

"We're just trying to make sure Justin feels listened to. If you stop with the nicknames, it tells him you care about how he feels. Deal?"

So I've tried to stop, and other things have changed at home, too. Some of it is clearly better, like Dad being less hard on Justin for liking video games. But for every good thing, there's something uncomfortable. Last Saturday, my mom randomly turned off a movie we were watching because it had a bullying subplot. Cue the most awkward five minutes of silence I can remember. And if I'm honest, I don't love the feeling that my brother and parents are having these big talks about our family in a place where I don't get a say.

I reach the end of the hall. With a sigh, I close myself into what my mom likes to call my Art Cave. The term makes me sound like a weird hermit, but I guess my bedroom is sort of weird. I've avoided showing it to Hailey, anyway.

At this point, my walls are invisible, every inch up to the ceiling plastered with posters, photos, and clippings. Some classics are mixed in—stuff like *Starry Night* and *The Persistence of Memory*—but most of the pictures aren't prints. They're just pictures that kick my brain in new directions. Shapes or colors that always feel fresh. I've got maga-zine cutouts of spaceships and deep-sea animals. I've printed photos of strangers from the 1920s off an online archive. Above my bedside table, I taped a cave in South America, filled with water so aquamarine it looks like chemical fire. I spent two whole weeks in art class trying to re-create that exact color blue.

My eyes catch on the NYU pennant by my window. I study it for a moment. I know my mom and dad have given up on me getting into their alma mater, but they're probably still hoping that the colleges I apply to next year will accept me. There's no doubt Ogilvy will help with applications.

I sigh, drop my athletic bag by my desk, and pick up the Ogilvy pamphlet with its smiling, multiethnic group of model children on the front. Flipping through it, I feel a tug of curiosity.

I pull out my phone. *Ogilvy S*, I type, and tap the result that autofills *Summer Art Institute*. I page through their site again, just to make sure there's nothing new, but it's the same spiel I saw when I applied: *Welcome to Ogilvy Summer Art Institute, the single most prestigious learning opportunity for artistically inclined high-school scholars.*

I roll my eyes and hit the back button. After scrolling past sponsored articles and college FAQ pages, I spot a post on a young artists' forum. *What's the Ogilvy Summer Art Institute like?* the original post says. *I'm considering applying!*

The first response reads: *haha those professors are crazy they 100% treat you like college students. my friend hooked up with 3 different people in 2 weeks and no one cared at all. vibes are good. apply for sure*

The second post says: *I heard they asked one kid to leave because he wasn't sufficiently dedicated to the program. Which is a lot.*

To my empty room, I say, "What."

But then I read the third response: *Ogilvy is AWESOME. I went three years in a row and it definitely helped me get into RISD. The professors are attentive and teach unusual classes you wouldn't get in high school. Plus the mid-camp trip upstate is beautiful, and the other attendees are some of the most talented, interesting people you'll meet. I met some of my best friends there.*

I toss my phone onto my bed, run a hand through my hair. I still don't get why they let me in, but it might be nice to have some time away from home. Maybe when I get back, the house will feel normal again. Maybe Justin will have worked through his issues in counseling, and he'll have realized what's already so obvious to me: He fits in with our exceptional family a hundred percent. I bet in five years he'll have no problem getting into NYU.

*Outsider feelings,* I think, rubbing my forehead. *Jesus.*

Without really thinking about it, I reach for an abstract sculpture that stands on the shelf above my desk. The piece is a foot tall, smooth and light in my palms. A delicate papier-mâché shell surrounds a carved piece of blond wood with a slender, graceful shape, like a single tongue of fire. The paper composite isn't bleached or painted. It's covered in Chinese characters, put together from a Chinese-language newspaper.

My mom married Phil when I was four, so I've always thought of him as my dad. It was Phil who taught me to ride my neon-green bicycle up the cul-de-sac, who whooped when he took off the training wheels, who hugged me in third grade when our beagle died and I cried so hard my head pounded.

This sculpture in my hands is the only evidence of my other dad. My biological dad.

My mom hardly ever talks about him. There's not much to tell: They had some one-night fling on Long Beach Island when my mom was doing her residency. She never managed to track him down again. I know that he was Chinese, obviously, and I know that his first name was the completely un-Googleable "Bo." And I know that he'd just finished this sculpture the night he met my mom. She'd complimented it, and he'd said, "If you like it, it's yours." I feel like his number would have been a more useful takeaway, but maybe that's just me.

Still, ever since I started getting into art back in middle school, part of me has felt drawn to my dad's sculpture. It's like nothing else in our house, maybe like nothing else in Landry Beach.

But now, as I look down at the printed columns of Chinese, Devin's and Hailey's words ring in my ears again. *You'll go great on their admissions pamphlets . . . It'll be a hundred other Asians, but like, legit Asians.*

I set the piece back on the shelf, suddenly annoyed with myself. For the first time, I wonder why I keep coming back to the sculpture. I don't know what my dad was trying to represent with it, and I can't read what's written on it. It doesn't make me more of an artist, or more in touch with the Chinese stuff. If anything, it should remind me how far away that other life is from me, the one I might have had if my dad ever knew I existed.

As it is, Hailey's right. I'm the furthest thing from a legit Asian. I get that people look at me and see someone Chinese, but my whole life has played out within ten miles of this house. If people could look inside my head, they'd see Landry Beach and its waves. They'd see my parents, Californians four generations back, raising me on Westerns and Bruce Springsteen. That's all. Sometimes people ask me where I'm from, and I say, "Here," and it comes out sounding urgent, like I need them to believe me.

I don't want to get defensive about this stuff—just want to make things clear. I have everything in common with the people around me.

I'm not unique. I belong.

# Chapter 2

ALI TAN

Even with Jessie and Elise sitting together on my suitcase, I still can't zip it closed.

"I think I'm going to have to downsize," I sigh, opening it up to see what I can purge.

"Did you pack your *entire* wardrobe?" Jessie asks, pulling things out haphazardly. "It's one summer. I don't think you'll need three different pairs of tights."

"Or a bright red faux fur coat. Unless there's some kind of Cruella de Vil–themed party that they forgot to mention in the application?" Elise throws the coat onto my bed behind us.

"It gets cold in the air-conditioning!" I protest, stuffing the coat back into my bag. I ignore the skeptical look on Elise's face. I *need* to pack the few cool and interesting articles of clothing I own. It's the *Ogilvy Summer Art Institute*. In *Manhattan*. The single most prestigious learning opportunity for artistically inclined high-school scholars. I'd rather show up dressed for the wrong season than wearing my usual boring, nerdy uniform of baggy T-shirt and out-of-style jeans. Which is why I have to fit that red coat into the bag.

"Well, if you forget anything super-important—" Jessie begins.

"—like maybe a pair of snow boots—" Elise interrupts.

"—we can always bring it to you."

"Thanks, guys." I sigh, collapsing on the floor between them and fanning myself in a mock-swoon. Jessie takes a casual selfie of us while we're flopped next to each other, then hands her phone to me to assess. Jessie's gap-toothed grin seems to take up half the frame; Elise's slim face and shy half-smile are barely in the photo. I'm squeezed in between, my eyes closed in laughter. We're all Chinese, but they're both full and I'm half, and my shoulder-length, mousy hair stands in contrast to their long, shiny black ponytails.

We all grew up together here in Flushing, the biggest Chinese neighborhood in Queens, and nearly everyone at our school—Queens Senior High School for Science and Math, a specialized public school that we all had to study our butts off to get into—is also Asian. By contrast, I couldn't help but notice during my many hours browsing the Ogilvy website, waiting for my acceptance, just how white the students and professors in the photos were compared to QSSM. All white, all creatively dressed, and, judging from the hefty sticker price—I got a full scholarship—likely all rich. I wonder if I'll fit in at all.

"I know it's only five weeks, and it's not that far, but I feel like I'm moving to a foreign country," I admit.

"Art camp is *totally* a foreign country," says Jessie. "How do you even grade art? Isn't it all subjective anyway?"

"I'm not sure if there are grades at Ogilvy. But I'm not going so that I can get good grades. I'm going so that I can grow as an artist and learn from some of the art world's foremost minds." I pause. "Also, it's not really a camp. It's more of a program."

"Well, I'm glad you've already spent some time memorizing their website," Elise teases. "I can't wait to see what kind of stuff you come up with. You're the best artist I know."

"That's not true," I protest. "Well, OK, it's probably true. But that's just because we don't know any actual artists."

"Soon you will!" says Jessie. "And you have to promise not to forget about us when your paintings are hanging at the Met."

I know she's mostly kidding, so I don't bother to tell her that my dream is the Whitney, not the Met, and that I'd be happy just being able to make art full-time. Like my dad. My eyes go to the picture on my bedside table of our family, taken ten years ago, when we were all still living here: my dad, my mom, my grandma, and me.

"She totally will," says Elise. "She's going to come back from camp all cool, with a nose piercing and a photographer boyfriend—"

I throw my pillow across the room at her. I've never had a boyfriend, or even admitted to having a crush on a guy. Elise and Jessie have an ongoing joke that I'm too cool for the boys at our high school and that someday I'm going to bring home some extremely handsome, older artist. This has only gotten worse since I got into Ogilvy, and I don't have the guts to tell them I hate the joke. I don't want a boyfriend, from our high school, or Ogilvy, or anywhere.

A girlfriend? That's a different story.

But Jessie and Elise are here for dinner whenever their parents work late, and I don't trust Jessie to keep her big mouth closed around Nai Nai. I've only told one person I'm queer: my mom. She's the one who suggested I not tell Nai Nai right away, that Nai Nai is a little old-fashioned and might not understand. Not that it's really relevant; I've never even been on a date with a girl, so it mostly just . . . hasn't come up.

To my relief, before Jessie or Elise can pick the joke back up, Nai Nai comes into the room with a Styrofoam container so large I can't see her face behind it. She sets it down next to my suitcase with a groan.

"I made you some food," she says, lifting the lid to show me what's inside. Columns of deli containers are stacked to the top, full of my favorite things: noodles, rice, and three different types of dumplings. "Need to put in freezer as soon as you get there. Should last a couple weeks."

"Nai Nai, there's enough in here to feed the entire dorm for a couple weeks. Besides, I don't even know if I'll have access to a fridge. All our meals were included in the price."

She shakes her head in a gesture that definitely means "We both know you'd rather eat this than that crap." Which is true, of course. But I don't want to show up with a whole box of food that's only going to go bad underneath my bed.

"I promise you that I will let you know first thing if there is a fridge," I say. "I'll text you about the fridge before I even tell you that I've arrived safely or that my roommate is a serial killer."

"In the meantime, I think you could probably use some help eating some of this," says Jessie, eyeing the noodles.

Pretty soon, the four of us are settled around our small kitchen table, chewing happily. I take my usual spot by the window, which is cracked to allow a cool breeze into the otherwise stuffy room. The sound of cars honking drifts up from the streets four stories below. All my senses are soothed by the familiar voices, sounds, and smells.

Nai Nai asks Jessie and Elise what their plans are for the summer, then sits back, content to listen as we chatter, more to each other than to her. I'm never sure how closely she's paying attention when we talk among ourselves. I think it just makes her happy to have a full and lively table.

"I'm working in a lab," Jessie says through a mouthful of food. "It's the same place my brother interned at a few years ago. Doing experiments on mice and stuff." This sounds like my personal nightmare, but for some reason, Jessie thinks it's the coolest way she could spend her time.

"I'm going to be shadowing a doctor at the hospital where my mom works," says Elise. Elise's mom is a nurse's assistant in an intensive care unit. The idea of being responsible for all those people hanging between life and death feels like more pressure than I could handle.

Nai Nai never graduated from middle school. She came from Shenyang to the United States in her thirties as a widow, when my dad was a teenager. She found work as a tailor in a dry cleaner's and raised me basically by herself. Sometimes I feel guilty about how many doors are open to my friends and me, just because of where and when we were born, when so much of Nai Nai's life has been just about getting by.

I've never said this to her—I don't think either of us quite has the words to talk about things like that—but I also know what she would say if I did. She'd tell me that the whole reason for the choices she's made has been so that I could do more than just get by.

I'm not sure if Nai Nai wishes I were doing something more academic, like what Jessie and Elise are doing. It's not like I'm going to the Summer Art Institute because I *can't* do science or math. It's just that art is the only thing that really gets me going. But Nai Nai gets quiet whenever I talk about my art, in a way she doesn't when I talk about school.

I tried to explain this to Jessie once, and she didn't really understand. "I get it," she said. "My parents really want me to do something practical."

I don't think Nai Nai is worried about art being impractical. I think she worries about me ending up like my dad.

My dad was—*is*—a sculptor. I have a few early memories of him. Not of his face, but of black T-shirts covered in dust and the way they smelled like sweat and clay and glue. I think he was gone from home a lot even back then, and when I was five, he left for good. Nai Nai never really talks about him, and I learned early on not to ask questions because it made her sad. She'd pretend to misunderstand the question, or busy herself in the kitchen and drift away from me. So, I don't really know anything about why he left, or where he is now, or if he stays in touch with her. My mom also refuses to talk about him—she says that if Nai Nai doesn't want to talk about him, we both need to respect that. I suspect she's partly using that as an excuse because it's such a painful topic and *she* doesn't want to talk about him.

The fact that art is my best subject, the thing I spend all my free time doing, is something that we mostly just don't discuss. I didn't even tell them I'd applied to the Ogilvy summer program until I'd gotten news about my scholarship. Nobody had tried to deter me from going; they didn't even appear disapproving. If anything, both Nai Nai and Mom had seemed studiedly neutral about the whole thing. I decided to take that as a win.

"Are you artistic, too?" Elise asks Nai Nai, laying her chopsticks down on her bowl.

Nai Nai laughs and shakes her head. This is not true—she's an incredible tailor, and she's made wedding dresses for some of the women in the neighborhood. But she wouldn't consider that *art*.

"Where do you think Ali gets it from, then?" asks Jessie.

I haven't told them much about my dad. I don't want them to feel sorry for me or ask follow-up questions that I don't have the answers to. They know he left when I was little, but I pretend that I don't remember him at all and that I'm perfectly satisfied with just my mom and Nai Nai.

I fully expect Nai Nai to respond with a shrug and a smile, her usual answer when she feels like being private, but instead she gets up and goes into her bedroom. The three of us look at each other, a little confused.

She comes back in and puts a binder on the table. "Ali's dad was sculptor," she says, opening the cover. It's full of amateurish photos of sculptures, clearly taken by someone who loved the artist more than the art, probably by Nai Nai herself, or maybe my mom.

I've never seen this before. I try and hide my surprise, irrationally worried that any dramatic reaction from me will break the moment and Nai Nai will take the binder away. Jessie begins to paw through the photos without so much as a glance at me, but I think Elise can tell that I'm a bit shocked.

"These are awesome!" squeals Jessie. "Why didn't you ever show us these before, Ali?"

I shrug. I feel frozen in place, like if I let myself move, I'm going to shove Jessie out of the way, grab the binder, and run to my room where I can pore over all the pictures in private.

Jessie and Elise page through curiously. I look on, too, suddenly wildly impatient for everyone to finish up, get bored, and leave.

That night, after Jessie and Elise have hugged me goodbye, I'm helping Nai Nai clean up. The binder sits on the table, somehow in my peripheral vision no matter which way I turn. I'm hoping that we'll sit down together and she'll tell me more about the pictures. "Thank you for the binder," I start.

Instead of taking the opening, she just smiles. "I'm going to bed. You finish cleaning up?"

I recognize this as her way to say that we aren't going to talk about it. Still, this is the closest I've felt to my dad since I was a toddler. I hurry through the dishes and finally shut myself in my room with the photos.

I lie in bed, poring over them until it's past midnight. It's a cliché, but looking at his work, I feel so inspired. I can't believe that starting tomorrow, I'll get to devote all my time to art, instead of squeezing it into a forty-five-minute period at school or evenings and weekends. Sometimes I feel like a superhero with a secret identity: an ordinary student by day, focused on my classes, an artist by night, freely myself. It's also a nicer way to think about being closeted.

My excitement about the summer is once again crowding out my anxieties, and a flurry of *what ifs* spins through my head: What if I find an incredible mentor? What if I really am talented, like my dad? What will it be like when I don't need to bury the sides of me that are incompatible with the version of myself I am at home? What will it be like to eat, breathe, and sleep art, and maybe even fall in love?

I wonder, as my eyelids start to grow heavy and the lullaby of muted street sounds quietly edges in over the stuttering roar of my air-conditioning unit, whether my dad felt the same all-consuming need to *create*. I feel like that must be true. Otherwise, why else would he have left?

I have one last goodbye to say before I leave. My mom moved to Long Island four years ago, right before I started middle school, to move in with Anand. Until then, she'd lived with me and Nai Nai. She had her own room, and Nai Nai and I slept in the other.

I didn't know enough at the time to think it might have been weird for her to live with her ex-husband's mom, but when you're a little kid, you think the world revolves around you. And I guess that impression was basically accurate: They lived together to make it financially possible for them both to raise me, different as they are.

Nai Nai did the cooking, Mom did the child-wrangling, and all three of us shared the cleaning. I was the go-between when they didn't understand each other; Nai Nai's English is pretty basic, and my mom's a white lady from Maine. After more than a decade under the same roof, Mom learned enough Chinese that she understands *some* of the things we say. Nai Nai and I found that out when we tried to plan a surprise birthday party in front of her and she interrupted, loudly, in English: "I hate surprises and I hate cake and I hate my birthday—you all know this about me already."

They have more than just me in common. Mom is a fashion designer. She worked in Nai Nai's tailoring shop to help pay the bills, and sometimes the two of them would sit late into the night, Mom with her sketches and Nai Nai with her sewing, while I drifted off to sleep in the next room.

When I was in fifth grade, Mom met Anand, who's basically the opposite of my dad in every imaginable way. He's an aggressively punctual math teacher whose small house on Long Island has no art whatsoever, only a million framed photos of his parents, cousins, siblings, and now, my mom and me. I moved into his house when she did and started a new middle school in the suburbs. It was OK. Anand is a nice guy and a great cook. I had more space than I'd ever had before, my own room, and a backyard.

But I ached with homesickness and missed Nai Nai, who hated venturing out of the neighborhood. I would beg to go back to Queens every weekend, and my mom would have to take me on the subway so I could sit in our old apartment. I heard her and Anand having hushed conversations about whether I was "adjusting" or not.

After a year, I asked if I could move back in with Nai Nai. My mom seemed sad but not surprised. Moving back to Flushing didn't solve everything—now instead of missing Nai Nai, I missed my mom—but it was better, being back in the apartment and neighborhood that felt like home. And unlike Nai Nai, my mom comes back to Queens every weekend, so I see them both more this way. Mom feels worse about it than I do, but Nai Nai just tells her these kinds of living arrangements are normal in China, that when parents leave the countryside to find work in cities they often leave the kids with their grandparents.

And six months ago, my mom—marching to her own beat as always—proposed to Anand, with a set of matching rings she'd designed herself. Since then, she's been deep in the weeds of planning their wedding, designing her own dress, sketching out floral arrangements, asking me what I think of the fonts on her invitations.

I'm sitting at the kitchen table, eyes flicking back and forth to the clock on the stove. I wanted to leave an hour ago, but she's late, as usual. She came into the city just to wish me goodbye, so I feel bad being critical, but I'm impatient for the summer to begin. My suitcase is packed, I'm dressed and ready to go. Where *is* she?

Finally, I hear the familiar sound of jangling keys and footsteps taking the stairs two at a time. My mom bursts through the door, blonde waves stuck to the sweat on her forehead, and my resentment fades away.

"I'm so sorry I'm late," she says. "I couldn't find my keys for twenty minutes, and then I decided to drive because I'd missed the train, and then I couldn't find parking in town—"

"It's fine. It's really OK."

She wraps me in a big hug. She smells like sweat and lavender, and for a moment it feels like the way things used to be, with all of us living under the same roof.

"I wanted to tell you something," she says, her voice muffled in my hair. "I'm going to India for the rest of the summer. So I'm going to be nine hours ahead of you."

I draw back. "Why?" I ask. It comes out sounding more annoyed than I meant it to.

"I've still never met Anand's grandparents, and he wants me to before the wedding. I thought the best time for the trip would be when you were busy with your program. Besides, Anand only gets summers off."

"Why can't they just come here?" I realize I sound annoyed because I am, in fact, annoyed.

"They're getting old, and . . . well." She looks at the floor, then smooths out the wrinkled fabric of her linen dress. "We can still call and text," she adds. "We'll have to be a little more organized about it, but they have great service at their house. Anand video chats them all the time."

"It's fine," I say. It's not, but I don't really know how to say that. *I don't want you to meet your future in-laws while I'm at a full-time program, because I want to be able to text you at every waking hour*, is not a reasonable request.

But I've never spent more than a night away from home before, and I'm already apprehensive. It feels childish, but I liked knowing how close they would be if things went wrong at Ogilvy. Besides, I know that "being a little more organized" about scheduling video chats is something Mom will talk a big game about but be absolutely incapable of doing.

She's looking at me with concern wrinkled into her forehead, her blue eyes enormous.

"Let's just go get bubble tea," I say. Following the movements of our favorite ritual is the easiest way to put these feelings away. By the time we're walking down the street together, sipping our sweet, cold drinks, I feel almost normal again.

Three hours later, Nai Nai and I emerge, squinting, from the subway into bright sunshine. She insisted on accompanying me, despite her usual reluctance to leave the neighborhood, and honestly, I don't mind. Obviously, there's only a river and a subway ride separating us, so if I truly get homesick, I can go home and it will cost less than three dollars. But I've already firmly promised myself that leaving is not an option. I don't know if I'll ever get this opportunity again.

There's so much I'm nervous about, though, that I'm glad to have

Nai Nai by my side. I'm nervous about the big things—like, what if my art is terrible, and I haven't realized it?—but maybe even more nervous about a never-ending list of small things—like what if the cafeteria food is inedible or if my roommate snores and I can't sleep a wink?

At the same time, the fluttering anxiety in my stomach mixes with my bubbling excitement, and I can't tell where one stops and the other begins. I have so much energy, I want to break free of my grandmother and sprint ahead like a dog off-leash.

It's no more crowded than our neighborhood, but I can tell Nai Nai feels out of her element anyway. There's something about *knowing* you can yell at someone who's in your way, even if you don't act on it, that makes you feel more confident. Nai Nai's English is totally adequate, but she's still shy in front of strangers.

One big difference, though, between this neighborhood and ours is that every storefront has been decked out for Pride Month. Walking past a bank whose windows are covered in rainbow decals, all of a sudden I'm self-conscious, as if I've been dragged out of the closet by a Wells Fargo.

I wonder if Nai Nai has noticed or if she's going to say anything. *Please don't*, I wish. I feel like if she says something negative, it will reflect on me doubly, like I'm a bad granddaughter for being queer and also a bad queer person for loving my grandmother. I think I prefer the limbo of not crossing the coming-out bridge until I have to.

But wait—what if I meet someone this summer and I want to cross that bridge? Won't it be better if I know what I'm up against? I quickly change my wish: *Please say something!*

She looks up at me and smiles. I'm small, but she's half a head shorter than me, even including the extra two inches added by her perm. She gestures toward a rainbow flag outside a bookstore. "Everything is rainbows now," she says.

*What? What could that possibly mean?* I open my mouth to ask her, but I nearly run into someone. There's a line snaking around the block, and a sign at the front reads OGILVY SUMMER ART INSTITUTE. We've arrived.

We join the line, and as we inch closer to the door, I can't help but notice that everyone looks older and cooler than me, and I'm the only person in line who's brought an adult. It suddenly feels juvenile to have my grandma drop me off on my first day of the Summer Art Institute. On the bright side, nobody seems to be paying me any attention, and it doesn't seem like they all know each other already. Everyone is glued to their phones, looking (or trying to look) nonchalant.

As we inch closer to the front, I entertain myself by studying the outfits around me, admiring the dress of a girl standing a few places ahead. It looks handmade, with a voluminous skirt made up of different brightly colored floral prints.

Finally, Nai Nai and I pass through the doors into the cool, sunny foyer. My heartbeat patters faster. The space is huge, filled with light and people. On a wall opposite us, twenty feet tall, hangs a line of portraits of imposing-looking white men—old Ogilvy presidents. The floor is a gleaming plane of freshly waxed stone, interrupted every so often by black pillars that display sculptures under glass prisms.

When we get to the front of the line, I sign in at a desk staffed by two college students. An extremely large, bearded guy hands me my ID badge while a girl with an undercut looks sidelong at Nai Nai and says,

"I'm not sure if you're allowed guests up in the dorm rooms. Security has been pretty strict all day."

"That's OK!" I blurt, secretly relieved to have an excuse to say goodbye. I don't want my roommate to think I'm not capable of spending a few weeks on my own, even if *I'm* not sure I'm capable of spending a few weeks on my own.

I quickly hug Nai Nai. "It's only five weeks. I'll see you so soon! I'll text you a picture of my dorm room." Before she can say anything, I roll my suitcase toward the sheer black wall, following the signs for the elevators. I reach the corner, where the elevators are dinging and whirring down the hall. By the time I look back, the line has moved on, and I don't even get to give her a final wave. I try to ignore the totally disproportionate wave of regret that this causes me.

I ride the elevator to the seventh floor and pull my suitcase through the halls uncertainly, looking for room 705. The dorm is exactly what I would imagine an art school to look like, if that art school were also in outer space. The deep-blue carpeting is so plush and dark. I can barely make out the numbers on the doors, since the doors are black and recessed into shaded niches, and the numbers are, inexplicably, a different shade of black.

Of course, I immediately forget to text Nai Nai a picture. In my defense, it's because I open the door and see my roommate for the summer balancing on the headboard of her bare twin bed, pinning a Pride flag above it.

"Hi," I call, tentatively.

She looks over her shoulder, nearly slipping. She curses, turns back to put the final pin in the flag, and hops off lightly. Only once she has landed on her feet does she greet me, sticking out her hand with a bored expression. She's white, nearly as short and thin as me, with bright, bleached blonde hair in a pixie cut and at least four visible piercings in her right ear alone.

"I'm Ali," I say, shaking her hand a little uncertainly. I'm not used to shaking hands with people who are under fifty.

"Brook."

I try not to feel intimidated. Brook looks older, like a junior or senior. And she's startlingly, carelessly pretty, with cool gray eyes and an amused mouth. And maybe I wish I could look that casual while hanging up a Pride flag.

Brook nods to the door. "I was about to head down for dinner. I can wait for you if you want to change, or . . . ?"

"Oh, I don't want to make you wait!" I exclaim.

"OK, see you down there, I guess."

I have not been clear, apparently. "No, I'll just come like this!"

Her eyes slide over my outfit, taking in the pit stains in my gray T-shirt, my ill-fitting running shorts, and my mismatched socks. She opens her mouth as if she's about to say something, seems to reconsider, and finally just walks to the door and holds it open for me.

I follow her down the hall. I know my outfit is embarrassing. I want to explain—I dressed for the weather, not for a first impression. But it would be rude to make her wait while I unpacked and found something better to wear.

I'm on the verge of saying this when she says, jabbing her finger against the elevator button, "Dinner's on the ground floor. It's smart to get there early, otherwise all the nearly edible food will be gone."

I laugh. "So, you've been to Ogilvy before?"

"This is my third summer here. I'm going to be a senior next year. I take it you're a freshman?"

"I'm going to be a sophomore in the fall!"

"Cool. Well, welcome to Ogilvy," she says, taking out her phone. "I was supposed to save some seats for a couple of my friends, but it looks like they're not getting in until later this evening." She pauses, as if considering. "We could sit together, I guess?"

I almost thank her, then think better of it. I, too, am an artist. I, too, deserve to be here. So I stand up straight, and then I, too, take out my phone, tap around aimlessly for a second, then say as nonchalantly as I can: "That sounds fine to me."

"Sorry," I mumble, lurching back from a woman who gets so close that I catch a noseful of fruity perfume. A few other New Yorkers shoot death glares at my suitcase, and I haul it out of the subway turnstile. The wheels squeal on the dirty tile as I back into a corner.

I've been making this last-second, guilty-looking move for hours. I didn't realize it until I got to this city, but apparently, I'm a slow, relaxed person who loves to take up space.

I look back down at the map on my phone. It's 11:15 P.M., and that little blue line connecting me to Ogilvy has shrunk to a centimeter.

*Almost there.*

I haul my suitcase upstairs onto the sidewalk, panting in the hot night air. Today I spent eleven hours navigating delayed flights and layovers, only to land in a heat wave. I've sweated so much that when I glance into a reflective storefront window, I see a dark, wet shape stamped onto the back of my T-shirt.

But somehow, I'm not miserable. Actually I've felt light all day, even hauling sixty pounds of luggage around. It's a relief not to be at home.

Technically, things are getting better around the house. Last week, the counselor pitched this idea that Justin and my dad should take a programming class online together. Now they spend every night at dinner talking about their coding projects and answering my mom's questions. As for my mom, she's started buddy-reading *Sense and Sensibility*, her favorite book, with Anastasia.

So things are getting back to normal, just like I wanted. I should feel good. I should be happy about the counseling breakthrough.

But instead, in the back of my mind, I've started to have this picture of our family growing closer and closer together, with me at the corner of the frame getting squeezed out to the side. And all because Justin hurt another kid. It seems like we're just pretending that part didn't happen.

I got written up a couple times in middle school. Being inattentive, disrupting class, that sort of thing. I didn't get bonding time with my dad as a punishment, that's for sure.

You can get away with so much when you're *such a brilliant kid with such a promising future*.

But for the first time in days, with Manhattan making noise around me, I can shove those thoughts away. I drink in the city as I tug my suitcase down the sidewalk. Cars tear down six lanes, drifting into and out of place with taps of their horns. Air conditioners hum, rattle, and drip, set into the brick and concrete buildings that soar up toward the grayish night sky. Thousands of silhouettes stir above me in yellow-lit windows.

Even when I follow the map onto a narrow one-way street, the noise of traffic doesn't vanish. The air has a different sound here. It's this subdued, ambient loudness, like the muffled roar of a jet turbine when you're inside the plane.

I roll my luggage past a line of row houses. Across the street, ivy tumbles down the face of a stone wall, and just beyond, there it is, lit up like an aquarium. OGILVY ART INSTITUTE stands out across a wall of sheet glass in bright white sans serif.

When I push through the glass door, the temperature plummets fifteen degrees. I stifle a satisfied groan and unsling my backpack, taking in the huge, deserted foyer. Its towering portrait wall. Its dozens of sculpture plinths. A few paces away, a heavyset security guard with a nametag reading *Stan* sits behind a welcome desk. Stan has watery blue eyes, a smooth bald head, and a crisp black button-down.

"Can I help you?" he asks briskly.

"Hey, yeah. I'm Niko Castadi. I'm here for the camp."

"For the Summer Art Institute?"

I hesitate. "Uh, right. Sorry I'm late—I called ahead."

"Yeah, I've got the note." The way he speaks is dismissive but not unfriendly. He picks up a landline, taps a few numbers, and waits, bobbing his head like he's keeping time to an inaudible song. "Arthur," he says. "Your straggler's here."

I wince. Great first impression.

Stan hangs up. "He'll be down." He eyes my clothes. "Long day, kid?"

An exhausted laugh tumbles out of me. "Yeah, you could say that."

Soon an elevator's *ding* comes from the corner of the foyer, where a hallway creates a break in the portrait wall. A tall, spindly man with a graying ponytail moves out of the corridor. He wears a three-piece suit the color of slate, and sweeps more than walks, like a bird of prey gliding down through the atmosphere.

"Mr. Castadi," he says, stopping before me. "I am Dr. Abbott, professor in two-dimensional mixed media. This way, please." He points me toward the hallway without even glancing at Stan.

"Thanks," I call back to Stan, who waves in acknowledgment.

As our footsteps echo across the foyer, Professor Abbott drops a paper bag into my hands. "Your student materials. ID badge and lanyard are to be worn at all times. You'll find your room assignment and schedule in the packet . . . and we do expect punctuality. Understood?"

"Yes," I mumble. My mouth has grown dry. From Abbott's vibe, you'd think he was here to bestow some kind of Nobel Prize for Art, not teach a summer camp.

We turn down the narrow corridor. A pair of elevators stand to the left, and the hall ends in an eye-wateringly orange wall with a set of double doors. "The Richard P. Stover Dining Hall," says Professor Abbott, indicating the doors, before directing me into an elevator. "Breakfast is served from eight to nine tomorrow."

He thumbs the eighth floor button, and the car hums up. "Curfew began at 10:30; I expect empty halls upstairs. Your roommate may already be asleep, so be conscientious."

I tug my welcome packet out of the bag and find my room assignment. Below my room number is information about my roommate.

**Andrew Hong, 16, Seattle**
**Interests: Frogs, bass guitar, Naruto**
**Medium: Photography**

My mouth is even drier now. I didn't list a medium on the roommate application.

"Feeling prepared, Mr. Castadi?" Professor Abbott asks with a look of cool expectancy.

I wonder if he can see my nerves. The truth is, the fancy foyer and the welcome wagon are driving home what I've signed up for. What if I fail out of Ogilvy? Abbott looks like he'd be delighted to sign off on that. What if they send me home, like that kid on the forum who got kicked out for not being sufficiently dedicated?

I want to ask if I'm supposed to have a medium yet, but I feel like "Dr. Abbott, professor in two-dimensional mixed media," would take that as a sign of weakness.

Instead I say, "Yeah. I feel great, thanks."

The elevator door opens, and I struggle to hide my surprise. After a few college visits with my mom, I assumed I knew how Ogilvy's residence halls would look: drab grayish carpeting, maybe some cheesy affirmation posters. Wrong. Ogilvy's eighth floor is a gleaming stretch of dark hardwood, and neon light fixtures zigzag across the ceiling. So many prints, paintings, and sculptures hang on the walls—with small white plaques, the whole deal—that I feel like I'm standing in some secret wing of a contemporary art museum.

We step out of the elevator, and Professor Abbott levels one hand at the door to our right. "My suite. I am the live-in supervisor for this session, so, in the event of a medical or . . . emotional emergency." He almost grimaces. "You know where to find me. Questions?"

"Um, yeah. Where's the bathroom? Am I allowed to take a shower?"

He points down the hall and gives my sweat-soaked T-shirt a withering look. "Showers are enthusiastically encouraged."

He disappears into his suite, leaving me to scowl at the closed door. Like, OK, guy who wears a three-piece suit during a hundred-degree heat wave. We weren't all born without sweat glands.

As I wheel my suitcase toward the bathroom, I slip my phone from my pocket and pull up a new text to Hailey. **miss you already**, I text one-handed.

Hailey never texts first, but she always responds within seconds. **Wow that's so embarrassing . . . do you like me??**

I smile. **idk where you heard that rumor but don't spread it around.**

She snaps me a picture of herself lounging on her sofa. Her long hair is splayed on a velvet cushion, soft and bright. An almost-smile teases at her strawberry-glossed lips. **So what's your plan for art camp?**

I slow, then stop in the middle of the hall. Murmurs and laughs are muffled behind the other doors. Exhaustion is starting to make my thoughts blurry, but Hailey's right. If I don't want to fail out of Ogilvy, I need a plan.

*You got in*, I tell myself, holding my phone more tightly. Sure, it was off the waitlist, and it was probably because Ms. Ryan wrote me a recommendation letter full of exaggerations, and obviously Professor Asshole Abbott didn't cast the deciding yes vote. But I *did* get in. That must mean that someone here thinks I can handle this place. Even that I deserve it.

I'm not an endless fountain of motivation, I'm not a high achiever, I'm not *such a brilliant kid with such a promising future*. But still. I'm here.

I feel a weird sparking sensation in my chest and realize it's pride. I don't hate the feeling.

**I think my plan for art camp**, I text Hailey, **might actually be, hold on, wait for it, to try at art camp?**

**Omg who are you?**

**Lol i don't even know anymore.**

**The next Dali?? ☺**

**maybe. :)**

I wake up in a room I've never seen before.

Last night, after the most satisfying shower in human history, I snuck into a pitch-dark room filled with the snores of Andrew Hong from Seattle. Now I check out the dorm for the first time. A tinted glass window stretches floor to ceiling, and on the walls, painted polygons of deep violet float across a base of pale blue. As for the opposite bed, it's a mound of clothes and cables and books, like my roommate dumped his suitcase on it before sprinting out the door.

I glance at my phone and startle halfway out of bed. It's already 8:30. I'm late to breakfast, not even nine hours after Professor Abbott's whole "we do expect punctuality" speech.

I throw on my usual outfit. Jeans that fit well. A single-color T-shirt, navy blue today, snug around my biceps if I flex. The same kind of Nikes that dozens of guys at Landry have. It's like a uniform. Wearing this, I could walk into any place back home and look average.

I don't bother unpacking, except for my dad's sculpture, which I tease out of its bubble wrap. First I set it on the corner of my desk, but then I hesitate. My roommate will probably ask about it if I keep it out. I crack open my dresser instead and tuck it inside.

I'm wasting time. I dash down the hall to the elevators, still massaging product into my hair, my ID badge bouncing on the lanyard around my neck.

The halls are deserted. I'm going to be the last one to show, again. Not a great start for my win-at-art-camp plan.

On the first floor, voices echo beyond the double-doors. I hold my breath before slipping into the dining hall, catching the door behind me so it won't slam and draw attention.

I guess I've adjusted to Ogilvy's vibes, because the industrial steel ceiling, the forty-foot-long mural of what looks like a single kidney bean, and the scattering of neon green tables barely register. As for the eighty kids sitting at those tables, no one sends a single glance my way.

Neither do the table of teachers near the opposite wall. Professor Abbott's head is bowed over a stack of papers.

I let out a long, slow breath and head for the buffet, my muscles relaxing.

As I wind between the tables, I eavesdrop, wondering what the other Ogilvy kids are going to be like. What I overhear isn't the most promising thing in the world. Two different groups are talking about this neighborhood (the "Lower East Side," apparently) like they've been here a thousand times, which makes me wonder—is this whole thing just going to be eighty kids from New York City, and a few stray imports like me?

I also hear one kid declaring something about "constructivism in the consumer sphere," which is sort of worrying. I barely know anything about art history. I could point to a Picasso versus a Monet, but even in advanced art at Landry High, Ms. Ryan didn't teach us about "constructivism in the consumer sphere," whatever that is. Her classes are studio time and more studio time, which is why they're famously the easiest A at Landry High.

I enter the buffet line. As I finish scooping eggs and sausages onto a plate, a chipper voice bursts out next to my ear, "Hi there!"

"*Aah.*" I cringe away and nearly knock my tray off the buffet rails.

"Ooh, ha ha, sorry," says the beaming man who's appeared beside me. The guy is roughly six and a half feet tall, and *huge*—broad-shouldered, big-armed, feet the size of ciabattas. Size aside, though, I've never seen anyone more nonthreatening. His rosy cheeks and bushy beard make him look like a novelty lumberjack toy. Also, he actually said the words "ha ha," so there's that.

"I saw you come in," he says. "I'm Chris Carlson, the Summer Art Institute director. You must be Niko."

"Um—yeah. Hi."

For a moment, I worry that he's going to lecture me about being late, but instead he ushers me toward the kidney bean mural, saying, "This way, here!"

I follow him across the dining hall. Soon he stops in front of a table full of East Asian kids, three boys and two girls.

Actually, as I glance around the dining hall, I realize it's the only table with East Asian kids.

"Everybody," says Chris to the table, "this is—"

"Roommate!" hollers one of the guys, jumping up. He looks younger than me, maybe sophomore-aged, and he's dressed as though he's trying to look like a cool college professor: tortoiseshell glasses, tweed jacket with sleeves rolled to the elbows, and tapered slacks. But he has an unpretentious face, a shaggy mop of black hair framing an easy, lopsided grin.

He bounds at me with hand outstretched. "What's up, man? I'm Andrew Hong. You're Niko, right?"

I shake. "Yeah, nice to meet—"

"Sorry I didn't wake you up! I was going to. I thought about it. But I wasn't sure if you got in at like 4 A.M. or something."

"Um, all good."

"Well, that's that!" says Chris. "I'll leave you all to it."

As Chris jaunts off, annoyance pricks the surface of my skin. Maybe he brought me to this table because my roommate's here, but it definitely feels like I got shoved in a box with all the Asian kids right away. What if I don't get along with any of these people?

To be honest, they don't seem like the type of kids I usually get along with. Back at Landry High, the art kids basically max out at dyeing their hair and wearing colorful makeup. They've got nothing on this table. The two guys beside Andrew are obviously brothers, one with a full sleeve of tattoos, the other with a destroyed Gucci sweatshirt. One of the two girls wears a black cardigan over a black turtleneck, with black high-waisted pants. She looks like an evil librarian. The other girl has hair dyed bubblegum pink, plus a dress that looks like it was cut from plastic bags and stitched together with Christmas-themed ribbons.

*She could be here for fashion design*, I tell myself, trying not to get too judgy. It's an art camp. Of course some people are going to dress like this.

Still, these are obviously kids who had no issue writing the "What makes you unique?" essay. And I don't know why, but that kind of person gets on my nerves. A lot of the time, with the loud, wacky Landry theater kids or the athletes-slash-class-clowns, I just find myself thinking, *Sit down and be normal. Appreciate how nice it is to feel normal.*

I glance over my shoulder longingly. Not even ten feet away is another table of kids who are wearing things like T-shirts. The guys sitting there even sort of look like Devin and Grayson.

But Andrew is pointing eagerly to the seat beside him and I'm not a *complete* asshole.

I sit and lift my hand. "Hey. Niko."

"Hi" bounces around the table. Pink-hair girl chirps, "Should we do, like, an icebreaker or something?"

"Yes, but it has to be Ogilvy-themed," says evil-librarian girl in a cool deadpan. "We can give our names, hometowns, and our favorite arcane fact about the life of Anselm Kiefer."

*Shit*, I think, forcing a smile while everyone else laughs. Here we go. I have no idea who Anselm Kiefer is.

"I'm Nathalie Xiao," adds the serious-faced girl to me. "This is Jen Soriano, my roommate."

The pink-haired girl flutters her fingers at me. Her smile is all dimples.

The two brothers nod my way, too. "I'm Wu Haoran," says the older one, whose tattoos look weirdly fancy under the rolled sleeves of his white linen button-down. "And this is my little brother, Wu Haolong. We flew in from Beijing yesterday."

"It was a long flight," yawns his brother, who looks like he might be a freshman. Along with the Gucci sweatshirt, he has an enormous golden watch buckled over his wrist, and both brothers have leather-detailed Burberry bags hanging over the backs of their seats, too. *They're actual Crazy Rich Asians*, comes a thought out of nowhere.

I avoid their eyes, mortified for thinking it. But even as I try to tamp down the embarrassment, I'm wondering about the order of their names, too. I know last names go first in Chinese, and tattoo guy introduced himself as Wu Haoran. But if *Wu* is his last name, which one am I supposed to use?

"Let me guess," says Nathalie across from me, still dead serious. My heart skips a beat. There's no way she could tell what I was thinking, right?

But then she says, "You've noticed some . . . demographic coincidences."

The others start chortling again. My stomach unclenches. "I *told* you," Jen adds to Andrew through tiny laughs like hiccups. "Didn't I say?"

"Uh, say what?" I ask.

Andrew shoots a look of tired amusement my way, an *I-know-you'll-understand-this* kind of look. With a sweeping gesture around the table, he says, "Behold! The roommate assignment people paired up all the Asians."

"How did they even know I'm Filipina?" says Jen. "Everyone in Louisiana always thinks I'm Latina because of my name." She tugs her hair out of its ponytail and starts winding a long, pink strand around her fingertip. "Not that I'm complaining. This is more accurate." She raises her right hand and says, "Asian as charged."

The others grin, except for Nathalie, who cuts a stern look toward the professors' table. "We *should* be complaining. I think it's tone-deaf of them. 'Hi, welcome to Ogilvy. You aren't white. Obviously you have to get along based on this one criterion.'"

"Jen, did you check the Asian box on the application?" Andrew asks.

Jen's mouth opens in a little "O" of realization. "I did. I forgot about that."

"Everyone here check the box?" Andrew glances around the table.

We all nod. I remember hesitating over the question, feeling weird about every possible answer. *White* felt like more of a lie than *Asian*, and *Choose not to answer* seemed suspicious, so . . . Asian it was.

"There you go," Andrew says with a sage air. "Never check the box. Especially for college apps! You don't know what admissions people are thinking about Asians."

Nathalie raises her eyebrows. "Yes, Andrew. If I don't check the box, no one will ever guess that I, Nathalie Xiao, am Asian."

The table breaks into laughs again, but when I try to force a chuckle, it sticks in my throat. God. I feel so awkward for some reason. Maybe it's because I've never hung out with a group like this before. There are a dozen Asian kids at Landry High, tops, and I don't run in the same circles as the others.

I glance between these kids. Nathalie's making notes in a small leather journal, Andrew is comparing his schedule to Haoran's, and Haolong protests as Jen tries to steal his baseball cap. I feel like they should be able to look at me and see that I'm different—that I grew up in a white family, that I've never been to Asia, that I don't feel like a real Asian.

"All right, everybody!" calls Chris from the staff table, waving both hands above his head for quiet. "Welcome, welcome to another year at the Ogilvy Summer Art Institute, and welcome back to our fabulous returning students. We are so excited for this year's programming. We've got an incredible lineup of teachers for you and fantastic classes designed especially for this session."

Chris's face splits into another big, eager smile. "I'm also so proud to announce that this is by far our most diverse year at Ogilvy. We've been developing a series of outreach initiatives over the past few years, and—well, you can see the results around you."

He aims his smile in the direction of our table but looks away quickly. Maybe he's seen the disgusted look on Nathalie's face.

My annoyance is back, too, stronger than before. So—what, did we all get in because of an outreach initiative? Is that what he wants the rest of the camp to think? Because I can see dozens of faces quickly turning away, having sneaked looks at us, and I'm pretty sure that'll be their takeaway.

I feel a fresh wave of discomfort. I wish I weren't sitting here.

Also, the announcement doesn't even make sense. At a scan of the cafeteria, this place seems barely more diverse than Landry High. Besides the kids at our table, I see exactly two Black kids, one girl who looks Indian, and maybe two or three who could be Latin. I saw more diversity in five minutes on the subway last night.

Chris is rolling along with his speech. "You might already have glanced over your schedules, which are at the back of your welcome packet . . ."

Sudden sounds of flipping and rustling fill the cafeteria. Chris laughs. ". . . or maybe not. OK, take a minute, look them over."

I page quickly to the end of my packet. A calendar shows the five weeks of camp split into color-coded scheduling blocks. Besides the required classes—workshop sessions, and something called Technical Foundations—I'm also signed up for classes called Art and Heritage, Overview of Art History, and Abstracting the Figure. The last one—*great*—is taught by Professor Abbott.

I try not to feel too disappointed. I'd put Abstracting the Figure and the history class on my list, but only as alternates, and I hadn't put Art and Heritage anywhere. But probably by the time I got off the waitlist, most of the classes were already full.

"As you can see," Chris exclaims, "we'll be taking a trip upstate for the second half of Week Two, and we'll end with a public showcase at the end of Week Five. We'll also have a dance at the end of Week Four, to let off some stress from working on those brilliant, gorgeous, world-changing showcase pieces."

Some laughs skitter through the cafeteria, but my gut has dropped. A showcase. Of course there was going to be something like this, some big final exam situation. All the Ogilvy kids probably thrive on stuff like that. They're probably the type who look forward to the SAT.

*You're an Ogilvy kid, too*, I remind myself. I reach for those sparks of pride I felt last night. I imagine cupping them in my hands, blowing on them so they flare.

I've done big art pieces before for Ms. Ryan's class. This doesn't have to be any different.

"Apologies to you returners who already know all about the show-case process," Chris goes on, "but for those of you who are new, let's talk through it. At the end of Week Five, we'll bring those showcase pieces out into the foyer, set up a professional-level gallery display for every one of you, and open the building to the public."

Chris gazes into the distance as though dazzled by the imaginary display. "You'll want to try your best with these showcase pieces, not only to push your abilities as an artist, but because the blue ribbon winner will be awarded the Alicia Barry Prize for Artistic Excellence. The prize comes with a $5,000 cash fund and will signal the winner as a young artist to watch—not just for college and conservatory admissions, but also to galleries here in New York City and elsewhere. This is the opportunity of a lifetime for young artists."

OK. So maybe it'll be different from the pieces I made in class back home.

Chris keeps up the energy, introducing the dozen other faculty members, but I've lost the thread. Their names and faces blur together. Across the table, Jen is whispering in a steady stream to Nathalie about the showcase components she packed in her suitcase. Nathalie gives the occasional approving nod, like she also did this.

I think back to studio hours with Ms. Ryan. Only now, facing down five full weeks of nonstop art, do I realize the approach Ms. Ryan took to teaching us at Landry High: She was trying not to scare us off. "Art is a place to relax," she always told us. "It's somewhere you never have to be intimidated or worried."

I liked that. There was never a wrong answer with Ms. Ryan. Here, though, I can feel the competition in the air, the pressure to be capital-g Great. Mostly, that makes me want to walk back into my dorm room and shut the door.

Mostly—but not completely.

Looking down at my watery eggs, I realize I'm imagining it just like Chris was. A gallery show in that huge light-filled hall, and a panel of judges moving between people's exhibits . . . stopping in front of something I made. Mixed into this feeling of pressure on my shoulders, there's something else. This weird idea that I could make something capital-g Great. And that feels different, like the slow rev of an engine at the back of my mind.

"So I'm messy," Andrew says as we head out of the dining hall side by side. "Like, room-wise. I'm really sorry about that ahead of time. Are you messy? If you're a clean person and you need things to be clean, please just tell me to fix my shit. I won't be offended."

"No worries. I don't mind mess, as long as it's—"

"On my side of the room? Absolutely. I won't let it get over the midway point. Promise." Andrew lowers his voice as a group of girls passes. "OK. Second important roommate question. What should we do if one of us wants to . . . you know . . . have some personal time with a lady friend?" He gives me a look of evaluation. "Or a guy friend? Or a friend of like, any gender?"

"Oh. For me it'd be lady friend. But, yeah, no. Won't be happening."

"Have some confidence!" Andrew crows, adjusting his glasses. "Everyone comes to this place wanting to meet somebody. It's basically a giant art-themed dating app. Here, let's go this way. Have you seen the sculpture yard yet?"

Before I can answer, or clarify what I meant about Hailey, Andrew holds a door open. We step out onto sun-dappled flagstones.

I glance up at the square of blue sky, surprised. From the street, Ogilvy looks like a solid glass cube, but this interior courtyard is big enough to hold a landscaped garden with dozens of sculptures lined along its walking paths. The pieces are glossed with morning sunlight.

Andrew strips off his tweed jacket and throws it over his shoulder, pushing the sleeves of his rumpled button-up to his elbows. "So, Nathalie and Jen are both, like, beautiful," he says in a low, secretive voice. "Actually, no, wait. Nathalie's beautiful. Jen is more pretty. Or cute, maybe?"

"Um," I say.

"You're right. The terminology isn't important. The point is, they're both, I *mean*. You know?" He gives me a hopeful smile. "Also, Haoran has a girlfriend back home, and Haolong is like just barely fourteen or something, so that's good for us. Good for me, I mean. If you're not interested, that's also good for me." Andrew gives me a once-over. "Great for me, actually."

I rub the back of my neck. "Thanks?"

"You're welcome." Andrew lets out a heated sigh. "Look, sorry if I seem weird about this. It's just, most of my friends are girls in Seattle, and none of them see me as dating material, I think because we've been friends for ages and stuff. But here I think my chances will be different." He brightens. "We're all into the same things, and Nathalie and Jen didn't know me when I was ten. Which has to be good. Right?"

"Right. But . . . uh. Which one of them are you interested in?"

"I don't know yet. Maybe both? We'll see!"

"Both?" I say, bewildered.

"Look, Niko." Andrew makes a gesture with his fists like he's trying to pull something out of his chest. "There's a lot of feelings in here. That's why I do art! If Nathalie or Jen liked me, I bet I'd like them back. They both seem cool."

I laugh, shaking my head. "Bro, I couldn't do that. I get one feeling for one person and I'm like, out of commission."

"Really?" says Andrew. "Weird."

"Pretty sure your thing is weirder."

He laughs, too. We've reached the end of the walking path. As we push through the east door and sink into the cool bath of air-conditioning, he asks, "What's your first class?"

"I have Art and Heritage. You?"

"The Organic Form," Andrew says cheerfully. "Like, bringing natural inspirations into your art and stuff. Shit is so perfect. I actually want to be a biologist, if the art thing doesn't work out."

**54**

"Oh, nice. Good to have a backup."

"See? So you *do* understand my girl philosophy." He laughs. "Sorry. I'm an asshole. I'm just kidding. I promise I'll be normal when we're all hanging out. See you later!" He salutes as he jogs for the stairwell.

I head on, feeling sort of overwhelmed. Mostly when I talk about girls with Devin and Grayson, it's two of us embarrassing the third, and the third person saying "shut up" in six different insulting ways. In the eight years we've been friends, I don't think Devin and Grayson have told me as much about their romantic feelings as Andrew did in the last five minutes.

Room 108 is ahead, and a few students have gathered in front of the door. They're reading a magazine clipping posted on a bulletin board: A BIG DEAL: LATONYA SHERMAN USES SCALE IN PORTRAITURE TO REENVISION HISTORY. As the others slip into the classroom, chatting in hushed, excited voices, I scan the article.

A photo shows a smiling, dark-skinned woman standing in a high-ceilinged art gallery. Her arms are lifted overhead, so the sleeves of her dress have pooled around her biceps, but her fingertips don't even reach halfway up the gigantic canvases on either side of her. Each painting must be sixteen, seventeen feet tall.

Both canvases are painted in psychedelic colors, their subjects' brown skin highlighted with streaks of cheerful orange or dabs of pale yellow. In one, a slender girl with short, glossy hair looks over her shoulder, her glasses reflecting a slash of electric pink. The other piece shows a woman in a wide-brimmed hat from a low angle, like the painter is gazing up at her from ankle height. The caption reads, *Sherman with paintings of Elise Dunnigan (l.) and Claudette Colvin (r.).*

I scan the article for details and find the names again:

. . . subjects like Elise Dunnigan, the first Black woman to work as a correspondent at the White House, where she reported for more than a decade before the civil rights movement. Claudette Colvin, at right, refused to give up her bus seat during segregation when she was fifteen years old, an action that predated Rosa Parks's famous protest by months.

Sherman describes the megalithic scale of the works as "the antidote to absence." In her collection, she explains, her subjects are reapportioned the space that generalized overviews of American history often deny to Black women . . .

I glance back to the portraits, hypnotized by the colors. For one of the women's dresses, pale blue paint is paired with red-violet, and it makes the cloth look so rich that I imagine pushing my fingers through the canvas and touching it. I can't believe that the woman who made these paintings is right through this door, about to teach *my* stupid ass about art.

Vaguely aware of footsteps hurrying down the hall, I shake myself away from the article and turn to enter the classroom. But the steps arrive faster than I expected. I'm halfway into the threshold when a tiny girl with dark blonde hair crashes into me and lets out a high, energetic noise like a startled cat. We both wheel off-balance on the waxed floor, and a folder in her arms goes flying, strewing images across the hall.

"Shit," I say, stooping to collect the pictures. "Sorry," we say at the same time.

"It's fine!" the girl says. "Totally fine. Here, I'll—" As she reaches for the photos in my hand, I spot the word "portfolio" written in block capitals across the folder. I return the photos, trying not to look at her art, but I glimpse the piece on top. It's pretty cool: a charcoal sketch of blackbirds sitting on a telephone wire. The shadows they cast on the brick wall behind them are done in different shades of colored pencil.

We hustle inside just as the woman standing at the front of the class turns from the whiteboard, where she's written "Art and Heritage." Even her handwriting is artistic: steeply angled italics, looping capitals.

"Ah, that's everyone," says LaTonya Sherman in a contemplative, honey-slow voice. "Good. Will one of you close the door, please?"

I nudge the door shut, and the blonde girl and I hustle to the two remaining seats, a pair side-by-side at a drafting table.

There's a moment of silence. Professor Sherman is watching the class with a small, closed-lipped smile. She stands with her feet pressed together, her elbows tucked close to her torso, while one long finger works thoughtfully at the corner of her mouth. In her striped floor-length dress, she looks like a collection of vertical lines.

She considers us for so long that I glance around the classroom, too. *Demographic coincidences*, says Nathalie Xiao's dry voice in the back of my mind. Of the eight kids in this tiny class, only two of them are white, counting the girl next to me. Art and Heritage is the exact opposite of the dining hall.

So, this is why the Ogilvy people assigned me to this class. I bite my cheek, annoyance itching at me yet again.

"Hello," Professor Sherman finally says, lifting her hand away from her mouth in a smooth wave. "I'm LaTonya. Please, no 'Professor Sherman'; I've always disliked that. Something"—she hesitates, lowering her long eyelashes—"yes, something artificial about it."

LaTonya ends on an upward inflection as though trailing away into thought. "This is the first time I've taught this class. How about that? I'm looking forward to exploring it together, the nine of us." She meanders around the front of the room, sidling past a rack of paintbrushes. "Art and heritage," she continues. "The two subjects go hand in hand, of course. Every artist inherits traditions, cultures, and worldviews, and whether we internalize or challenge those inheritances, in art as in reality, that's up to us.

"So, that might mean creating work about your family. It might mean reacting to your artistic lineage. Your influences; you've inherited those, too, whether you realize it or not. It might mean commenting on the place you come from, celebrating the parts of the culture you love or critiquing those parts you can't stand." LaTonya glides to the whiteboard, where she traces a second printout of the article with her huge-scale paintings. "It might mean filling in some blanks where other people see empty space, where you care and other people don't seem to."

After a tense silence, she lets out a warm, rolling laugh. "So, clearly we're going to have to get personal here. Let's get loose, OK?" She shakes out her long-fingered hands. "Let's get comfortable. Today, we'll get to know each other a little bit."

With that, the class introduces ourselves, and LaTonya follows up with our first task. "I want you all to find out something unusual about your seat partner's personal history to share with the class. And dig in.

I don't want a fun fact here. We're looking for discomfort. Something we can reach into and find art. OK?"

I wait for more explanation, but apparently that's it. Pairs turn toward one another and chatter fills the classroom.

I glance over at the blonde girl beside me, who also looks surprised that we haven't been given more specific instructions. I forgot her name during introductions, but I remember she's a rising sophomore. Even that's older than I would've guessed. She looks like an eighth grader, round-faced and stubborn-chinned, although her darting gray-green eyes are perceptive.

"I'm Niko," I reintroduce.

"Ali."

"Cool. Um, do you think I could borrow a sheet of paper? And a pencil?"

She looks confused. "Sure," she says, rummaging in her backpack.

"I left my stuff in my dorm," I explain. "I thought I'd have time to get it after breakfast."

"Oh. Right." She hands me the supplies, but her gaze flits around to the other tables, like she's confirming that she's the only one whose seat partner came unprepared.

Operation Win at Art Camp is really not going well.

"So, I guess we should . . ." Ali trails off, untangling her honey-colored hair. There's an uncomfortable silence. I wonder how seriously everyone else is taking LaTonya's instructions, but the kids at the other tables are speaking too quietly to hear. I drum my fingers on the drafting table, trying to look like I'm sorting through thousands of deep, interesting moments of my personal history, all of which I'd be totally fine with confessing to this total stranger and then our entire class.

It's horseshit, obviously. Hardly any part of my family life has been "interesting or unusual," and the things that *are* feel even less on the table. I wouldn't tell any of these people about the Justin bullying situation if they paid me.

Then there's my parents. The class is called Art and Heritage, after all. I bet that's the kind of thing LaTonya's looking for. What it's like to have my looks in a town like Landry Beach. What it's like to be half-Chinese while not knowing anything about China.

A stubborn knot forms in my chest. I don't want to talk about that with anyone. I don't want Ali to look at me like I'm an alien or a tragedy, like my life is so different from hers just because she's white.

Beside me, Ali looks reluctant, too. Her body has hunched up over the drafting table, as though she's looking down at something she's hoarding to herself.

I find myself speaking. "How personal can it be if we're going to tell a bunch of strangers?" I try to sound careless, maybe a bit sarcastic.

"I know," Ali says. "Happy first day of Ogilvy, right?"

We both let out awkward laughs. Ali sneaks looks at the other tables with those sharp eyes. "We do have to finish the assignment, though."

I feel myself relax. We're on the same page. She's not going to try and shove me into giving her my life story—and I bet the rest of the class is having the same reaction. This is an icebreaker, that's all.

"For me," I say, "let's go with—I'm a surfer. I've been on boards since I was little, because I'm from a beach town."

"OK, cool." Ali copies my answer into her binder word for word. "Mine can be that I saw a Monet for the first time when I was six. My grandma took me to the Met for my birthday, and after that I couldn't stop drawing. And now . . ." Ali pulls on a huge smile, as though trying to make herself excited again. "Ta-da, here I am!"

I keep expecting LaTonya to call the end of the exercise, but the seconds tick by slowly. Ali and I quickly run through all the small talk you can get out of "I'm from New York" and "I'm from California."

"So you're a rising senior?" she says. "Where are you applying to college?"

"Um. CSU Monterey Bay, for sure. It's right out on the beach. Probably a couple of the UC schools. I'm not really sure, beyond that."

She can't quite erase the confusion from her face. "Oh. Cool! I love the beach. I mean, I've never been to California, but I go down to Coney Island sometimes."

"How about you?" I ask. "Thinking about colleges yet?"

"Definitely. I mean, my big question is, conservatory or college? It all depends on how my art goes the next couple years. I'd *love* to go to SCAD, but then it'd also be nice to have the flexibility of a more traditional university. So, I mean"—she laughs—"for that I'd want to look at Brown, Yale, and Columbia, obviously, and NYU. I'm also considering women's colleges! Barnard would top that list, but I'm also doing more research about Smith."

I am slightly terrified by this answer. "Wow. You really know . . . a lot about . . . yeah."

"Yeah," Ali agrees.

"So that's why you're doing this camp? For college?"

Ali's nose scrunches up as though she's smelled milk that's gone bad. "It's not really a *camp*. The Summer Art Institute is super-prestigious. 'Camp' makes it sound like we're playing capture the flag."

Somehow I know that if I laughed, she'd take it as me demeaning Ogilvy even more, so I just say, "Right, sure."

Another endless silence. Finally, LaTonya calls the end of the exercise. The pair of us face forward and loose grateful sighs at the same time.

"So, what do we have?" LaTonya says, drifting around the classroom now. "Personal history. Let's start with Bhavna and Liliana."

I prepare myself to hear bland anecdotes about everybody else, too.

"So, when Liliana was twelve," Bhavna says, "her grandmother died in this car accident. And Liliana was supposed to see her on her thirteenth birthday two weeks later, and the funeral wound up being just one day before that."

I glance at Liliana, a tall, curly-haired girl with a flush darkening her cheeks. Bhavna keeps going. She talks about how Liliana started having recurring nightmares and had to take the driving test four times because it made her so nervous, and about how her birthday every year still feels hard instead of happy. I peer over at Bhavna's notes. They fill an entire page.

When Bhavna finishes, LaTonya nods slowly. The professor's hands are clasped, her expression pensive. "Thank you so much for that honesty, Liliana. There's so much there that you can draw on in our next exercise. What did you learn about Bhavna?"

Liliana gets to her feet and explains how Bhavna got diagnosed with depression two years ago. She describes Bhavna's thought patterns, and the way she had to try out four therapists to land on someone who helped her, and the way that she got closer to her father, who used to struggle with the stigma of mental illness, too, growing up in Mumbai.

By this point, my heart is going too fast. I glance over and see an ashen-faced Ali.

Five minutes later, we're hearing about a kid named Max Bargiel's family, and the way that his dad's immigrant status has shaped Max's views on American foreign policy. I feel a sharp jab against my knee and glance over. Ali is pointing to three words she's scribbled on her sheet of paper: *THIS IS BAD*

I nod. She starts to scribble again: *We need something else!!*

But before I can write anything in response, LaTonya is walking over to us. Ali quickly folds over her sheet of paper to conceal the notes.

"And what have you two discovered, Ali? Niko?" says LaTonya, the small, gentle smile on her lips again, and then I actually feel bad. I feel low in a way I never do when teachers slide my mediocre grades onto my desk facedown. The way she's looking at me—it's like she expects something good from me.

"Um." I stand up. "Ali . . . she . . . her grandma took her to the Met when she was six, and she saw a Monet, and that was kind of when she knew she wanted to be an artist, and . . . yeah."

There's a pregnant pause. Ali's face reddens as she stares down at the drafting table.

"I see," LaTonya says slowly. "How about you, Ali?"

Ali stands up quickly, fumbling with her sheet of paper. "Niko's a surfer," she blurts. "He's been surfing his whole life because he lives on the West Coast."

I think about how nice it would be to die immediately and then have my remains melt into the ground.

"Hmm." LaTonya's expression is mild, but her smile has faded. "All right. Thank you both. Now, Adrian, how about you and Gabi?"

Ali and I are back to avoiding each other's eyes.

We spend the rest of the class using our stories to make what LaTonya calls an emotion map, exploring which feelings rise from the memory we picked. Then we do some sketching, testing out different shapes, colors, styles, and mediums to pair form with feeling.

I'm expecting consequences the whole class, so I'm not surprised when the clock hits 10:30 and LaTonya says, "Niko, Ali, could you stay afterward to speak with me, please?"

I try to delay, shuffling my sketches around like it matters that they're organized. At the next table over, Liliana and Bhavna are speaking in low, eager voices. "I've never had a class like this before," Bhavna says, tying back her curly hair.

"Me neither," Liliana gushes, her cheeks flushed. "I had no idea sketching could feel like that. It was so vulnerable."

"Right? I feel like I just had, like, a whole new creative outlet open."

"*I* feel like I just got out of a weirdly fun therapy session."

They pack up and leave with everybody else, excitedly discussing their mood pieces. Once they're gone, Ali and I shuffle up to the front.

"I'm so sorry, LaTonya," Ali blurts out the second we reach her desk. "I don't think we really got what we were supposed to do."

LaTonya's eyes glimmer with amusement. "Ali, please don't sell yourself short."

Ali blinks, looking surprised.

"I think the both of you knew exactly what I was asking you to do. But you saw yourselves standing at the edge of your comfort zones and stepped back. Is that right?"

Ali and I both swallow, then nod. An identical downward jerk of our heads.

"All right. Well." LaTonya tucks her pen behind her ear. "I'm not angry with either of you, but I think you deprived yourselves of the point of the exercise. We've got to reach that place of openness. I'd like you both to work together on a short essay about personal history. Maybe one or two pages, all right? Tell me what role you feel personal history plays in making art, and include some details about yourselves. You don't have to say anything painful, of course. But give me something that's you, OK? Give that to each other." She smiles. "Give that to yourselves."

# Chapter 4

I'm fuming as I shove the door open to the studio. I *really* don't want to do that assignment. I'm surprised by the strength of my own feelings. That guy Niko seems fine, and the essay is short, so I'm not sure why the project bothers me so much.

I sigh. I'll just have to worry about it later. It's time for the thing I've looked forward to most, the reason I'm here: showcase workshop. We have class in the mornings, but afternoons are dedicated to our showcase projects.

Of course, I've been imagining what it would be like to win the Alicia Barry Prize, like everyone else, but I'm trying to stay realistic. I know I'm only a sophomore, and one of the seniors will probably win. But even if you don't get the ribbon, a good project here can make a big difference with college and conservatory admissions and scholarships.

College might seem far off, but I want to seize every opportunity I can get, since it's not like I'm going to get a lot of help art-wise. Neither Mom nor Nai Nai went to college, so their advice is limited to encouraging me to "do my best" and "work hard," and we don't exactly have money in the bank earmarked for "Ali's Continuing Art Education." The Queens Senior High School for Science and Math, shockingly, doesn't send a lot of kids to art school every year.

I don't want to badmouth QSSM. I applied because Jessie and Elise did, along with most of the other kids my age from the neighborhood, and I was lucky to get in: There's no denying it's a huge leg up on my chances at any college. Test prep, essay prep, AP classes, the brand name on my resume—it feels incredibly ungrateful to complain. I just wish that there were more of these types of classes.

That's why I'm so excited to spend meaningful time on my art this summer, to be surrounded by teachers and classmates who can help me grow. I can feel it crackling in the air as people excitedly talk to each other about their ideas. Some kids have brought in materials from home, partially finished paintings, sculptures, and collages sitting on high tables in front of them.

I wonder for a moment if I should have done that, but quickly dismiss the thought. No, this summer will be a fresh start, a chance to create something that leaves everything else I've done in the dust. I've been working primarily in charcoal recently, but I'm excited to get back into painting and maybe even try my hand at sculpture.

The studio is bright and enormous, and the room is buzzing. It's cold inside, even though the far wall is lined with plate-glass windows pouring sun. Students are gathered on stools around the high tables. If the room wasn't cluttered with easels, sculpture materials, and mysterious lumps under canvas, I might have imagined it was a science lab. A quarter of the program's students are in this workshop section, artists of all media. I see Brook at a table nearby, hugging a Black boy with closely shaved hair and blue nail polish. She spots me over his shoulder and hesitates before waving me over, too.

When I reach the table, the boy is saying to Brook, "About time you showed up. Do you know how many good-looking guys I've had to turn away while I've been saving this seat for you?"

There's one other girl at the table. She's tall and gangly, with pale, freckled skin and a mess of reddish-brown curls. I recognize her as the girl ahead of me in line yesterday, the one in the patchwork floral dress. Today she's wearing a pair of enormous paint-splattered overalls, like an exaggerated idea of what a painter looks like.

"Guys, this is my roommate, Ali," Brook says, waving vaguely in my direction while she looks at her phone again. "Ali, this is Grace and Jeremiah. Jeremiah and I have both been coming to Ogilvy for the last couple years. Grace is one year above you, Ali. We met her at an event at the Whitney last year for young queer artists."

"There are events at the Whitney for young queer artists?" I ask. "That's so cool! I had no idea." What I really want to ask is, how do I get into this world? How is it possible that the four of us had such different experiences growing up in the same city?

"Yeah," Brook says. "Basically all the young queer artists in the city already know each other through those kinds of events and obviously programs like Ogilvy."

"Well, not all the young queer—" I start to say.

Brook has already moved on. "I was super disappointed with my class this morning," she says. She speaks quietly and angles her entire body toward Jeremiah, so it doesn't feel like she's welcoming any follow-up questions from me.

Grace gestures at the empty seat next to her, and I sit, relieved. Dinner with Brook last night was a little uncomfortable, to be honest.

She's just so much worldlier than me, even though she's only two years older. But Grace gives me a big, open smile. "So nice to meet you," she exclaims. "I guess you can tell, we're all from the city. I'm from Brooklyn. Where are you from?"

"Queens, actually."

"Practically neighbors!" She's wearing a bunch of hair ties and woven, handmade-looking bracelets up and down both her skinny, freckled wrists, and she plays with them as she talks. "I'd hoped Ogilvy would put me and Brook together, but it's great to make new friends, too."

"Well, I don't know anyone here, so I'm really glad I met you." That sounds weirdly intimate, so I quickly clarify. "All of you, I mean!"

Our eyes meet. Grace's eyes are round and blue, almost surprised-looking, with lashes a shade darker than her hair. I look into them for just a moment longer than I meant to, and she looks away suddenly, down at the table. I avert my eyes, too, my face suddenly warm.

"So, Ali, where are you from?" Jeremiah asks. He's wearing a bright blue bomber jacket, the same color as his nails. He has a wide, easy smile and makes intense eye contact, instantly striking me as the polar opposite of detached, uninterested Brook.

"She's from Queens," Grace jumps in. She turns to me. "Brook and Jeremiah told me there are always a ton of kids from the city. It's nice because then we can keep hanging out after the program ends!"

"Another city girl." Jeremiah gives me a big smile and squeezes my hand across the table. I smile back. I've been here less than twenty-four hours and I already have friends. You could even say that I'm already part of Ogilvy's queer community.

"So, what are you all thinking about doing for your showcase pieces?" I ask the others.

"I'm a photographer," says Jeremiah. He lays an expensive-looking tablet on the table, carefully angling it so we can all see, and swipes through a huge range of photos. He skims through portraits and landscapes, both in color and in black and white, before stopping at a photo of a rat. "I'm currently working on a series about the animals of the city. Not, like, pets, but wild animals, stray animals. You know, the unloved ones. My heart has always kind of gone out to them."

He makes me want to sell everything I own and buy a film camera. I'm sure that to our respective friend groups, Jeremiah and I are both "the artistic friend," but it's so obvious to me that we are in completely different leagues. I wonder if Ogilvy made Jeremiah's talents what they are, and I harbor a secret hope that when I'm a senior, the younger kids will be the ones *ooh*ing over my portfolio.

"I paint canvases," says Grace, "and then show short films over them in loops." She pulls out her phone and all of us lean around it, watching the short films. My favorite is a painting done in bright blocks of color; over it she's imposed a black-and-white film of an older couple dancing.

"My grandparents," she explains. "They were actually just dancing in the kitchen that day, totally spontaneous, and I happened to catch it on my phone. It ended up being my favorite thing I've shot."

"It's very Fred Astaire and Ginger Rogers," says Brook, and Grace nods vehemently, like Brook really *gets it*.

I keep quiet. I know Fred Astaire and Ginger Rogers are old-time dancers, but I don't have a mental image of them. Honestly, I don't know much about the arts outside of what I've taught myself. We're not one of those families that has a bunch of books on shelves or watches old movies together. Togetherness just looks very different for us than it seems to for other people.

A wave of homesickness hits me, so acute I feel it'll knock me off my stool. I'm imagining myself in our tiny apartment, bent over my schoolwork at the kitchen table as I hear Nai Nai cooking, the smell of frying garlic and ginger as it wafts across the room to me.

"Earth to Ali," Brook says with a laugh.

"What are you thinking about doing for your project?" Jeremiah asks, obviously repeating himself.

"Sorry!" I exclaim. "I have so many ideas, actually. Maybe you could help me narrow it down? I want to go in an entirely new direction from everything I've done before, so I don't have any photos to show you all. I've been going through a charcoal phase recently, but I want to do something bigger and brighter this summer."

Jeremiah and Grace are nodding eagerly. Brook is staring out the window. My cheeks burn. *Am I really that boring?* I plow on anyway. "One idea I had is using book jackets that all have sort of a related theme and forming an image that's related to that theme. Or a series of paintings that represent the people I know through metaphors. Like a still life of items that make me think of that person. Another idea I had was, like, a commentary on fast fashion using clothes found in the trash or on the street."

"That's already been done to death," says Brook, suddenly turning back to the conversation. I must look visibly hurt, because she seems to feel bad and adds, "The book jackets and portraits sound cool though."

"I love all those ideas," Jeremiah says. "Don't feel pressure to commit to one just yet. I wish I'd used my first summer at Ogilvy to explore more."

Despite Brook's lack of enthusiasm, I'm not worried. Those were just the first few ideas that came to my head—I have a list two pages long in my notebook, and I can ask our teachers for advice on narrowing things down.

"Hello, everyone! Welcome to your first showcase workshop," says the man at the front of the room. "My name is Brian Rosa. I don't want you to think of me as a teacher. Instead, I'm going to be your guide for the next five weeks. This class is different from others you'll be taking here; it's a largely unstructured, creative time for you to explore and grow as artists. During the first week, we'll be doing a series of exploratory exercises before you commit to one showcase project. Today's theme is simple."

He gestures to an easel behind him. The fact that it's kind of small and the room is so big undermines the dramatic effect. We all squint and crane to read it.

"You," he says impatiently. "Today's theme is You."

When this fails to have the desired—or any—effect, he sighs and says, "This afternoon, we're going to reflect on our experiences and how they shape our art. What is the unique perspective *you* bring to your art? What do you have to offer the world that nobody else does? And, on the flip side, when you approach your projects, why are you the right person to create them? For the first hour, I want you all to work in complete silence, journaling. Then, we'll have a brainstorming session for your final project, basing ideas on what you've recorded."

"Not sure an hour of journaling is exactly what my parents had in mind when they sent me here," says Brook, but she pulls a notebook out of her bag and begins to write furiously, so it's clear she doesn't think the assignment is a *total* waste of time.

I also take out a binder. I'm not much of a writer, but I keep this binder to jot down ideas, assignments, or anything that pops into my head. I stare down at the page, eager to begin, and realize that I have absolutely no idea what to write.

Instead, I look around the room at everyone with their heads bent, writing away. It seems that I'm the only one who doesn't have anything to say. *Why am I the right person to create what I want to create?* This feels like the wrong question. *Why am I the right person to create any-thing at all?* Making art has always just felt like something I need to do. I don't want to start overthinking the role of art in my life. It's the one thing that works without any real effort on my part.

I doodle half-heartedly on the blank page and shiver in the cold room. This is going to be a very slow hour. My mind wanders back to the extra assignment from LaTonya's class, and now it clicks why that assignment bothers me. It's the same reason this journaling "You" exercise is getting under my skin. It's because I know what the *right* answer is for these teachers. It's the college application formula: All I need to do is write a two-page paper on how growing up working-class Chinese in Queens gives me this unique insight that nobody else in the art world has. If I want it to be a three-pager, I just need to throw in some part about how being abandoned by my father created a childhood trauma that I work through by making my art. That's the right answer, that's the A paper, the packaged vulnerability with a feel-good message attached.

And I *don't* want to write that paper. I don't want to make art that only a fifteen-year-old half-Chinese girl from Flushing with daddy issues could make. I want to make art that speaks to lots of people, art that has nothing to do with what bubble I have to fill in when I take standardized tests, nothing to do with my relationship with my family. I don't think my race is an interesting thing about me, let alone *the* most interesting thing, the thing to center my art around, but I know that the world doesn't necessarily agree. That's why, when I filled out the Ogilvy application, my cursor hovered for a minute over the "Race/Ethnicity" question, until I eventually skipped it entirely.

During the year I lived on Long Island, I went to a primarily white middle school near Mom and Anand's house. It was almost completely fine. But there were things that annoyed me—things I couldn't put into words at the time because I was eleven years old, things that are only coming back to me now. I remember making some friends on the first day of school. Then, on Friday, Nai Nai came with my mom to pick me up.

On Monday, my new friends asked me why I didn't tell them I was Chinese, like I'd done something really rude or lied to them. When we unpacked our lunches, one of them made a face and asked why my food smelled bad. I'd brought in the exact same meal the week before and nobody had commented on it. They'd all eaten Chinese food before. It wasn't a weird thing to eat, unless, I guess, you were a Chinese girl with a Chinese grandma, in which case it was weird and stinky and different from what you might get as takeout with your white family.

I'd never thought of myself as anything other than Chinese, so I was surprised to realize that my classmates had thought I was white like them. But once I reflected on it, it wasn't a crazy assumption.

My mom is blonde—a shade of blonde most people have to pay for—with blue eyes, and her genes clearly worked hard to make themselves shown in me. My hair is a light honey brown, my eyes a grayish green.

The way I looked didn't make much difference to me growing up in Flushing. I went everywhere with Nai Nai, holding her hand, and nobody questioned that I belonged to her. It was probably more obvious to outsiders that I was part Asian given the context.

But once I started to get older and go places on my own, I noticed that people treated me a little differently when I was by myself. More attentive, friendlier. I assumed it was because of the way I spoke and carried myself, like an American, like I belonged anywhere in this city, unlike Nai Nai. Jessie and Elise had teased me in elementary school for being a "secret Asian," looking whiter than any of the other halfies in school, but until those girls in sixth grade confronted me about it, it had never occurred to me that I didn't just look *more* white, I looked, well, *white*. Or at least, I looked white to people who didn't know a lot of Asians.

I'd never lived anywhere as white as that town, so it was also a surprise to learn how people thought of Chinese food and culture. When we read *The Good Earth*, my English teacher called on me, referenced "our newest arrival's exotic background," and asked me which part of the book rang true to me.

Considering that the book was about peasants in China in the early 1900s, and I'd spent all eleven of my years in Queens, I couldn't relate to the book at all. But I was embarrassed not to have anything to say, so, grasping at straws, I said that I knew a lot of people who had the same name as the main character, Wang. The teacher pursed her lips, clearly hoping for a different response.

I spent the rest of that year feeling slightly out of place in a million tiny ways, some to be expected—inside jokes that classmates had that I didn't understand, being new—and others more frustrating, like when an eighth-grade girl fell into step beside me in the hallway, asking me if my family was part of the Chinese Communist Party, and was I aware of the human rights abuses occurring in Tibet and Xinjiang? Mostly I just remember hiding my papers, a sea of A's. I'd been proud of my good grades in elementary school; here, it felt like I couldn't shake my classmates' snide comments about them: "*Well, obviously Ali had to get an A.*" They hardly ever called me an "Asian nerd" outright, but I knew it was implicit, every time.

I never said anything about this to my mom. It felt like it would have been a betrayal of Nai Nai, somehow. Mom would have felt bad, but she couldn't do anything about it, and I hated the idea of making her feel sorry for me and Nai Nai for no reason.

At the end of my homesick year, I moved back with Nai Nai full-time, and when I walked into my new middle school in Flushing on the first day of seventh grade, I felt a huge relief. Until I'd left, I hadn't known how nice it felt to be surrounded by people like me. It felt like when Nai Nai would come up behind me doing homework and press my shoulders down to un-hunch them for me, like I hadn't even noticed the slight tension I carried with me every day.

I love how basically everyone at my high school is also Asian, mostly Chinese. We don't get treated differently, because being Asian is just normal. If I spoke up at school to say that I wanted to share my unique experience as a Chinese girl, everyone would laugh—it's not a unique experience there. Maybe here at Ogilvy it is, but not where I'm from.

Now, when I go back and visit my mom and Anand on Long Island, I just . . . blend. Since I'm not in school there anymore, I'm not part of a community where everyone knows my name. If I'm out with my mom and we go to her psychic to have her aura read, she doesn't assume I'm Chinese, and to be honest, I kind of like it that way. My gut tells me that my mom's psychic—a fifty-something white woman named Janine—would be absolutely *thrilled* to ask me about my personal insights into the World of the Orient.

So yeah, I guess I do have *some* life experiences based on my race, but the idea that they made a Big Impact on my worldview seems, mostly, stupid. I don't think my worth as an artist comes from a light teasing in math class. I don't think my whole perspective was shaped by rolling my eyes at girls who were a little bit racist about Nai Nai's cooking.

What I've experienced isn't adversity or oppression. To put it in the same category as the discrimination that the women in LaTonya's portraits faced feels like the opposite of inspiring: "Ah yes, my lived experience as an Asian girl in the most diverse city in America has led me to face great suffering which I can only express through my art." No, thank you. My thoughts, my feelings, they're mine. They belong to me as an individual. It feels reductive to make me express myself through some lens that I didn't even choose for myself. Monet didn't paint as a white man.

I sigh loudly. I regret taking Art and Heritage. I maybe even regret coming to Ogilvy.

I look at the clock again. We have another thirty minutes. I have nothing else to do with my time, so I write down everything I just thought of. It's more of a nonanswer than an answer, but at least now I look like I'm participating.

At one hour, Professor Rosa tells us to move on to the brainstorming portion of the exercise. This, I'm ready for. I flip back to my two-page list and begin adding more. I think about Grace's film and painting creations and write down some ideas of adding film elements to the kind of work I've been doing lately. Projecting a brightly colored video over a black-and-white sketch could look really cool. Maybe Grace could help me with the film part. Thinking about Jeremiah's New York street animals photography project, I consider a series of photographs of the streets outside the Summer Art Institute. I could take pictures every day, and collage the photos over time, showing how the streets, and my relationships to them, change each day.

Before I know it, it's time to leave. I'm still in my head as we walk out, still coming up with new ideas—until the moment cool fingertips touch my bare shoulder.

I startle, turning, and catch a quick breath of Grace's light, flowery perfume. Jasmine. We're close together in the crowd of other kids, and I find myself disappointed when she pulls back.

"Sorry!" she exclaims. "I could tell you were in the zone."

"It's OK. That brainstorming session was exactly what I needed. Now I just need help narrowing it all down."

"Your energy is inspiring," she says. "I like that you're trying to branch out and take a risk."

"Is it a risk?" I ask.

"I mean, not risky like *paragliding.* Just, it's nice to see someone stepping out of their comfort zone."

This makes me break into a big smile. *Take that, LaTonya,* I think. Stretching my comfort zone doesn't just have to be about diving into awkward personal topics. "Thank you!" I say. "I'm so excited to experiment this summer. How was your morning class?"

"Oh, it was amazing." Grace lights up. "I was in The Organic Form. I'm really interested in floral motifs. I usually make them abstract, but this class is helping me understand more about the details and what makes a realistic-looking plant or animal. It was actually more like an anatomy class than an art history course, and all the other students were so impressive. I love being around people who are so curious. How did your morning go?"

I think about LaTonya's essay, and I consider telling Grace about the feelings in my journal. I feel like maybe she'll get it, since she seems so open and kind. But then I think about how quick my middle school classmates were to treat me differently once they knew I was Asian, and I dismiss the idea. I start to tell her instead about how Niko and I misunderstood our assignment, spinning it to sound like a funny, embarrassing story.

I don't think Grace would be racist, but sometimes it's nice to fly under the radar. And Grace—stylish, summery Grace, with her cutting-edge art and her old film references and her curls that smell like jasmine—I want her to see me as an individual, like I see her.

When Grace and I arrive for dinner at the dining hall, I stop on the threshold. At breakfast and lunch I was too busy to take much notice, but now I'm struck by how the other kids look. Last night, everyone was wearing comfortable traveling gear, but today, Grace isn't the only one who looks like she's DIYed some of her clothes. I'm wearing combat boots with a short floral dress. The boots and dress felt like the edgiest, coolest outfit I owned when I put it on at home, but here I look like someone who's never met an art student trying to dress like an art student. Which is, I suppose, what I am.

As Grace and I continue to scan the room, I notice how few other Asians there are. They're all sitting at one table together—weird to see when my school cafeteria is overflowing with Asian tables. Not that any of these kids look like my friends from home. First there's Niko from Art and Heritage, who probably has more muscle mass than my entire friend group put together. Beside him, a taller girl with massive amounts of black eyeliner sits braiding the pink hair of a shorter girl, poking her to get her to stop fidgeting. And across from them are three boys wearing, in order, Gucci, tweed, and Versace, the branding visible from a mile away.

Well, I guess Jessie might wear tweed, but only because her parents sometimes force her to dress like a 1960s secretary.

Grace spots Jeremiah and Brook, and we hurry over to join them. "So," Grace says, sitting down. "What do we all think so far?"

"Honestly," Jeremiah says, "given all that talk about improving diversity, I would have hoped for some meaningful change from last year. But no, Ogilvy is still the whitest place I've been all year. And I spent June in the Hamptons." He throws this line away like a joke, and we do all laugh, but I can tell from the way he's fiddling with his napkin that he's not sure if he should have said this out loud. "No offense," he adds, looking quickly from Grace to Brook to me.

"I know, right?" I exclaim. "Like, there's only one table of Asians."

He gives me a weird look and then laughs. "Um, OK."

I realize how odd my comment probably sounded, coming from someone who looks white. It's one thing to notice where your fellow Asians are sitting, but another thing to be a white person who's tallying up and commenting on where the minorities are.

I turn red. "Oh, I'm actually—" I begin, but Jeremiah is already launching into a new story about his roommate, who he says flew in last night from Texas on a private jet. The evidence for said private jet is scanty, and he, Brook, and Grace begin to argue about whether Jeremiah is making this up.

I stay silent, suddenly feeling conscious of my secondhand clothes, thrifted by necessity rather than just creativity. I wonder if the others can tell that I've never been to the Hamptons or met anyone who's flown on a private jet.

But maybe it's good to feel uneasy. "Out of my comfort zone," like Grace said. As my eyes pass over the unfamiliar faces in the crowd, my excitement rises again. This world feels enormous, full of possibility. I feel like I've spent my whole life in just one position, and finally I'm able to get up and stretch and try new poses. My new friends have access to parts of this city I've never seen—I have so much to learn from them. I already know that by the end of five weeks here, I'll be a different person. My eyes linger on the Asian table for a moment as another thought begins to form in the back of my mind. I'm still embarrassed, but maybe I'm glad Jeremiah cut me off.

After dinner, Grace tells me that Jeremiah and some other kids are playing video games in the rec room—apparently there are some minor Twitch celebrities in our presence, Jeremiah among them. "Do you want to come? It's OK if you don't really game, we can also just watch."

I want to, but I need to start thinking about what I'll do for LaTonya's extra assignment, so, feeling like I'm missing out, I head back to our dorm. Before I start working, I open my browser to solve an even more time-sensitive problem: my wardrobe. I close my eyes and envision everyone's outfits from today: Grace's oversized overalls, Brook's black mesh crop top and black leather shorts, Jeremiah's vintage jacket. I reach for my wallet and take out the credit card my mom gave me strictly for emergencies. I've never used it before, but I'll ask for forgiveness when I get back. Ogilvy is a different world. I have to fit in if I want to fully take advantage of it.

I don't even know where I can get clothes like the ones people have here, so I just type into the search bar: "black mesh crop top," "oversized overalls," "80s bomber jacket." I find a cheap retailer that somehow sells all of these items and add everything to my cart. Two-day shipping is $20. I hesitate, then select it. In for a penny, in for a pound, after all. I need new clothes as soon as possible.

That mission accomplished, I turn to my next task and open a Word document for LaTonya's essay. Unlike most assignments I do for school, where it's clear what I need to do for the A, this one has me stuck.

Sitting at my desk, looking at a blank screen while I can hear the other kids screaming from down the hall—I'm aware of how uncool I am right now. "Asian nerd" bubbles up in the back of my mind. This is all I can think of as I reflect on LaTonya's prompt.

The thought that occurred to me earlier, when I made the comment about the "Asian table," begins to take on more form. Nobody at Ogilvy knows I'm Chinese. Nobody at Ogilvy can put me in an overachieving nerd box. At Ogilvy, I'm finally free to be seen how I want to be seen.

My sigh echoes in the quiet dorm room. I love being Chinese when I'm around other Chinese people, when it's something we share. Being Chinese in a world full of *other* people, though—it just sets me apart. *Art and Heritage.docx*, reads the screen in front of me. I want to stand out for my art, not my heritage.

Maybe I shouldn't have signed up for the class. I thought it'd be about famous artists' histories and cultures. Instead, it feels like LaTonya wants me to fixate on the person I've been all my life, to reflect instead of change. But I want to focus on the future.

And I definitely don't want to share these feelings with some random guy who can't even come to class prepared.

OK. That was mean. But I saw the way Niko tensed up when LaTonya lectured us after class. He felt bad. And the thing is, he's Asian, too. I don't want him to drag me into writing that "My Life Is So Hard as a Working-Class Asian Girl" essay.

My phone buzzes. Nai Nai is calling. I feel a wave of homesickness and reach for the phone.

But just then, there's another burst of laughing and talking down the hall. My hand falters.

Instead of picking up the phone, I stand. I close my laptop hard. I came here to be with other artists. Not to be some nerd who sits alone in her room, writing an essay about the same boring life she's always lived, taking calls from her grandma like she can't even be on her own for a full day.

I leave my phone on my desk, grab my ID badge, and slip out into the hallway, beginning to smile.

# Chapter 5

NIKO CASTADI

"Hey, Ali—"

The words are barely out of my mouth when Ali says, "Sorry, got to run!" She zooms away from the dining hall double-doors, where we're all heading out from lunch, and around a corner, the bright color of her too-big bomber jacket the last thing I see.

"Bro," I say to nobody.

I sigh and set off for showcase workshop. *We've got time*, I tell myself. It's Wednesday afternoon, so Ali and I still have five days before LaTonya's punishment essay is due.

But time at Ogilvy doesn't seem to work the same way it does in California. I thought I could stay on top of things. I took seven classes in junior year, after all. Wouldn't four be easy?

No, apparently. Not at all.

Showcase workshop passes slowly as I hunch over my sketchbook. Half my mind is on the page, swimming around in the sea of shapes and colors—waiting for instinct to latch onto something and turn it into an idea for a real piece.

But the rest of my thoughts are stuck inside my backpack, jammed between stacks of unfinished readings. I'm not a great reader at the best of times. I get distracted by my phone, or by creases in the printouts, or by noise around me, even sounds as small as the air conditioner turning on. And my classes have all assigned thirty or forty pages of readings for this week, a mix of articles and textbook excerpts.

Then there's Technical Foundations. Our pixie-like professor, Dr. Ziegler, was basically rubbing her hands together with glee yesterday when she described the course as a "workhorse class." For next Tuesday, she's assigned us this exercise on a two-by-three-foot grid that involves shading seventy-six different surfaces.

I sneak a look around the showcase workshop. Is everyone else feeling as overwhelmed as I am? It's tough to say. I've been making excuses not to work with Andrew and the others. The first and only time I joined their study group, I took one look at the jaw-droppingly detailed sketch that Haolong dashed off for one of his classes, and that was it. I decided to work in private. I don't want people like that seeing the garbage I come up with when I'm sketching.

The second LaTonya dismisses us—she's also the showcase supervisor for my section—I hustle out to an empty classroom nearby, empty my backpack on the table, and start Ziegler's shading exercise.

It's better than the readings, at least. I sink into the grid, working my pencils into the corners to create sharp angles and consistent shadows.

At some point I realize the light has changed. I glance up. It's already 6:30.

I swear under my breath. After three and a half hours, I haven't done even half of the assignment. I was so sure I could finish the whole thing by six. Do I stay? Keep working?

*You have to eat*, I tell myself. It's only that thought that forces me to slide the exercise into my new Ogilvy-issued portfolio case and head toward the dining hall.

I check my phone as I walk. Devin and Grayson are having an intense back-and-forth about the new DemonForce game, and Hailey has responded to my message from earlier today. **Soooo have you made camp friends yet?**

I drift over to one side of the hall and pause in my tracks. **yeah i sort of got assigned a friend group lol**

**Wait really? How?**

**haha. the camp director walked me over to this table with all the other asian kids. he was like here . . . your new home**

Laughing emojis from Hailey. **Omg really? That's so funny**

**yeah. it felt kind of weird tbh**

After a moment, she follows up with: **See this is why you should come back home :) That's the great thing about Landry Beach. Here you're unique, in big cities you're just another Asian boy haha**

I feel a twinge in my chest and reread the message a couple of times. I don't really know how to reply. I guess when I told her it felt weird, I was hoping she'd ask why, not make a joke.

But this is Hailey. She never says anything earnest unless she's layered humor on top. I let my eyes settle on the important part: **come back home :)**

I send a smiling emoji back. **want me to bring you anything from nyc? lol**

**Only you & your awesome art.**

Now I really am smiling. Besides Ms. Ryan and my family, Hailey is the first person who's seen my art. When I submitted my Ogilvy application, I sent her photos of the half-dozen pieces I attached for the portfolio. I got so nervous right afterward that I almost texted her to say, *Wait, stop, don't look at them*—but before I could, she was sending me a list of what she loved about every piece.

The clouds of stress that have been hanging over me all day begin to clear. I set off for the dining hall, my thoughts beginning to bloom with new ideas and new colors, the brown-gold of Hailey's freckles, the shining red of her polished nails.

I can still do this. I can make something great here, something that Hailey loves, something that might even impress my family.

I'm probably just about to hit my stride.

On Friday, I make a point of getting to Art and Heritage early. Ali, on the other hand, dressed today in what seems to be a kiddie-goth outfit, seems to make a point of getting there just on the cusp of late. "Hey," I say the second she sits down. "We've got to start that essay, remember?"

"Oh, right," she says, looking carefully distracted as she pages through her binder.

"How about—"

But then LaTonya welcomes us back and asks us to take out our readings on Māori wood carving. At the end of class, I turn to Ali right away, but she beats me to it.

"So, the essay," she says. "We can each write our half tomorrow and then stick the halves together on Sunday. Sound good?"

Blindsided, I flounder for a second before finding words. "Wait, that isn't—"

She stands, stuffing her binder back into her overfull backpack.

"We should probably both write a page. It'll look better than if we just have one page between the two of us."

"But—"

"Cool. I'll find you during breakfast on Sunday. Later!"

Then she's off again, darting through the threshold.

I swear quietly under my breath as I exit the room. What's her deal? It's not like I'm so thrilled about the essay, either, but the whole point of LaTonya's assignment was getting us to work together.

Maybe she's avoiding me because I forgot all my stuff the first day. Maybe she thinks that if she spends too much time talking to me, her grades will slowly start to slip by association.

Or maybe she comes from a family of bank robbers or something, and writing about her family would expose them, and she's trying to throw us off the scent. Although you'd think someone with a bank-robbing family history would stay away from classes with names like "Art and Heritage."

As I cross the courtyard, I amuse myself by cooking up increasingly ridiculous things Ali might be trying to cover up. Like, maybe she's secretly forty years old or is the Zodiac Killer. But my amusement deflates when I imagine LaTonya's face if we turn in something as half-assed as our assignment on Monday.

We only have three days now, and I'm still not done with that shadow exercise, and yesterday Ziegler added another time killer to the stack: a study of light temperature that has us duplicating the same colors under different light conditions. Then there are my Art History readings on Egyptian and Mesoamerican art, which are bound to take up half my weekend.

So—no. I haven't hit my stride yet.

I try not to think of my parents' reactions if they got a call from LaTonya telling them that, even after my miracle waitlist acceptance, I still managed to let them down. With a lurch of guilt, I shove my hands deep into my pockets and shoulder my way through the double-doors into Abstracting the Figure.

Professor Abbott, ponytailed as always, with that hawklike look on his thin face, is clicking through projection slides unblinking when I enter the room and jog down the steps into the lecture hall.

Turns out I don't hate Abstracting the Figure. It might even be my favorite class. On Monday, Abbott talked us through a series of photos and highlighted objects like lampposts and chandeliers, showing us how they could remind us of human bodies if we took pieces out of context. On Wednesday, he described a list of bizarre theories that ancient and medieval cultures had about human anatomy.

Since both of those talks, I've caught myself looking at the world differently. This morning, the curves of the chairs in the dining hall made me think of cupped hands. Looking at my own torso in the mirror, I imagined one of those medieval diagrams, all the organs crowded around out of order.

This morning, I was excited to see what Abbott might have set for today's lecture, but now I'm just picturing Ali's cagey expression as she zoomed down the hall.

Andrew and Nathalie have saved me a seat in the front row as usual. "What's up?" Andrew says when I sit stiffly beside him.

"Nothing."

"Very convincing," Nathalie says.

"I thought you liked this class," Andrew says.

"What?" I say. "No, I'm fine with the class. That's not . . ."

I sigh and check my phone. We've got a few minutes until the lecture, so I tell them both about the Art and Heritage situation, starting with Monday's presentation fiasco.

I tell them as much as I can, anyway, without admitting how much the workload has been killing me. Yesterday I found out that Andrew was way underselling his "interest" in biology. He apparently won an international science fair for some project he did with frog stem cells. As for Nathalie, every time she says a sentence, I learn a new word that would have boosted my terrible SAT score. They've probably already realized I'm the moron of the group, but I don't want to add hard evidence to the list.

". . . so," I finish, "basically, I have to yank this girl kicking and screaming into this essay, and the essay is already pretty . . ."

"Invasive," Nathalie finishes, her mouth thin. "Wow. Niko, that whole assignment sounds so inappropriate."

"It does?" I say, surprised but reassured.

"Yeah, that sucks, man," says Andrew. I expected him to find some positive spin on the whole thing, but he looks glum. "Sometimes it feels like if you want to get taken seriously, you have to go all-in on the private stuff."

"Not like that's surprising, when so many people confuse art for exhibitionism," says Nathalie, both irritated and casual, as if it's a sentence she's said a thousand times.

"Yeah, for real," I say, trying to sound like this is an opinion I both share and understand deeply.

At this, Nathalie's face registers a hint of amusement.

I go on quickly. "So, neither of you have done that sort of art before? Art about, uh, being Asian?" The words feel clumsy from my lips.

"No, I have," Andrew says, brightening. "It was great. I did this photo series last year about my grandparents and what they brought with them from Korea when they immigrated." He shrugs. "I don't feel like that's private, though. My grandparents were excited about it. They kept making suggestions and whipping stuff out of drawers, like, how about this? Or this? And they got all flattered when my friends from school were interested in the series."

He tugs out his phone and shows us the Instagram account he dedicated to the project. "Sometimes," he adds, "I feel like all people know about Korea is like, K-pop and *Squid Game*, so I thought it was fun, sharing something more personal."

"Mm," Nathalie says. "And you didn't feel like that reduced your art to an educational tool?"

Andrew laughs. "Art can be two things."

That gets a rare smile from Nathalie. Andrew rests his chin on his hand as he smiles back, his eyes glazed and dreamy.

Nathalie doesn't seem to notice. "I've done identity-based art before," she tells me. "But I don't know if I'd do it again. My freshman year, I used calligraphy for a set of paintings that showed everyday scenes in my house. You know, telling the diaspora story through Song dynasty language. Small-town Idaho plus centuries-old artistic heritage. And I still think the series is worthwhile, but sometimes when I was putting it together, I felt like a sellout. Like I was using my culture to seem interesting." Her eyes, which had found her lacquered nails, flicker back to me. "It seems like that's what this professor wanted you to do. It makes sense that you wouldn't want to do it."

"Yeah," I say automatically, but that's not quite right. I get where Nathalie's coming from. She feels weird mining her background and putting it on display. I have the opposite problem, though. I feel like I wouldn't have anything to mine if I tried.

Also, thinking about the way LaTonya said "Give that to yourself," I don't feel like she wants us to sell ourselves out. It seems more like she wants to open us up. It's not her fault I want to keep some doors closed.

Andrew claps me on the back and says, "Don't worry about the essay, bro. Once it's in, you can just coast on the A and not think about it."

I almost laugh. That's me. Coasting on A grades. Definitely not struggling to scrape out Cs.

Nathalie and Andrew both wait for my answer. I open my mouth, but just then, Professor Abbott dims the lights and flips on the projector, and silence drops. I settle into my seat, relieved. I really didn't want to lie to their faces about my grades.

As Abbott takes roll call, I run my hand through my hair. Honestly, I like this camp group a lot more than I expected to. Yeah, sometimes Andrew is cringy, but he's also way nicer than Hailey's crowd, or even Devin and Grayson. And the others are all intimidating, especially Nathalie, but they're funny, too. They bring up subjects I'm not used to talking about, battles in ancient empires, artificial intelligence theories, deep-sounding ideas from weird-sounding novels. Their interests and curiosities are all over the map.

And they treat me like I'm part of the club. Like I'm someone who's good at school, and who has their background, and who always gets where they're coming from.

I remember the knowing look Andrew gave me at breakfast that first day, when he said, *They paired up all the Asians*. I think about how everybody smiled sheepishly, like we were all watching a movie together and subjected to the same embarrassing scene. And the laughter when Jen joked *Asian as charged* to the rest of us—it felt so different, versus the stuff I've said before to Devin, Hailey, and Grayson.

Abbott has started his presentation. On-screen, a painted canvas shows a red doorframe standing open. On the other side of the threshold are a white marble floor and a hanging light fixture, and between them, a dark pink carpet rolls down a set of steps. At the top of the steps, darkness.

"Impressions, please," Abbott says.

Several people raise their hands right away.

"Cartwright," Abbott calls.

"It's like a horror movie," suggests Ella Cartwright at the end of our row. "A creepy haunted house."

No response from Abbott. "Davenport?"

"It's sophomoric," says a cool, uninterested voice from a few rows behind me. I glance back and see a blonde girl smoothing down her pixie cut with one jewel-studded nail. "The artist clearly wants you to figure out it's a mouth. What is there to get from the piece after that?"

"Wow," Nathalie says quietly from my left. "'Sophomoric.' And I thought I was going to be the most pretentious person at Ogilvy."

Andrew and I stifle laughter. "So," I whisper, "you're saying we're allowed to call you pretentious?"

"Only on weekends and holidays."

Grinning, we all look back to the painting of the door, and I feel a contented rush. *This class is fun*, I think as Professor Abbott breaks into a new, vigorous lecture about what he calls "the body language of architecture."

I consider the sculpture on my desk upstairs. *Were you like this?* I find myself thinking, picturing the papier-mâché shell around the tongue of fire. Was my dad part of a group of Chinese artists, like my group here? Was he part of the art world, a world like Ogilvy?

I feel annoyance creep in and shake the questions. If I wind up doing well at Ogilvy, it won't be because of something in my DNA. It'll be because, for once, I'm trying my hardest.

I don't know what Ali's deal is, but I'm not going to let her get in the way.

"Ali?" I say.

Ali and her three friends look up at me from their cafeteria table. To Ali's left is another younger girl, pretty and pale and bohemian-looking, wearing a floral sundress. The two kids opposite look closer to my age. One of them is the girl who made that "sophomoric" comment during Professor Abbott's lecture.

Ali's cheeks turn red. "Yeah?" she says, looking determinedly away from me.

"We should meet up tomorrow. Work on that project."

"Oooh," says pixie-cut girl with a smirk, nudging the guy in overalls next to her. "Ali, you didn't tell us you were getting into a *joint project* with someone."

"*Brook*," says Ali, so red now that it looks like a painful sunburn.

I sigh and roll my eyes in Brook's direction. "Dude, it's an essay. I'm not into tiny freshmen."

"Yeah," Ali says a bit too loudly, "and—and I don't even swing that way. So."

She makes a whole thing out of unsticking the zipper on her jacket. But I see the girl to her left shooting Ali a furtive look, something brightening on her face. By the time Ali finishes with her zipper and scans the table, though, the other girl has gotten involved with the cheesecake on her dinner tray.

Ali's blush has retreated into more of a glow. "What's there to meet up about, anyway? I thought we already made our plan. Write our halves of the essay, then put it together."

I pause. If we turn in what she's suggesting, LaTonya will be even unhappier than before. But I'm not going to give Ali some lecture in front of her friends about the point of the assignment. Her friends are older; I bet she wants to impress them.

I shrug. "We can talk about it later. Just want to make sure we're on the same page."

Her shoulders loosen, and I glimpse relief on her face. "OK," she says. "Cool."

"I'll be reading in the eighth-floor lounge tonight. If you have a minute, we could talk then." I lift my hand in an easy wave. "Later."

Before I return to my friends' table, I think I see curiosity mix into Ali's relief.

She finds me in the lounge about twenty minutes after dinner. As I fold up my Mesoamerica reading, she shifts awkwardly, one hand curled loosely around her other forearm.

"Look," she says before I can greet her, "I'm sorry about this week, all right? And thanks for not going into everything in front of my friends."

"No worries. Thought you probably wouldn't appreciate it."

Ali lets out a shaky laugh and perches on a neon pink armchair across from me. "I wouldn't. How could you tell?"

"I don't know. The look on your face."

"Yeah, my friends at home tell me I have an obvious face, whatever that means."

I smile. "They're not wrong."

There's a short silence, but it's more relaxed than the one that's been hanging over our shared desk all week. We both glance around the lounge. Half a dozen other kids are gathered at a table in the opposite corner, playing some card game that involves a lot of shouting and slapping each other's hands. A heavyset professor is connecting a laptop to a projector and making enthusiastic suggestions to Professor Abbott, who's tugging down the screen at the front of the lounge with a long-suffering expression.

"It's a weird assignment," I offer to Ali. "I don't really want to do it, either. But I'm pretty sure LaTonya wanted us to—"

She grimaces. "I know. You're right. I just have a tough time making myself . . . anyway, let's just tear off the Band-Aid."

"Yeah." I hesitate. "I guessed you didn't want to write it together because your family are secretly bank robbers. But you can just tell me up front about that stuff. I can keep quiet."

I expect her to laugh, but instead she points a menacing finger at me. "Yeah, but how can I be sure you won't steal the gold bars I smuggled into my dorm?"

I grin. "Oh, I already stole those. Sorry you have to find out like this."

As Ali grins back, a voice from behind me calls, "Niko!" Andrew is jogging across the lounge, his hair flopping with every step. He points to the screen that the professors are setting up. "Are you here for trivia night?"

"Um—"

Before I can say no, Andrew plops down on the couch beside me and goes on. "Good, 'cause we need four people for a team, and there's no way we're winning without a sports person. I think Haolong and Haoran are weirdly into football, but they're video chatting with their parents." He checks his phone, looking hopeful. "I invited Nathalie and Jen, though."

I snort. "Nathalie won't come."

"What? Why not?" Andrew's face falls. "Did she tell you?"

"No. Just doesn't seem like a Nathalie thing." I can imagine her deadpanning, "*Trivia is, by definition, trivial.*"

Andrew glances across the coffee table to Ali. "How about you? What's your trivia specialty? And don't say art, because everyone here's going to be an art geek. Also, hi, I'm Andrew."

"Ali," she says with a wave.

"Oh! From that whole Art and Heritage thing?"

"Um, yeah," she says, giving me a startled look that clearly says: *You told your friends about it?* I rub one hand over my face, making a note to myself. Never trust Andrew with sensitive information.

Andrew notices nothing. "I can handle any and all biology questions," he says. "And Niko knows about basketballs, and whatever. How about you?"

Ali bites her lip. "Oh. I was going to find . . . I wasn't really planning on . . ."

"Yeah," I add, "I don't know about trivia, Andrew. I have a shitload of reading to catch up on."

Andrew scoffs. "We all have a shitload of reading to catch up on."

"You do?"

"Yeah! Oh my God, we got sixty pages from Rosa for *The Organic Form*. Sixty pages! It's like, bro, do you think your class is the only class we have?"

"Wait, yes," I burst out with a rush of vindication. "Lowery gave us this Mesoamerica reading for Art History, and I'm like—" I tug the rolled-up reading from the edge of the sofa and let it flop open, showing the thick stack of paper and the minuscule text. "How am I supposed to get through that by Tuesday?"

Andrew and Ali both let out sympathetic, mildly disgusted noises. Relief floods me. Apparently this *is* hard. Apparently I'm not the only one who thinks so.

"Just take the night off," Andrew wheedles. "You too, Ali. It'll be so fun. You can do Mesoamerica later, Niko."

Ali glances over her shoulder and goes still. I follow her sight line. Flowery sundress-girl is standing by the door, scanning the lounge. She spots Ali, and as she beelines for us, a smile forms on Ali's face.

"Totally!" Ali says. "I'm in. We can stay and play, for sure. That's my friend Grace." Ali's tensed in her seat, her fingers picking at a worn spot on her jeans. "Um, Niko," she says, not even looking at me, "you're playing, right? Four for a team?"

I grin. "OK. Fine. But only because I'm a good wingman."

Ali turns bright red. "What? Shut up. I don't know what you're talking about."

"Sure, sure. And—essay tomorrow?"

"Essay tomorrow," she agrees. Then, with a small, sheepish smile, she adds, "Thanks."

After our team comes in a solid ninth place in trivia, Grace announces that she's going to study downstairs with Brook and Jeremiah. Part of me wants to accompany her, but I'm having too much fun with Niko and Andrew. Andrew is the only person I've met at the program who feels like someone I would have been friends with outside Ogilvy, and that familiarity feels surprisingly comforting.

"I can't believe there wasn't a single art round in trivia at art camp," Niko says.

"Institute," I correct him without even thinking about it.

"I think people would get too competitive," Andrew says. "Violence would erupt. Heads would roll. It just wouldn't be worth the lawsuits afterward, you know? And think of the press!"

"I thought all publicity is good publicity?" I joke back.

"'Parents demand answers after trivia competition at *prestigious* Ogilvy Institute ends in riot,'" Niko says. He draws out the word "prestigious" with a long, pretentious sounding "e" sound and the three of us collapse in laughter.

When the others leave for bed, I decide to go find Grace. I want to tell her that my offhand remark in the cafeteria today was me coming out for the first time. With the warmth that she's shown me all week, the advice she's given me on my art, the way she's welcomed me into her friend group, I feel like she'll be excited for me, too.

But when I go down to the study room, it's empty. She must have gone to bed already. Disappointed, I go back to my floor to get ready to sleep.

Grace has lent me a floaty yellow cotton dress. Despite the difference in our heights, it looks nice on me. It has puffed sleeves and ruching on the bodice, and the skirt comes down to my ankles. Some of the other new clothes that I've bought make me feel like a kid in a costume. This dress, by contrast, makes me feel like myself. I hang it up lovingly, sad that I have to give it back to Grace tomorrow.

I nestle into bed, replaying the moment in the dining hall over and over in my head, a stupid grin on my face. I came out to multiple people, and it was fine. In this moment, I wish that the Summer Art Institute could go forever.

At lights out, Brook still hasn't returned, but fifteen minutes later, I hear voices in the hall, one low and cool, one melodic and cheerful. They stop outside my door. I can't make out what they're saying, but I hear a lot of laughter. When Brook opens the door, I catch a glimpse of curly hair illuminated in the bright light of the hall, and Grace's voice whispers, "Good night!"

My heart sinks. Grace and Brook. Was that just a friendly conversation, or something more?

Suddenly I'm remembering my first conversation with Grace, when she told me she was hoping Brook would get assigned as her roommate. What if Grace has been hoping to become more than friends with Brook for months?

I deflate, suddenly embarrassed at how eager I was to debrief my moment with Grace earlier. This is probably not a big deal for her at all. She was probably born out. She probably had a girlfriend in preschool and has no idea what it's like to have to surprise her family with an announcement they may take badly.

I decide that instead, I'm going to play it cool. Nobody needs to know that was my big moment.

I *know*, I think, smiling into my pillow as I turn over. That'll be good enough.

On Sunday, I head to Niko's room, hauling all my books with me. I'm surprised by how heavy the workload has been. If I were really doing my best, the way I do at school, I would only be getting a few hours of sleep. But I've been letting the school side of things slack a little, skimming some readings instead of trying to retain everything. My portfolio, by contrast, is more important.

I walk down Niko's hallway with a spring in my step. I'm still buoyant, riding the high from Friday night. His door is propped, so I let myself in. "Hi!"

"Hey." Niko is lounging on his bed with his shoes still on. I recoil instinctively and resist the urge to comment on how gross that is.

I drop my backpack and sit at Andrew's desk. It's a mountain of mess, with readings bulging out of the drawers, sketches crumpled up in the corners, and pencil shavings scattered over a pile of stationery with "ARH" monogrammed on it.

Niko's clothes are super-basic: blue jeans and a gray T-shirt. Mine are basic, too—denim shorts and a yellow T-shirt I borrowed from Nai Nai because it was so old it had started to look vintage. Unlike me, he makes his anti-fashion fashion look cool and deliberate, like his outfit is just as much of a look as Grace's over-the-top bohemian style or Brook's angles and leather.

I take out a piece of paper and write "Essay Brainstorming" at the top. "OK," I say. "Let's figure out what we want to say with the essay."

He nods. "You could always write your part about how you're, like." He fiddles with a leather bracelet on his wrist. "Not straight or whatever."

I laugh. "Be more awkward about it, please." But his awkwardness tells me Niko's also from a world where coming out can feel like a big deal. The excitement I've been holding back from the queer kids at the program bubbles over.

"You know," I admit, "I've literally only told one person before—my mom, and she's sworn to secrecy. It felt so good to tell people, but I definitely don't feel ready to write about that in an essay."

"I feel like the whole *point* of this essay is to write about whatever makes us most uncomfortable," he sighs. "It's so weird."

"I know. How is telling the class about my absentee father going to help me become a better artist, you know? I can do my emotion map by myself."

He nods. "At least only LaTonya is going to read this. I feel better writing an honest paper for her than I did about that stuff on Monday. I don't really get how everyone in the class was so OK with just diving into, like, their family drama or whatever."

"So what is it?" I ask.

"What is what?"

"Your family drama."

"You're trying to get me to go first, aren't you?"

"Guilty as charged," I admit. "So how about it?"

He shrugs and takes a deep breath. "OK, so I've always felt pretty lucky at home. My family's happy. Two doctor parents, three kids, and everyone basically gets along. But in the last six months, things have gotten super weird." Haltingly, he tells me about his little brother, Justin. At first, I can't help staring when he explains what Justin did. All kinds of sibling dynamics are totally foreign to me, but this is on another level.

"That's crazy," I say. "How could you not know? Was he nice at home?"

He winces a little. "Yeah, I had no idea. There's the whole idea that bullies are usually unhappy at home, but Justin obviously isn't. Or like, if he is, it's not because of us. He's like the golden child. Or was." He pauses, rubs his temples, and looks away from me. "No, he still is." He gives a rueful laugh. "He didn't even get in trouble for it. My parents are treating it like he's sick or something, like if they just *diagnose* what made him do it, then everything's fine."

"Are your parents big disciplinarians normally?" I already know the answer is no.

"No, never," he says. "It's all about like, talking about how we feel and stuff." He sighs. "Which is usually OK, because usually nothing is too wrong. It's like, Anastasia stealing Justin's books or Justin hogging the PS5 or whatever. But now . . . I don't know. Talking about it feels like shit. It kind of shattered how I saw our family. Like, if I could miss this, what else am I missing that should be obvious?"

I scoot the chair to the bed and give him an awkward pat on the shoulder. "All families keep things from each other. I know all about that."

"Because of the whole, being-gay thing?" He's balled up a loose sock and is tossing it up and down, staring resolutely at the ceiling.

"Yeah, but it's not just me holding back in my family. There's so much we don't say to each other. I don't think it means we care about each other any less." I draw in a deep breath. "My dad left when I was little," I admit. "And we just . . . don't talk about it at all. Some things are painful to talk about, or can't be solved by talking. I don't know if that's what was going on with Justin, but I guess I just want you to know you shouldn't blame yourself."

He stops tossing the sock and looks at me. "What do you mean you *don't talk about it*? Like, do you pretend that he doesn't exist?"

"I mean we focus on everything else. We don't talk about him in the same way that you don't talk about some boring family down the street who you don't know. He just doesn't come up." I pause. "He was an artist, too, though. I think it's where I get it from."

"Hey, my birth dad was an artist, too!" he says, sitting up. "There must be something genetic about it, right?"

"Maybe," I say, a little skeptical. "I don't know if I believe there's like, an *art gene* or anything. But yeah, I like to think I get my artistic side from my dad."

"So was your dad any good?" Niko asks. "Mine gave my mom this one sculpture, and I kinda love it. It's mine now." He unfolds himself from the bed and crosses the room to his dresser. He pulls a small statue out from behind a big tangle of wires, electronics, and other junk. It's light wood, covered in Chinese newspapers.

I completely lose my breath. I *know* this statue. I know it because we have several just like it at home.

"Niko," I say. "I've seen those sculptures before."

"Don't tell me that. The last thing I want to know about my dad is that he was copying some museum piece."

"No. That sculpture is exactly like the ones we have at home. Like, *exactly*." I reach for my backpack and grab the binder Nai Nai gave me, flipping through to find pictures of the sculptures.

"What are you saying?" he says, although his eyes have narrowed, and he's studying my face. I know he's already thinking what I'm thinking.

"I'm saying that I think your dad is *my* dad," I whisper.

I hand him the binder so he can see for himself.

# Chapter 7

I can't tear my eyes from the photo album in my lap, from the snap-shot of the sculpture I've set on my desk. As for Ali, she's staring at the sculpture like she's trying to memorize every contour.

My heartbeat grows louder in my ears. "No way," I say. "This can't be real."

"Did your mom ever live in New York?"

"I . . . yeah. She went to NYU, and she was here for med school, too. I guess she would have been here fifteen years or something. She met my dad on a weekend trip to Long Beach Island."

"Then it *can* be real. I think it is." Ali takes the photo album from my motionless hands and lets it snap shut. The sound breaks me out of my reverie.

"But how—" I laugh nervously. "Right? How is this happening?"

"Maybe we're being secretly filmed or something. Maybe Ogilvy is, like, an elaborate prank show?"

The disbelief bubbles higher in my chest, and I bury my face in my hands. Then we're both laughing. There's a wild edge to it. The whole situation feels off-kilter.

"Wait, holy shit." I look up, slightly dizzy. "Does this mean my dad is in Queens right now?"

The laugh curdles on Ali's face. "No idea. I haven't seen him since I was five." She looks away. "He basically disappeared off the face of the Earth."

The excitement that had shot through my body fizzles. "What do you mean?"

"I mean he doesn't call and doesn't write," she says shortly, "and his name is Tan Bo, which has, like, a half-million Google results."

"*Bo*." I can't help blurting it out. "That's my birth dad's name. That's, like, one of the three things I know about him!" My head whirls faster—I actually have to brace my hand against the wall to steady myself. "Are you in touch with any of his friends?" I press. "Did he grow up here? Where did he go to college? Maybe I can—"

"He went to Pratt. It's a dead end."

I wait for Ali to explain, but she keeps quiet for so long that I demand, "Why?"

"Because." Impatience is creeping into her voice, too. "I did some college visits last summer. And when I was visiting Pratt, I asked the faculty if they'd heard from him, or anything. There was only one professor who was teaching when he went there, and she didn't remember him, so . . . no trace, OK?" She winces, then bursts out, "God, that makes me sound so pathetic. I promise I don't actually think about it all the time. It's not like I'm sitting there just hoping he'll come back or something, I *do* have a life."

"I know you do," I say, my frustration evaporating. Suddenly I feel like an idiot. Our dad never even knew about me, but he lived with Ali until she was five. She has plenty of reason to be defensive about him—and angry with him.

A weight forms in my stomach. I've always imagined my birth dad as some hip artist, cool and free. And, knowing basically nothing about him, it's been easy to assume he was kind and generous, too. A good guy. Why would I expect anything different?

But now I look at the girl opposite me and picture a laughing, squishy little kid, wanting to play outside or make messes with paints. I picture the kind of man who would look at her and think, *Not my problem.*

I swallow. "Hey, um, I didn't mean to be pushy."

"No, it's OK." Ali makes an effort at a smile. "You didn't know him, so . . . anyway, let's not think about that, right? I mean, you're my *brother*. I have a brother! That's—it's . . ."

She trails off, struggling for words, and I understand why. When I think of my siblings, I think of years' worth of jokes, tussles, and petty arguments. Anastasia losing a tooth when she cracked her mouth on the coffee table, and Justin yelling when he saw. Justin's guilty laugh when I caught him sneaking into my room to borrow my colored pencils, the fancy ones with the crisp tips that our grandparents got me for Christmas. But Ali . . .

In terms of DNA, I'm just as related to her as I am to Justin and Anastasia. But I'm suddenly aware of how little I know about this girl.

"Should we . . . tell people?" I ask. "Our families?"

Ali shakes her head. "I guess, but how do we say that? It's so unbelievable. What if—"

She breaks off, her hands suddenly rigid on the photo album.

"What?" I say.

"Oh, wow," she breathes. "Niko. The showcase at the end of camp.

There are going to be journalists there. You know—art journalists." Ali's eyes are alight when they meet mine. "If we're right . . . this would be an amazing story for them to cover. Human interest! Right?"

She scoots forward to the edge of the bed. "Listen. What if we team up on our showcase piece? We could make a brother-and-sister art piece that's about us finding each other here! How could that *not* win first place?" Her face flushes with color until she's practically glowing. "Just picture it. A spread in the Arts and Culture section of the *Times*. It's like: *Long-Lost Art Genius Siblings Win Alicia Barry Prize after Finding Each Other at Prestigious Ogilvy Institute.*"

I'm grinning now. "Art genius is sort of a lot."

Ali waves her hands impatiently. "I'm being serious! This could be a huge deal. Artists need a breakout. This could be ours."

It all feels surreal, like rules no longer exist in our world. Despite myself I'm starting to picture it, too: a photo of Ali and me standing next to one of those plinths in Ogilvy's foyer. Lit up on the plinth, adorned with a massive blue ribbon, is something we made.

I picture the NYU pennant on my bedroom wall. My grandparents, aunts, and uncles cooing over Justin and Anastasia's accomplishments but floundering to find anything to talk about with me. My parents wistfully talking about motivation. If Ali and I win this thing, none of that would ever happen again.

I lick my lips. "Yeah. I mean. It could be cool."

"Yes!" Ali leaps to her feet, darts to the backpack she left in Andrew's desk chair, and tugs out that omnipresent color-coded binder. She flips to a new tab, whips out a pen, and says, "So, what are we going to make?"

"I guess . . . I guess it depends. I take a breath, try to clear my head, and roll with it. What medium do you use, mostly?"

"I work across media! I like lots of different styles. I used to paint, primarily, then went through a charcoal phase. I've been painting again since I got back to Ogilvy. The quality of the paints here is way better than what I could get at my high school, so it's fun again. How about you?" She frowns. "I haven't actually seen any of your art yet. Do you have a portfolio?"

I hesitate. I was hoping I'd be able to get through the whole five weeks without showing anyone the pictures I sent in for the application. Andrew, Nathalie, and the others haven't been too pushy, but somehow I think Ali, with her list of artistic inspirations and her conservatory dreams and her whole vibe, will insist.

"Yeah," I say, trying to sound unconcerned. "Here." I pull up the album and hand over my phone.

There's silence as she swipes through. I stare at a point a few feet to the left of Ali, my shoulders hunching. I prepare for her to call off the idea. Obviously she'd be on a different level.

"Niko." Her head rises. She's wearing a breathless smile. "I love these."

"You do?"

"Yes! This one? Wow." She flashes the screen at me. It's the abstract I did based on that cave with the aquamarine water: chalk and charcoal, the brilliant blues and whites and greens caged in by jagged slashes of black.

I smile, sitting up straighter. "Thanks. I really like your stuff, too."

She jots a few notes in her binder. "The only thing is, we have such different styles. I was thinking one unified piece, but I don't think we could pull that off. Your stuff is so, like, raw and visceral." With her non-note-taking hand, she's still swiping through my portfolio pictures, and honestly, that impressed look on her face is doing wonders for my ego. Ali is an *art person*. She's made it her whole identity, and she's acting like my stuff is worth taking seriously.

The wheels in my mind are really starting to turn now. "What if we each did half a piece?" I suggest. "One canvas split into two parts? But—no, maybe that's kind of cheesy, with the half-siblings thing."

"Yeah, we don't want it to look like a gimmick." Ali paces to the window, cradling the binder in her arms like it's her child. "We could both do sections of a sculpture. That wouldn't look so half-and-half, because there wouldn't be a literal dividing line."

"What would we sculpt, though? I mean, we want something that has to do with us being related, right?"

"Definitely." She jots another note. "Yes, we want to stay on-theme. I don't think it would be that fun a story if it's like, you know, here are these great siblings and they made this giant bird together, or whatever."

I laugh, settling back onto my bed. "OK. The thing about sculptures, though—I've only made one or two. I'm just not as good. If part of your pitch is genius art siblings . . . I don't know."

"I've only tried sculpture once before," Ali admits. "So we'll stay with 2D?"

"Yeah. Good. Something 2D that lets us do different styles without being cheesy." I close my eyes and watch colors pass in front of my vision in the dark. "I mean, series are a thing. Multiple drawings, or matched sets, or . . ."

"Yes! We could just do a pair of related pieces! And what we make will have to do with our lives in some way. Right?"

I sit back up so fast that the blood rushes from my head and I sway, dizzy. Ali's face swims around in my vision for a moment, her flushed cheeks, her bright eyes. I break into a wide smile.

"Idea?" she says.

"Idea," I say, rising to my feet. "I'll do a portrait of you. You do a portrait of me."

A dreamy look comes over Ali's face. The binder droops in her grip. "Yes. That's perfect. It shows our different influences and how that changes how we see each other."

"Should we work on them together?"

She nibbles her lip. "No, I think that gets in the way of the idea. I think we should interview each other and find out as much as we can about each other's lives. Then we can make the portraits privately so we don't get influenced by each other's ideas. Otherwise it won't feel truthful. And once we're done—"

"Curfew in ten minutes," calls Professor Abbott's stern voice down the hall. "Get ready for lights out."

Ali stops in the middle of a frenzy of writing, looking as disoriented as I feel. I'd forgotten for a moment that other people existed, that a couple hours ago, this felt like a totally normal Sunday night.

Even weirder—"We, uh," I say, "we still need to figure out what we're doing for LaTonya's paper."

"Oh. Oh! Right. That."

We both let out awkward laughs. Since we last talked about that paper, it feels like we've toppled headfirst into a new reality.

"OK," Ali says. "We can write down what we talked about earlier. You with your little brother and me with my"—she grimaces—"dad stuff."

"Sure. And we'll collab on an ending where it's like, here's what our families don't really talk about, and even if we don't make art about it or anything, it's still part of where we're coming from. Cool?"

"Cool." Ali sets aside the binder carefully, whips up a Google doc on her laptop, and proffers it to me. I sigh as I type my email address into the share field: surf4life04@gmail.com.

An impish grin spreads across Ali's face. She opens her mouth.

"I know, I know," I groan. "I was ten."

She laughs, then grabs up her stuff and heads for the door. "See you tomorrow, Surf for Life."

# Chapter 8

At the beginning of showcase workshop, Professor Rosa informs us that those of us who haven't begun work on our final projects should begin today. He pointedly looks at me and two other kids in the class with empty workstations. "Don't forget that starting Wednesday you'll be on the retreat upstate. You want to have a strong beginning that you can spend that time reflecting on."

I tune him out. No more spinning my wheels. I know that Niko and I can make up for lost time. I can already see the shocked looks on the professors' faces when we reveal our project—and our story.

I pull out my notebook, determined. I start to sketch out some ideas. I jot some words down that make me think of Niko but quickly move on to drawing. I doodle some waves and a figure atop them—he's a surf bro, after all—a picket fence house to represent his picture-perfect family, and the sculpture, the one that looks just like the ones we have at home. I get into that art flow state, where nothing else seems to exist, and my doodles turn into drawings, getting bigger and bolder on the page.

At the end of class, the people around me begin gathering their things and heading out. I'm putting the final touches on another sketch when I feel that familiar light touch on my shoulder.

My head jerks up to see Grace brushing her hair from her eyes, her smile pushing a dimple into her right cheek. "So, I'm guessing you've settled on your final idea?"

"Yes!" I exclaim. I slam my notebook closed in excitement and my papers go flying. We both laugh and start to gather my things.

"Can I ask what you're working on?" asks Grace as we all leave the studio.

"I don't want to spoil anything. I don't want to say until it's finished because part of the piece is the element of surprise."

Brook looks mildly interested. "Cool. Looking forward to seeing what you make." She actually sounds like she means it, and I thrill a little. I text Niko: **About to grab dinner—first interviews afterward?** He responds with a thumbs-up.

A few minutes later, I'm seated with my tray of food at a table with Brook, Jeremiah, and Grace. I'm flattered that these three people, who are honestly aspirational for me—out, queer artists, amazingly talented people—have chosen me to be part of their group.

"OK," says Jeremiah, pointing his fork at me, a grin on his face. "Who was the single first artist who you remember being totally obsessed with?"

"That's easy for me," I say. "Mary Cassatt. All those mother-and-child scenes really spoke to me, since I was raised by my mom and grandma."

Brook gives me a sharp nod, to indicate respect. "Who was yours, Jeremiah?"

"Picasso."

"So cliché." She rolls her eyes. I already knew this would be her response, but Jeremiah is the one person who never seems like he's trying to impress Brook. Often, I feel like he deliberately says uncool or unsophisticated things that will get a reaction out of her.

"It's my honest answer," he says. "My favorite color was blue, and I liked that the people had body parts in funny places."

"I still like Picasso," Grace chimes in. "For exactly the same reasons."

"Who was your first great love?" Brook asks her.

"I was totally obsessed with Giacometti before I even knew who he was. Probably before I knew the name of any artist," she says. "We had a bunch of replicas of his statues around the house, because my mom was a big fan. I used to love picking them up and playing with all the long, skinny limbs and the textures. I liked the dog sculpture since we were never allowed to have a dog. I named it McKenzie and would drag it around the house on a leash."

"You named your fake dog McKenzie?" Jeremiah laughs. "That's such a weird dog name."

"This will probably shock and surprise all of you," says Grace, "but I was a weird kid."

"No weirdos here," says Jeremiah, turning his entire body away from her, pretending to shun her. Grace leans over and bobs her head around him, trying to get into his field of vision. She accidentally knocks a slice of pizza off his tray, and it lands face down on the floor. Grace, Jeremiah, and I crack up. Brook tries for a moment to look embarrassed but gives up and laughs, too.

"I'll go get you another slice," I say, getting up. "I wanted to get seconds anyway."

As I make my way through the cafeteria, I survey the scene. Everywhere I look I see people being their loudest, craziest, most expressive selves, and it gives me a warm, cozy feeling. I love my friends back home, but I'm not down-to-earth like Elise and I'm socially awkward in a way that Jessie never is. I think of Jeremiah saying "no weirdos here," and how, as someone who often feels like a weirdo, it made me feel seen in a way I never have in Queens.

In a room full of people letting ourselves experiment, Niko's restraint winds up sticking out—like a guy from a stock photo pasted onto a Picasso. I catch his eye as I'm walking back to my table with pizza for myself and Jeremiah. He gives me a knowing, friendly nod, and I smile back, our secret pinballing off the inside of my head.

When I get back to the table, Jeremiah has moved on to a new thought experiment. "If you could have dinner with any two artists, living or dead, who would you pick?"

As I mull over the question, Grace says, "Obviously Van Gogh and Gauguin. I want to hear all the juicy roommate insider information."

"You just like to stir up drama," says Jeremiah, and we all collapse in laughter.

"What about Ai Weiwei?" I suggest.

"Yeah, but then you'd have to speak Chinese," says Brook.

"I feel like if we're bringing people back from the grave, we also have access to translation technology," Jeremiah says, rolling his eyes. "Besides, I seriously doubt Grace's favorite French impressionists spoke any English."

I could also pipe up and add that I do, in fact, speak Chinese, so I'd be totally equipped to navigate a conversation with Ai Weiwei, but I keep quiet. It's weird how at home, I'd never try to hide being Chinese, but I'm afraid to mention being queer, while here I feel like there are so many other queer kids, but I don't want it to come up that I'm Chinese. Unbidden, the thought of Nai Nai pops into my head, and I realize with a rush of guilt it's been two days since I texted her last. I feel my stomach turn. Then Brook turns to me and asks what I think of LaTonya as a professor, and I'm back in the moment, guilt forgotten.

After dinner, Niko and I hunker down in one of the study areas. I've prepared a list of questions that I think would be useful to ask. Before I can start, he grabs the list out of my hand and starts reading it out loud.

"What, if anything, were your formative experiences with art?" He laughs. "Come on, man. What is this, the Ogilvy application process all over again?"

"I think it's *important*," I say, grabbing the paper back. "This portrait project won't make any sense if it doesn't come from a deep place of knowledge and understanding. There's a huge difference between a portrait done by someone who really knows the subject and one that you just hire some rando to make. We need this to be in the first group, otherwise it's just like . . . what, you painted a reasonably accurate likeness of each other and also cool, surprise, you're siblings, that's weird!"

I grab my sketchbook and show him the caricature of him surfing. "I mean this nicely, but you're basically just this guy to me right now. And that's what a portrait of that guy looks like. So, I'm sorry I prepared for the assignment, but we don't exactly have a lifetime to become sibling-level close."

"I just think it would be more normal if we had, like, a free-flowing conversation. Like, if you just run down this list of questions, then you won't learn anything about me that you didn't set out to learn."

"It was just a starting point," I say. "Can we try it, at least? It feels weird to me to go deeper without an icebreaker."

"Sure. But I reserve the right to refuse to answer anything that sounds too much like an application question."

I laugh. "It's a deal. OK, first question: What's your very first memory?"

He looks up at the ceiling, his eyes going so far up that it looks like he's trying to spin them around to search his brain for this memory.

"I'm not sure if this is my first memory, but I remember being in a park with my mom and dad. The grass was super green, and we had this big, soft picnic blanket, and I remember being scared of the grass."

I laugh. "Really?"

"Yeah. I didn't want to go anywhere near it. I have this very strong memory of feeling afraid when I looked at it."

"And then what?" I press. "Did your parents take you over to it?"

"I don't remember that. This memory is like, a snapshot. Blanket, comfy. Grass, green and scary. Me, three years old."

"That's so cute," I say, writing down *grass = scary* on my paper.

"I was a cute kid," Niko says.

"I mean, everyone is a cute kid. No need to brag about it."

"I was actually exceptionally cute," he says. "I was voted Cutest Baby in my town three years in a row."

"Really?" I ask. I write that down, too: *Cutest baby 3 years in row*. "Wait, but like, wouldn't you be too old to compete after three years?"

"I'm kidding," he says. "There was no cutest baby competition in town. Or if there was, I was not chosen as the lucky winner."

I laugh. "I could have been voted Cutest Baby in Queens."

"That I refuse to believe. I'm sure you were an adequate baby or whatever, but there must be like, ten million babies in Queens."

"There are not even ten million people in all of New York City," I huff. "Whatever, those are your own genes you're insulting."

I read my next question: "Who are the most important people in your life?"

"My family." He looks away from me when he says it. I also look down at my paper. It's too weird to know that objectively, scientifically, *family* includes me, when we both know that's not what he means. He goes on: "My mom, dad, brother, sister. And my friends. We've been surfing together for years. We have the kind of friendship where we don't need to say things out loud. We just kind of get each other. Like, if one of us is feeling down, we just . . . I dunno, rally around that person until it passes. Do you have any friendships like that?"

I think of Jessie and Elise. "Yeah, I have a couple great friends from school. We're pretty different, but we've grown up together, and that feels really important."

"Oh, and also my girlfriend, Hailey," Niko adds hastily. He looks embarrassed. I'm not sure why. "We've only been together for a couple months, but she's awesome."

"What do you like about her?" I probe.

"She's just like, funny. And cool."

"Is she into surfing? Art?"

"No, she plays volleyball," he says. His eyes glaze over for a moment, like he's thinking of something. "What's the next question?"

We go through my list, questions about his family, his friends, surfing, California. He turns the questions back at me, too, except for the ones he deems too "application-y." I wonder if he's just anxious about college applications. I would be too, if I were a junior.

Not long before curfew, we get onto the subject of our other classes, and I realize I still don't have a great sense of his artistic identity. The portfolio he showed me was only half a dozen pieces, after all. "Do you think I could see some of the sketches you've done this past week?" I ask.

He hesitates before saying, "Sure. One second." He tugs a folder out of his backpack and begins to leaf through assignments, hunched over the papers. I lean closer, curious.

The grades at the top of the pages leap out at me. He flips past three Cs in a row. Then a D, circled at the top of a page where he's barely written a few sentences. His handwriting is big and messy, like he's trying to take up more of the lined paper to disguise how little he's done.

My heart drops. That's why he's hunching—he didn't want me to see his bad grades. I avert my eyes, but I can feel him looking over at me. I wonder if he knows I saw.

I knew that Niko wasn't the most academic person in the world, between his deer-in-the-headlights look when I asked him about his college plans our first day and coming to class unprepared. But I don't understand. I see him carrying his readings around all the time, and he was the one bugging me to do LaTonya's essay. I didn't think he was the type to slack off on assignments like this.

I don't say anything about it, and neither does he. I'm relieved when he reaches the section of the folder with his sketches and begins to spread them across the desk. And they're just as confident, colorful, and dynamic as his portfolio.

I guess he's the type of artist to coast on natural talent and not put any effort in otherwise. I almost envy that. I've never known how to make things look easy.

The next few days pass like this: meals with my friends, free time spent with Niko, and intense sketching in workshop, which raises more questions about him—*How does Niko stand on a surfboard? What do his best friends look like?* I squeeze my other assignments in around the edges. I ditch the list of preplanned questions. The ice feels broken enough to me.

Meanwhile, everyone at Ogilvy is beginning to buzz about the trip upstate, where we'll have basically no supervision and spend time in nature, working on our projects. I'm a little hesitant to break my flow, with everything going so well here, but when Grace talks about nature, and camping, and even things like bug spray and sunburn, a tinge enters her cheeks that makes her look like a painting.

The outdoors isn't my thing, but maybe it could be, this summer. Sometimes during lunch or showcase workshop, I catch myself imagining Grace and me whispering between bunks and sneaking out to stargaze, Grace moving the hem of her nightdress so it doesn't catch on tree bark. I picture us sitting close together on a log by the campfire, laughing as marshmallows droop off our skewers. And sometimes I lie awake in my dorm, look across at Brook's figure under the covers, and wonder if she's imagining the same thing.

# Chapter 9

The pastel tip blunts as I glide it against a piece of scrap paper. As pale green transfers to the page, the patch of vivid blue there becomes more subdued and more complicated, closer to the color of Ali's eyes.

Closer, but not quite right.

I draw a deep breath. I love the smell of the showcase shop: wood shavings, paint, and water. I never thought I'd find a smell I loved as much as the beach, but this place is becoming a close second.

Even better when it's this quiet. Most people are packing last minute for the upstate trip, since the buses are due outside in an hour. So, there are only three other people in the shop, working in silence at the sunlit spread of tables.

I nestle the green pastel back into the tray and pick up a light gray. Maybe this one?

Bingo. The second I touch it to the scrap and pull, the exact shade of Ali's irises surfaces out of the mix. Smiling, I scribble down the numbers of the pastels I used and clip the scrap to a stack of other references.

I think of the stack as the Ali bible. It has her skin tone, lip tone, and hair color, posture references, and sketches of some of her wackier clothes and accessories, like the kite-shaped sunglasses and the glitter-encrusted shoelaces. I seal the bible into a plastic bag so I can pack it upstate, then hunch over a sheet of paper littered with pencil marks. My plan is taking shape.

I go through with a more confident pencil, marking out a view of Ali's street in Queens, courtesy of the Internet. It's a narrow one-way lined with small, polite-looking sedans. Scrawny trees stretch their arms in front of old but well-kept brick buildings, and rusted balcony rails peek over awnings printed with strings of Chinese. I want to amp up the color of the awnings to match them to the bright tones Ali wears, make them both pop against the neutrals of the city. I want the whole scene to feel as energetic and enthusiastic as she is.

I feel like I'm beginning to *get* Ali. Obviously we still don't have the dynamic that I have with Justin and Anastasia, but I'm starting to predict the way she acts, at least. Her energy has no middle ground. During our interviews, she has these long, lip-chewing periods of thought that explode into excited exclamations. When I ask about her art ambitions, her gaze flies around the room like she's looking into a million possible futures, and then she begins to overexplain at a hundred miles an hour.

Ali's a fast, loud, New York City extrovert who's used to a fast, loud life. And like a lot of the kids here, she's probably used to being the biggest personality in the room. I imagine she strolled into Ogilvy with no worries at all.

I wonder what she's got planned for me. Maybe she'll wind up setting me inside my house with my family. She asked a lot of questions about my life at home—obviously family is important to her. Another Ali thing.

The neighborhood's basic shapes have formed. I go over the sketch in charcoal, avoiding the complicated Chinese characters for now.

Next I start in on Ali herself. I mark out the rough angles of her frame, but it's really her face I want to practice. I check my reference photos and mark the point of her chin. Next the line of her nose, which forks upward into the inquisitive slopes of her eyebrows.

*I can kind of see it in the eyebrows*, I think.

I shake the thought, annoyed with myself. Obviously to make these portraits, we have to get comfortable with each other's looks. But it still feels kind of invasive, maybe borderline racist, staring at Ali and having thoughts like, *Are her eyebrows kind of Chinese-looking, or am I making that up?*

I bet loads of people around the world have eyebrows like Ali's. There's no such thing as an inherently Chinese eyebrow. It's stupid even to notice or care.

Still, this morning, I caught myself studying my own face in the mirror, playing a weird game of compare and contrast with my mental image of Ali. At one angle I felt like there was something similar in the shape of our chins or the slopes of our foreheads. But then I tilted my head and it disappeared, and it seemed like there was nothing in common. What's written all over my face is hidden around her edges. There one moment, gone the next.

As the lines of Ali's face grow clearer and darker, something tightens in my chest. It's a minute before I realize the feeling is envy.

I set down the charcoal, frowning down at the emerging Ali on the portrait.

I try to stamp the feeling out. I know I should be happy with the person I am, and whatever—every cheesy message I've gotten from every cheesy high school movie. But I can't help thinking: If we'd had a different roll of the genetic dice and I'd wound up the one with sandy hair and greenish eyes, my childhood would have been so *average*. No comments from random tourists in Landry Beach asking me in loud, slow voices where I'm visiting from. No weird feelings when I look at family photos and see myself sticking out so obviously. Just . . . none of it.

My whole life, my parents have gone on about how appearances don't matter, and how I'm exactly the same Justin and Anastasia. But in the past few years, that's just made me feel like I'm doing something wrong, like I'm bringing this stuff on myself somehow. By "this stuff" I mean the guys in my Algebra II class who decided out of nowhere to nickname me Shang-Chi, even though I don't look like that actor at all. I mean the girl at school last year who asked me how to pronounce the lyrics to some K-pop song. When I said I had no idea, she said, "Wait, why? Aren't you . . . what are you?"

I walked away with my jaw clenched, feeling weirdly humiliated. Even now, I feel embarrassed thinking about it.

As I look at the background I've sketched, my imagination spirals away into another alternate life. What if *I'd* grown up in Queens? Yesterday afternoon, Ali told me all about her best friends Jessie Deng and Elise Chu, and her grandma's tailor shop with its million spools of thread, and the humid basement cafeteria where you can get the best noodles you've had in your life for seven dollars. If I'd grown up in Ali's world, I'd talk about it with the same casual air she does. I'd be so much more confident in actually *being* Chinese.

*Hailey*, I think, reaching for my phone. I open our text conversation and scroll back to last week, to that message she sent on Wednesday.

I didn't realize it had stuck under my skin, but I navigate right there, like I always meant to come back to it.

**Come back home :) That's the great thing about Landry Beach. Here you're unique, in big cities you're just another Asian boy haha**

It was a joke. Right?

I rub my hand over my face and feel another jealous twist in my chest. Joke or not, nobody would say that to Ali.

Trying to cheer myself up, I scroll through our communications and pause on Hailey's beach selfie on Monday—**bet you miss these waves. :)**—and yesterday, a photo of a mystery novel in her lap as she sat in her backyard swing. She sent a heart emoji with that photo. Hailey isn't a mushy romantic. She's never sent a heart before. I imagine her working up the effort to show her feelings even that little bit.

I haven't told her about Ali. I'm not sure why. We talk about family stuff all the time—she knows everything that's happened with Justin, and she's told me about her weird relationship with her mom. Last year, when Hailey got invited to senior prom as a sophomore, her mom started pinching her underarms and her thighs in the leadup to the dance, making little comments like, "You've got to work a little harder if you want those photos to look good!"

"She said *what*?" I asked Hailey when she told me.

Hailey shrugged. "I know she feels like shit about her own weight, so she's just taking it out on me." Her voice was weirdly flat—but she did tell me.

For some reason the Ali situation just seems different than discussing our families back home. Like it'll make her see me differently.

I exhale. I'll tell her later. After all, I haven't even told my parents, and they should get the news first.

Instead, I snap a photo of my messy workstation and send it to Hailey with the caption, **i wonder if dali had people who cleaned up his stuff?**

When I turn off my phone, I see myself in the screen and flinch. There are charcoal marks all over my face. Every stressed-out touch left a dark streak.

At the sink, I wipe my face clean, then glance at myself in the mirror. *Back to normal*, I tell myself. But even as I think it, I'm envisioning Ali beside me in the glass, our spot-the-difference puzzle. I'm wondering how Hailey really sees me—*unique* or *just another Asian?*—and wishing I could edge away from both possibilities. I'm seeing myself alongside my camp friends, who laugh along with me like they understand me but who don't know anything about how I grew up.

I turn away. I think I'm starting to lose track of how normal feels.

"Hey!" Ali whispers as we stand in line for the second bus.

I glance back. "Uh, hi," I whisper back. "Why are we whispering?"

"Because. I'm checking how Secret Operation Joint Showcase Project is going."

I chortle as I hoist my suitcase into the coach bus's storage area. "That's the worst secret operation name ever."

"No, it's not," she protests. "It's—" Whatever defense she had devolves into a squeak as she tries to lift her suitcase onto the stack. She nearly unbalances.

"God, let me get that," I say, trying not to sound pitying. "You're going to pop your arm out of its socket."

"Oh, sorry we don't all have *deltoids*. Some of us were born with serious medical conditions where we don't have any arm muscles."

I grin. "Yeah, sure." I lift her suitcase in one-handed, because I can, and it's fun to watch her scowl deepen. "Anyway, showcase is going fine. How about you?"

Her scowl evaporates. Immediately, she's back to secretive-smile Ali. "The operation is on to Phase Two," she stage-whispers, tugging her binder out of her backpack and paging to her master plan. "Are we on schedule to finish rough drafts upstate?"

"I could do that." I tap her bulleted list as we climb up onto the bus. "Do I need to like, set up a Google Calendar so that you can check in on my ETAs or whatever?"

Ali snaps the binder shut. I grab my hand back just in time, and she sniffs. "Mine is going well, too!" she chirps, navigating down the aisle over people's legs and backpacks sticking out from seats. "I can't wait to show you. Ooh—OK, this is me. Later! Don't get carsick. Buses suck. Bye!"

She topples into the seat beside her friend Grace. God, she's such a dork. I'm still smiling as I head toward the back of the bus, where most of the older kids are sitting.

Andrew leans into the aisle and waves me over. He's sitting next to Jen. Behind them, the seat beside Nathalie is open, clearly being saved for me.

I give Andrew a puzzled look. Last night, as we were packing for the trip, he told me, "I have to sit next to Nathalie on the bus, bro. This is important."

"Uh," I said. "Why?"

"Because! This bus ride is basically long enough to count as a first date. Haoran told me that last year he sat next to one of his hookups on the bus ride up, and two days later they were spending all their time making out in the woods."

"Wait, hang on. *One* of Haoran's hookups?"

"Yeah, he hooked up with like four people."

"In five weeks?"

"Exactly! So clearly he knew what he was doing. Although he does have the tattoos, so he's got an advantage. Anyway. Bus ride!" Andrew flung aside his usual blazer and muttered, "No, I've worn that like sixty times."

Now his carefully selected outfit—green corduroy pants with a black-and-white optical illusion button-up—is clashing outrageously with Jen's pink-and-orange ensemble. I bend down as I pass their seat, pretending to tie my shoe, and whisper to Andrew, "What happened?"

Andrew glances over. Jen is leaning over her seat to talk to Nathalie. "Jen yanked me into this seat. Like, with her hands."

"Oh." I raise my eyebrows. "You think she . . . ?"

Andrew shrugs but aims a hopeful glance back at Jen. "I don't know. Jen is so cool, too."

I grin and shake my head, getting back to my feet. I have no idea how Andrew operates like this.

I sink into the seat beside Nathalie. "Hey."

She looks quickly away from Jen. "Niko," she greets, just on the borderline of formal as always.

Jen waves hello, too. She shoots Nathalie a knowing little smile, then sinks back into her seat beside Andrew.

That smile sounds an alarm bell in my head.

I lean forward to mess with my backpack, buying some time. I think I'm pretty good at reading people. And Jen's smile was a wing woman look.

*Nathalie?* I think. *No way.*

As I straighten up and settle back into the bus seat, I glance over at her. If Nathalie likes me, it could explain why Jen was all aggressive about getting Andrew to sit with her.

I shift uncomfortably in my seat. I don't get how Nathalie could be interested in me. Serious, intimidating, analytical Nathalie? I guess we both like art, but even then, she treats it like a religion and I'm pretty obviously going off my gut. What else do we have in common?

Then again, maybe Nathalie doesn't think about having stuff in common when she's into someone. No, she probably has some mental algorithm that involves calculus and four different philosophy books.

"Head count, Bus One," Professor Abbott intones over the coach bus's speaker system. We shout out numbers up to forty-two, and soon we're peeling away from Ogilvy, heading up past the row houses toward the busy street ahead.

I'm still thinking about Nathalie as the bus honks and lurches out onto the main road. I'm dreading all the stuff that comes next here. I'll have to hurt Nathalie's feelings, and Andrew might get awkward around me when he finds out. Maybe he'll even resent that she likes me instead of him.

Until Hailey, my whole love life was a series of pathetic one-sided crushes. I've never had two girls like me at the same time.

I frown and catch myself rubbing my forehead for probably the eightieth time today. Why haven't I mentioned Hailey to my friends yet? After ten days of Ogilvy I haven't even mentioned her name. What's wrong with me?

In front of us, Andrew and Jen have struck up a cheerful conversation about color theory. I'm too aware of the silence between me and Nathalie, and the fact that these seats are pretty small and my knee is about two inches from hers.

I clear my throat and gesture vaguely with my phone. "Uh—sorry I'm not super entertaining right now. I'm just waiting for my girlfriend to text me back."

"Oh," says Nathalie. Mild surprise touches her features, but if she's upset, she doesn't show it. "Of course. Is this a girl from California?"

"Yeah. Her name's Hailey." I pull up a picture of us on the beach and show Nathalie.

The corners of Nathalie's mouth lift. "She's beautiful. You two are very aesthetically appealing."

"Thanks." I swallow. The worst is over, but for some reason, the back of my neck is still prickling with heat. *Aesthetically appealing*, I think. "Um. Are you dating anyone back in Idaho?"

"No, not me," says Nathalie with a wry smile. "My parents are the 'no dating until college' type. So, I'd want to really like somebody before risking being disinherited. No offense to Idaho boys."

I laugh, and feel a confused ego boost—so, if Nathalie was making moves to get together with me, it means she likes me enough to piss off her parents?

Before I can think of anything to say, my phone lets out a cheerful *ding!* I look down and see new messages from Hailey arriving in response to the picture of my workstation.

**Ooh wow look at my artist boyfriend**

**Are you going to make me something?**

I glance over at Nathalie, feeling guilty. She smiles with genuine warmth and says, "Go ahead," with a nod at my phone. Then she pulls out an enormous hardback called *Motifs in Chinese Art at the Turn of the Millennium* and cracks it open.

I sink down in my seat and begin to search for the next right answer.

# Chapter 10

By the time we get to our cabin site upstate, it's after dinner and beginning to get dark. We go straight to our bunks.

I heave my things onto the bed with a little more energy than I need to. I slept the entire bus ride up and I'm feeling revitalized, ready to let this four-day break inspire me. I can count on one hand the number of nights I've spent outside the city in my life.

Grace is one of the last to enter the cabin. She ambles in next to Brook. Their heads are close together, and Grace is nodding intently. They're probably discussing their showcase pieces. Grace has been looking forward to filming some nature clips to show over the painting she's been working on. Suddenly, Grace lets out a shriek of laughter and shoves Brook playfully. "You are so *bad*," she squeals.

OK, maybe they aren't having a conversation about showcase pieces. I turn away so nobody can see disappointment spread across my face. I wish I hadn't gotten my hopes up about meeting a girl at camp, and I especially wish I hadn't let myself get attached to Grace. Brook is glamorous and sophisticated in a way I can only aspire to be. Next to her, I feel like a scurrying little creature, eager to please and easily impressed.

A shadow looms in my peripheral vision as I'm pulling things out of my bag.

"Hey stranger! You don't mind if I take the top bunk, do you?" It's Grace.

"Of course not," I say. "That is, unless you're tired of me, ha." I intend this to sound funny. Instead, it sounds awkward. *Scurrying little creature*, I think.

She doesn't miss a beat. "Better the devil you know, right?" She grins and clambers up to the top bunk, throwing herself down so heavily the springs groan. She leans over the edge. Her curls are so long, they nearly come down to my own mattress. "What are you most excited about for this week?"

I stop unpacking and think, staring out the window. We're right by the woods. The last of the light is nearly gone, and all I can see is a block of dark, dense green leaves silhouetted against the deep sky, fluttering slightly in the breeze.

"The beauty." I sigh, as if to myself.

"Ali! Such a romantic. I was going to say s'mores, but now I feel like I need to say something more profound."

"I'm excited about s'mores, too," I say. "And the absence of the hot-garbage smell."

"Yesss. I wish we were *actually* camping, you know?"

"Totally," I say. This is a complete lie. I already feel like we are *actually* camping, and we have bathrooms and showers attached to our cabins. I have never been *actually* camping, by which I assume Grace means sleeping in tents, at the mercy of ticks, bears, and rain, and I never plan to. I steer the conversation back to her so I don't have to keep lying. "Your family camps a lot, right?"

"Yeah," she says, that flush of enthusiasm coming into her face again. "Basically every year for our family vacation. Last Christmas we went to Utah. Have you ever been to Utah?"

I have never left the tristate area, so I just shake my head.

"Oh my gosh, you absolutely have to go. You would love it. The *beauty*!" She laughs gently. "I've never seen anything like it. It's amazing, but also such a weird place. There are all these red rock formations. Huge stone arches and columns. We spent a day in Bryce Canyon, which is like, if you imagined being lost in a giant's carpet, but the pile is all rock. You're wandering through these dense columns of red rock dozens of feet high. It's a trip."

Despite my complete lack of interest in ever sleeping outside, ever, I wish I could tag along on a trip like that with Grace's family.

"Can I see pictures?" I ask.

"Sure!" she says. "But you're going to have to come up here. I'm settled into my top bunk life and I'm not moving."

My breath hitches. She's inviting me up to her bunk. *Be natural*, I tell myself. *It doesn't mean anything.* A little awkwardly, I climb up and sit gingerly at the foot of her bed, trying my best to arrange myself so that I'm not completely on top of her.

"Get over here!" She grabs my arm and pulls me down so we're lying next to each other. My cheeks burn and I'm sure they're bright red, but she's looking at her phone and doesn't seem to notice. She flicks through her pictures with a long, manicured nail until she finds the ones she's looking for.

"They're called hoodoos," she says. "These column things."

There are several pictures of her family, looking sporty and outdoorsy in matching puffer coats, arranged artfully in front of several columns of red rocks. Grace is in the middle, with one brother who looks like he's a couple years older and one much younger brother, impossibly cute, with several missing teeth that he shows off in every photo. Her mom looks just like her, but where Grace is careless and unpolished, her mom looks elegant and put-together, her mess of curls artful rather than perpetually out-of-control, her face free of freckles.

"Your family looks like they're selling whatever coat brand that is," I joke.

She laughs. "Yeah, my mom is very image conscious. We probably spent a quarter of the time at Bryce just trying to get these pictures to turn out how she wanted. She's a museum curator, so it kind of comes with the territory. She loves all of our outfits to 'speak to each other' in family photos." She snorts a little. "I wish I were making that up."

"I think it's cool, actually," I say. "My mom is a fashion designer, but she doesn't care at all what I wear. She's very subscribed to the idea that you can't tell your kids what to do. Do you and your mom go shopping together?"

"Ha. We used to, but I had to stop letting her come with me. We both have a very clear idea of how I should dress, and we do *not* always see things eye to eye."

She scrolls through idly, stopping on a picture of her older brother in a tux standing next to a pretty Asian girl in a black sparkly cocktail dress.

"Prom?" I ask.

She nods.

"Who's his date?"

She makes a dismissive sound. "That's Whitney, his girlfriend." The word *girlfriend* is full of disdain. I can't help tensing up. Maybe Grace *is* weird about Asians?

I tread carefully. "Sounds like you're not a huge fan."

"Ugh, not at all. To start, she ignores me one hundred percent of the time that she's around. We've been at the same school together since I was in kindergarten and she was in second grade, and she's completely on her high horse about it. Also, she dumped my brother for, like, two weeks to go out with this other guy and went crawling back as soon as he dumped her. It was all very dramatic. Basically I don't think she's very nice to me *or* him."

Perfect. This saga has taught me a little bit about how much more dramatic Grace's school is than mine, and absolutely nothing about how she or her family might feel about her dating someone Chinese.

It's fully dark now, and people have finished unpacking. The rest of the girls in the cabin are either curled up in bunks in groups and pairs, chatting, or already tucked into bed with books and phones.

"How about you?" Grace asks. "What's your family like? Do you have siblings?"

"Oh, I, uh." I'm bursting to tell her about what Niko and I have figured out, but it's not my secret alone to divulge. I sidestep the question: "It's actually just me and my grandma at home. I used to live with my mom, but now she lives with my stepdad on Long Island." Everything I've said is technically true, but framed in a way to minimize the weirdness of our former living arrangement to people who might not get it.

"And you said your mom is a fashion designer. Which explains where you get your great sense of style from."

I feel again like I'm glowing, but this time from within. "Thank you," I say. It feels inadequate, but I silently congratulate myself for not babbling.

"What's your grandma like? Are you close?"

"Yeah," I say. "Not like, going-shopping-together close, or tell-her-everything close, but a different kind of close." It would be so easy for me to mention something that makes it obvious my family is Chinese: tell Grace what neighborhood we live in, or mention what my favorite foods are at home, or talk about what language we speak at home. It would be so easy to mention my heritage that it almost feels like I'm lying if I don't, since she so clearly believes I'm white. But I really, really like her, and I don't want her to think of me any differently. What if she starts acting like the girls in sixth grade? Still friendly on the surface, but *off*, too, in ways that only arise every so often?

"You should come over when the program is finished!" Grace says suddenly, as if she's just thought of the idea. Meanwhile, I have been thinking about this possibility basically since the second that she told me she was from Brooklyn.

"I would love that!" I say, and we lie there quietly for a moment, side-by-side, as people whisper around us. Grace continues to flip through pictures on her phone.

LaTonya pokes her head in the door and sings out, "Lights out, ladies!" She flips the switch and the cabin goes dark. I feel the hairs on my arm prickle. Grace is so close, and the dark makes it feel like everyone else has disappeared and it's just her and me.

Then a voice rings out from across the room: "I do *not* like Taylor!" A cascade of giggles follows the outburst.

Our silence goes from companionable to slightly awkward. I don't want to broach the topic of whether Grace has a crush on anyone. I'd rather just avoid thinking about the near certainty that she likes Brook, who at this moment is lying several bunks away from us, just out of sight but certainly not out of mind. And I definitely need to avoid thinking about the fact that our calves are resting slightly against each other. And that I can smell the faint hint of jasmine from her pillowcase.

"Anyway," I say too loudly. "You should come visit, too. My grandma would cook you a feast."

"I would love that. I love meeting my friends' families."

"Of course you do," I tease. "You're like, every parent's dream."

"Not always," Grace says. She turns off her phone and puts it away. "I had a girlfriend this past year, and her parents did *not* like me."

"Oh," I say. "I didn't mean it like that. I mean, I know not everyone's parents are accepting. Actually, my grandma doesn't know that I'm, you know. Queer. I just meant that you're so outgoing and friendly. It feels like you always know just what to say to people." Babbling again. Scurrying.

"I don't really feel like that most of the time," she says. "At school I'm a little weird. I spend all my time in the art room. I've been going to the same school since I was in kindergarten, and it feels like if you didn't make your friends in kindergarten, then you just . . . won't have friends until you graduate high school. I have dyslexia, and when I was little, I was always getting special attention or being taken out of regular class. And I couldn't read out loud when I got called on, and it would embarrass me so much I used to cry. Anyway, nobody wants to be friends with the weird crying girl, so it was lonely for me in elementary school. Then I found art, and I had something to do with all my time. I guess that's also why I talk more like people our parents' age than people our age. I spend more time with my teachers and parents."

"Well, I'm so glad that I've gotten to be friends with you at camp," I say. "And . . . I really admire you. As an artist, but also as a person."

Somehow, for once, this feels like enough. Grace smiles at me in the dark, and my heart races.

The next morning, I wake to impossibly loud birdsong and an uncomfortable cramp in my neck. I realize I've fallen asleep in Grace's bunk, and I'm simultaneously thrilled and embarrassed. The light outside the window is a rosy gold, and from a quick glance around the room, nobody else seems to be up yet. I inch my way to the very bottom of the bunk. My skin is bathed in the rose-gold glow from the window, and it feels not so much like a trick of the light as a manifestation of the joy bubbling inside me.

I glance back at Grace. In sleep, her light brown lashes are fanned over the top curves of her cheeks, and her lips are slightly parted. There's a curl of hair falling over one eye. For the first time, I'm letting myself believe that she might feel the same way about me that I do about her.

I climb into my dark, cool bunk for another hour of sleep.

I wake up properly when everyone is stirring around me. The dawn light has given way to a bright, harsh glare, and with it my giddiness has been tempered. I shouldn't get my hopes up.

Sure enough, Grace and Brook sit next to each other at breakfast, talking so quietly that nobody else can hear what they're saying. Jeremiah tries to join their conversation several times, and each time they just nod and turn back to each other. He raises his eyebrows and turns to me instead.

"Studio time?"

"Studio time," I agree firmly. We bus our trays and head out of the cafeteria. Brook and Grace don't even seem to notice that we're leaving.

In typical over-the-top Ogilvy style, rather than herd us into a multipurpose room, they've brought up "portable studios"—climate-controlled trailers where we can work on our pieces. Unlike workshop back at Ogilvy, where we're divided into groups for several hours, here we all work together with no official start time, end time, or real supervision. Today, LaTonya is nominally on duty, but she's sitting in a corner with headphones in while the rest of Ogilvy paints, sculpts, and draws furiously around her.

Jeremiah and I set up shop in a quiet corner of the studio, and he lays out some of his prints from the city. As chatty as he was in the cafeteria, he falls silent almost immediately upon entering the studio, as if the change in setting caused an automatic change in disposition. I know he's really been looking forward to our time upstate, since it'll allow him to get totally different shots from what he can get in New York.

Niko saunters in just as I dive into work. He greets us, takes the station opposite us, and also immediately hunkers down, headphones on, to work on his canvas. So far, we've both kept to our promise that we won't look at each other's work until we're done, but I'm *dying* of curiosity to see Niko's draft. Since we're not in the same workshop, I haven't even had a sense of what media he'll be working with, but today I see him pull out a set of pastels. *Interesting*.

Despite my jokes with Niko about how I only see him as a surfer caricature, I've decided the beach really is the best place to set his portrait. Where he's from seems so integral to who he is as a person.

He's so laid-back and confident, nothing seems to ruffle him. He's the opposite of the tightly wound, overachieving New Yorkers I've grown up around.

I went to Google Maps street view to get a sense of what the beaches in his hometown look like, and I'm glad I did. The long, pristine expanses of sand are nothing like the crowded, narrow, strips of urban beach I've been going to my whole life.

I squint at the real-life Niko standing across from me and compare him to the version that's developing on the canvas. The likeness is good, and I think I've captured something about him—his whole body and even most of his facial expression are at ease, but I've also managed to capture some of the intensity that comes out in his eyes during moments when he's working on his canvas or talking about surfing or his family.

I work for a few more hours. As I paint, an idea comes to me: Seeing Niko at work reminds me so much of Nai Nai at work, sewing other people's clothes. The way his brow furrows is just like hers; the way he doesn't even take a break to wipe the color off his hands or have a sip of water is just like the intensity that she gets. Thinking of her, I decide to add fabric detailing to the picture. It will give it some extra depth, some visual interest—and it'll imbue the portrait with additional meaning.

We're allowed to go into town as part of Ogilvy's summer-camp rules. Buses leave after lunch, and we can shop for supplies, take photographs, set up our easels in town. Anything goes, as long as we sign out first.

I'm starving, so I run to the cafeteria to grab food. When I return to the studio, the room is basically empty. Niko and Jeremiah have both left already. I look at my canvas and think about what I want to add.

White lace for the caps on the waves; that's easy. Maybe old patchwork Hawaiian shirts for Niko's clothes? Might be a little kitschy, but I like the idea. It's worth a try. Shiny gold velvet would be nice for the sand.

I write it all down and run for the bus.

There's a flea market in town, and it's absolutely perfect. I'm not sure how long I've spent bobbing from stall to stall, picking up a scarf here, an old T-shirt there, each only a couple bucks. There's no way I can fit *all* of it into Niko's portrait, but some of the fabrics have inspired concepts for other portraits—a purple taffeta makes me want to do a portrait of Nai Nai right by the sign for the 7 train near our apartment, and a green tulle makes me think of my mom sitting in the bright grass of her new suburban house.

Then I spot a yellow sundress across the room, and it reminds me of the dress I borrowed from Grace. I run over to try it on. It's a *little* big but fits well enough—and it feels *right* in a way that my impulse online purchases haven't, really. Looking around at the racks, I realize that I *love* the look of everything I see. Long cotton dresses in bright prints and patterns—perfect for the summer heat and totally unlike any of the clothes I have at home.

I grab things willy-nilly, as if there were a mob of ravenous shoppers behind me, even though the market is basically empty. By the time I check out, I've added to my bag of materials two dresses for myself, as well as a scarf and a pair of sandals. As I'm pushing through an entire rack of sarongs, I catch a glimpse of Niko across the room, flipping through some old comic books. I rush over to him, eager to share my progress.

He smiles when he sees me.

"Hey!" I exclaim. Things between us have grown more natural as we've spent more time together. It used to feel weird to share a big secret with someone who was essentially a stranger, but I don't feel like he's a stranger anymore. I would even call him a good friend.

"Hey, how's it going?" he says. "Nice shopping bag." He nods at my overflowing bag.

"I got inspired," I admit. "I had a great breakthrough when I was working on your portrait today. It's coming along so much faster than I expected. I think it's because I feel like I really know you now? Anyway, this morning I realized I was basically already done with the main section and now I just want to perfect it. And I had this idea to add some fabric to it. So here I am!"

He's nodding enthusiastically, like he really gets what I'm saying. "Me too," he exclaims. "Like, I've *never* gotten so much done so fast. I think it's got to be how good an idea this project is. Kudos to you for that."

"I was about to go get ice cream," I say in a flash of inspiration, feeling the need to celebrate. "Want to come?"

He agrees enthusiastically and we push open the door to the street, squinting in the bright light.

As if I'd brought it into existence by sheer force of wanting it, there is in fact an ice cream store across the street. A bell rings as we enter, and I feel like I'm the main character in a sitcom about people in a small town. The blast of cold air against my sweaty skin sends a pleasant shiver down my spine. A blond guy with acne, probably around Niko's age, lounges against the counter dressed in a red-and-white striped shirt. I examine the flavors one by one.

"Can I try the caramel?" I ask. "And also the strawberry, actually."

"Sure," he says with a smile. "Anything for you?" he asks Niko.

"No thanks," says Niko.

"So where are you from?" he asks, still looking at Niko as he hands me two small spoons of ice cream.

"We're from a summer art program in the city," I say with my mouth full. "We're here for a few days."

He looks amused and still doesn't look away from Niko. "No, like where are you *really* from?"

Niko's brow furrows deeper. "California," he mumbles.

The blond guy nods. "But like, originally, I mean." He gestures at his own face, smiling.

All of a sudden, I really don't want ice cream anymore.

"Let's go!" I exclaim. "I just remembered I told Jeremiah I'd meet him at the park! Sorry thanks bye!"

I grab Niko by the sleeve and pull him out of the shop, power walking us both down the block.

Niko gives me a bemused look. "What was that all about?"

"I didn't want to buy ice cream from that *racist* guy!"

He laughs and looks away, stretching his arms behind him. "So . . . I guess that's never happened to you before," he says.

"Not *literally* that," I say. I tell him about the white girls I was friends with in sixth grade, and how weird it is when Nai Nai and I go out together in Flushing and people take my light hair and eyes like an invitation to have a whole conversation about my parentage. "It's so annoying for that to be the constant conversation starter, you know?"

"Yeah," he says. "I feel the same way about it as you do. I know that guy doesn't mean to be racist—"

I inhale, ready to disagree, but he steamrolls over me. "I know you think he should know better, but I don't think he means badly. It's like you described: It's just annoying that it happens all the time. I think it just comes with the small-town territory for people who look like me. I never really thought about what it would be like in a city, until I came to Ogilvy. It's probably nice, living in a neighborhood like yours."

I take a moment to think. "It is. For me it's less about *looking* like the people around me, since, well, I obviously don't in Flushing." It feels awkward to acknowledge this out loud. We haven't really talked before about the difference in our looks. We're both avoiding each other's eyes, although I can tell Niko's still listening. "But . . . it's nice knowing that I share a culture with them. That we have something in common that most other Americans don't."

I mull over my own words as we amble down the street in silence. I meant what I said, but at the same time I like how at Ogilvy, I don't share a culture with the people around me. I share something else—a love for art, a desire to be my own self.

As we approach the bus pickup spot, I have an idea. "OK, I know we agreed we wouldn't show each other our portraits until we were done, but . . . I honestly already feel so good about mine. And it sounds like you do, too."

"Should we show each other what we have so far?" Niko asks.

We go to our phones to find the most recent versions of our work.

"Swap on three?" I ask. Niko rolls his eyes at the unnecessary drama, but he agrees.

We hand each other our phones. I'm waiting for a gasp of approval from Niko, or an encouraging word, but I don't hear anything. Then I forget to be offended by his silence, because my eyes have focused on the screen in front of me, and I *hate* what I see.

There's a generic-looking girl in the foreground, but she's totally overshadowed by the chaotic background scene around her. She's standing on my street in Queens. Obviously Niko did the same thing I did and googled to see what my neighborhood looks like, but unlike me, he's made the whole portrait about the background. In real life, my street is quiet, sedate even, but on the canvas, large, campy-looking signs with Chinese characters jump out in bright pastel, while the girl in the front could be anyone. With her fair hair, she looks like a tourist in the luridly drawn neighborhood.

I don't understand why he's chosen to focus so hard on the city view. We were supposed to be focusing on *each other*, not our hometowns. The beach in Niko's portrait is pretty but very clearly part of the background. Whereas this portrait on Niko's phone—this is not at all what we had agreed on. I even feel a little hurt. All those evenings hanging out, getting to know each other, and he's just slapped a picture of a girl onto a background he found on Google? Where am *I* in this picture? Does he just think that the only noteworthy thing about me—despite *all of our conversations*—is the fact that I grew up in a Chinese neighborhood?

Blood rushes to my face. The more I think about it, the angrier I get.

"What do you think?" he asks, eagerly.

I don't want to hurt his feelings. He's obviously worked hard and done research.

"I think the pastels were a great medium to get such vibrant color into the scene," I start. "But I feel like the background kind of overwhelms the foreground?" I'm aware it sounds kind of bratty to say, "Your picture of me doesn't focus enough on me!"

"But that's kind of the point," he says. "I wanted to put you in your background, in your element. I think the city part is just as important—more important, actually—than what you look like because it's made you who you are."

But I'm not *purely* a product of my city or my neighborhood, I want to say. We don't all emerge from Flushing as identical beings with identical personalities just because we all grew up in the same environment. Everyone from *his* town isn't the same; being from *his* town isn't the most interesting thing about him. It's hard to think of how to say this out loud without sounding defensive. As I'm contemplating how to say this, he speaks up again.

"I like that you included the beach in the background of my portrait," he begins, slowly. He's also unhappy, I can tell immediately. He's also starting out with a compliment, just like I did. It's how everyone at Ogilvy gives negative feedback: a slow, hesitant compliment, followed by all the things you actually hate about the piece. The less sincere or more stupid the compliment sounds, the more it means the person giving feedback hates your work. Niko really, really hates the portrait. "I just don't . . . this sounds petty, but I don't think it looks like me."

"What do you mean?" I take my phone back and look at the portrait. "It does look like you." This is such an insulting piece of feedback that I think I'm about to lose my temper. The most basic thing you can do when making a portrait is make it look like the person. All of us at Ogilvy who do portraiture have figured out how to make a portrait "look like the person."

"I mean, I get that you're painting in a more impressionist way or whatever, but I feel like you didn't keep any of the things that make me look myself. My eyes don't look like that. My nose doesn't look like that." He hesitates, then says, "You kind of made me look like a caricature of an Asian guy, which is . . . weird."

"I did not," I say, shoving my phone in my pocket. "It's going to end up more detailed when I'm done, to start with. But it already looks like you. Everyone who's seen this portrait knows I'm doing a portrait of you."

"That's because there are four Asian guys at this entire program, and everyone knows you and I are friends."

"At least I bothered to try and paint you," I say. "I didn't just draw a generic picture of Queens—a place you have never been—and add another face to the crowd."

"That's what I'm *saying*," he says. "It's *not* me. It doesn't *look* like me."

"I put a lot of work into this," I continue, in a low, angry tone. "I've been tearing out my hair trying to get this right. I feel like you didn't even try with mine."

"There's more to *trying* than writing down a page of questions and treating every project like a research paper for class!" he says. His voice is raised now. I'm so angry I can barely see six feet in front of me, and I can feel that I'm about to start crying.

"I don't think you know what it means to try," I say.

Instead of yelling back at me, Niko just turns around and storms away, leaving me to wait alone for the bus.

# Chapter 11

Ali's words ring inside my skull as I stride through the outskirts of town and into the surrounding woods. The shade gives me some relief from the heat that's lancing through my limbs.

I've gone maybe a mile down the trail when I stop, breathing hard. I close my eyes, feel the wind coasting over me, and try to imagine the salt air of the beach back home.

It doesn't work.

*I don't think you know what it means to try.*

This is just like the argument I had with Justin the week we found out about his bullying. He was so aggressive at home, moody and obnoxious and taking everything like an insult, until one day I snapped at the dinner table. "Bro," I said, "stop taking it out on us because *you* couldn't act like a normal person at school."

Like he'd had it prepared, he snapped back, "So I should act like you instead and just fail at everything?"

That's how my little brother sees me. It's probably how my parents and Hailey see me, too. Of course Ali's the same. I *knew* she saw my grades that day I showed her my sketches—I knew she was secretly judging me.

My nails dig into my palms. I've stopped at a section of the trail that overlooks a shimmering lake. The water looks clean and bright, fed by a river to the north and draining out through creeks to the southeast.

*She's younger*, I tell myself. Ali's barely out of freshman year. I shouldn't care so much what she thinks—about my portrait or who I am.

Except I do. I've seen Ali's portfolio. I know she's good at art. So, what, did she just not try with the portrait she made of me?

The heat is making me itch. I stride toward the lakeside, where a smaller trail leads toward an ancient-looking dock. I strip off my shirt as I storm forward, my thoughts turning in tight, furious spirals. I wish I'd never seen that portrait. The hair, the eyes, the mouth—why did she have to stylize it like that? All her talent, and she used it to flatten me into the same stereotype I've been trying to get away from all my life?

When my own sister looked at me, that was what she saw.

I reach the dock and barrel down the weathered planks. My breaths are sharp in my chest, and questions are beginning to pelt me. Is this the reason I have to deal with people's jokes at school, and Chris Carlson's *diversity smile*, and even stuff as unimportant as that ice cream guy's *where are you really from?* Does all this shit happen because I *don't* belong in my own country and never will? I stop dead at the end of the dock, head pounding. Maybe it's time for me to grow up. Maybe I should just accept that when people look at me, they don't see themselves.

I kick off my shorts and shoes, tear off my socks, and hurl myself into the lake.

The water explodes around me. Then I sink. For a long moment, I hold my breath under the surface and listen to my hard, fast heartbeat.

My hair floats upward, off my scalp. Cool water slides between my toes. The gentle currents eddying from the river glide over my skin, and my pulse slows in my ears.

. I let myself float up toward the surface, exhaling streams of bubbles to control how quickly I rise. Then my head is pushing gently into the summer air.

It no longer feels like ninety degrees. The breeze is cool over my wet face, and I can smell the trees that surround the lake, and the old wood of the dock, and pollen. The sounds of the woods, which I hadn't registered before with my blood running so hot, suddenly seem peaceful. The rustle of leaves. The birds singing back and forth, half a dozen songs. The shift of water against the dock's supports.

As I push my body around the lake, powering myself through the water with stroke after stroke, I realize how much pent-up energy I've been holding in my muscles the past week and a half. At Ogilvy, I didn't think about trying to find a gym or make time in our packed schedule to work out. I flip onto my back and close my eyes, the sunlight tickling my navel.

Ali's portrait of me swims up out of the darkness.

I move my hand over the slopes of my face. Was it the portrait that upset me so much, or the reminder?

The reminder, I think. But—I don't hate how I look. Do I?

I like working out because it shows me the ways I can change. I don't think I hate myself, though.

The thought is weirdly comforting.

Sure, I wish things were different sometimes. Wasn't I mentally swapping lives with Ali just the other day? Even before then, I guess I've had the thought that if I were white, like an equivalently good-looking white guy, would I have spent the first seventeen years of my life having doomed crushes, feeling totally undesirable?

But I know that's not just me. Grayson tenses up whenever there's a joke about short guys in movies. Devin had this whole complex with his hair in middle school where he buzzed it off because kids at school kept making fun of the color. Even Hailey. She pretends she doesn't care, but sometimes I catch her looking at herself in profile when we pass by glass storefronts, frowning and sucking in her stomach. I know it's not exactly the same, but it's in the same ballpark. None of us can get out of our bodies, I guess, no matter how much we want to.

I swim until I'm breathing hard and my calves are twinging. Then I pull myself out of the water and sit on a bench at the end of the dock, twisting water out of my boxers.

I consider texting Hailey. She's my girlfriend—shouldn't she want to know if I'm feeling like this? But I don't reach for my phone. She wouldn't know what to say if I tried to explain.

I don't know how long I've been staring at the water when a voice calls, "Niko!"

Footsteps beat at the other end of the dock. I grab for my shorts and pull them on, and when I turn around Andrew, Jen, and Nathalie are ambling my way, Andrew waving, Jen already sunburned, Nathalie wearing a baseball cap and sunglasses.

I force a smile, trying to think of a way to leave without being rude. "Hey," I call back. "Where are the Wus?"

"With the other international kids, in the studio," says Andrew. "Like we probably should be, but oh well."

Nathalie tugs irritably at her braid. "I'm glad they're getting some use out of it. I mean, if we're going to kill the environment dragging that air-conditioned monstrosity all over the—"

"Wait," Andrew says, sounding appalled. As they reach my end of the dock, Andrew flings out his arms to stop Jen and Nathalie in their tracks, like I'm an alligator on the attack. "Niko, since when are you *ripped*? Why do you have like sixteen abs?"

Jen lets out a bubbly little laugh. "Shouldn't you have known that? Being his roommate?"

Andrew shakes his head. "No, he's been sneaking to the shower or something. I would've noticed this! Would've seen!"

"Stop making it weird, Andrew," Nathalie says, and maybe she's just sunburned, too, but her cheeks look red.

"Yeah, shut up, Andrew," I say, but I'm grinning, and I'm only sort of embarrassed as I pull my shirt back on.

Actually it feels good, like their comments are running a balm over a spot that just got rubbed raw.

"No, I'm serious, though," Andrew says, slipping off his flip-flops and sitting on the end of the dock to submerge his feet. "Are you like a weightlifter or something? Along with the surfing?"

I wonder if he's giving me a hard time, but there's only genuine interest on his face. I settle back onto the bench and shrug. "Yeah, kind of. These past couple of years I've gotten more interested in bodybuilding. Like—you know. Meal plans. Macros."

It feels stupid to say, but as Jen joins Andrew in soaking her feet and Nathalie sits on the bench beside me, they look interested. "What are macros?" Jen asks, smearing a palmful of sunscreen down her arms.

"Uh, it's short for macronutrients." I explain how you can plan different ratios of calories in your diet—proteins, carbs, and fats—to try and cut weight or build muscle. "I bet Andrew knows more about this than me," I add. "Biology stuff."

Andrew laughs. "What? No. I don't know everything about biology. I mean, obviously I know nothing about weightlifting, look at me."

He waves his lanky limbs, and his forearm catches Jen's cheek, smearing her sunscreen into her mouth. "*Andrew*," she splutters. She spits sunscreen into the lake and shoves him. Soon they're laughing, slapping lake water at each other.

"What is it about bodybuilding that interests you?" Nathalie asks me.

I look back out at the lake, trying not to read too much into the fact that Nathalie sat beside me instead of Andrew or Jen.

*It's just sitting*, I tell myself. I'm overthinking.

I lift one shoulder in a half-shrug. "Guess I just like watching it happen. Cause and effect sort of thing." I try not to be self-conscious about how I'm phrasing my answer. When Nathalie talks, it's kind of beautiful, but I always feel like I'm trying to express something and can't quite get there. "I put energy in, and I can see that in the mirror."

"Is that why you were out here?" says Andrew. "Catching up on workouts?"

Andrew's cleaning his glasses and squinting up at me through the harsh sun. He and the girls look so relaxed, so calm, that I almost feel calm, too. Some of my tangled feelings have cleared away, like blockage down a river.

"I've been feeling sort of weird," I say.

The words surprise me as they come out. Probably if Devin or Grayson heard that, they'd say, *Weirder than usual?* And we'd just mess around until the air cleared.

But Andrew and Jen look at me with curiosity, and Nathalie takes off her sunglasses. "Everything OK?" she asks quietly.

"Yeah, what happened, man?" says Andrew.

A lump rises in my throat. I look back out at the lake, confused to feel my eyes stinging. "Nothing. I don't know."

"Art stuff?" says Jen sympathetically. "Is it one of your classes?"

"Not really. I mean—" I draw a slow breath, and a reckless feeling comes over me. "Well, yeah. The classes are all kind of hard for me. I actually got in off the waiting list. I know y'all talk about the classes being hard, but you still get A's on everything. I really don't. And I'm trying really hard. I'm just not smart that way. So. That sucks."

"Bro," says Andrew, looking dismayed. He pulls his feet out of the water so he can face me fully. "Why aren't you in our study group? It's way tougher to get through all this stuff by yourself."

I avoid his eyes. "I don't know."

"Is it because I ask people what grades they got on things?" Jen says, looking stricken. "I'm so sorry. It's such a bad habit. I can stop." She fiddles with one of the straps on her bathing suit, which looks handmade, edged with a silver fringe.

I let out a shaky laugh. "You're fine, Jen. It's just . . ." I push my hand through my hair. "You guys are really fucking good at everything, you know? I mean, Haolong's sketches, God."

Andrew lets out a relieved laugh. "But that's Haolong. He's, like, a prodigy."

"Dude. *You're* a prodigy. You won an international science fair."

"Yeah, so what? If you put me on a surfboard I'd drown in four seconds. Like, you're good at stuff, too."

Nathalie has been quiet, but when she shifts on the bench, we all look her way. I can only meet her eyes for a second. "So, is this why you always change the subject when we ask about your portfolio?"

I shrug. "I mean, you can see my portfolio. I don't care." I pull out my phone. Despite what I've just said, I hear my pulse quickening in my ears as I open the portfolio folder and hand it to Nathalie. Jen and Andrew hop up, too, and peek over Nathalie's shoulders.

Suddenly my stomach twists. It's so stupid. I already did this with Ali. You'd think I'd be more used to it after the first time, but I feel just as exposed.

"Niko," says Andrew, sounding disbelieving. "What the fuck."

"I can't believe you hid these from us!" Jen splutters. "They're amazing!"

A smile pulls at my mouth. I look down at my lap. "You'd say that no matter what they looked like."

"I wouldn't," says Nathalie.

A laugh works its way out of my throat. "Yeah," Jen agrees, "she really wouldn't."

"And they *are* great pieces." Nathalie's expression is gentler than I've seen it before. "This one with the blue. It's like—I don't know. It makes me think of rebirth or baptism or something. I'm not even religious. But it feels like that."

"Dude, you've got to show me how you pick colors," Andrew says, swiping through to a landscape of an abandoned town. "This bit here with the moon reflecting on the satellite dish is so cool."

"Was that the only thing?" Nathalie asks. "You were worried about your art?"

I sigh, running my thumb over a dark knot of wood in the bench. It's like she already knows. "There was also . . . I don't want to get into it too much, but there was this portrait thing, and . . . I don't know. I didn't like the way I looked in it. And I started wondering, like, do I actually just not like the way I look, full stop?"

The breeze picks up in the silence.

"Sorry," I add. "Killing the mood."

"It's OK," says Jen. Her normally chirpy voice has grown small. "I have three sisters, and they're all prettier than me. I wish I looked different a lot of the time, too."

"Me too," says Andrew. "Like, um, I don't know. Every morning. Ha." He returns to the edge of the dock and looks across the water. Guilt pools in my stomach. I know I have it easier than Andrew, who's younger and smaller and always cracking these self-deprecating jokes about his acne.

I steel myself. I've already told them this much. I might as well do the whole thing. "For me, I think it's because I'm around a lot of—of white people all the time."

The words feel wrong in my mouth. I don't talk about people being white. Not my family, not my friends.

"I'm half-Chinese," I go on, "and my mom remarried. So my family is white. Also my girlfriend and all my friends."

"Hey, objection," Andrew says. "*We're* not white."

"What?" says Jen, feigning shock. "You're not white, Andrew Hong?"

I try to smile. "Right. All my friends are white except you guys. But it means I haven't ever"—I wince, tug at my hair—"talked about this shit before. Because how could they get it, and it also doesn't seem like it matters."

"Of course it matters," Nathalie says. "How could it not matter? I used to have ten metric tons of internalized racism, like, toward my own parents, even. I used to feel awful about myself all the time. That mattered."

"You *used* to?" says Jen. "Wait, Nat, do you have a magic solution for self-esteem problems? Share, please."

Nathalie sighs. "Fine. I will. My strategy is, every time I start thinking about how great it would be to match some ridiculous, arbitrary, Eurocentric beauty standard, I force myself to be angry at having those standards imposed on me instead."

"So you spend a lot of time being angry," I say.

"Yes. Probably sixty percent of my life."

I realize, then, that I'm smiling. Nathalie's lips twitch.

Andrew laughs, kicking the lake water. "Whatever. I have lots of white friends in Seattle, too, Niko. They just listen to me complaining about racist stuff and they're like, that sucks. Or if I'm talking about how awesome it is to visit Korea or speak two languages, they're like, we're so jealous; and either way we all get on with our lives. Just talk about stuff. Your white friends will deal."

"Well, when you put it *that* way, it sounds so simple," I mumble.

"It is," Nathalie says firmly. "You don't have to make everybody comfortable. "It's not your job to be a frictionless surface that everybody else glides over."

"Advice from the highest-friction person I've ever met," says Jen, flicking water at Nathalie from her acrylic nails.

Our chuckles echo across the water.

Jen squeezes droplets from her long, pink hair, looking pensive. "Seriously, though, Niko. Talking about it helps." She shrugs, making the silver fringe on her bathing suit quiver. "When I come across Filipino art, sometimes I feel like it's especially for me. Also, thinking about my family, I've got my grandparents' recipes, and stories from my parents about Manila, and my aunties speaking Tagalog with me. There are good things, too. Family things and community things."

I feel a pull in my chest, imagining Jen with her family at home.

"There are the friends, too," Andrew says, nudging Jen's shoulder with his.

"The friends are OK," Nathalie says, looking out over the lake.

I smile. Silence falls again, and as another breeze sweeps over the dock, the day suddenly seems sunnier.

When I think of Ali's portrait, I realize the anger is gone. What's left instead is the dim shape of guilt. I envision her careful brushstrokes, the steady gaze of the guy in her painting. She wasn't trying to reduce me to anything. She was painting her honest artistic impression of how she sees me, and I put something onto the portrait that had nothing to do with her, or the art.

"Thanks, guys," I say. "For that, and for . . . yeah."

I search for more words, but none come out. They seem to understand.

When I get back to camp, I run back to the cabin, hoping desperately I won't see anyone I know. The cabin is, mercifully, empty, and I curl up on my bunk with my face in my pillow. Thoughts are swirling around my head: the irritation that blossomed when I saw Niko's portrait, how he said that I treat everything like a research project for class. It makes me cringe to think that's how I've been coming across here at camp: not really an artist, just a dorky, list-checking overachiever. I've been hiding my whole background from my friends, scared that it will make them see me that way—but it's how I come across anyway.

Thinking of the portrait awakens an even bigger swirl of emotions. On the one hand, it feels meaningful that Niko made the effort. I think of him finishing up one of the Chinese signs, making sure to get it right, and thinking, "Ali will like this. I want to make it look like home for her." This thought—the huge gap between his intentions and how the portrait makes me feel—is what sends me over the edge. Hating the portrait feels like I'm rejecting not just Niko but also Nai Nai and where I'm from.

I don't understand these feelings; I love where I'm from, I love Nai Nai, and I know I'll love my brother someday, too. But there is a part of me that feels like I want . . . not to reject where I came from, but to chart my own path.

Something hard and pointy is digging into my shoulder. I sit up and realize my sketch pad is on my bed; I must have tossed it there before I left this morning. Feeling heavyhearted, I open it up. I turn to a fresh page and grab a pencil.

I start to draw, and once I start, I can't stop. I end up filling several pages with my sketches, all representing the portrait I wish Niko had drawn: a girl seated at an easel in the Ogilvy workshop studio, a girl walking alone through the streets of Manhattan, a girl sitting at a bench in the woods like the ones up here.

I work until my hand cramps and I realize the room has grown dark around me. I use my finger to blend a couple details of the last one and close my sketch pad. I feel like I'm awakening from a deep sleep, like the last few hours just completely disappeared. There's a crick in my neck from hunching over for so long. The anger from earlier feels distant.

As I flip through the four sketches I've made, I realize that this girl, just like Niko's girl, is still interacting with her environment. The environment never stops mattering—after all, who are we if we're totally removed from our surroundings? The difference is that these scenes represent choices I've made for myself.

It's fully dark outside now, and I start to smell campfire smoke. I stretch and amble down to the fire pit to find Niko.

He's sitting alone on a log in the back, his silhouette—backward baseball cap, hunched shoulders—illuminated by his phone. When I approach, he puts his phone away and scoots over to make room on the log for me.

"I wanted to apologize—" I start.

"I'm sorry—" he says at the same time. We laugh nervously. "Ladies first," he says.

"I wanted to apologize for what I said in town," I tell him. "I wish I hadn't said what I said about you not knowing how to try. It's clear to me how hard you tried on that portrait. And it was really nice of you to show where I'm from and try to get it right. I guess . . . it kind of elicited some feelings in me. I'm starting to feel like where I'm from doesn't fit me right anymore? That's why it's been so cool to come here, to Ogilvy, where I can figure out what it means to be myself. It's a really *good* portrait, Niko. It's just not how I see myself right now."

"I also wanted to apologize," says Niko. "I guess . . . I felt like yours kind of did the same thing. It just seemed like you emphasized my Asian-ness so much, and everyone at home does that, too. My little sister, Anastasia, she's still in the phase where she draws these really terrible cartoony pictures of our whole family, and I always look like this weird dark-haired interloper." He laughs. "I guess I hoped that you might be someone who doesn't see me as an outsider."

"I don't, though!" I protest. "Everyone I know is Asian, except my mom, basically. You're actually like, the least Asian person I know!"

He grins, and I take a skewer from the fireside and begin pushing marshmallows onto it. "I painted you to look Chinese because you are Chinese," I go on, less jokingly. "It doesn't have to mean you're on the outside of anything."

"Yeah." He picks up a skewer and lowers a marshmallow over the fire beside mine. "Yeah, I know."

We sit there in silence for a minute. As our marshmallows turn gold, I realize the next problem that's staring us in the face.

"But what about the actual project?" I ask.

"The showcase?"

"Yeah. I mean . . . should we just keep going with them the way they are, even though we don't really like them? Or should we start over and make new ones?"

"I . . . don't know," he says, exhaling and slumping down a little on the log.

I slump, too. Two out of five weeks done at Ogilvy, and we're talking about starting over.

The next day, we wake up early and pile into the buses to be ferried back to the city. I'm a little sad to pack up my canvas and load it onto the portable studio, not knowing if I'll be able to use it as my showcase piece. It makes me anxious to be so close to our final deadline and not know if we've made any progress. But early this afternoon, on the way back to Ogilvy, we have an excursion planned to the Museum of Modern Art. I hope desperately that a museum visit will help inspiration strike.

I've been on field trips to museums before, and the chaperones spent more time corralling us than letting us see the exhibits; so I'm pleasantly surprised when we arrive at the museum and LaTonya tells us to find a buddy and meet back at the entrance in three hours. I'm even *more* pleasantly surprised when Grace asks if I want to be her buddy.

"I love how much freedom they give us here," I gush as I follow her to the main staircase. "They treat us like actual adults."

Grace looks amused. "I mean, it makes sense. We're all working in different media and expressing different perspectives. We should be able to choose which exhibits will help us the most."

I'm quiet as it becomes clearer to me: Grace is used to this because her private school has the resources to let students be independent. My high school would never do that; the risks are too high. Most of us will be the first in our families to go to college. Mistakes cost more for us than they do for the kids at Grace's school.

For a minute, I envy her; but it's not her fault she's lucky.

"There's a temporary installation on immigrant voices in New York City on the second floor," I suggest, reading the first thing that I see on the museum map.

"I don't know if that really feels like our thing," Grace says, skimming the blurb. "We only have a couple hours."

*Wait, what*? I think. Is art only "our thing" if it's created by an American-born artist? Also, so many artists lived in adopted countries—Van Gogh emigrated from the Netherlands to France, and I know Grace loves him. But I guess the immigrant label never stuck to him. I wonder why.

"Can I take you to my favorite exhibit?" she asks suddenly.

"Of course," I say, setting aside her "our thing" comment. We head up to the third floor, and she leads me into a darkened room. All I catch on the placard outside is that a fifteen-minute film will play on loop.

Although it's enormous and we're the only ones there, the seating is limited to a tiny bench in the back. We settle in next to each other. The material of my shorts grazes the material of her dress, and it's enough to make my hair stand on end, distracting me from the film. I watch a series of bucolic scenes flit before my eyes, noticing every time Grace shifts her weight on the seat beside me.

"What did you think?" she says afterward.

*I think you're amazing,* is what I want to say. "I really liked it," I say instead. "What makes it your favorite exhibit?"

"I love how even without sound, the film totally transports you to these other places. I think the silence heightens the experience—you focus on what you're seeing instead of your other senses. When I'm feeling stuck with a film for one of my own projects, sometimes I come to this room and watch this on loop like five times in a row."

"That's incredible," I say. "All the way from Brooklyn?"

"It's my absolute guarantee to get myself unstuck," she admits. "It's worth it."

I wonder if Grace is feeling stuck in her showcase project right now. I'm about to ask her, when all of a sudden my phone vibrates. It's Niko.

**omg come to the 2nd floor rn**

**gallery 213**

**it's urgent**

"Hey, I'm sorry about this," I say to Grace, "but I have to run down to the second floor. Can you wait here, and I'll be right back?"

"Sure. Honestly, I'll probably watch the film again."

"Great, amazing," I say. "I'll be as quick as possible."

When I get to the second floor, I hurry to Gallery 213. It's one of the rooms hosting the New York immigrant exhibit. A big sign by the door reads URBAN EAST ASIAN DIASPORA.

Niko, too, is alone. He's standing with his back to the entrance, hands clasped behind his back, facing a huge red mass. As I get closer,

I realize it's a brick wall, a temporary installation. As I draw nearer, I start to recognize Chinese characters overlaying the brick.

*He found an artist who inspired our dad,* is my first thought; but—no. Although it's in color, and on a massive scale, I immediately register the similarity between the style of this installation and the sculptures Niko and I have at home. It's too close to be a coincidence, and the date is a mere five years ago, making it younger than our sculptures.

This artist didn't inspire our dad. This artist *was* our dad.

# Chapter 13

"This is it," I say, low and excited.

"How do you mean?"

"How—our dad's *in the MoMA!* We can find him, track him down. We can ask him for advice about our showcase!"

Ali nibbles her lower lip. "We're supposed to do the showcase on our own, though."

"Ali," I say in disbelief. "We have a chance to reconnect with our dad. You want to throw that away?"

Ali makes a noncommittal noise. She isn't quite crossing her arms, her elbows cradled in her palms.

My excitement is turning to impatience, so I return to the project. "Look, you wanted to have a big breakout piece. Our dad already had his. He knows how to do this, he's a professional. I haven't come up with a new draft idea for the portraits yet. Have you?"

"No," she admits.

"Then what's the problem? We can call him, or—"

"How?" Ali says stiffly. "Do you have a working number for him? Because my family doesn't."

"Hold on." I whip out my phone. Ali watches in silence as I pull up Google and search **cang long nyc artist**.

"Cang Long?" she asks. "But that's not his name."

I point at the placard beside the piece. *This installation was created by Cáng Lóng. Translated as "Hidden Dragon," the pseudonym nods to the prominent wuxia film* Crouching Tiger, Hidden Dragon *(Ang Lee, 2000) and underscores the artist's anonymity.*

Ali takes a cautious step toward me and bows her head over the phone, too.

"OK," I say slowly. "This doesn't look great."

The first three articles refer to our dad as a "notorious recluse," an "obsessively private eccentric," and a "pseudonymous unknown." A fourth says, "The artist could not be contacted for comment." The Wikipedia page is hardly more than a laundry list of his pieces and where they appear. He has no website.

I try to rally. "Well—" I point to the placard again, at the title: *Alley Face of Chinatown Restaurant, Manhattan, New York City (2018).* "This was pretty recent. If he stayed in New York that long, he's probably still here, right?"

Ali jerks her shoulders in a shrug. "Like I said, I haven't seen him since I was five. He could be anywhere."

She looks away from the placard, away from me, but I catch a glimpse of hurt on her face. Her forehead is furrowed as though she's trying to calculate something.

"Look," I say carefully, "there could be lots of reasons he didn't get in touch. We can't know unless we find him. And . . . I mean, you have that album of all his sculptures. I know you like his work. Don't you want to learn from him? Like, as an artist?"

She fiddles with the frayed hems of her shorts.

I take a breath. I try not to sound too desperate. "Ali, I really want to meet him."

Ali squeezes her eyes shut briefly, then says with purposeful brightness, "Yeah. I . . . you're right. We have artist's block, and he's an artist. We're making a piece about being family, and he's family. It makes sense."

Relief spreads through me.

She sounds like she's mostly talked herself into it, but I add for good measure, "It might be cool to reveal this during the presentation, too. Like, that we didn't even know our dad had an actual career as an artist until now."

Her smile becomes more genuine. "Yeah. That's true."

The tension eases as we study the sculpture before us. No answers there. No answers on the plaque, which talks about the restaurant in Chinatown like it was a place that existed a thousand years and an ocean ago.

I wet my lips with the tip of my tongue. I've never believed in fate before. But as Ali and I stand dwarfed by our dad's piece, I feel like I'm looking down on the pair of us from far away, two tiny figures sharing our art, sharing this summer, and now, finally, colliding with this piece our dad made.

I remember Jen wringing out her hair on that sunlit dock upstate, musing about her grandparents' recipes and her parents' stories. *There are good things, too. Family things.*

Standing here, I understand what she meant. That family feeling touches me, almost electrifies me, connecting Ali and me to something bigger than ourselves. It feels like a root into the earth, feeding me fresh water when I didn't realize I was thirsty.

*Maybe*, I find myself thinking, *this is what I could belong to.*

A sharp intake of breath from Ali brings me back to myself. "Wait," she says, whirling toward me. "Of course. Niko. Pieces don't just end up in museums on their own. They're curated. Someone here discovered this one."

It's so obvious that I laugh. "Wow, we're geniuses. So, we've just got to find the curator?"

"Exactly. Let's try the front desk." Ali checks her watch. "And we should hurry. We've only got half an hour."

The sculpture curator who comes out to speak with us at the request of the information desk is an older woman barely taller than Ali with short silver-gray curls. "Ogilvy students?" she exclaims, clapping her hands together. "Lanette Winters. It's wonderful to meet you. I love talking to the next generation."

"Thank you so much for taking the time, Ms. Winters," Ali says.

"Sure! I have to leave for a studio visit in"—she checks her watch—"fifteen, but I'm all yours until then. What's your question?"

"We were wondering about one of your pieces in the Urban East Asian Diaspora exhibit," I tell her. "*Alley Face of Chinatown Restaurant*?"

She nods. "Great piece. Love that exhibit. It's been in the works a long time." Her voice grows somber. "That's the future of the museum, you know? Diversification. Art that the average person might not otherwise pause for."

I open my mouth, then close it again, vaguely annoyed on my dad's behalf. I feel like anyone passing that sculpture on the street would have stopped to take a second look.

"Well," Ali says, "we were wondering if you had the artist's contact information from the acquisition. We'd love to talk to him about it, um, for one of our classes."

Lanette's brows draw together sympathetically. "We don't, unfortunately. The restaurant owner sold that particular piece to a patron who noticed it and also happens to be a board member here."

"Do you have the owner's name?" Ali asks eagerly.

"His name might have been . . . Ming . . . or, Ling . . ." Lanette's cheeks color, and her eyes flit to me. "Well, the restaurant was called Eight Tastes," she tells Ali hurriedly. "It might still be there. I'm not sure if it was demolition or renovation they were going for. Either way, thank goodness we were able to save the piece! Right?" She lets out a loud laugh. "The museum as an institution can go a long way to legitimizing outsider art, and if we're doing that, we're doing our job."

Her eyes move from Ali to me again. A proud smile spreads over her face. "Finally, an equal playing field! It's taken this country too long. Inclusivity. I'm sure you'd agree."

I can't help exchanging a look with Ali. Then, for some reason, I feel the urge to laugh. "Yeah," I say, keeping my voice steady. "Totally."

"Thank you so much for your time," Ali says, voice wavering. We hurry off.

In the elevator, we make eye contact. For three seconds, we hold it together.

Then we dissolve into laughter. "OK, that didn't have to be that weird," I say.

"Seriously," Ali says. "Our dad isn't even an outsider artist. He went to Pratt." She breaks into fresh giggles, holding her forearm over her eyes.

"Whatever," I say, still grinning. "I guess they don't know that." I pull out my phone and type "Eight Tastes Restaurant" into my maps app and feel a leap in my chest. "But hey," I say, holding up my phone. "Guess what?"

"What?"

"The restaurant's still there."

The ride back to Ogilvy is sleepy and contented. Everyone's bused out by this point, and my friends are either napping or buried deep in homework. I try to catch up on readings, too, but I get two paragraphs into my latest history packet—twenty pages on the rococo style—and have to call it quits. The sight of our dad's piece is still buzzing around my brain like a bee in a jar. Part of me wants to go up to the front of the bus and announce it over the intercom.

Our trip upstate seemed a lot longer than four days, somehow. When I think back to the way I acted on my first day at Ogilvy, I feel like I'm considering a version of me that's a year younger, not two short weeks. Some part of me feels more settled now—more calm, more self-aware. Or maybe it's just that I feel closer to the kids on the bus around me.

After a glance over at Nathalie, who's sleeping silently against the bus window, using her Ogilvy hoodie as a pillow, I sink down into the seat and bring up my new message from Hailey.

**Kelsey wore me down . . . we're going to be cocaptains**

I reply with a grimace emoji.

**I know lol**, Hailey says. **I love Kelsey but we're going to spend wayyy more time partying than practicing, with her as cocaptain**

**Whatever,** she adds almost immediately. **Are you back to Manhattan yet? Or still wandering through the woods?**

back in manhattan. we actually stopped by MoMA today so that was cool

**Omgg we went there last summer. Most modern art is so stupid lol**

I hesitate for a long moment before deciding on: **yeah it's not for everybody haha**

Hailey doesn't reply. Wrong answer.

I add, **there was this next-level stupid exhibit on the top floor that was like. seven thousand paper clips scattered on the ground. so that definitely made me a better artist**

**Right?** she says at once. **So silly**

I hesitate for a long time, biting my tongue. I want to tell her about my dad's piece. Some instinct is holding me back, but I think of what Andrew said upstate. *Just talk about stuff, they'll deal.*

I begin to type.

**something crazy actually happened while i was there**

**What?**

**i found a piece in the museum made by my dad. like my birth dad**

**WHAT? Are you serious???**

I smile, relief making my skin prickle. **yeah i know! suddenly i'm going through this Urban East Asian exhibit and his work is just there**

**Do you have a picture?**

I send her a few photos I took of the exhibit: a close-up, plus one I snapped from across the gallery, which shows the way my dad's sculpture stands out from the paintings on either side.

She types for maybe thirty seconds before the message comes: **It's cool!**

i think so too. :D it reminds me of a sculpture he left with me. actually the only thing of his i still have.

**Are those paintings his too?**

oh, no those are just the exhibits on either side

I zoom in on the paintings. One of them is the San Francisco skyline, brush-painted and watery among swirls of cloud. The other is a fleshy-looking abstract with a red-and-gold strip of cloth bisecting the canvas.

Hailey's next message is: **So the museum was picking out stuff from Asian artists? That's lucky for them**

I look down at my phone, suddenly aware of the rumble of the bus engines, and Nathalie stirring gently to adjust her sweater-pillow, and Haolong murmuring to Haoran in the seat behind us.

I start typing. **well that was the theme of the exhibit, but I liked**

I delete the message, biting the inside of my cheek.

**yeah,** I start again, **it seems like the museum is trying to be more inclusive and**

I hit delete again, harder this time. Why am I parroting that curator lady's talking points?

I reread Hailey's message. "Lucky for them." For artists like my dad. For artists that the average person might not pause for. For "outsider artists" who need to be "legitimized."

Lucky for artists like me.

**they didn't just get into the museum because they're asian,** I type.

My palms moisten as I reread the unsent message. I find myself glancing over at Nathalie again, at her slight frown in sleep. I remember the cool hardness of her voice as she said, *You don't have to make everybody comfortable.*

And this is actually what I'm feeling, I think. I don't want Hailey to think my dad only got into a prestigious museum because he checked some Asian box. I don't want her to think that's how I'll live my life, either. I want her to think I'm talented for real. Like anyone else could be.

I hit send.

A long pause. The time at the top of my phone screen changes from 2:36 to 2:37. I reread my own message. **they didn't just get into the museum because they're asian**

Then Hailey says, **That's not what I said.**

**but you said it was lucky for them. like they wouldn't have been in the museum otherwise**

**Well . . . haha I mean, the exhibit is literally an Asian themed exhibit. You just told me that. So yeah. Those pieces ARE there because they're Asian??**

My phone slips in my sweaty hands. **ok yeah but I'm saying, the pieces would still have been good enough to be in the museum, even if the exhibit wasn't about Asian art**

**Idk lol**, she says.

I stare at my phone, a knot forming in my chest.

**Your dad's is awesome**, she adds quickly. **His is really cool and definitely good enough. But the other paintings . . . lol**

She goes on. **I meeean they're not Monet you know? haha**

The knot in my chest tightens. I'm typing fast, barely reading what I've written before pressing "send." **but none of the other artists in the** moma are Monet either. why do these people have to be Monet to deserve to be there

Oh my God, Hailey says. Why are you in such a bad mood

i was in a great mood ten minutes ago.

OK then go enjoy your good mood, thanks for putting ME in a shitty mood. Just because I was trying to say it was cool that your dad got into the museum. God.

I stuff my phone into my backpack. I don't want it touching me right now.

The bus's sleepy atmosphere suddenly seems suffocating. Did that conversation actually just happen? Did I just pick a fight with Hailey?

I wipe my palms on my jeans and close my eyes. My pulse is going in my stomach.

"Niko?" says a quiet voice sometime later, I'm not sure how long.

I open my eyes. Nathalie is awake, her Ogilvy hoodie unrolled in her lap. There's a furrow between her eyebrows. "We're pulling up," she says, pointing through the bus window toward the approaching Ogilvy building. "Are you all right? You look kind of sick."

For one moment, I imagine showing Nathalie the text messages. Because I know somehow that she would understand what bothered me. And she could probably put what I was feeling into words in an actually articulate way, and when she described it, the whole conversation would make more sense to me, and maybe I'd feel better.

But then her eyes move from mine, just for a moment, down to my mouth and then away with this guilty twitch of her expression. And she busies herself with taking down her ponytail, and my attention tumbles with her sleek black hair to the smooth skin of her collarbones just above the scoop neck of her T-shirt, and in my memory Andrew is saying, *Nathalie's beautiful.*

I look away from her immediately, my neck flooding with heat. No, I'm absolutely not showing her those text messages. And I'm not sitting by her on the bus anymore, or in class.

"I'm fine," I tell her.

Andrew breathes deeply on the other side of our dorm. He fell asleep an hour ago. I'm turned toward the wall on my side, my phone still held six inches from my face, a window of light in the darkness.

I should be asleep. I should be tired, at the least. It's 11:45, and I got barely three hours of sleep last night, tossing and turning in my bunk bed upstate while trying to think of new ideas for our showcase portraits. But I'm staring at the same photo I've pulled up a hundred times today: the MoMA listing of our dad's piece.

I type "Eight Tastes Restaurant" into my maps app. As the route forms a blue snake along the Manhattan streets, I shove my phone into my pocket and slip out of bed.

Andrew's never woken up before when I've used the bathroom at night, and this is no exception. When I slip my sneakers on and crack the door, he doesn't even stir, even though a stripe of light falls across his face.

I hesitate, looking at his peaceful expression with a pang of guilt. As we were getting ready for bed tonight, he said, "OK. I have a plan. My parents are coming into New York in a couple weeks, like, just before the dance. It's my mom's birthday around then, so they're going to sign me out of Ogilvy for dinner sometime that week. I think I'm going to ask one of the girls if they want to come."

I laughed. "You're going right to meeting the parents on the first date?"

"Why not? It'll be a really nice dinner," he said, unfazed. "I still don't know who to ask, though. Jen is so sweet, right? I mean, it's like I forget everything else when I'm with her. But I think I might be more into Nathalie. She just seems—complicated, you know? Like, she seems deep. And she likes LCD Soundsystem."

"Yeah," I mumbled. "She's cool."

And that was all I said, because I'm a coward. Also, I still don't have any solid proof that Nathalie likes me, and I'd look like an egomaniac if I said that and it wasn't true.

I shake the thoughts and exit our dorm.

Usually, the Ogilvy hallways are comfortably noisy. Besides the voices and laughs echoing out from dorms, there'll be music seeping under the cracks of closed doors, or weird droning sound samples in the lounge from kids working on videography projects. Right now, though, the hall is as silent as my own house back in California.

I move cautiously. Most of the professors commute in for classes at the start of each day, but Professor Abbott is still in his suite at the end of the hall.

I creep toward the elevator doors and pause mid-step. If I call the elevator in the middle of the night, will I trip an alarm? Will the *ding* as the car stops be enough to wake Abbott up?

Better not to risk it. I dart into the stairwell and sneak downward.

My heart's beating fast. I've skipped class a dozen times, and I've snuck out of my bedroom window twice that many times for night walks on the beach, but none of that has felt like this. Not the risks—what was going to happen at home, me getting grounded?—or the temptation.

Out in the foyer, I see a silhouette at the front desk. I freeze, retreating into the shadows. Stan's back on the night guard.

There's got to be some other way out. The cafeteria, maybe. I'll bet the kitchens have a way out for trash disposal. I back around the corner and down the hall, moving slowly so that my sneakers don't squeak on the waxed floors.

I slip into the dining hall and feel my stomach plummet as a voice says, "Hi!"

Cold sweat prickles all over my body. "Ali!" I hiss. "What are you doing here?"

She shrugs, standing up from the cafeteria table. "I knew you'd try this."

"How?"

She pulls out her phone and reads aloud from our text thread earlier today. "Ahem. You: 'We should go to Chinatown.' Me: 'How are we supposed to get out of the building?' You: 'Idk, we can figure it out. What, have you never snuck out before, lol.' I didn't have to be Sherlock Holmes."

"OK, well, keep your voice down, the security guy's out front." I wave her into a corner of the dining hall, where the hum of a fridge offers cover for our voices. "You could've just texted me instead of waiting in the cafeteria alone like an assassin or whatever."

She scowls. "*You* could've texted *me*. You're the one who was going to leave me out of this."

"I wasn't trying to—" I sigh and rub my forehead. "What, do you *want* to come?"

"Yes. But not in the middle of the night. What if we get locked out?"

"I was going to prop the door. And unlock a window just in case."

"OK, but what were you actually going to *do* in Chinatown? Just stand there and look at a renovated brick wall in the dark?"

When she says it like that, it sounds so pointless. I guess I'd imagined some pilgrimage where I'd find a clue at the end of the road, or—I don't know. I remember that connected feeling I had beside Ali in the museum, that rooted feeling, tangled deep into our dad's art. My blood is still pumping, and I'm still replaying my conversation with Hailey, too. *Lucky for them.*

"Is something up?" Ali says, looking uncertain.

I consider taking out my phone. It'd be better to show Ali than Nathalie, for sure.

But if Ali sees those texts, she'll get the wrong idea about Hailey. She was so quick to call that guy at the ice cream shop racist. I don't want her to think of Hailey that way, too.

The knot of frustration in my chest tightens again. I don't think Hailey was being racist, but she didn't seem to care what I was saying. I don't even need her to apologize. I'd be happy if she just said she understood what I meant.

I remember the way she snuggled into me in her basement, the soft feel of her hair beneath my fingertips. The *thump-thump* of my heart the first time she reached toward me in class with some stupid made-up excuse to touch my hand. I don't want to lose her over this.

*You could apologize*, says a little voice in my mind. If I apologized, the whole thing would just go away.

It's just that I don't think I said anything wrong.

I realize how long I've been quiet when Ali says, "Look, Niko, I get it. I want to go there, too. But if we're going to find out anything useful, we need to go when the restaurant is open."

"Right," I say, snapping back to the present. Our dad—the restaurant—the fact that we're almost half-done at Ogilvy, and the only thing we've got for our showcase is a pair of drafts that we both hate. "Yeah. Of course."

"We can sneak out later this week," Ali goes on. "I looked over the schedule."

"You did?"

She pulls a square of paper from between the pages of her journal and unfolds it. She's neatly highlighted a few events in yellow, written "*potential??*" beside them, and circled a block on Thursday labeled "Movie Night."

I stifle a laugh in my throat. "Of course you did this."

Ali shrugs. "*You* weren't making a functional plan. Clearly."

"OK. Burn. Shut up." I lean over to check the schedule more closely. "Movie Night does make sense," I say slowly. "We can wait for it to start, then make excuses and pretend we're going to our rooms. I can pretend to get a headache, and you can pretend to get food poisoning or something."

She wrinkles her nose. "Why do I have to get food poisoning?"

"I mean. You can have the headache. It doesn't actually matter."

"It matters if I'm basically announcing to my friends, 'Hey everybody, news flash, I have explosive diarrhea.'"

I find myself grinning. "Yeah, you should say it exactly like that. Also send it in a mass text."

Our stifled laughs break off as there's a creaking sound outside the cafeteria door. We both go still, shrinking back behind the fridge.

No one comes in. We exchange glances. "Let's get back upstairs," Ali whispers. We dart for the door and slip through, navigating into the stairwell.

"I can't believe you waited down there for like an hour," I whisper as we climb past the sixth floor.

"I'm dedicated." She flits past me onto the landing. "And I can't believe *you* were going to wander around the city all night when we still don't know how to fix our showcase."

I sigh. "Thanks, Mom."

"You're welcome," she says. As we stop on her floor, her amused look fades. "But—look, Niko. About the showcase, and our dad."

"What?"

She perches on the steps. "I'm up to try and find him. I am," she insists, when I give her a searching look. "But we might not find him right away. Or, like, at all. We can't just stop our whole showcase project until we can talk to him."

I let out a slow breath and settle on the steps beside her. Ali's right. In the gallery, it felt like I could reach out and touch some part of my dad, but here, in the Ogilvy building, finding him seems like a way longer shot.

*It's going to happen*, I reassure myself. But we've got to think practically.

"OK," I say. "What are we supposed to do? I've never actually had an art block before. Usually art just sort of—happens to me. You know?"

"I know. Me too." Ali smiles. Then her eyes widen. "Wait, that's it!" She whips out her journal again and starts flipping through its pages, finally stopping near the center. "These are all the showcase concepts I had before we came up with our idea. What if we combine one of these with our portraits?"

I take the notebook from her and stifle a laugh. "Ali, there's like two hundred ideas here."

"I know," she says, sounding proud.

I scan down the page. My eyes stop on *metaphorical portrait series—represent people in my life through metaphors/still life??*

"Hey," I say slowly. "Wait. This could be really cool."

Ali peers at the idea under my finger and brightens. "Brook said she liked that idea during our first showcase workshop!"

Somehow, hearing that Brook Davenport liked the idea makes me less enthusiastic about it, but I don't tell Ali that. "OK," I say, ideas already beginning to circulate. Ali represented by her pair of beat-up white sneakers with glittery shoelaces. Ali represented by the crammed-full binder she hauls to classes. "So, same plan as before?" I add. "We make the pieces in private? We only see them once they're finished?"

She hesitates. "I *do* think that's the only way to make sure there's no, you know, stylistic cross contamination. But . . . you don't think it'll go the same way as last time?"

I bite my cheek, wondering if she's right. We can't afford another fight, another setback.

But as I consider Ali, I think, *It's not going to happen.* I spent my whole last sketch thinking about her from the outside: the city where she grew up, and the street where she lives, and the way she looks, moves, and talks, as though she were a picture on a screen. Looking back at our interviews, it's like we were collecting lists of data.

Now, when I look at Ali, I see the hurt and embarrassment on her face when we started fighting at the bus pickup stop, and the closed-off evasion when we were standing in front of our dad's piece. I remember how self-doubt crossed her features when she apologized at campfire night. Ali isn't just the go-get-'em city girl I thought she was. She's not just big loud colors and center stage. I know that now.

"It's going to work this time," I tell her.

"How do you know?"

"Just trust me." I smile, stand, and head up the steps. "I'm the older sibling."

# Chapter 14

Brook is in the bathroom, and I'm admiring myself in front of the full-length mirror. It's my new morning routine. Once I'm alone, I catapult myself out of bed and yank on one of the new dresses I bought upstate. Today I'm wearing one in red cotton. It's calf-length, sleeveless, with a tiered skirt and a light floral pattern. It's a little loose around the torso, but I think it gives me an air of nonchalance. I feel immediately older and more sophisticated when I put these clothes on.

Next, I apply red lipstick. I was inspired by Brook, who lent me hers the other day. I was surprised that it suited me too, so I made a mental note of the brand and color and bought the same one.

I look like a different person, and when I turn from side to side in the mirror, it feels like one of those trick images that looks different from different angles: From one angle, I look like a kid playing dress-up, from another, I look just like myself but *better*.

As I turn, examining the red of my lips and the way the dress swings as I move, my mind goes back to my dad. I wonder how he reinvented himself when he left. I'm sure he changed more than just his name. Did he cut his hair? Buy all new clothes? Change media or techniques in his art? Although buying a new dress and lipstick isn't quite the same thing, it sort of makes me feel connected to him, like I also understand what it means to feel stifled by my life and need to shed the past.

I switch off the light and head out for class, texting Nai Nai as I wait for the elevator.

*Meatloaf for dinner last night,* I text. *Never missed home so much before.*

She responds almost immediately with a vomit emoji. Nai Nai is a frequent and creative user of emojis. I laugh and put my phone away when the elevator dings. Since I got back from upstate, I've been calling and texting her again every day. I feel bad that I went so long without talking to her during the first two weeks at Ogilvy. But I'm sensing a distance when we speak. All of a sudden, I'm hiding everything important from her. Not just being queer, not just my feelings for Grace, but now also the fact of having a long-lost brother and discovering my dad's piece in MoMA. During the school year, I'd come home every day and tell her all the details of what happened, but here, I give her only the blandest facts of my day, worried I'll give something away if I speak too freely.

My painting for the project is coming along. I've decided to keep the ocean motif, but now I'm representing Niko as a boat filled with objects. I like the idea that he, like me, is finding his own way. Some of the objects are obvious: a surfboard, an easel. Some of them would only make sense to people who know him well: our dad's sculpture, a volleyball representing his girlfriend. Finally, there are some that mean something only to me, and I'll have to explain them to him. A bowl full of wontons, because even though he didn't grow up eating our food, I know he'll love it anyway. A little tree, to represent his two family trees: our shared family and his blended family back in California.

I also keep getting inspiration from the people around me. Jeremiah's work in black-and-white photography has inspired me to leave part of the canvas uncolored, outlined instead in black and white, like a comic. Grace mentioned a painter called Hilma af Klint offhandedly, and I ended up falling down a rabbit hole, looking at her psychedelic, colorful canvases. Following that, I added abstract patterns to some of the surfaces. The overall effect is, I have to admit, very contemporary looking, almost edgy. I'm still using fabrics too, and now that the painting is primarily of objects, the fabrics play a more natural role, adding texture to each of them.

I'm pleased with how the piece looks, but at the same time, I feel like it's missing something big, something revolutionary. I consider finding our dad, and for the first time, when I think about him, I feel anticipation for the future rather than sadness about the past. He might be exactly the right person to advise me on what this project needs to make it exceptional. I picture his little wooden sculptures, the ones that Niko and I have. They're nice, but the bright red wall in MoMA? That was *revolutionary*.

Now that we're into Week Three, everyone is knee-deep into constructing their showcases. The painters and more traditional sculptors in the program don't require much more than what we can find in the Ogilvy building, but for those of us who need nontraditional materials, the professors organized a few field trips out into the neighborhood to shop. There was so much to discover right here on Ogilvy's block. On Monday, in a Salvation Army, I found a corduroy jacket with amazing silver buttons that I knew would be perfect for my project. I also, incidentally, found a pair of baggy low-rise jeans that looked just like what every girl I saw on the street was wearing. I bought both and tucked the jeans lovingly away in my dorm room closet before bringing the jacket down to the workshop, where I spent the last hour of class deconstructing it.

"Wait," said Niko yesterday night in the lounge, where we'd met up to discuss our strategy for Thursday. "If you've been getting off-campus for these trips, why can't we just use them to sneak out?"

I sighed. "We have to check in every half hour. That's not enough time to get to Chinatown and back, let alone do anything useful. Movie Night is going to work, OK?"

He didn't say anything.

"How's the art been going?" I asked tentatively.

"Um—not bad. Could be worse." He rubbed a tired-looking eye. "Yeah. I'm nearly back on top of the Art History readings, and I finished those figure sketches I was late on for Abbott."

"You look tired."

"Yeah. Stuff with Hailey." He paused. "We haven't texted in a few days."

"Oh, no," I said. "Want to talk about it?"

He gave me a shifty look. "Not really. Let's—yeah. Let's just focus on showcase stuff. I've got a couple of ideas I'm considering for Meta-phorical Ali. How's it going for you?"

"So much better," I told him. "I'm getting ideas from everywhere. Just walking around the workshop and looking at everyone's projects has been really inspiring. Grace and I were talking about how much we love pointillism, so I added some of that to some of the background! Sorry for the spoiler."

"Hmm," he said, brow furrowed, but then his friends arrived in the lounge and headed over to join us, effectively cutting off the conversation.

It's OK if Niko doesn't get my project. When I think about my evolv-ing showcase, I can see so many different influences in it. It's a new kind of art for me—all of this is new. I feel a rush of adrenaline as I step out into the muggy heat of the sculpture yard in my long, light dress. It feels weird and amazing to have transformed myself like this, my clothes, my art, just because I wanted to.

It's so different from home, where every part of me seemed like it was laid out for me in advance. Where everything about me was predictable, uncreative, constrained: I could only do art in my limited free time, and the materials were always in short supply. Here, I have access to everything. So many possibilities have opened up, not just for my project but for myself. Finally, Ogilvy is living up to its promise. It's showing me who I am.

Halfway through Thursday, I realize I'm nervous.

I text Niko this. **Hi, so, you've sneaked out before, right?**

**yes obviously lmao,** he says.

**And it went fine? You didn't get caught?**

**i never get caught**

**relax,** he adds after a minute. **our plan is airtight. we're going to be fine**

I don't really believe him, is the thing. Niko has an easy, relaxing presence, but should we actually be relaxed about sneaking out from under the professors' noses?

As the movie night gets closer, I try to reassure myself with thoughts that they won't expel us right away if we get caught. We haven't done anything wrong before, so they'll probably just give us a stern talking-to and then tell our parents.

OK. That isn't reassuring at all. Nai Nai can't find out about this.

"Are you OK?" Grace asks as we enter the lounge for Movie Night. "You look really pale."

I figure I might as well start the lie now. "I'm fine," I tell her with a forced smile. "My stomach just feels a little weird."

We settle onto a couch with Brook and Jeremiah, and I scan the room for Niko. He's sitting near the door with his friends, but notices me and nods.

The lights go down, and suddenly I feel as nervous as though a spotlight were about to come up on me. As a list of producers glows on the projection screen, I check my phone every thirty seconds, making sure we're on schedule. Niko slips out unnoticed at the five-minute mark.

At the ten-minute mark, I clutch my stomach and make my best noise of mild pain. I lower my voice and whisper to Grace, "I've got to go to the bathroom. I think I have food poisoning. Don't wait up for me."

"Oh, no. Seriously? Do you want me to come with you? I think I have some Tylenol, if—"

"No, no, it's fine! I get an upset stomach sometimes. I brought stuff for it." I get up to a half-crouch. "Just enjoy the movie! I'll see you later."

"OK," she whispers back, still looking uncertain.

I slip out of the lounge, then dash down the deserted hall for the stairwell.

Niko is sitting on the steps, reclined. "There you are," he says, not even bothering to whisper as he hops to his feet.

"Keep your voice down!" I hiss.

"Why? Everyone else is in the lounge." Niko waves me down the stairs. "Like I said. It's going to be fine."

Still, my palms are pouring sweat as we sneak into the darkened cafeteria, then through the kitchen with its industrial steel counters. We decide to go with the unlocked-window method, figuring that propping the door would be too obvious.

"No one should be back here until morning, anyway," I whisper to Niko as we creep toward the door. "I spilled something at dinner on Tuesday night to make sure. When I was helping the custodian clean up, I asked her if she worked all night, and she laughed and said they were all out of here by 8:30, and—"

"Ali, you told me this already," Niko sighs, nudging through the back door.

"Oh. Right. OK." I follow him through, and the moment the door closes behind us, I feel my nerves settle.

The summer night smells like pollen and hot asphalt as I draw a deep breath. The whole night is ahead of us, and we've got a restaurant to find. "That was . . . kind of easy, actually?"

"I told you," he says with a grin. "OK, Queens. Which way?"

I lose Niko in a crowd of drunk, screaming people on the way into the subway. I don't notice until I realize I'm alone on the platform, totally confused as to where he's gone, so I retrace my steps. The poor boy is *still at the top of the subway stairs*. There's a steady stream of people descending the steps and he lets them pass one by one, seemingly unable to insert himself into the flow. I sigh and trot back up toward him. I can't believe he was so relaxed sneaking out of Ogilvy, but this is somehow beyond him.

"Isn't California the land of the freeway? *Merge.*" I grab him by his elbow and pull him into the crowd. When we get to the platform, the subway is about to close its doors. I accelerate and we squeak through just before the doors close on Niko's backpack.

"Do you all just do this every day? Don't you get like, hypertension or something?"

"This is the pace the civilized world moves at," I say. The subway jerks into motion. I'm too far from a bar to hold on to, so I plant my feet at shoulder width and sway.

He observes me. "You'd be a pretty good surfer."

"Really? Thanks!" I bask in the glow from the compliment for about a second and a half before he brings me back to Earth.

"You have a low center of gravity, so that's good. You're very possibly the dinkiest person I've ever met." I hit him with my backpack.

Ten minutes later, we're walking down Mott Street. I pass storefronts that feature waving cats, ads for discount facial treatments, and Chinese New Year posters several years out of date.

"What's your Chinese zodiac sign?" I ask Niko.

"I, um," he says. "I don't know. I was born in September."

I almost laugh and hold it back just in time. "It's based on the year," I say, as if I were explaining it to Grace.

"Ohh, OK. I was born in 2004."

I do a quick Google. "That makes you a monkey."

"What does that mean?"

I pretend to read the words on my screen. "Monkeys are . . . good at surfing, art, and annoying their siblings."

He shoves me, and I laugh.

"This place is busy," he says, eyeing a packed shop that sells rolled ice cream.

"Isn't it? You should see it during Chinese New Year. I came here to celebrate last year with my grandma."

"With whose grandma now?" He raises an eyebrow.

"With *our* grandma." I roll my eyes, mostly for show, but to be honest, it weirds me out to hear him claim Nai Nai. With Mom finding Anand, and with Jessie, Elise, and me moving in different directions as we grow older, sometimes I feel like Nai Nai is the only person on earth who's truly mine. The idea of sharing her with Niko makes me feel jealous in a visceral, almost physical way. I wonder if maybe I can get away with never introducing them to each other. Maybe I could tell him it would upset her, and he could go back to his happy family in California. I'm sure once the bullying thing with his brother calms down, he'll lose all interest in Nai Nai. After all, he already has a family.

"Tell me about her," he says, seriously this time.

"She is . . ." I hesitate. How do you describe the person who's raised you from birth, the person who represents the only home you've ever known or imagined?

I finally settle on: "She's very . . . short."

"Excuse me?"

"Yeah," I say. "She's like, four foot nine maybe?"

"And you are . . . taller than that? Are you sure?"

"Oh my God, I am five feet tall," I say, which makes me sound, somehow, even shorter. Like how adding "and-a-half" makes you sound younger than whatever age you said you were.

"I meant like, her personality," he clarifies.

"I knew what you meant," I say. "I'm just trying to decide how to describe her."

"Tell me what it's like to live with her. What's a day in your life like?"

"Well, she gets up super early. She's a tailor and she works at a dry cleaner. She opens it at six thirty and works until three. That way she's always home by the time I get back from school. These days, I'm at school until basically dinnertime, and when I come home, the house smells like whatever she's been cooking. It gets really humid inside; it's like walking into a cloud of dumplings or noodles or something. I usually do my homework through dinner, but she sits with me and always refills my bowl without me even noticing. She does all the household stuff, which makes me feel super spoiled and guilty, but when I try and clean, she gets mad and swats my arm and tells me I need to study instead. Usually she watches TV while I finish my homework and then she goes to bed early."

"I would love to meet her," Niko says. "I mean, if you wouldn't mind."

"Sure, maybe." I say. "I mean—if it wouldn't upset her too much. She's obviously still traumatized about my dad leaving, so it might be a lot. Maybe in the future though."

I hope this is enough to get him to stop pressing the subject. Nai Nai and I have this perfect balance at home. I'm so afraid of throwing off that balance, especially lately. I already feel like I will, if I ever tell her that I'm queer.

My throat feels thick, and I can't say anything else or I might actually cry. I settle instead for a tight smile and look quickly away—right up at a white, rectangular sign that says EIGHT TASTES RESTAURANT.

There's no question: We are in the right place. The restaurant's brick front is painted bright red, and set into the wall is another one of our dad's pieces, six feet by six feet, the wooden carving in the center of its niche seeming to throw light outward. Like the wall in the museum, it's bright crimson. He's layered red envelopes, red streamers, and shiny red paper in several overlapping layers. It looks like he mostly used Chinese New Year decorations, but I catch a glimpse of shopping bags, too, and ads from magazines.

It's a beautiful piece, but the thing I like best is how different it is from the stuff in his binder. Instead, it resembles the bold wall we saw in the museum, which he made when he was probably in his forties. This piece resembles his early work in some ways: The wooden carving is a similar shape to the ones Niko and I have, and the collage of paper also resembles the surfaces of our sculptures. Yet, at the same time, they're dramatic opposites. This piece, and the wall in the museum, look nothing like the earth-toned, natural-looking, faded-newspaper print aesthetic of his work I've seen. His old aesthetic was subtle and elegant. But his later style—it's bright and vibrant and in-your-face, and I adore it. I run my fingers over the edge of the piece and feel a tug of longing and hope.

"He really did reinvent himself," I say quietly. "He didn't just change his name. It's only because I know his other pieces so well that I can see the resemblance."

Niko is already on to the next step. "I wonder if the owner is still in touch with him. Let's go ask."

I follow him into the restaurant. Gray tiles squeak under our sneakers, and the hot steam and smell of frying garlic and ginger hits me. It's the first time I've walked into that smell since leaving for Ogilvy, and it makes me more homesick than I've felt all summer.

Niko walks to the back of the restaurant, where a middle-aged man is taking orders from a shuffling line of a dozen people.

"Hi, excuse me," Niko says. "Are you the owner here?"

The man looks confused. "Sorry?" he says, thickly accented.

Although I'm sure his English is fine, with the noise, the chaos, and our weird request, I think it's probably better if we have the conversation in Chinese.

"Hi, I'm Ali," I say in Chinese. I note confusion on his face before he evaluates my features, decides he "gets it," and returns his attention to what I'm saying, all in a split second. "We wanted to ask the owner of this restaurant about the artist who made the piece out front. We're trying to get in touch with him."

"Ah," he says, nodding. "We don't know anything about that. We just bought this restaurant a few months ago. If you want to ask the old owner about it, you should ask him directly."

"Do you have a phone number for him?" I ask.

"He's not really a phone guy," says the man. "He opened up a new restaurant, though, called Envy North. Maybe you could try them?"

"That's great, thank you so much!" I exclaim.

I turn back to Niko. His hands are behind his back, and he's studying the paper menu in front of him very intently, a frown on his face.

"How does that sound?"

"How does what sound?"

I realize like an idiot that of course Niko didn't understand a single word we just said. I quickly translate for him. He doesn't say anything.

I can't tell if something is bothering him or if he's just already mentally planning the next stage of our search.

I, however, can't think about anything besides eating. I've just realized how hungry I am. I barely ate anything at dinner, thanks to nerves.

"Hey," I say, checking my phone, "we still have an hour and a half until curfew."

"I know what you're thinking," Niko says, "and I approve."

I grin. I place an order for two bowls of wonton soup, and soon we are cozily ensconced in a corner. I'm slurping happily, while Niko is spending more time studying the contents of his bowl.

After a little while, he says, "Was that Mandarin? Earlier?"

I nod, my mouth full.

"So our dad speaks it?"

I swallow too much at once and wind up coughing. "Ye-ep! It's his first language. He was around my age when he and Nai Nai left Shenyang."

"And is this the kind of stuff you eat at home?" Niko asks, gesturing to his bowl.

I gulp some water, and finally my eyes stop watering. "Yeah, sometimes. This is like, comfort food. We eat pretty simple food when it's just the two of us, but when Elise and Jessie come over, Nai Nai goes all-out. Even on a regular weeknight."

Niko leans forward, looking unusually intense. "Tell me what she'd make. I want the whole menu."

"Why?" I laugh. "You've had Chinese food."

"I've had P.F. Chang's," he says. "I'm guessing it's a little different from stuff our dad's side of the family makes, like, traditionally."

"OK, you're right. It's definitely different. Lots of noodles, obviously. Both cold and hot. Preserved and pickled vegetables, like cabbage and potatoes, and some others . . . I actually don't know all the names in English, now that I think about it. Oh, and pork sausage—that's my favorite."

Niko sighs. "We are a no-pork household back in California."

"Really! That's a tough restriction with Chinese food, I think. You don't eat any pork at all?"

"I eat everything," he clarifies. "But Anastasia read somewhere that pigs are as smart as dogs, and I guess my parents found that convincing."

"Oh, I hate that," I say. "Well, she also makes tofu, and mushrooms, and fish. There's something for everyone."

"It sounds amazing," he says, and I'm surprised by his wistful tone.

Feeling suddenly guilty about how I brushed off his request to meet Nai Nai, I hastily stuff several more wontons into my mouth.

We're careful to be home well before the movie ends. I sneak up to my room and freeze in the doorway. Grace is sitting on my bed, as if she's been waiting for me to come home.

"Where have you been?" she demands. "I made Brook let me in here when you didn't come back to the movie."

"I was in the bathroom."

"Don't lie," she says. "I checked the bathroom."

"I—I went to one on a different floor. I was embarrassed. About the food poisoning. Did you enjoy the movie?" I add.

"Don't try and change the subject. Where did you go?" Her voice falters. "Is everything OK?"

I sigh. I can't think of a quick lie that would explain everything, and besides, I don't really want to lie to her.

"I'm going to tell you something crazy," I tell her. "But you have to swear you can keep this all a secret."

A concerned look flits across Grace's face. "You can trust me," she promises.

I go straight to the most important part. "You know Niko, that guy from California? Turns out, my dad, who walked out on me when I was five, is his dad, too."

"What? Did you know before coming here?"

"No," I say. "We found out because we both have pieces of his art. And here's the craziest thing: It turns out he's a famous artist still living here in the city. He changed his name and got famous after he left us both. Niko *found one of his pieces at the MoMA*. That's why I ditched you," I admit.

"Yeah, I thought that was a little odd," Grace says, not adding the part I know she's thinking—*and rude*. "How sure are you about all of this?"

"I'll let you decide," I say. I open my phone and flip to a photo of the sculptures I have at home. "We both have these at home. My dad made these, and his dad made this." I flip ahead to the near-identical sculpture that Niko brought to Ogilvy.

Grace slowly exhales. "You sure it's not just a copycat thing?"

"One hundred percent. Niko knew my dad's first name, and he looks exactly like photos of my dad when he was younger."

She squints at my face, something dawning. "Wait, but I'm confused. Niko is Asian."

"We're both half," I say, hoping we can move past this quickly.

"I don't see it." She's still looking at my face. My skin burns. I feel embarrassed, like I'm being examined by the doctor. I smile awkwardly and open my mouth to say something, anything, but she continues. "Wait—yes, now I totally get it. Your eyes. Your eyes look Asian. And like, your cheekbones?"

"I look like my mom," I say. "Anyway—"

"Wait, but your eyes are green. Or gray. Shouldn't they be brown? I'm just remembering biology class."

"I have no idea," I say. "Genetics are crazy, I guess."

"It's just so weird that I didn't guess!" she says.

I suddenly feel conscious of my entire physical being. My face is hot, and my hands instinctively reach to fiddle with my sleeves. I stare down at the plush carpet rather than watch Grace study me. I've finally caught her undivided attention, and it's for this reason. Why would she have guessed? Why would she need to guess? Why does it matter whether I look more like my white mom or my Chinese dad? And what does it say about me that my heart is skipping a beat for a girl who's suddenly hung up on my ethnicity? If I really respected myself, wouldn't I shut this down somehow? I don't even really know what's rubbing me the wrong way, though, let alone how to put it into words. I change the subject. "OK, let's focus on the much more interesting thing here," I say instead. "You know, my secret sibling and secret famous artist dad?"

"Ah, of course!" Grace exclaims. "What are you going to do?"

"We're . . . actually trying to find him right now," I admit. I fill her in on the showcase idea, the portrait drama, and our hope that he'll be able to set us on the right track. Grace is as good a listener as always, bubbling over with excitement, but sometimes she looks at me strangely, like she's searching for something in my features. I wonder if she's curious about me like you'd be interested in some exotic zoo animal, or if she's interested in my life, my feelings, who I really am—and I wonder how I'm supposed to tell the difference.

Abbott's face is unreadable as he slides my homework assignment, then Nathalie's and Andrew's, onto our table. The second he moves on, I flip it over, daring to hope. I worked hard on this one—a response to a fifteen-page article we read about anthropomorphism in automobile design. At our study group on Tuesday, both Haoran and Jen read it over for me, while I looked over their perspective sketches for Ziegler.

The grade written at the top is a small red B.

I want to break into a smile, but I restrain myself, pushing the paper into my backpack. "All good?" Andrew whispers to my side.

"Pulled a B."

"*Yes!* Nice, bro!" Andrew claps my shoulder, looking delighted.

Now I do smile. It's funny how the same guy who'd be devastated if he got a B himself is so excited that I managed one. You'd think it would feel condescending, but I doubt Andrew could condescend if he tried.

At the front of the class, Abbott says, "Well done. These papers overall met a high standard." I could swear his eyes move in my direction before he turns away. "I'll see you all after the weekend."

As the three of us pack up, Andrew glances over at Nathalie. "How'd you do?"

She lifts her shoulders. "OK."

"What," I say before I can stop myself, "you get an A minus?"

"No," she says too quickly.

I laugh. Her dark eyes meet mine. I look down at my backpack immediately.

Andrew doesn't seem to notice. He also hasn't seemed to notice that I've carefully positioned him between me and Nathalie in every class, meal, and study group since we got back from upstate.

I zip my backpack up, my excitement about the good grade wavering. It's been almost five days since my fight with Hailey—we still haven't texted—and it's probably not fair, but I've started to feel frustrated not just with Hailey, but with Nathalie, too.

It's just that she said I didn't have to make everybody comfortable, and so I sent that text message, and now Hailey and I aren't speaking. It's just that Nathalie put this idea in my head that if I treated this stuff less like a joke, it'd make things better. But it made everything worse instead. It's just that Nathalie's here, and Hailey's not. And I'm doing things like avoiding her eyes, and making sure Andrew sits next to her instead of me, and glancing over when I make jokes in our study group to find out if she cracked a smile. And that's enough to make me feel like I'm doing something wrong.

I need to swallow my pride and fix things with Hailey, that's all. I'm already halfway across the country. She could be meeting up with her guy friends right now, realizing that it'd be so much easier to date one of them instead.

"I'll catch y'all at lunch," I say as we exit the lecture hall. "Be there in fifteen."

Instead of rounding the corner with the others, I shoulder out into the sculpture yard. It's a dark, overcast day, a summer storm gently rumbling overhead, but no rain yet. I settle into a bench beside a bubbling birdbath and take out my phone.

I'm just about to start writing a text to Hailey when a message pops up from my mom.

**Hi sweetie! Long time, no text! Ogilvy still going OK?**

hi, I reply. **yeah it's going good so far.**

I hesitate, suddenly tempted to tell her about the grade I just got in Abbott's class. True, it's not an A, but Abbott's the hardest grader we have, and I was a straight-C student in all my classes last year except art.

I start to type, but my mom answers first: **So glad to hear it. You'll have to call us sometime and tell us what you're learning! Everything is great back home. Wonderful strides in counseling. Your father and Justin battling it out for highest scores in their programming class! Anastasia misses you. She is zooming through some books you used to love too!**

I delete what I'd written, which was: **actually i wanted to tell you about a good gr**

Instead I type, **cool i'll ask her about the books when we call sometime ok? got to go to lunch. thanks for texting. love you**

My mom sends a heart.

I let out a slow breath and look around the sculpture yard. It was just one B grade. Was I really about to tell her like it was some newsworthy thing? On Wednesday, when Ali and I got back a B on LaTonya's punishment paper, she gave me a sheepish smile and said, "Asian fail." Which, apparently, is anything below an A.

I shake the thoughts. No more delays or distractions. I lift my phone again, open my texts with Hailey, and take a slow, steadying breath.

**hey**, I type. **i miss you.**

It takes me a full minute to write these four words, and even longer to make myself press *Send*.

No reply. I wait two minutes, then add, **i'm sorry.**

Then, just like that, she's typing. Even that much, that beginning of a response, feels like a ray of sunshine pushing at the cloud cover overhead.

**I miss you too**, Hailey says. **It was stupid**

**yeah**, I say. **reset? never happened?**

**Never happened. :)**

**wow it's so weird**, I text, smiling now. **i just woke up from this 5-day nap and have no idea what you've been up to. you'll have to catch me up**

**That's such a funny coincidence, I spent the last five days trapped on a desert island? Soooo I feel like I'm missing stuff from you too?**

Happiness spreads through me as I sit in the windy warmth, catching up on her week. She isn't angry. She isn't dumping me. She's willing to forget the whole thing, and it's barely more than two weeks until I see her again.

"Niko!" calls a voice. I glance up. Ali is jogging through the courtyard toward me. "What are you smiling about?" she says breathlessly.

"Hailey," I say, gesturing with my phone. "We're all good again."

"Oh, I'm so glad!" Ali hops onto the bench beside me. "Do you have a second?"

"Sure." I text Hailey a quick talk-later message and pocket my phone. "What's up?"

"It's . . . well, did you look up that restaurant? Envy North?"

"Oh. Yeah."

We exchange grimaces. From what the cashier told Ali last night about the last owner opening up a new restaurant, I'd pictured another location like Eight Tastes: linoleum floors and fluorescent lights, a simple sign that looked like it was screen printed at a same-day turnaround store, and sizzling street food flipped over a glass counter at dizzying speeds.

I was wrong. This next restaurant that we're apparently just supposed to waltz into, Envy North, is a Michelin-starred, ten-table room that's filled Google with gushing critics' reviews. I tried to look up contact information for the chef, Meng Tao, and got redirected to a "Public Speaking" page, where I can pay $5,000 an hour to see him in the flesh.

I glance around the courtyard to make sure we're alone. "How are we going to get in to see the guy?"

"Also, how are we going to get out of Ogilvy again?" Ali whispers. "I've looked at the rest of the schedule. We're basically campus-bound for the rest of the program."

"And we've got to somehow sneak into a restaurant that only fits, like, thirty people."

"I know. I can't see any way to get . . . unless . . ." Ali trails off, her eyes growing unfocused. "OK. I have an idea."

"What's—"

"No promises, though. I've got to ask someone."

"Who?"

She hops up from the bench and dashes toward the door. "Meet me at your room during study hour!"

I watch her disappear, bemused.

Once she's gone, I lean back against the bench, trying for the hundredth time this week to think of the perfect object to represent Ali. Last night showed me another side of her, free from all the rules and patterns of Ogilvy, but if anything, that just makes it harder to think of a single thing to represent her.

The whole night feels like a blur, looking back. As we moved through Chinatown, I wanted to stop to peer into the shops, which looked like little oases down the dark street, with their huge, welcoming, illuminated signs. It was only thanks to Ali yanking me out of the way that I escaped getting trampled by people with AirPods.

But after I'd fallen into her don't-fuck-with-me walking rhythm, the feeling of being an obvious tourist faded. I started watching the people around us, knowing this was how Ali grew up: surrounded by faces that looked like mine. Suddenly I felt like I was standing outside my body, seeing myself mixed in with everybody else, and I looked like just one of the crowd. It was like a kind of invisibility. Maybe for the first time in my life, I felt physically average.

Then we turned a corner, and that fast, I was back inside myself. I remembered that I'm not Ali: I don't live in this city, don't go to school here, don't understand the rhythms of life or even what the signs say. For every way I belonged in those crowded streets, there were a dozen ways I was missing some understanding.

This week, I've felt so aware of how little I know about my Chinese half. It's not just what Ali and I talked about at Eight Tastes—that I don't speak Mandarin, that I don't know anything about Chinese food, that I couldn't point to Shenyang on a map. It's a whole upbringing. Ali and my camp friends think about their futures differently. They do schoolwork differently. Their parents raised them differently. I know that with Andrew being Korean, Jen being Filipina, and the Wus being mainlanders, we're a pretty diverse group background-wise, but I've heard them make jokes like Ali's, too, laughing at the idea of an "Asian fail," these standards they all have in common.

I guess my whole childhood, I thought that all this had nothing to do with me—that it just wasn't my life and never could be. But this week, I've started picturing myself differently. It's like I'm an empty glass. If we find our dad, I can have a relationship with him that'll fill up that space inside me. There's so much I'll start to understand in an authentic way.

As for learning Mandarin, or knowing literally anything about China, I can't understand why I never wanted to do it before. At home, I shoved it all away from myself so hard, I couldn't even see what I was missing.

But now . . . I don't know. I'm starting to feel like I really *am* just like Andrew and Jen and Nathalie. Like if I can just reach out and open some door, take a few steps forward, I'll find myself in some place they've stood all their lives.

I remember, as we got near the restaurant last night, Ali darted across the street, holding up a hand to a slowly rolling car in what somehow read as both an apology and a don't-you-dare-hit-me gesture. Watching her move so confidently, even though her features stood out in the crowd, I felt another jolt of envy. Ali had it all, and she seemed to feel so casual about it.

Gazing up at the shifting clouds, I wonder if I could use something from last night for her portrait, but the thought fades fast. She already told me she doesn't want to be defined by her upbringing. Whatever I pick, it has to have her future in it, too. She wouldn't want me to choose something like the wonton soup we shared for her portrait—no matter how cozy it is, no matter how much I feel like I'll remember that forever, now, when I think of her.

I still like my first couple of ideas. There are the sneakers with the glitter laces, which I could set on a city sidewalk. It's definitely a more subtle way to bring in her New York identity, and I think I could nail the color contrast. Or there's her binder, bursting with her color-coded tabs. But I'd have to be careful with that one, too. Ali's never looked more hurt than when I went after her for being a high achiever. I'd have to capture her uniqueness in the binder somehow.

My leg is jittering. I need to start drafting again. We're at the end of Week Three here. I have only a couple of weeks to execute, and I have to get it perfect this time. Not just for me, or even for Ali, but for our dad, too. This can't be some little achievement, a B in class. He has to look at what I've made and think, *That's really worth my time.*

When I get back to my dorm after lunch, Ali is waiting for me at the door with her curly-haired friend.

"Grace," I say, trying not to seem surprised. "Um. What's up? How is . . . your showcase going? Ali and I were meeting up to talk about . . ."

"She knows," Ali says. "I explained everything last night."

"Oh, God." I let out a long breath. "OK. Here."

I unlock the door, and we slip inside. Technically we're supposed to keep the door open if we're in our rooms with friends, but Ogilvy famously doesn't care about enforcing this so-called rule.

"So," Grace says, "Ali told me you two need to get into Envy North."

"Yeah. Any ideas?"

Grace smiles. "It was Ali's idea. My parents are involved with the art scene in the city, and she figured, if this restaurant guy commissioned your dad, maybe he is, too."

"I was looking at the website," Ali adds, "and Envy North is *covered* with art. I mean, you can barely see the walls."

Grace nods. "So I texted my parents, and they said they know him."

"What?" I say, not understanding. "They know him? Like, personally? Doesn't New York City have eight million people or something?"

Grace and Ali both laugh. As always, when talking about New York with New Yorkers, I feel like someone who's just had an inside joke described to them.

"You're right," Grace says, "but some circles are really insular. Anyway, it's not like my parents are best friends with the restaurant guy. They just know the people who did the interior design."

"Right," I say slowly.

"The point is: My parents told me Envy North is catering this gallery opening next week. I told them you were Ogilvy students, such amazing artists, the whole thing, and they said they can get you on the guest list if you want to come."

The door opens. We all whirl around.

Andrew sticks his head inside, his face full of accusation. "Gallery opening?" he says, looking between us. "Wait, who's secretly going to a gallery opening?"

Ali, Grace, and I all wince. "Keep your voice down," I hiss, waving him inside.

Andrew shoulders the door shut, grinning. "Sorry. OK. What's happening?"

"Nothing," Ali says brightly. "Grace and I are both from the city, so . . . so we're planning something for after the program ends!"

"Wait," I say, an idea striking me. "Hang on. I think he can help."

"Help with what?" Andrew says.

"Are your parents still going to be in New York next week? And are they still signing you out for dinner one of those nights?"

"Yeah," Andrew says slowly. "Why?"

I exchange a look with Ali. She nods.

So—I tell him. All of it. Andrew's eyes widen, and he hops up to sit on his desk so clumsily that he knocks the lamp off and has to snatch it out of midair.

". . . so," I finish, "that's why we're trying to sneak out again. We know this Meng Tao guy commissioned our dad five years ago, so he'd have recent contact information. We've got to get hold of him."

Andrew's mouth is now fully open. He looks at Ali, then back to me, then at Ali again.

"Wait, so you're . . . Asian?" he says to her.

I elbow him. "Really? That's the part you can't get past?"

Grace laughs. "I had the exact same reaction."

"I know, I know," says Ali, rolling her eyes. "Very surprising, why are my eyes not brown, et cetera, et cetera. Can we please focus on helping my secret long-lost sibling and me find our estranged, pseudonymous, famous father?"

"Look, Andrew," I say, "I know you wanted to invite Nathalie or Jen to dinner. But what if you pretended you were inviting us instead? It might be our only chance to get out of the building for the night."

Andrew's expression falls, and I feel another guilty pang. Between this and my suspicions about Nathalie, I've never been a worse wingman. "It's OK," I say quickly. "We can find another way. Maybe—"

"No! I'll do it," he says, schooling his expression. "It'll work. But the camp admins will call your families to get permission, so you'll have to tell your parents and set everything up like you're actually going. Then, on Tuesday, I'll show up at dinner alone and tell my parents that you had to stay behind last-second to work on your showcases or something."

"I don't know," says Grace, looking unconvinced. "Andrew, won't your parents come here to pick you three up?"

Andrew waves a hand. "I'll ask them to call an Uber. Then Niko and Ali can get off halfway through."

I hesitate, still feeling guilty. "Thanks, man."

"Yeah," Ali bursts out. "You two are the best. Thank you so, so much for helping us."

"Thank *you* for having the most ridiculous life story ever," says Andrew. He turns and prods me on the arm. "You owe me, though."

"I know. How can I get you back?"

Andrew flops backward onto his bed. "You could scope out my chances for the dance." He flips over so that his face is buried in his pillow. I barely hear him groan, "God, I can't believe you found a long-lost sister before I could find a date."

We laugh. When Andrew tilts his head out of his pillow, he's grinning, too.

"Who do you want to ask, Andrew?" Ali says with a mischievous smile.

"He doesn't know," I answer. "He's been going back and forth between Nathalie and Jen for three weeks. Don't ask him to make a choice on the spot like this, it's too cruel."

I expect Andrew to laugh and agree, to make some self-deprecating joke, or to compliment Nathalie and Jen in over-the-top ways. Instead, redness tinges his cheeks, and he rubs the back of his neck. "No, um—I wanted to ask Nathalie." He lets out a sheepish laugh. "I actually can't stop thinking about her. I feel like we've been talking all the time since we got back from upstate."

My stomach drops. He's right. They *have* been talking all the time since we got back, because I've been physically arranging it.

And suddenly that seems like the stupidest thing I've ever done. What if Nathalie *does* like me, and now I've put Andrew in a situation where he's fallen for her?

On the other hand, what if she likes him back? Yeah, Andrew's younger than us, but he's smart enough to be in college already, and he's funny, and I've heard Nathalie complimenting his art. That idea gives me a rush of hope—but there's some other feeling mixed into it, too.

*Fuck,* I think, really panicking now. I don't *want* Nathalie to like me. Do I? That would be so messed up.

I think of Hailey, and it's blissfully simple. Her beauty, her poise, the hold she has over me and everyone else. The crazy feeling of luck I still have whenever I consider that she chose me. *Yes,* I think with relief. I want Hailey to be here, I want to hold her, I want to be with her. Whatever other feelings I have, they don't matter.

"So, what do you think?" Andrew says. "Can you check out the terrain for me, Niko?"

"Yeah. I got you."

Andrew holds up a hand. I high-five him. He adjusts his glasses and turns his smile on the girls. "What about you two? Ali, Grace? Asking anyone?"

Ali clears her throat, suddenly examining one of her bracelets with too much interest.

"I'm not sure," says Grace. "It might be sort of fun to go alone, right? And then you can dance with everybody and there won't be too much obligation."

"Yeah," says Ali, smoothing down her long, woven dress. "I'm not sure, either."

"You should go with Niko," Andrew says.

"First of all," I say, "what the fuck."

"I mean like as a sweet brother-sister dance thing!" he protests. "Like how fathers and daughters dance at weddings! Then you don't have to deal with all the dance-asking politics."

"Yeah," I say, "except that nobody outside this room knows we're siblings, so, gross. And—" I narrow my eyes at Andrew. "You can't tell anyone, OK? The showcase is supposed to be a surprise."

I glance at Grace, too, who smiles. "Ali already swore me to silence."

"I'm not going to tell anyone." Andrew props himself up on his forearms, looking affronted.

I raise my eyebrows at him.

"Niko, come on. Why would I?" Andrew snorts. "Everyone would think I was making it up." He hesitates. "You aren't making this up, right? It's not just a huge joke?"

Ali removes the binder of our dad's old work from her backpack. "This is my grandmother's," she says, handing it to him. Then she points to the sculpture on my bedside table. "And Niko's had that since he was a baby."

Grace peers over as Andrew pages through the binder. He stops on the photograph of the sculpture. Grace shakes her head, making her curls sway hypnotically in the light, while Andrew pinches the bridge of his nose just beneath his glasses.

"Yeah," he mutters, "this is breaking my brain. Also—" He hefts the binder in his hand. "How much does this thing *weigh*, Ali? How did you have space to pack this?"

Ali laughs. "I may or may not have gotten two of my friends to sit on my suitcase so I could zip it shut. I have an overpacking problem."

A smile spreads across my face.

"What?" Ali asks.

"Nothing," I say. But that's it. It's perfect. I envision the suitcase she hauled up to the coach bus, scuffed and bulging at the zippers.

That's Ali's portrait. Something that strains to hold every colorful part of her life, no matter where she brings it.

LaTonya paces slowly between our tables, fingers steepled. "Today, we're going to talk about homage. How artists speak and refer back to each other. How inspiration can become art."

Niko is slouched beside me, twirling a pencil, but there's no mistaking it—his attention is riveted on LaTonya.

She shows us some examples of references in art, how one artist might pose a subject to deliberately recall another famous work. Then, she sets us loose to work on our own homages. I seize on Giacometti, Grace's favorite artist. I pull up a photo of that skinny dog sculpture she told us about, and I get out my sketch pad. I sketch the dog from every possible angle, including ones where I have to use my imagination, like from directly underneath.

"Giacometti is one of my favorite artists," LaTonya says, as she looks at my sketch pad. I blush, pleased, but after she walks away, I realize that she hasn't actually praised my sketch.

A little annoyed, I lean over and look at what Niko's drawing. He's working on a drawing of a sculpture, covering it with Chinese characters. He keeps bending over his phone and typing things. I can only assume he's translating everything he wants to write from English into Chinese.

"What artist could you possibly be paying homage to?" I whisper.

He covers his paper, defensively. "I don't make comments on every-thing you draw in this class!" He seems a little embarrassed. I wonder if he's worried that I can see mistakes in his Chinese characters, but I can't read Chinese, only speak it reasonably well, so I would have no way of knowing whether what he's writing makes any sense.

Still, annoyed at his defensiveness, I say nothing and turn back to my own work. Done with my Giacometti-inspired sketches, I turn to the next page and start to doodle cartoons of little old ladies sewing long swathes of colorful fabric, tall blonde women twirling in white lacy dresses, and a gangly little teenager in a bright yellow dress.

LaTonya's shadow looms past me again. I cover my page, embar-rassed to have been caught not working on the assignment. I grin up at her, nervously. She doesn't smile, but I swear her eyes twinkle at me. This time, she doesn't say anything at all. Her thoughts, as usual, are a complete mystery to me.

Later I'm in the workshop, bent over my piece, when suddenly light floods the room. I blink, disoriented. If it's light now, that means it was dark before, which doesn't make sense, because I got here right after lunch and . . .

My stomach rumbles just as I glance at the clock on the wall and realize that eight hours have passed instead of the two or three I'd assumed. I've been hard at work, tweaking details here and there, but my painting is still missing that something *exceptional*. I look up and see Grace standing in the door with an eyebrow raised and a Styrofoam box in her hands.

"I take it you didn't see my text asking if you wanted me to wait for you to eat dinner," she says.

I respond with my most abashed smile.

"Anyway, you'll be glad to know I didn't wait. And I brought you dinner." She walks over and puts the box down in front of me. "You missed Brook showing us photos of her supersecret portfolio."

Brook has been cagey from the start about her work, and I haven't really seen any of it. All I know is that she's also a painter. She works with her easel facing the wall so you can't see what she's been doing.

"Ugh, I'm so jealous!" I exclaim. I keep my cool for one second, then burst out, "So . . . can you tell me what she told you?"

"I know, I'm sorry to make you feel left out!" Grace looks down and I swear she blushes. My heart sinks a little. "She says everything has a common theme of trying to disorient the observer. She has a whole series of landscapes painted at odd angles so the horizon isn't where you expect it to be. But enough about Brook! I want to hear about you. No day of rest, huh?"

"I need the weekend to catch up and focus," I say, through a mouthful of lukewarm cabbage.

"Well, don't burn yourself out. It's just camp."

I'm a little surprised to hear Grace say that. I kind of liked how she and everyone else here seemed to view Ogilvy as so much more than camp. I feel a little foolish, like she thinks I'm pouring myself into something that doesn't matter that much.

The feeling fades, though, when she leans in and looks closer at my workstation. "What are you working on at the moment?"

I gesture to the pile of fabric on the table. "I initially had this as a mixed-medium painting with fabric designs, but it got a little busy. With all the objects I'm already including, plus the different visual styles I'm incorporating, I don't really think there's room for the fabric as well."

She frowns. "I liked the fabric. I thought the variety in texture gave it something special."

"Funny, Brook liked the fabric, too. I was asking her for her thoughts, and she said that she liked the more ethnic-looking fabrics." I gesture at a scrap of red fabric that I cut from a tattered qipao I found in a trash can in Chinatown. "She said it gave the piece a sort of a craft-like quaintness. But, you know, craft-like quaintness wasn't really what I was going for, so I think it might be more in line with my vision if I take it off."

Grace picks up some crumpled fabric from the table and smooths it out. "Brook is smart, but she's not the only authority at Ogilvy," Grace says. "I think she gives good feedback, but you should also know when to tune her out."

"I mean, she *liked* it," I point out. "I'm actually doing the opposite of what she said."

"Well, it's your piece. I think it looks great either way." I can tell she doesn't agree, and I feel worse than ever. I look at the pile of cloth on the table and feel weirdly sad about the idea of throwing it all away. I liked the fabric, too.

She gently pushes the material to the side and looks directly at me. "So how are you feeling about everything else?"

"What else is there?" I ask. "Oh, you mean the whole secret-sibling, quest to find my absentee father thing?"

She laughs. "Yes. That little thing."

"Well, it's hopefully the weirdest thing to ever happen to me!" I say, with a laugh. I expect Grace to laugh too, and move on, but instead she just waits, her blue eyes holding mine, as if she knows there's more.

And there is. I've just been nervous to examine it. I'd rather plow forward into elaborate plans and research than reflect inward and poke at this raw, newborn feeling.

"It's really . . . exciting," I say eventually. "It feels like my world just got twice as big. I love living with my grandma, but it's insulating to only be so close to one person. It makes me feel like there's only one way to be. And . . . I want to be different. I want to have adventures, to be brave and create art and make my mark on the world, you know? I've always kind of assumed I might get that side of me from my dad. I don't really remember him, and now I might actually find out how far our similarities go."

As I say this, I realize that there's another side I'm even more afraid to admit, which is that for every part of me that's excited, there's two more parts that are nervous, for the exact same reasons. I barely remember my dad. What if he's not how I imagined? What if I'm not what *he* imagined? I've always been proud of my art, and all my life I imagined he'd be proud too—but what if he isn't?

Grace is studying my expression, as if she can tell there's something I'm not saying, but she doesn't pry. "Well, I'll let you get back to it," she says, getting up. I give her a nod; I'm still staring at the piece, trying to decide what's missing.

It's only after the door closes that I realize I forgot to say goodbye.

Once she's gone, I look at my painting. I've peeled off nearly all the fabric pieces. I was hoping that would be what I needed to bring the whole thing together and make it look more cohesive. But still, there's something missing from it, spiritually, and I don't know what it is. Frustrated, I put the frame away and look at everyone else's projects for a moment.

I can't really look through Jeremiah's without getting my greasy fingerprints all over the photos, so I leave them be. I've seen them when he's handling them, and they're all beautiful. He's stuck with the animal motif in city scenes, squirrels on park benches and pigeons on top of old phone booths, but he also has some shots of nature scenes from upstate.

Grace's is, predictably, amazing. She has a canvas six feet tall propped against the wall, and she's painting it with vibrant flowers that look almost photographically real. There's a big white lily in the middle, and that's going to be what she broadcasts her film against.

I can't see Brook's, which is facing the wall as usual. But what Grace said has given me an idea. *Disorienting the viewer*.

I take my canvas and turn it upside down, looking at it from this angle. It looks *much* more interesting from this perspective. Possibly even revolutionary.

"Niko, what do you have for me here?" LaTonya has glided up to my workstation, serene in a glittering green dress.

"I picked something."

"I can see that." She smiles down at the drafting table, which has transformed in the few days since I chose my idea. Dozens upon dozens of drawings litter the surface, charcoal on bright, heavy card stock. One shows a tiny stall selling papayas, another a warped wooden hoop. On the sheet closest to me, I've sketched a piece of wood like a tongue of flame, surrounded by a shell of papier-mâché.

These sketches show our dad's pieces from Ali's binder. A corkboard stands against the wall behind my station, covered with photocopies of his sculptures. Our dad's art is going to come together to create Ali.

Most of the sketches are only half finished, pencil lines underlying the charcoal shapes, but I've been working fast. I know I can finish before the showcase. Before me stands a large canvas, two by three feet. Right now it's a mess of outlines, but I can picture the way it's going to look ten days from now.

I unpin a reference photo of Ali's suitcase from the corkboard.

"I have this friend," I say to LaTonya. "I want to represent her through this suitcase. And her dad's an artist. So, I'm collaging the image together from his work."

"I see," LaTonya says. "And what do you hope to say with this piece?"

My hand, holding the sketch, falters. I try not to let my disappointment show. LaTonya doesn't look impressed, or even sound excited about the idea. Everything—from her voice to her posture—reads neutral. Is this how she reacted to the others when they told her what they'd decided to do?

I set the sketch back on the table. "Um, I guess the point is—when you put his art together, it makes an image of her. And since the subject is a suitcase, it's like parts of her past creating her future."

But now I'm avoiding her eyes, because that's not my idea. That's what Andrew said to me yesterday over text. I'd told him my plan, and he'd replied in bursts,

**Bro that's a great idea!**

**Like, showing how Ali's background makes this path forward for her**

**And then also showing how you, being the artist, put your perspective into how you see Ali! And the parent you guys have in common!**

**It's so cool, there's so much going on, LaTonya is going to love it!**

I immediately latched onto what Andrew said. It sounded impressive and sophisticated, like a real artist's statement.

But now, when I look at the canvas in front of me, something else comes to mind. I imagine a tall silhouette in front of the piece, our dad seeing his own work reflected back at him. He'll see the way I've already inherited something from him, and how much more he has to give.

I'm trying not to get my hopes up. There's no guarantee that we'll be able to talk with Meng Tao at the gallery opening tonight. Even if we do, maybe the chef didn't stay in touch with our dad. Maybe our dad left New York, or even left the country.

Still, I can't help imagining the possibilities.

I look away from the canvas and back at LaTonya, the vision fading. She's regarding me, gentle and piercing as always. "Niko, I think it's wonderful that you're creating a piece that has to do with your friend's heritage. Frankly, I'm touched by it, given our work in class."

Uncomfortable, I nod. "Sure."

"Do you feel this piece is a tribute to her father's work?"

"Um, I guess partially. I mean, I always thought this one sculpture"—I tap the one with the wooden flame—"was cool. His designs are awesome." I sneak a sidelong glance at her. "Don't you think so?"

"He's certainly a talented artist."

There's something she's not saying. I look back at the canvas. Did I do something wrong?

"I love your focus, Niko," she goes on. "And these sketches, individually taken, are striking. This collage will be sure to have a lot of visual appeal." With a confidential smile, she rests one hand against the canvas. "All I'll say is: There's a lot going on here. The abstraction of person into item. This homage to someone who isn't, strictly speaking, your subject. And then you, the artist, and your perspective. Make sure not to lose Niko-the-artist in those feelings of tribute. Or that loss will be felt in the art."

She glides away, leaving me frowning after her. How could I get lost in the art? It's my idea. I'm making the piece. Didn't we *just* have a class the other day about how artists respond to each other?

Worries start to cloud my mind. Is LaTonya right? Is there too much going on? I still haven't seen Ali's new portrait of me. What if hers turns out worlds better than mine? In that case, the whole showcase-unveiling plan is shot, because it'll be embarrassing if only one of the siblings has a good piece to show.

Worse, what if Ali's having just as much trouble and the whole thing falls to pieces? What if she and I don't even manage to make something worth looking at, let alone something that our dad will want to touch?

Another image comes to me, this time of my parents' faces. My mom and Phil are wearing glazed expressions, preparing to give me some good-effort speech. *We're so glad you tried your best. Now come home.* Exactly like they expected from me. That vision of the blue ribbon is blurring, falling away, my dad's turning his back . . .

I can feel myself spiraling. I spread my hands on the table and breathe. *LaTonya said it'll have visual appeal*, I remind myself. She liked the sketches. That's a more direct compliment than I've gotten from her since the beginning of camp.

I just have to stick to the plan. For now, I'll focus on the sketches but won't start assembling. Tonight, Ali and I *will* find Meng Tao at this gallery opening, and he *will* get us in touch with our dad, and if there's something missing in my concept, he'll know what to do. He'll bring us together; he'll deepen the roots; he'll fill the gaps.

This is going to work.

At 6:15 P.M., Andrew, Ali, and I gather in the Ogilvy foyer, and Professor Rosa arrives to check us out at the desk. I silently thank God it's not Professor Abbott, who'd probably see through us with one glance at our faces.

"What time do you think you'll be back?" Professor Rosa asks Andrew.

"I told them before eight thirty," Andrew says confidently. It's unsettling how good a liar he is. His smile is exactly as cheerful as usual, and there's no hint of nerves as he slings his messenger bag across his back.

"All right," Professor Rosa says. "I'll wait here to let you in around then."

"Thank you so much, Professor Rosa," says Ali. She, unlike Andrew, clearly can't lie to save her life. Her eyes are fixed on a spot over Professor Rosa's shoulder, and she keeps fidgeting with one of the corduroy pockets on her new dress.

"That's us," I say, pointing to a Toyota that's pulling up outside the building. "See you tonight, Professor."

We slip out into the summer evening. The scents of warm pavement and hot tire stir around us, wind brushing up the streets, until we enter the car, which smells like strong deodorant and pine air freshener.

"Andrew?" says the driver.

"That's me," says Andrew.

We take off through the city. I exhale slowly, trying to iron out my nerves. Ali, beside me, is fidgeting more than ever. The air freshener quickly starts to give me a headache.

The thing is, even though Grace's parents managed to get us on the guest list, I have no idea what to expect from a gallery opening. How easy will it actually be to get celebrity chef Meng Tao on his own?

On this, at least, Ali and I seem to be on the same page, because she suddenly says, "You don't think we have to buy something to stay at the event, do you?"

I hadn't considered this. "Um. Shit. I hope not. Won't everything be like four thousand dollars?"

Andrew laughs. "Yeah. No way they'll think you're there to buy fancy art. We're teenagers."

"Grace is a teenager," Ali mumbles, "and she was telling me about how her mom takes her along to help select art from galleries."

"Fun," says Andrew cheerfully. "Anyway, it's going to be fine. My parents and I are having dinner at Eataly. You can come hang out with us if everything goes wrong! It'll be great. There'll be pasta."

I give him a half-smile. "Thanks, bro. You're still the best."

"And you still owe me," he sighs. "You haven't talked to her?"

"Not yet. I will, though. Promise," I say, my mouth only a little dry. Nathalie and I have been polite and friendly and nothing else since getting back from upstate, and Hailey and I are texting nonstop, too. I don't have anything to feel guilty about.

It's true that things are different between me and Hailey these days. I thought it was normal, at first, but everything seems kind of careful now. She doesn't ask questions about my life anymore, which comes off as shitty and uninteresting, like I'm not worth her time. Sometimes I think it's my fault, since she was asking about my life when we got into the fight; I know that if I'd just laughed along, it never would have happened. Sometimes I want to say something about it.

But whenever I think about the fight itself, I bump into this steel part of me that just can't turn around on it. Because that's my dad she was talking about. That's me. That's our lives, and when Ali and I find our dad, my heritage is only going to become a bigger part of my life.

So I don't say anything. I ask about Kelsey and Gigi, and her dad's case. I text back the right answers, casual and flirty, and so does she, and we keep up our rhythm. It's just that the rhythm felt like music before, and now it's like a hollow drum.

The Toyota turns up a narrow street with dozens of storefronts: perfumeries, soap shops, boutiques with two or three expensive-looking outfits dangling off sticklike mannequins. Nearly every window has gone dark for the night, but near the end of the block is an illuminated sheet glass window with a dark cloth display.

We halt in the line of cars trailing up to a stop sign. Andrew says, "Hey, they're going to get out here, is that OK?"

The driver grunts over the muted voices of a podcast.

"Good luck," Andrew says. Ali opens the door, and we climb back out into the night.

We slow as we approach the gallery. The sheet glass is etched with the name ANDERSON JENNING GALLERY, and the dropcloth beneath begins, *Anderson Jenning is pleased to present UNBECOMING: the first exhibition in thirteen years by Lyza Schumann, featuring over fifty photographs spanning two decades of the artist's most intimate and confessional work . . .*

Ali and I stop in front of the door, exchange nods, and enter.

Empty, the gallery would look like a tiny parking garage, with its bare white walls, the industrial pipes spanning its ceiling, and a concrete floor that slopes up and around a corner. But the angled spotlights and quick, quiet jazz music give the place a clandestine feeling, and it's packed with well-dressed adults carrying champagne flutes.

"Hello," says a voice to our right. We turn to find an attendant giving us a toothy smile. "I'm *so* sorry, but this event is invitation only."

"We should be on the list," I tell him. "Niko Castadi and Ali Tan."

The attendant narrows his eyes dubiously before looking down at the clipboard in his hand. "Of course," he says, doing a weird little half-bow as he steps back. "My mistake. Please enjoy the opening."

Ali tugs me forward, and we begin to move between clusters of adults. I wonder if this is what everyone at Ogilvy is going to look like in twenty years, a sea of open-necked linen shirts, strange shimmering sack dresses, and acrylic shoes that remind me of Jen's favorite pair. Some of the party guests give us looks of puzzlement or mild interest. Near one of the largest photos, we pass a group that I'm pretty sure includes the artist, a dark-haired woman in a formal, wine-red gown who's speaking to a cluster of ten or so silent listeners.

"There," Ali whispers, pointing around the corner. Near the back, where a fuzzy-sounding trumpet line is spilling from a pair of speakers, stands a caterer's table and bartender. ENVY NORTH is written in barely legible cursive across a tablecloth where silver platters gleam.

"Hi, excuse me," Ali says, approaching the table. The black-shirted woman plating the hors d'oeuvres glances up. She looks Chinese, in her thirties, with hair dyed violet.

"Do you work at Envy North?" Ali asks.

"Sure do."

"Meng Tao is supposed to be here tonight, right?" I ask.

"Oh, yeah," says the woman. "He loves these things. Never on time, though. I doubt he'll show up for an hour or so."

Ali and I trade a look, then check our phones. It's still only 6:47. "Should be OK," I mutter. "Andrew said 8:30."

"Are you fans?" the woman asks, grinning. "Aspiring chefs?"

"Artists," Ali says, smiling back. "We're students."

"Oh, right on. Well, he'll be here sometime, promise. Want some food while you wait?"

She gestures with a pair of tongs at the displays of food, which, honestly, seem more like art installations than like food. Tiny pinkish cubes, which could be some kind of meat or maybe frosting, sit atop crisp black wafers. These are arranged checkerboard-style with cream-colored wafers, which have been dashed with red gel. Another platter holds a hundred jellylike hemispheres that shiver when Ali accidentally bumps the silver tray with her hip. Threads of green garnish float on top of the hemispheres in identical X formations.

"Is this . . . um . . ." I begin.

"Asian fusion," says the woman with the violet hair, giving me an ironic wink. She points at the hemispheres. "Soy and black pepper bonbons with lemongrass garnish." She indicates the wafers. "Sesame and black rice wafers topped with shrimp or pork and chili emulsion."

We take one of everything on small plates and back away toward the wall.

"Meng Tao should teach a sculpture class at Ogilvy," I say, prodding one of the hemispheres with my plastic fork. I'm intimidated to touch the food, let alone put it in my mouth. "I mean, talk about negative space."

"Yeah," says Ali skeptically, mashing her fork into the hemisphere without pause, "I don't know if I really value negative space in my food. With food, I'm more about things like mass. And volume."

Ali and I grab waters from the bartender's stand, and for a while, we circulate around the gallery like everyone else, pointing out the photos we like, muttering quietly about the ones we don't. We keep a careful eye on everyone who comes into the gallery, but as the clock hits 7:00, there's still no sign of Meng Tao.

It's nearly 7:15 when a trio of adults drifts up beside us. They pass through a tinted spotlight, turning their pale skin teal for an instant. One, a tall, full-figured redhead wearing florals, points at the photograph next to my head. "That's the one. Sorry, excuse me," she adds to me.

"No, my bad." I duck away. "Go ahead."

"Yes," says one of her companions, a small, balding man with circular rimless glasses. He's also scrutinizing the photo. "I see it."

Ali and I shy further away so the third of the group, a mustached man wearing a tweed cap, can offer his opinion. He does: "Very tasteful. Yes, *very* tasteful. I understand what you mean."

I exchange a glance with Ali and see my own curiosity in her face. There's basically no art scene in Landry Beach, and even though Ali grew up here, she described her upbringing as pretty unglamorous. I find myself wondering what actual "art people" talk about when they come to galleries. The photo before us shows a rusted bicycle leaning askew against a wooden fence, looking so unbalanced that it seems like it could drop out of the frame at any second. What kind of deep meanings are these people getting from this photo that we can't understand?

"At the same time," the woman sighs, "I already have three sets of prints in the front room—you know, the Murakami is the anchor piece of the room, obviously—so then the question becomes, if I buy this one, am I risking a cluttered look?"

*Oh*, I think.

I meet Ali's eyes again and see amusement there. I feel my own lips twitching and I'm about to turn away when the man with the tweed cap says to Ali, "I love to see young people at these events. They're not letting you in on the wine, I hope?"

"No, no!" Ali says with a little laugh. "Of course not."

"Tell us," says the woman in florals with a smile, "who here do you know?"

"My friend Grace LeBlanc . . . her mom—" Ali begins.

"No! Emilia LeBlanc?" exclaims the man with the glasses. "Such a small world! Emilia, you know"—he waves toward the other man and woman—"Emilia from the board for the Brooklyn Historical Painters' Foundation." They all make sounds of delighted recognition. Glasses Man beams, his blue eyes seeming to glow. "So, I assume you two are budding young artists, too?"

Ali and I both stand a bit taller. "We are!" Ali says. "I'm Ali, and this is Niko. He's here for the summer from California."

"San Francisco?" guesses Tweed Man, looking at me.

"No, I'm from a town called Landry Beach."

"Sounds sunny," says the woman. They laugh and sip their wine.

"And you?" Glasses Man asks Ali.

"I live here in the city," Ali says.

Much more enthusiastic sounds from the group at this. "Here in Manhattan?" asks the woman.

"Queens."

"And what type of medium do you both work in?" says Tweed Man with a knowing little smile at his friends, like, *let's indulge the children.*

"A lot of my background is in painting, but I've been getting interested in textiles recently," says Ali.

"I'm into charcoal," I say. "I spent some time with pastels last year, so I'm pretty comfortable with that, too."

Tweed Man's eyebrows rise. I can tell this is already a more serious answer than he expected from us. "Oh ho," he says. "Very exciting. I suppose you'll both be thinking about art programs for college?"

"Definitely," says Ali at once. "We're actually students at the Ogilvy Summer Art Institute right now, so that feels like a great opportunity to define ourselves as artists before we have to submit applications."

I can tell the adults are impressed by the mention of Ogilvy, or maybe just by Ali. Their eyebrows have risen, and when Glasses Man speaks again, his voice is more serious. "So, what kinds of subjects interest the pair of you?"

Ali glances to me, so I say, "I'm all over the map. Um—did a series last year about water, and light coming through different kinds of water, and for that I was interested in how we see colors in the moment, but then remember them in bigger, kind of more dramatic ways later. I really like pastel for that feeling. And for charcoal I'm more interested in motion and figure work. Right now, for Ogilvy, I'm doing a mixed-media portrait of, um, a member of my family."

My whole spiel takes me by surprise. Because none of it is bullshit, unlike what I told LaTonya this morning. Before Ogilvy, I wouldn't have been able to describe what I was trying to do with that cave water drawing, even while I was working on it. I guess our hundreds of pages of readings have been saturating my brain for the past weeks, showing me how to talk and think about art.

So—why couldn't I describe my portrait of Ali to LaTonya like that? In a way that felt like it meant something?

All of the adults are nodding. "Would you say you're often drawn to work about family?" asks Tweed Man. "I know the family unit is of chief importance among, you know . . . in the East."

"Not really?" I say with an embarrassed laugh. "I don't usually make art about my own life. Mostly I'm more interested in the world around me."

"Of course, of course," says Tweed Man quickly. "And how about you, Ali?"

"Oh, I'm just like Niko! I have a million interests. I have lots of ideas for found and recycled art. The passage of time is a theme I really want to dive into, maybe a graduated series of pieces that I create over a long period. I'm doing something family-related at Ogilvy, too. And then there's textile, and how it falls on the body, and how woven fabrics evoke traditionalism! I don't know. Maybe someday I'll settle down and pick one medium. Maybe not!"

She laughs, and we all laugh with her. A shimmer seems to settle over the night. It feels otherworldly, standing here in this gallery with Ali and these strangers. I wonder if this is the future she's always aspired to. For me, at home, art was always just a place to go in my own mind. But for Ali, living in this city—she's probably walked past a hundred galleries like this, looked inside and seen hundreds of events like this one.

Maybe that's why she wants it so badly and why her feelings toward her own neighborhood are complicated. This isn't the same New York she's described from her childhood. This is all something else. But it's right here, pressed up against her New York, close enough to tempt her.

The adults are asking Ali about her ideas, and I can't help but notice that none of them are asking her about themes "of importance in the East." But just as I have that thought, Glasses Man turns to me and says, "You know what, Niko, I just remembered something. If you're planning to apply to art programs in New York, you should really look into the DYCA Mentorship program."

"The—what is that?"

"Diverse Young City Artists," says Glasses Man. "It's a great opportunity. Tell them I sent you." He takes out his business card and scribbles on it in pen, then hands it to me. "They can pair you with an older, established artist of color in the city, help you network, build community, explore possibilities for your future career. I think we can all agree"—he glances among his friends—"that art as a community-building tool has been, for a long time, wielded in exclusionary ways. Can't fix it overnight, but, well, now you have that."

I look down at the business card with the man's writing. *Referral – DYCA Mentorship*, scribbled above his name, Jonathan Atwood.

I'm very aware of Ali standing next to me. Of the two of us, she's the one who's more likely to apply for programs in New York. I glance at her, wondering if I should mention that we're both half-Chinese. This program could be useful to her. She's not Grace. She didn't grow up strolling through galleries in private events like this.

But Ali's head twitches in the tiniest shake.

She doesn't want to admit it, I realize. She doesn't want to say she's an Asian artist.

Puzzlement, then frustration rises in me. Of course, Ali wouldn't want to feel like she got an unfair head start. Neither do I. But—she has this whole background, one that I've been thinking about nonstop for the past week and a half. She's authentic, real, a legit Asian. And she's just turning away from that?

*So did you*, whispers a voice in the back of my head. Every day in Landry Beach I told myself being Asian had nothing to do with my life. It's just that I couldn't get away with it, not with the way I look.

In this moment, I really wonder: If I looked like Ali, would I spend my whole life keeping quiet, slipping under the radar? I remember envying the way she looked when I was making that first draft of her portrait, but now it seems kind of sad. She has to make the choice. Reject half of herself or choose the thing I've spent most of my life trying to escape.

"Thanks, Mr. Atwood," I say finally. "I appreciate this. I'll email them if I wind up applying somewhere out here."

Atwood beams, and I do genuinely feel grateful toward him. He opens his mouth to reply, but just then Ali sucks in a breath and grabs my arm.

"I'm so sorry," she says, all smiles to the adults. "I just saw someone we were supposed to meet here."

They wave us away with cheerful goodbyes, and Ali drags me forward.

"Where is he?" I whisper, scanning the gallery.

"He just went back outside," Ali hisses. "No! He can't leave!"

"OK." I snatch her water glass. "I'll deal with these. Go after him. Now."

"But you—"

"I'll be right behind you. *Go.* You're a girl. You're, you know, you look ten. He won't blow you off unless he's a real dickhead."

"I don't look *ten*," she says, but she's already maneuvering around a group of people and disappearing, while I get stuck behind the crowd at the bar.

I dodge guests in cocktail dresses, moving for a side table full of abandoned glasses. This is happening. *Please*, I find myself thinking. *Don't let the trail go cold here.*

I forge back through the gallery, craning my neck, trying to peer past dresses and suits. Then I break through to the front and see them. Ali, standing across from the man we came for.

Meng Tao is a short, slender, tattooed guy holding a cigarette. His tattoos come up above his collar line, colorful tendrils at the sides of his neck, and extend to his wrists. I push through the door into the smells of hot asphalt and smoke.

Ali points at me. "That's him! That's Niko."

"Shit," says the chef. "I mean—crap," he adds, glancing at Ali. "Sorry. It's just—Christ, you look exactly like Bo." He sticks out a hand. "I'm Tao."

"Hey. Niko." I shake with a lump in my throat. I don't know why, but it never occurred to me that I might look like my dad. I guess my grandparents make a big deal out of that with Justin, but I never thought of it as something that could apply to me.

"So, I was telling your sister," says Tao. "Your dad was never good at keeping in touch, especially when he was making something new. I tried for a while. Used to send him texts when people asked about the piece at Eight Tastes, but that dropped off after the MoMA sale. He lived at the same address for ages, though. It's in this neighborhood, actually; you'd think we'd have run into each other at some point. It's possible he moved, but if you wanted to try going there in person—"

"Yeah," I say at the same time that Ali blurts out,

"Yes, please!"

Tao nods, his phone already out. "OK. Here. Ready?"

Ali and I both write down the address.

"Thank you," Ali says.

Tao nods. "Good luck." Then he stubs out his cigarette on the pavement and reenters the gallery.

Ali and I stand in silence for a minute, watching each other. Ali's face is tense, her lips slightly parted. She's breathing unevenly, like she's taken a flight of steps too fast.

I know how she feels. Meeting Tao went better than we imagined. Finding our dad now seems more possible than ever. It's like I could reach out and touch a future where we're all standing in the same room.

"It's only 7:30," I say. "We could go there. Now."

"Do you want to?" Ali says.

I swallow. The reality of it is bringing in new thoughts, things that hadn't occurred to me yet—every negative possibility. Our dad could be in serious financial or medical trouble. Maybe he got addicted to something, or got arrested at some point, and couldn't stand to face his mother.

Or worst of all: Maybe he's doing completely fine but has so little interest in seeing Ali or me that he shuts the door in our faces.

I picture that silhouette turning away from my canvas.

I remember Ali's look of hurt as she stood in front of his piece at the MoMA.

Panic surges at the back of my throat. He can't just do that. He can't deny me this whole part of my life and background, the full person I could become. And he can't do that to Ali, either—this is her home, her city. She'll have to tell her grandma what happened, and her home life will be wrapped up in it forever.

For the first time, I wonder if this whole thing was a bad idea. There had to be a reason he was local but never bothered to get in touch with Ali and her grandma.

*No*, I think forcefully. He could be surprised and happy to see us, excited that we're artists. That could be what we focus on as a family. We could show him in-progress pictures of our showcase, and our portfolios. I could ask him what it was like, moving across the Pacific at Ali's age, starting over in New York. I could ask about Pratt and see whether he's more like Ali, organized and motivated, or—like I privately hope—more like me, kind of erratic, not perfect when it comes to structured stuff. Maybe he could teach me Mandarin. I imagine all-summer trips to see him and Ali, trips to museums the three of us could take together.

I imagine our portraits displayed side by side in the Ogilvy foyer.

"Yeah," I say hoarsely. "I want to."

At once, Ali begins to type furiously. "The maps app can't find us," she says. "Come on, you stupid—" She holds her phone high to try and get a location read.

Impatient, I lift my own phone—only to find a message from Andrew, sent several minutes ago:

**SOS RED ALERT!!!! Dinner's over and parents were like "we'll walk you back to Ogilvy"!!!**

My stomach drops. **wtf no**, I text back. **shake them off.**

**I can't! They're insisting. We're like 20 min away! They're going to drop me at the door and Prof Rosa is going to see!!!**

I swear loudly. "Ali," I say, "we can't."

"What?" She waves her phone in my face. "It picked us up! It's only 840 feet away—"

"If we don't want to get kicked out of Ogilvy, we need to run back to campus," I say, showing her the texts. Her eyes fly wide open. "Come on."

We sprint down the streets. I glance at my phone every other intersection, watching the minutes count down, picturing Andrew and his parents strolling through the balmy evening. I imagine LaTonya, or Professor Abbott, or Professor Rosa, gliding through the Ogilvy foyer— any of them could see, and that'd be it. I'd be on a plane home first thing tomorrow.

"Almost there," Ali gasps, wiping her forehead with the back of her hand.

**eta?** I type one-handed. We hurtle across a crosswalk past a guy walking six dogs and a woman loudly negotiating a business deal on her phone.

**4 min**, Andrew says.

With two minutes to go, we turn onto the familiar one-way and see Ogilvy's building glinting up the street. Ali throws out her arm to stop me.

"What?" I pant.

Clutching at a spot just below her ribs, she points ahead. I see Andrew and his parents a block away, ambling idly toward Ogilvy.

Trying to catch our breath, we creep up the sidewalk behind them.

**behind u**, I text Andrew. **say goodbye fast pls**

Andrew checks his phone and glances over his shoulder, then shoots us a secret thumbs-up behind his back. Hardly fifteen seconds after he and his parents have stopped at the glass Ogilvy doors, he's hugging them goodbye, and they're continuing along, down the block—out of sight.

Ali and I hustle up the sidewalk just as Professor Rosa comes into view, jogging across the foyer.

He pushes the door open. "Andrew! You're back early. Sorry I missed your parents, I just saw them—where are Ali and Niko?"

"Here, Professor Rosa!" Ali says breathlessly, hurrying up to the door. "We hung back to get a photo, sorry!"

Professor Rosa considers us. For a moment I'm terrified he'll guess that we just sprinted halfway across Manhattan to get here. But then he smiles and says, "Well, come on in."

Ali, Andrew, and I exhale, exchanging sheepish grins, as we sidle in behind him.

"Any luck?" Andrew whispers.

"Yeah," we whisper back.

In the elevator, wordlessly, Ali hands me her phone. I lift it to my eyes.

I'm looking at a street view of our dad's apartment. It's tall and narrow, made from red-brown brick, with strips of concrete underscoring the black-framed windows. A fire escape zigzags down its front, casting shadows on the windows, keeping everything inside out of sight.

**How was dinner with your friends?** Nai Nai asks.

I stare at her text, confused, before I remember the lie about going out with Andrew's parents.

**It was nice!** I say. **Good to have a change of scenery.**

**I'm glad you make new friends at camp** ☺

New friends. If she only knew. I respond with a single smiley face and turn back to my easel. I'm in workshop, painting. Like Brook, I've started painting with my easel and back to the wall, so that people can't look at what I'm doing. I'm worried it will look stupid if anyone sees it before I'm done. I'm also a little nervous that if someone saw it without context, it might look like I've taken Brook's idea. But that's not what I'm doing, I'm making it my own. Like in LaTonya's class.

I take a moment to look at my canvas. I like it; I'm really proud. Turning it upside down has made a big difference, but there's still something nagging at me about it that I can't put my finger on. Something is missing, despite everything that I've added to it. I think the painting is *good*. Maybe the best thing I've ever done. But I'm not confident that it's good enough to win the prize. I'm squinting at the painting, tilting my head back and forth, when I notice someone hovering in my peripheral vision.

I turn and am surprised to see it's Niko.

"Oh, hey," I greet him. "Shouldn't you be in your workshop?"

"I'm on a bathroom break," he says.

"This isn't a bathroom," I point out, but I'm excited that he's here. "I know we said we wouldn't show, but do you want to see mine? It's nearly done."

Niko examines the piece, his head tilting from side to side.

"Looks cool, right?" I say.

"Yeah, I like it," he says eventually. I can tell it's a real compliment this time around, but he also looks confused. "Why is everything upside-down?"

"It forces the viewer to engage with it more. All the objects are familiar objects, but when it's upside-down you have to linger on each item a little more, just to figure out what it is. Putting it upside down makes the viewer take in the individual pieces rather than the painting as a whole."

"Or maybe they'll just focus on it being upside-down. Besides, what does it say about me that it's supposed to be a metaphor for me and it's upside-down?"

"It doesn't have to be a perfect metaphor," I say, irritated. I angle the easel away from him. "Anyway, why did you stop by?"

He lowers his voice. "The dance on Friday." He's staring out the window as if trying to act natural, even though there's no way anyone can hear us with all the ambient noise from forty of us working on our projects. "It's our chance."

"Are you sure?" I'm dubious. The dance is my opportunity for Grace to notice me in a new light. Even though I've been slowly improving myself all summer, she probably hasn't really *seen* the change, kind of like how I don't notice my hair growing until Nai Nai tsks loudly and sits me down at a chair in the middle of the kitchen. But at the dance, I'll hopefully look so good that she can't help but notice me.

"It has to be during the dance," says Niko.

"Why does it *have* to be during the dance?"

"Because! The showcase is only a week after that. What if our dad looks at our pieces and sees huge issues with them? We've got to leave time to make changes. It's got to be soon. We need time with him. If . . . if we want a shot at the prize."

He's shuffling a little bit. I realize he's staring out the window not as a sneaky cover for our conversation but because he's anxious.

"OK," I say. "Friday."

He nods once, sharply, then turns and heads out of the room.

I meant what I said about Grace, but there's more to my reluctance than my excitement for the dance. A pit of doubt about our plan to find our dad has been slowly growing in my stomach since last night. Meng Tao had been so casual about the fact that he'd been here the whole time, but the revelation had felt like a slap in the face. Back when I believed he'd left the city entirely, I could imagine reasons—some possible, some far-fetched—why he'd never called. Maybe he couldn't afford to be an artist in the city anymore, and he was ashamed. Maybe he moved back to China and didn't know how to get in touch. Maybe he took a vow of silence and was living in an art commune in the wilderness.

Instead he was a subway ride away. He had time to make art for a Michelin-starred chef, but not enough time to watch me grow up. Is this someone whose door I want to knock on? Do I want to pull back the curtain and learn why he left? Every possible answer to that question seems crushing. I was already nervous about this idea; now I'm more sure than ever that it will end badly.

But—I remember the look of determination on Niko's face. I want to keep my promise to him. And maybe, I think, a flicker of hope returning, if we do this just right, and my showcase is absolutely perfect—I can show our dad he was wrong to leave.

"OK, team," I say, spreading out a big sheet of paper on one of the workshop tables. Grace, Andrew, Niko, and I have gathered here during dinner, when it's empty, to figure out our plan for sneaking out during the dance. "They'll be paying close attention, so it's important to make sure everything goes right."

"We won't have Andrew's family as a cover this time," Niko adds.

"So we need to come up with something else. Here's what we had in mind." I begin to sketch a floor map of Ogilvy on the paper.

"We can't go in and out of the front door," says Niko. "Stan watches it like a hawk."

"The dance is going to be in the cafeteria," I say, drawing the map of the cafeteria and the door to the kitchen. "We can get out using the kitchen, but it's going to be a lot tougher when the entire program is right next door. We're going to need to distract whoever is watching that door so we can sneak in and out."

"That's where you guys come in," says Niko. "When we're about to leave, you're going to have a little too much fun dancing and spill a drink on whoever's there."

Grace and Andrew look dubious. I can tell they're both thinking about how upset they'd be to have any drink spilled on their respective outfits.

"You can spill water if you feel bad spilling a Coke," I say. "Just spill enough that they have to go and change their shirt or whatever."

"Fine," says Andrew, with a sigh. "Just know that as a man who takes care of his wardrobe, I find the whole thing distasteful."

"When we're on our way back, we'll text," says Niko. "Which means you've got to keep your eye on your phone, no matter how much fun you're having. You'll run another distraction and we'll sneak back in, and no one will be any the wiser."

"Wait," says Grace, her brow furrowing. "Are you saying we need to spill on this poor person's clothes twice in one evening? Won't that be sketchy?"

"Or come up with another distraction," I say. "Be creative, you're art students."

"She's right," says Andrew. "How weird a coincidence for the same guy, who's standing by the door to the kitchen, to get conveniently distracted twice."

"And what if you get back toward the end and the room is practically empty?" says Grace.

"OK, OK, you're right," Niko says. "What should we do instead?"

"What about the front door?" Grace suggests.

I begin to draw a map of the lobby on the paper in front of me.

"What, like just waltz in?" asks Niko. "Stan sees everything. He's going to be very confused when we walk in, and he never saw us leave."

"I have an idea," says Andrew. "When Niko and Ali are back, they'll wait outside and text us. Grace, you and I will come down and you'll tell Stan you thought you saw a stranger on your floor. Insist that he come up and investigate. Since you can't see the elevators from the front door, I'll hang back and give you a signal when Stan is safely in the elevator."

"Seems simple enough," says Grace. "I resent being the damsel in distress, but I'll do it for you two."

"Did you really need the whole blueprint thing?" Niko asks me, waving down at the map. I've also drawn a map of the lobby, because I could.

"No harm in a little practice sketch work," I say.

"I think you just wanted to look like a character in a heist movie."

I have nothing to say to that; he's right, and what's more, I didn't even realize that was what I was trying to do. I laugh, embarrassed, then rip up the drawing. Just in case the maps look suspicious, I put half of the pieces in the trash can and save the other half to throw away in my trash in my room. Another thing that a character in a heist movie would think to do.

With our plan set for Friday, I stay late in the showcase workshop room on Wednesday, and even later on Thursday. That hazy silhouette I've imagined standing in front of the canvas is solidifying. And while LaTonya hasn't said anything that makes me think she really loves my idea, she also hasn't told me anything negative. I've been putting the finishing touches on my sketches tonight, all thirty, which means that the second I get our dad's input, I can start assembly. I should finish the portrait with days to spare.

What's even crazier is that I'm still on top of my homework. I'm not making Ali's grades or anything, but I'm finishing the readings, and yesterday I earned my first A in Abstracting the Figure.

I'm almost annoyed about it, with Professor Abbott being Professor Abbott, but I'm realizing his is the first class I've ever taken that I'd say I love. On Monday, he gave this lecture about the way bodies go elastic in cartoons, and I spent half of lunch glued to an article he passed out about hand-drawn animation.

I check the clock: ten minutes to curfew. When I glance around, I realize I'm the only one still here.

I wipe my charcoal-dusted fingers on a wet cloth and start to pack my things, but as I zip my backpack shut, my eyes catch on one of my final sketches. One of the shaded areas could use deepening. I pick up the charcoal again, the stick squeaking under my fingertips, and draw a few careful lines.

"Almost done?" says a voice behind me.

I startle and whirl around to see Nathalie eyeing my sketches. "Nathalie. Um. Hey. I didn't realize you were still here."

"I wasn't. I passed the window and saw you still working. I thought I'd tell you it was curfew, in case you didn't realize."

"Oh. Thanks."

I feel a guilty drop in my chest. After the excitement of Tuesday night, and with our plans for tomorrow, I still haven't asked Nathalie what she thinks about going to the dance with Andrew. But it's not too late. I know he hasn't asked her yet.

Nathalie takes the stool at the workstation beside mine, and the squeeze of guilt turns to something else, some other awareness. I haven't been alone with her for a while. I forgot how intense her silences are.

Nathalie points at my project. "You're pretty obsessed with this, aren't you?" She says it neutrally, but a quirk of her mouth gives me the sense that she approves.

I make a dismissive sound. "Everyone here is more obsessed with art than I am."

"Really?" She gestures around at the empty room. "All these people?"

I laugh and set down my charcoal. "OK, yeah. But I'm not like you. I don't know everything about Postimpressionism or whatever."

"Mm. Major oversight. You should memorize that Wikipedia article right away."

Her unaffected expression makes me want to smile. There's something nice about her quiet confidence—how she knows the type of person she is, but doesn't take it so seriously that she thinks life begins and ends with knowing about art.

I glance back to my workstation. "Look, I wanted to ask you something."

"Oh?"

"Yeah. This isn't for me, because—yeah, obviously—but are you . . . like, looking for anybody to ask you to the dance tomorrow?" This is the least clear I have been in my life. "I mean, are you into the idea of any specific person asking you?"

The workshop suddenly seems very quiet.

"Are you asking for Andrew?" Nathalie says, low and tentative.

I move my head in a jerky nod.

Nathalie tucks her dark hair behind her ear with a quick motion. She swallows, looking upset. "Um, if he did, I don't think I'd say yes. I don't want to give him the wrong idea. I'd go with him as friends if he wanted that, but if he's asking you to ask me about it . . ."

"Yeah."

Nathalie closes her eyes, covering half her face with one hand and rubbing her fingertips into her hairline. "Can you tell him I didn't want to go with anybody because dances are like, a type of psychological torture?"

I let out a guilty laugh. "Yeah."

Our eyes meet for a split second and we both look away.

Frustration lances through me. I hate this feeling. I hate that some tiny part of me is relieved she said no. I hate that the same part of me wants to ask, *Is that true, that you didn't want to go with anybody?* And I'm not going to say that; I never would. But as I stare at the linoleum floor, I'm wondering if there's a tiny part of her that wants to come out with something like, *But if you didn't have a girlfriend . . .*

Nathalie's eyes move to my hand, which is compulsively spinning the charcoal. Her hair has come free from behind her ear. She tucks it back again and stands. I do too. I hadn't noticed before that she's maybe six inches shorter than me. She always seems to loom, just from the way she keeps her distance and watches.

"So—" I say.

At the same time, Nathalie says, "I guess—"

We both wince. "It's late," I start again. "I'm going to—"

Then I see motion over her shoulder, out in the hall, through the plate glass windows.

It's Andrew. He's taken a step back, watching us. I feel another wrench of guilt. And I don't know if it's shown on my face or if he's just seen enough already, because he's turning and rushing down the hall, his tweed jacket flapping as he goes.

"Andrew," I say after entering the bathroom, because it's past curfew and he's not in our room, so this is the only place we're allowed to be.

"Go away," he says from the locked stall at the end.

But before I can even tell him that I won't go away, he's speaking again. "I can't believe you. Like, do you have a problem or something? What's your problem? You—you're into Nathalie? And you've just been listening to me being an idiot about her for weeks?"

"You're not an id—"

"And you have a girlfriend!" he bursts out. "What happened to your California dream girl? What about her?"

The words ring off the bathroom tiles. I let them fade before saying, "Hailey and me are fine. And nothing is going to happen with me and Nathalie."

A long silence.

"But it fucking *could*," Andrew says in a small, miserable voice. "If you didn't already have a girlfriend. Tell me I'm wrong."

I lean back against the tiled wall. "I don't know how Nathalie feels. I didn't ask her. I don't want to know."

"That's such bullshit, man."

I close my eyes.

"I'm just—" Andrew lets out a pained laugh. "You kept making it so I'd sit next to her. Right? That's what was happening? Because it was weird with her, or something, and you could tell. Why didn't you just say it?"

"Because I didn't know for sure. I didn't want to sound like a huge asshole and assume she liked me because of—I don't know, because of one time Jen smiled at her in a weird way."

"Niko, open your eyes, Jesus. You can make assumptions like that. Look at you, look at who you're dating."

And now I'm angry, somehow, even though I know I'm the one who messed up. Because we all talked about this upstate, and I thought Andrew understood. "Bro, I don't know who you think you're talking to, but Hailey's my first girlfriend and we haven't even dated for three months. My whole life, I've done this, too, I've always liked people who don't like me back. I told you at the lake, I basically fucking said I hate how I look! You don't think I have any reason for that?"

The stall door bangs open as Andrew shoves his way out. His eyes are reddened. "I never said you didn't have a reason. But shut up, OK? Just actually shut up. Because if you hate how *you* look, how do you think that makes *me* feel?"

I splay one hand over my face. My head is starting to pound. I wish I were with Devin and Grayson right now. A friendship wrapped in a dozen kinds of comfortable silence. It's all too direct, talking about things like this. It's like staring into the sun.

"I'm sorry," I say hoarsely. "I thought you and Nathalie could be good together. I thought, you know, I have Hailey. It doesn't matter how I feel."

Andrew takes off his glasses and wipes his eyes. "Yeah. Fine. You're right, it doesn't matter."

"Andrew—"

"Forget it."

And for once, he leaves it at that, just two words. He strides past me and out the door.

Andrew's not in our room when I wake up the morning of the dance. When I go down to breakfast, he's not at our table, either.

"He was here for a little while," says Haoran absentmindedly, swiping through a page on his tablet, "but he said he had to go catch up on some showcase things . . . Jen, what did you have for number four on this?"

I don't look at Nathalie. So, Andrew hasn't told anybody.

I feel selfish for even thinking about it, but I wonder if he's still planning to help me and Ali sneak out of Ogilvy again tonight.

*It doesn't matter*, I tell myself. Grace can handle our distraction plan alone. Andrew doesn't owe me anything.

Classes are canceled for the day as a celebration for the dance, which is a relief, because the idea of walking into Abstracting the Figure with Nathalie and Andrew is painful. Instead, after breakfast, I head into the sculpture yard to call my family. They've been trying to make it happen all week.

"Niko!" my mom says in such a loud, high-pitched voice that it makes my phone audio peak. "There you are!" I adjust my headphones, settling into one of the benches.

"We thought we were never going to see you again," my dad says with a laugh. "You two. Stop messing with—get in here." He leans off-screen and drags a protesting Justin and Anastasia on-screen.

"Hey, you two," I say, trying to smile.

"Hi, Niko," Anastasia says in singsong tones, while Justin rolls his eyes and lifts his hand in hello.

I can tell, even from across the country, that something has sealed over in the time I've been gone. Justin's expression is sort of moody and embarrassed, like always, but the way he's sitting at the kitchen island is relaxed and open.

"How is that showcase project going, sweetie?" asks Mom. "Have you settled on a final idea?"

Dad cuts in. "Of course he has. He's only got a week left, right, Niko?"

He says it dismissively, but I know this trick of Dad's. He's done it before when he suspects I'm floundering with something. It's a reassurance to Mom but also a gentle reminder to me to step it up if I haven't. Which, usually, I haven't.

I should want to tell him I'm eighty percent there, that I've got a plan, that I'm pretty sure my final piece is going to be the best thing I've ever made. I could even tell them honestly that I feel like I'm in with a shot at the top prize, if everything goes right.

But I just find myself saying, "It's going OK."

My parents look relieved. They're saying how excited they are to see pictures next week, and if I just work hard and finish strong, I can make something I'll really be proud of.

It's weird. I remember sitting in my dorm across from Ali when she first came up with the joint showcase idea. That night, I imagined how excited my parents would be if I won the ribbon.

But now I look at them—at my mom's arms fastened around Anastasia's waist, at my dad describing his coding projects with Justin—and I feel distant from them. So much has happened these past few weeks, and it all feels like it's in vivid color. My expeditions with Ali. That huge full-body shock I got, walking into that MoMA exhibit. Compared to all that, California seems faded in my memory.

Anastasia is talking about her dance camp now, and I'm nodding along, but my eyes have settled on my parents, and I'm surprised to feel a kind of disappointment spreading through me.

I've never felt this way before. I've always taken my parents' approach to our family as pretty much perfect—we've had our ups and downs, but I've never wanted them to change.

But now I'm looking at them and thinking, *They could have given me these full-color feelings before*. They could have done things differently when it came to my Chinese half. It would have been easy to drive me an hour to San Diego and take me to a Chinese cultural center or something. They could have tried to fill this gap.

Maybe they didn't even realize the gap existed. If that's true, I guess it's reassuring in some ways—that they didn't think I was missing anything. But in other ways, it's even more disillusioning. The idea that my parents, so smart, so worldly, could be that naive.

As we start to say goodbye, I feel weirdly nostalgic, like I'm saying goodbye to a version of myself. I think of my parents reassuring me that I'm just the same as every other kid in Landry Beach. For a while it worked, for a while they could convince me. But I don't think I'll ever be able to feel that way again.

When I imagine my future, it doesn't look like the past my parents designed for me. It looks like my other half, like Ali and my dad and this city. That's the belonging I could never completely find with the four people waving to me on-screen.

I return to our dorm room in late afternoon, twenty minutes before the dance. Andrew is standing in front of the mirror on his side of the dorm, wearing a dark blue suit jacket and messing with his hair.

He meets my eyes in the mirror, then looks away.

I begin to get dressed. After a minute's uncomfortable silence, Andrew hits play on his phone, and some trance EDM music begins to thud from a portable speaker stashed in the chaos of his desk. The beat is a relief. I can almost pretend we're just having one of those days where we're tired, not in the mood for conversation.

I tug on khakis, button up my white shirt, and shrug my black blazer on. I have my tie halfway through its loop when Andrew says,

"So. Are you and Ali still going through with tonight?"

His voice is too stiff, and I'm too casual as I say, "Yeah."

That's it. Andrew glances at me in his mirror one more time and looks away.

I don't know what to do or say. I already apologized last night. What else is there?

I don't want to spend the next week at Ogilvy like this. It'll ruin the rest of camp for both of us, and probably for Nathalie, too.

I mess up my tie and restart, hands clumsy. Frustration is tensing every muscle in my body. Nothing is even going to *happen* with Nathalie, because I'm with Hailey. I'm so lucky to be with Hailey.

*I'm lucky*, I remind myself.

My tie is too tight now. I loosen it, muss my hair up, and take a picture of myself in my mirror, holding the phone at chest height, one hand in my pocket. I send the picture to Hailey with the message, **thoughts on your date for the dance?**

**Haha your hair! You look like one of those K-pop guys**, she says.

Irritation jolts through me, hot and sudden.

My whole body is even more tense now, my neck so stiff that I can feel the tightness in my scalp.

**Hailey. i'm not korean**, I type. After a moment, I force myself to add to the end of the message, **lol**

I hit send. She doesn't answer.

I force myself to swallow. I feel like I'm back on the bus, my stomach beginning to churn. She's going to be mad again, and we're going to fight again, and I really don't need to worry about this tonight, with what Ali and I are already planning.

I set my phone too hard on my dresser and grab a pair of socks from my drawer. I'm halfway through pulling one on when my device buzzes again.

I nearly trip getting back to the dresser.

Hailey's message reads, **Oh nooo lol I'm so sorry for comparing you to hot famous people? Are you going to make this a thing again?**

My jaw clenches. My hands are viselike around my phone.

The irritation is lighting up into real anger. *Oh nooo lol I'm so sorry.* Her sarcasm feels worse than anything so far.

It was so stupid, I realize, to say our last fight "never happened." Neither of us can forget it. Obviously Hailey didn't forget. And obviously she still thinks I was being unreasonable the first time around.

As for me, I can't forget the way I felt sick on the bus, and the way I wondered—if I ever managed to make it as an artist—if Hailey would assume I just got "lucky." And I can't forget that other text she sent, when she said that in New York I'm "just another Asian boy." What did that even mean? What does it mean that if I ever react to her Asian comments with anything other than a laugh, I'm apparently *making this a thing?*

Blood is rushing in my ears, blocking out the music. As angry as I am, I somehow feel pathetic, too, and confused. Is this actually the only thing she thinks, seeing a picture of me when I'm trying to look good? I don't want to be sensitive like this; I don't want to feel this way.

"Niko?" says a cautious voice.

I look up, blinking rapidly, at Andrew. He's approached me with a wary expression. I didn't even notice.

His eyes drop to my phone.

I shake my head. Force a swallow. Then I'm pushing the phone into Andrew's hands and sitting hard on my bed. My hands clamp around my knees.

"Um," Andrew says loudly. "What is this? What is she talking about, *make this a thing again?*"

It's hard to make myself speak. "Scroll up," I force out. "To last Sunday."

His thumb flips over the screen again and again, then taps to stop the flying texts. As his eyes pass back and forth over the messages, his eyebrows rise, and he holds the phone closer to his face like he can't believe what he's reading. "*What?*" he says again.

I draw slow, shaky breaths. I sneak a look at Andrew's expression. He's staring at me now.

"What?" I repeat back at him, defensive.

"Um, nothing, just—" He lets out an incredulous laugh. "Why are you dating this girl? How often does she say stuff like this?"

"Not that often. I don't know. I mean, it's not every day."

"*Not every day?* Niko. You never have to put up with this. Like, ever. Have you told her this stuff bothers you?"

"It doesn't bother me. Didn't. Until I came here. I'm just being—"

"No," Andrew says. "You're not being anything, this is her problem. Tell her you don't like this stuff, and if she won't stop, then dump her. I'm serious."

"I can't break up with *Hailey Maxwell*, are you crazy?"

Andrew's look of disbelief fades, leaving a sad look of comprehension behind. It's almost pitying.

"Man," he says, "no wonder you started liking Nathalie. She'd jump off a roof before acting like this." He gives my phone a disgusted look and tosses it on my bed. Then, with a sigh, he sits next to me.

I glance over at him.

"This sucks," he says. "It just sucks sometimes."

"Yeah," I mumble back. "Look, I'm really sorry again about . . . I guess I'm not good at any of this stuff."

"Terrible at it," he agrees. But he pats me on the back when he says it, and my stomach settles. A smile tugs at my mouth.

Andrew checks his watch. "You're going to be late meeting Ali."

"Shit." I jolt off the bed and grab my phone, my wallet, my lanyard.

Soon we're riding the elevator down with several other kids decked out in dresses and suits. In typical Ogilvy style, the colors and fabrics are nothing like you'd see at Landry's prom. The guy next to me is wearing sequined slacks, and one girl's dress is a raggedy punk band T-shirt that hits at mid-thigh.

We exit on the first floor to find the hallway darkened and the double-doors propped open. Colorful disks of light spin out into the corridor. Ogilvy has hired a DJ, and dozens of kids are already dancing inside the dining hall, the bass thudding through the building and echoing around the foyer.

Andrew and I stop before the double-doors. "Um," I say, "you don't have to—"

"It's fine," he says. "I'll help."

265

"Thanks, man."

"Yeah." Andrew sighs, but gives me a smile.

Ali and Grace find us immediately when we enter the dining hall. "Ready?" Ali says, bouncing on the balls of her feet. She's wearing a bright blue romper and black leather jacket. Both look a little too big for her, like she's borrowed them from someone. She sees my face and stops bouncing. "What's wrong? What happened?"

"Nothing. Just nervous." I draw a deep, shaky breath and push away my thoughts of the phone in my pocket. Tonight is about me and Ali. My family, our future.

And whatever else happens, I think things are going to be OK with Andrew. I'm going to make things right with him; I'm not going to take him for granted.

Ali searches my expression for another moment, but then she nods.

"OK," says Andrew. "Diversion plan . . . go."

We move casually toward the corner of the room where the side door leads back to the kitchen. Professor Abbott is nodding his head to the music, guarding the corner.

"You have two hours," Grace whispers. "Andrew—come on."

She and Andrew launch into a clumsy dance, laughing as they whirl each other around in motions that don't match the music. A second later, Andrew is tripping, catapulting forward, and spilling punch all over Professor Abbott's pant leg. Abbott recoils, staring at them like they've just spat on the *Mona Lisa*.

"Oh my goodness," Grace squeaks. "We are so sorry, Professor! Can we get you some napkins, or . . ."

I don't hear the rest of the excuse. Ali and I sidle behind the standing speakers that have been set up near what's usually the pasta station. With Professor Abbott turned toward the wall, we're soon behind his back and through the kitchen door.

It clicks shut behind us, stripping the treble out of the music. By the time we're out the back door, all that's left is the distant pulse of bass.

I can't help grinning. "Abbott's face," I say.

"I know," Ali says with a stifled, guilty laugh.

We set off at a brisk walk. The sun is low, but the evening air still clings to me, warm and moist, and within a minute I'm tugging off my blazer and pushing up my sleeves. We hardly speak at all—a couple of stray questions about my suit, her outfit, what our friends are planning for the dance. Mostly we're heading down the noisy city streets with dense silence hanging between us.

It's not until we reach the edge of Chinatown that Ali says, "Still nervous?"

I exhale as I turn left, following the Google Maps route. "Yeah. I keep trying to tell myself, you know, no big deal. If we don't find anything, we just . . . for the showcase, we just present what we've got. Right?"

"Right," Ali says with a small, nervous laugh, "and then there's no risk that we show him our pieces and he thinks they're totally unsalvageable."

"Yeah." I make myself laugh, too. We glance at each other, and there's an evasive look in her darting eyes, and I know Ali's not really thinking about the showcase prize, either.

The rest of it closes in on me as we pass through the bustling streets. For the first time since Hailey's message, longing tugs at my chest. I want more of this. The meaty, gingery scents that intermix from nearby restaurants, the exasperated conversation of a nearby couple in Chinese, even the buildings themselves, which I read about on my phone. The renovated townhouses and tenements that were transformed with the waves of immigrants who came here. I don't just want to know the story. I want to feel like it's *my* story.

I stop on a corner. I draw a shaky breath and look down at my phone. "There," I say, pointing down the street. "It's that building."

We approach. The bricks are turning from red to gold in the lowering sun. Rust spots on the fire escape look like old paint.

Ali and I head up the concrete steps. When I see the door is ajar, excitement shoots through me. I try not to feel like it's a sign.

I'm about to reach for the door when Ali says in a small, whispery voice, "I'm scared."

My hand falls away from the knob.

"I want to see him again," she rushes on, "but not because I tracked him down. I want him to come back because he wanted to be part of my life again. He stayed away for so long. Why would he want to see me now?"

My throat tightens as I look up at the building. The dusty windows are reflecting the crimson sky. "I know," I manage to say. "It's hard for me, too, and I can't imagine what this whole thing has been like for you."

She swallows, looks at the ground, and eventually nods. "OK. Let's be brave." She pushes open the door, and we enter.

The building's interior is musty and narrow. The tiny hexagonal tiles of the entrance hall are chipped, the carpet on the steps shabby, but the place looks well-kept otherwise, no accumulations of dust or dirt.

"Third floor, right?" Ali whispers.

"Third floor."

I go first. I feel like I should. We jog up the steps and halt at a tiny landing with a wooden rail, in front of a door with a brass number "3."

Ali and I exchange looks. I raise my hand and knock.

The knock echoes through the building, back down the stairwell, up to the poorly lit fourth floor landing. It circulates, circulates, and then fades.

"Here," Ali says urgently. She reaches out her hand and bangs hard on the door with the flat of her hand. "Hello?" she calls. "Dad? It's me. It's—are you home?"

No answer. My heart is beating hard now. *Come on*, I think. Let someone answer. Anyone. Even if he's moved, even if the trail ends here.

"He—he could be out for dinner or something," Ali says, checking her phone. "No texts from Grace or Andrew. We can wait. We can just go and walk around for an hour, or something, and come back. OK?"

I nod. She's speaking quickly. I don't think I'll be able to make a sound for a little while. I loosen my tie some more.

We climb back down the steps. As we're approaching the second floor landing, I hear a jangle of keys from below.

Ali sucks in a breath. "Hey," I call, nearly tripping down the steps as I throw myself into a run. "Hey! Is someone there?"

Sweat pops on my palms. I use the banister to fling myself around the stairs, imagining a head of dark hair coming through the door.

An older woman with salt-and-pepper bob has just left the ground-floor apartment. She's paused near the landing, her wrinkled face angled up toward us. "Excuse me," I say, jogging down the steps. "We're looking for someone. He lives on the third floor, or used—"

"No English," she says, waving a hand at her mouth. She follows this with something in Chinese, eyeing me.

I shake my head and stand back to let Ali maneuver around me, down the narrow steps, to fill in the gaps.

"We're looking for Tan Bo," I say. "We're his kids. We're art students, at the Ogilvy Art Institute." I know this is a stretch of the truth, but I don't want her to shoo us away, as if we're just a couple of kids. "We haven't seen him since we were little, but we got this address from someone who knows him. Do you know him? Is he home?"

She pauses. For a brief moment her brows furrow and lips tighten, as if she's having an internal argument. "I . . . did," she said. "He lived here, but he was killed in a car accident several years ago."

"Are you sure?" I say, my voice rising. I feel cold all of a sudden, the air in the stairwell clammy and metallic. "Are you sure it was him? And not someone else? Maybe it's a mix-up?"

She looks at Niko. "I can tell just from looking at your brother that we're thinking of the same person. I'm sorry to be the one to tell you." She hesitates before the front door, and as if she recognizes there's nothing she can say to make it better, she pulls it open and heads out into the night.

"What did she say?" Niko says, urgently. "I know it was bad, I can tell by your face. Please, tell me what she said."

"He died," I say, my voice low and tight.

"What? Are you sure?"

"Yes, I'm sure," I say sharply. I don't share what the neighbor said, about the two of them looking alike. It's so inappropriate, but I'm *jealous*, like Niko has something of my dad's forever that I'll never have.

"OK, I guess we should go back then," he says, his voice quiet, monotonic.

"I guess we should," I say. I wish he wasn't here right now. Anger is bubbling low in my stomach. Why did Niko have to suggest that we try to find our dad? I wish he'd left well enough alone. I'm angry at myself, too, for not convincing him otherwise. I should have trusted my instincts.

I take the rest of the steps two at a time, shoving open the door, Niko close behind me.

I feel the tug of a dull sense of duty, like I should find the right words to say to him, but I don't want to. I don't have it in me to comfort; I need someone to find the right words to comfort *me*. The best I can settle for is keeping my anger private.

I stare down at the sidewalk. If we'd just waited five minutes more before leaving, we would have missed the neighbor in the stairwell. We would have knocked and the door would have gone unanswered, or maybe answered by a stranger who couldn't give us any more leads. We wouldn't know what had happened. The trail would have ended, and I would have been exactly where I was at the beginning of the summer—blissfully unaware.

We walk in silence back to the subway, Niko half a step behind me, following. More than anything, I feel foolish. How stupid, to get my hopes up that I'd find the father who left me and what, have a *relationship* with him? Make him *proud*?

I think about my mom and Nai Nai and their love for me. I wish I'd been wise enough to be content with that. Instead I just went running after disappointment. I glance down at my outfit and feel embarrassed. I borrowed the jacket from Brook, the romper from Grace. I'd dressed tonight in so much excitement—wanting to look like an adult, to show my dad I'd grown up, that I'd followed in his footsteps, that I was a real artist, not just a little kid.

Ogilvy might be less than a mile away, but now it feels like an alternate universe, everything there meaningless.

I feel a pang for the small hope that has blossomed and unfolded in me the last couple weeks, the hope I didn't want to admit to, the hope I was afraid to nurture. I'm angry at myself for letting it grow, angry at Niko for bringing this possibility into my life. It's weird that this hope was a one-time thing: there's no future, anymore, in which I can hope to meet him, to patch things up. Now I just . . . know. And yet there's so much I don't know. I don't know if he regretted leaving us. I don't know if he would have ever come back at some point.

As we stand on the subway platform, Niko clears his throat. *Oh no,* I think. *Does he want to talk about it?* I know he said his family is all about talking about their feelings, but I can't think of anything I'd like less.

"So . . . I guess there's still time to go to the dance," he says instead. "I mean, since we're all dressed and everything."

I'm not at all excited by the prospect anymore, but I nod anyway. Maybe it will be good for us to go in and try to be normal. Maybe this feeling of shock and sadness and anger will fade fast. After all, did we really lose anything tonight? It's not like either of us knew him. The only door that closed, closed on an idea.

My thoughts continue to swirl as we ride the two stops back to campus and weave our way through crowded streets, full of college students and other people enjoying the summer evening. I'm about to walk through Ogilvy's front door when Niko grabs me and pulls me back.

"Have you lost your mind?" he asks. He jerks his head at the enormous outline of the security guard sitting at the front desk.

"Right," I say. "Sorry, sorry." I've completely forgotten all our plans. My mind is still back in that stairwell, on my fist raised over the door, footsteps that never came. How narrow those stairs felt as we walked back down past the neighbor, the stricken look in her eyes, and how the breeze when I pushed the door open to the street raised goosebumps on my skin even though I was wearing a jacket. I shift my weight from foot to foot as Niko texts Andrew. The shoes are killing my feet.

The door swings open suddenly. It's Andrew.

"Hurry," he says. "Jen's distracting Stan."

We quickly cross the lobby to the elevators. Andrew is practically running, anxious about the security guard's return. He doesn't notice that we're silent.

"Wait, why Jen?" I ask. "Where's Grace?"

"Couldn't find her at the dance," Andrew says. Finally we reach the side corridor. The music pulses ahead in the cafeteria floor, but we stay in the hallway, where the bass isn't so loud.

"That's weird," I say.

"I don't know if it's *that* weird," he says. "I saw her with that girl—the annoying one, you know, in Niko's year. The blonde. They were dancing. Looked pretty close." He looks over at Niko.

*Brook*, I think. Of course. Grace and Brook, finally getting together, and Grace couldn't even be bothered to wait to help Niko and me with our plan. The last bit of willingness I had to appear at the dance slides away from me. I know I can't show up and pretend everything is OK, not when I don't even have the tiniest hope left to cling to.

I quietly press the call button for the elevator. Niko is staring into space, as if he hasn't heard Andrew speak at all.

"What's up, guys? Did you not find him? You weren't gone for very long." Andrew furrows his brows.

"We didn't," Niko says.

The elevator doors slide open. I just catch the beginning of Andrew saying, "Hey man, are you—" and I'm hurrying into the car, slamming my palm onto *close doors*. I can already feel a heavy sob building up in my chest, and I can't wait to kick off my stupid shoes and take off this uncomfortable outfit and curl up in my favorite old T-shirt and lie in bed.

When I get up to the room, I don't knock—why would I, when Brook is clearly off somewhere with Grace?—I just push open the door.

Brook looks up, clearly startled, from where she's been sitting on her bed alone in the dark.

"Don't you knock?" she asks, angry, before I can even switch on the light.

"I'm sorry," I say. "I thought you were with Grace."

"Well, obviously I'm not," she says. "I'm kind of in the middle of something. Do you mind?" I realize with a start, as my eyes adjust to the dark, that her eyes are red.

"Are you OK?" I ask, taking a step closer.

"Get out!" she snaps.

I hurry out the door and close it behind me. Why would she react like that? Aren't we friends? I turn and hurry down the hall. I don't know where to go, so instead I head back down to the dance.

Grace and Jeremiah are standing right by the punch table, both looking at the ground.

"Hey guys," I say. They offer half-hearted nods. "What's up?"

"Oh, nothing," Grace says. She's normally bouncy, buoyant, eager to greet with a hug. Now she's refusing to even make eye contact. I turn to Jeremiah, who is uncharacteristically silent.

"OK, obviously something happened," I say. "You can't keep me in the dark. I just walked in on Brook looking really upset. Is everything OK? Did something happen?"

Grace shoots Jeremiah a pleading look. He loudly announces that he's going to get a drink and would anyone else like one. Then he's gone before we can answer.

Grace edges closer to me. "Brook and I were dancing," she says. My heart sinks again. This can't be good. "She tried to kiss me, but I wasn't into it."

"What?" My head snaps up, surprised.

"No, I told her I . . ." She looks at me, holding my eyes. Even in the dark, her eyes shine a bright blue. "I told her I like someone else."

*It's me. It has to be me. That's why she's looking at me like this, right?*

"Uh, who is it?"

Grace grabs my hand. "You, obviously."

"But," I start.

"Why do you think I wanted to bunk with you upstate?"

"But," I say again. "I thought you liked Brook."

"I love Brook's art," Grace says. "And I feel comfortable with her, because she's one of the only people I knew before Ogilvy. But I don't like her like that."

Suddenly it feels like everything else is falling away. The dingy stairwell, the curious neighbor. The long, slow walk back to campus. The dance, and the people around me. It's just me and Grace and the cheesy lights of the disco ball lighting up her face and her freckles and her hopeful smile.

"Do you . . . want to dance with me?" she asks, hesitantly.

"Wait, I have a better idea," I blurt. "I want to show you what I've done with my showcase piece. It's almost finished now." I'm so excited about it, and I think Grace will love seeing how far it's evolved. Forget a dance, nothing could make me feel closer to her than showing her my work. She already knows about Niko, so she'll understand what I'm trying to do. And I can't wait to show her the influence that she's had on it, along with our other friends.

We leave the dining hall as if we're going to classes, then sprint to the workshop hallways. I grab her hand and we run, laughing, into the showcase studio.

"I was really inspired by you and Jeremiah and Brook," I say, hurrying to where my painting is propped against the wall, "but it's meant to be a portrait of Niko using metaphor."

I reach for the canvas and pull it out to show her. Instinctively, she turns it right side up, with the sky on top.

"It's supposed to go this way," I say, flipping it back. She frowns.

"What's wrong?" I ask.

Grace hesitates. "I'm sorry if I'm wrong," she says, and pauses again, uncertainly. "It's just . . . isn't this Brook's idea?"

"What do you mean?"

"It's something she was working on for her portfolio. The disorienting, upside-down landscape thing? I told you about that."

"Yeah, I liked the idea," I say. "I wanted to incorporate a similar theme into my work."

"But that's *her idea*." Grace is looking at the darkened window, around the studio, everywhere but at me.

"All artists are inspired by each other," I say. "It's normal! I haven't even seen any of Brook's paintings."

"Yes, but there's a limit to that." Grace's voice is becoming steadier, surer.

"I don't think it's so obvious," I argue. "There's a lot of inspiration in this piece. The bright colors are inspired by our conversation about Hilma af Klint. The part I left black-and-white is inspired by Jeremiah's portraits." I point to each part of the canvas as I speak. This feels so unfair. Why is she zeroing in on this one thing?

Grace frowns and goes silent. She seems to be thinking hard.

"Ali, I'm saying this as a friend," she finally says. "But I think . . . I think you do this in other ways, too. Like the first few days at Ogilvy, you wore different clothes. But since then, you've been dressing just like Brook and me. And I'm glad you like my clothes! But I also think you're great the way you are. You don't need to be more like us."

I'm mortified. I'm almost more embarrassed about her bringing up my style evolution than I am about the painting. I toss the canvas onto the nearest table facedown and turn away. My face is burning.

"You all were so cool, and so close already, and I wanted to be part of your group," I admit. "I just wanted you to like me." I wanted to knowledgeable and confident like Brook and Grace. I felt like at Ogilvy, I could be that person, too, the glamorous queer artist, the opposite of how I feel like I've been seen all my life. But saying any of that out loud feels impossible. We stand in silence for what feels like minutes.

"Please just go away," I say, finally. "I'm so embarrassed."

Grace lingers for a moment, opens her mouth as if she's going to say something, and then closes it. "OK," she says.

The tears I've been holding back since we left Chinatown are about to explode out of me. Once Grace has left, I collapse on the floor, bury my head in my arms, and let myself cry. Loud, messy, babyish sobs echo around the cold, empty room.

Never, ever in my life have I felt more detestable. Grace is right. I stole Brook's idea and it completely backfired, as I should have known it would. It makes me feel like learning about my dad's death tonight is punishment for the person I've been all summer. What part of myself have I lost in trying to impress Grace and the other kids here? Taking someone else's idea isn't who I am, or at least, it isn't who I want to be. I should have turned in a crappy project, or no project at all, rather than go that far looking for inspiration. I should have accepted that Grace would like who she liked—maybe me, maybe Brook—rather than attempt to impress her by trying to be more like Brook. And after all that, it turns out, she liked me just fine.

Well, I've managed to ruin that, too.

I know it's illogical, but I feel like if I hadn't done all these stupid things, spending money we don't have on clothes, letting one offhand comment change my entire painting, *copying other people's ideas*, if I hadn't tried so hard to be this cool artist version of myself, and lost myself in the process, then maybe the universe might not have had this in store. I know my dad died years ago—it was not *literally* my fault, and I don't *blame* myself exactly—but it does feel like I deserved what I got tonight, and that makes me feel like there's some kind of order to it after all. I wonder if there's something deeply wrong with me, something deeply unlovable, that my dad figured out all those years ago.

I think about the piece at the restaurant in Chinatown, how I'd admired it so much when we saw it because of what a *break* it had been, with his past. Why did I admire that, of all things? His past was me and Nai Nai. He left us forever, and for what? So he could make a pretty brick wall? The image of the wall swims before my eyes—I'm literally seeing red. I wish I could take a sledgehammer to that wall and destroy it.

# Chapter 21

NIKO CASTADI

"I'll catch up in a minute," I tell Andrew as we emerge into the dance. "Just need something to drink."

"Sure," he says, still looking tense. "Yeah. But I'm so sorry, dude. I can't imagine. Are you sure you're OK? We can go chill in our room or something."

After Ali dived into the elevator, Andrew had wanted to know what happened. He could tell something was wrong, because of course he could, and I admitted the truth. Now I'm wishing I hadn't.

"No, um, I'm fine. I didn't ever know him, so it's not really like . . . it's just weird." I force a half-smile. "But thanks again for your help. Let's just . . . I'll see you over there, OK?"

"OK," says Andrew hesitantly. As he moves toward the dance floor, I head toward the table with the punch bowl.

*Nothing happened*, I tell myself as I ladle juice into a cup. No change. It's just another wave breaking over me. Soon it'll recede. I just have to ride this out.

I drain the cup and refill it, realizing how thirsty I am. We walked for probably an hour, but I didn't feel much on the way back. Even my thoughts seemed distant.

Now my body is acting strangely. I keep shifting my weight and running the back of my hand over my forehead even though I'm not sweating. The breaths I take seem to punch down into the lowest reaches of my lungs—a sharp, painful place.

I refill my cup and step into the corner, pulling out my phone. I scroll through a few apps. Devin's posted his usual stream of beach stories today, two full minutes. Grayson's family has apparently headed to L.A. for the weekend, so there are some videos of him and his brother sticking their heads out the car window while his parents yell at them. A weak smile tugs at my mouth.

I put my phone away, aware that a couple of songs have elapsed. I'm OK. I can be normal.

I spot Andrew and the others moving off the dance floor toward one of the round tables set up at the periphery. I swallow the last of my punch and follow, determined to act natural until I feel it. But as I approach their table, I hear snippets of Chinese, and my steps falter.

It goes on for minutes. I stand stupidly by a group of other kids, waiting for my friends to say something I understand.

Finally, Nathalie breaks back into English. "My mom's Cantonese is much better than mine. All I know is, like, *zou gong fo*!" She makes an emphatic pointing gesture.

Andrew laughs. "What is that? Stop messing around?"

"Do your homework."

"Oh, yeah," says Jen. "Well, comes with the territory."

Everyone's laughing and agreeing, and Haoran and Haolong and Nathalie are back into Mandarin again, and I'm just standing there pulling at the sleeves of my suit jacket. I think of Jen reminiscing about her family on the dock upstate, her aunts' language and her grandparents' recipes and her parents' stories. I remember those rooted feelings I had in the museum. It's like those roots have been slashed away.

Just hours ago, I was looking at my family on my phone screen, feeling the barrier rising between us—somehow feeling OK about it, because I'd convinced myself I had a chance at this other kind of life. But even if Ali and I had found our dad, how naive was it to convince myself that finding him would be some golden ticket to feeling like I'm the right kind of Asian, or that I'd fit in with other Asian kids? I'm almost eighteen. I'd still be the same person with the same upbringing, the same blind spots.

With horrible clarity, I finally understand LaTonya's issues with my showcase. It wasn't about Ali. It was a shallow bid to get the approval of someone I thought could affirm my belonging.

My hand makes its shaky way across my forehead again and I find that I am sweating now. My fingers are sticky, and my eyes are burning. I turn away from the table and wind around the edge of the dance floor.

Then I'm out of the dining hall, alone in the long corridors lined with plaques and paintings. I duck into a nearby bathroom and sink back against the wall, the row of stalls blurring as tears prick behind my eyes. I draw harsh breaths, blinking hard.

After a few minutes, I'm able to gather myself. I wipe the wet streaks from my cheeks and drift over to the sinks. I splash my face with cold water until my breathing steadies.

Numbness has spread through my body. I move back out into the hall, then take out my phone and open up my text thread with Hailey.

**Are you going to make this a thing again?**

**yeah**, I reply, typing slowly, steadily, without deleting or rewriting. making it a thing. sorry. could you stop with the asian jokes and references and stuff? i don't actually like them. they make me feel weird.

She types for a while. **You want me to totally ignore the fact that you're Asian?**

no i just don't like that it comes up all the time

Hailey types for a while. When the message pops up, it's long enough to push the rest of the conversation up off the screen.

Ok I'm just going to say it. It feels like I can't do anything right here. You literally joke all the time about being Asian so I've been trying to treat it the way you do. And now every time I say something about it it's somehow the wrong thing. I'm not going to pretend you're not Asian bc that's stupid. And if you want me to then it seems like you have a complex or something you need to work out.

i didn't ask you to pretend i'm not asian. i'm just asking you to try making fewer jokes about it

Omg. "try making fewer jokes" that is so condescending haha. Maybe if you try really hard you can do it Hailey!! Like I need a life coach, to stop doing the same thing that you do. Also you're acting like I said something racist?? Getting compared to K-pop stars is a COMPLIMENT. I literally bent over backward to say nice stuff about your dad's art even though you know I think modern art is stupid. Also if I had a problem w asian people why would we be dating??

I try not to focus on the "bent over backward" comment. I try not to focus on anything except the question I'm trying to ask.

i haven't been making jokes about being asian for a while, bc i realized i don't like them, like i said. i'm asking if you can do that too.

Again, she types a long time. But this time, all that shows up is,

I just really don't like how this is happening

hailey, i'm just asking a question. i'm just telling you i don't like the jokes and asking if you can stop. that's all.

Ok except that's not what's happening and it's not what happened last time. You're making all these little suggestions that I'm being racist and I'm not a racist so of course I'm going to be upset.

My heartbeat slows. I look up from my phone. The hall is shadowy and quiet. The music is distant, almost inaudible.

I draw a slow, shaky breath and type, I don't think you're racist. But I also don't think we should date anymore.

She doesn't answer. One minute passes, then two.

I say, Maybe you're right and I have a complex. I've definitely been going through some stuff this summer and thinking really hard about who I am. But I asked if you could try to do one thing to make me a little happier and it seems like the answer is no. So, I don't know where to go from there.

OK so you were testing me. I'm glad I failed your test. I don't want to be with someone who plays games.

hailey, this was never a game to me.

I put my phone in my pocket and turn off the sound.

I didn't lie to her. The jolt through my whole self when she touched me, that wasn't a game. Neither was the happiness when she kissed me, like I was becoming weightless, or the way I stayed up checking my phone under the sheets to see her messages.

But I think back to how Andrew reacted earlier, and I realize he guessed Hailey would react like this. He could tell.

I think maybe I knew, too. That's why I never brought up Ali, or how we were trying to find our dad, or our trips to Chinatown, or my conversation with my friends at the lake. I was armoring part of myself, afraid something like this would happen.

I consider my next move with a hazy distance. I know I can't go back to the dance, can't pretend to be normal right now. My dorm is out, too. Andrew will show up after noticing I'm gone. He'll want to talk, because he's a good friend, probably a better friend than I deserve. Telling him no will just make me feel worse.

The showcase workshop isn't far. The thought of my sketches, my canvas, even just the smell of paints and wood shavings, makes the numbness recede a bit.

I accelerate down the hall.

The windows are darkened, but when I push through the door, I hear a small, surprised sound. I turn toward it, saying, "Hello?"

No answer. I hit the lights.

Ali is sitting on the ground in a corner of the room. She's never looked smaller, folded in on herself with her knees hugged to her chest. Her face is red and puffy, but she hurriedly wipes her nose and eyes as though I won't be able to tell she's been crying.

"Hey," I say, taking a few cautious steps toward her.

"H-hey," she chokes out.

"I know. It sucks." My words have never felt clumsier. "I wanted us to find him, too."

Ali folds her arms over her stomach. "It's not just that," she says through sobs. "I—I'm a terrible artist. And a terrible person."

Before I can protest, she's bursting out with the whole story: that she took one of Brook's ideas for her final showcase, that Grace found out, that she just wanted Grace to like her.

My heart sinks. I crouch and place a tentative hand on her back. "Hey," I say quietly. "It's going to be fine."

"It's n-not. Grace hates m-me."

"No, come on. You just made a bad call, OK? I make bad calls all the time when I'm surfing. You don't beat yourself up about it for hours or you'll wind up drowning. You've just got to get back on the board."

She's still sniffling, but her mouth twitches in what could be a smile. "I can't believe you're giving me surfing metaphors."

"I mean, what other kind of metaphors do you think I've got?"

A full smile this time.

"Also," I go on, "I swear I'm not just saying this because we're related, but you're way cooler than Brook, anyway."

Ali elbows me. "Shut up. You don't have to lie to my face."

"I'm serious. I get why you and Grace would think she's cool, because she's like, smart and bored and older." I consider. "And hot. I guess. But everyone in our grade thinks she's kind of a pretentious poser."

Ali buries her face in her hands and looses a muffled laugh. "Sorry. I know that shouldn't make me feel better, but it does. She's actually so rude sometimes."

"Is she not rude all the time?"

Ali pushes her hair back, revealing her guilty grin.

I sigh and settle cross-legged onto the floor beside her. "Look, whatever your friends think, I like who you are, OK? Even if you're still figuring it out." I fiddle with the end of my tie. "I'm figuring some shit out, too."

"You must feel so ready to go home," Ali says.

"Yeah," I say, closing my eyes. A stream of images passes through the darkness. The curve of a wave, the glitter of white sand, Hailey's eyes—then the narrow streets of New York, and a cloud of steam rising from a vent beside a light-glossed dumpster, and the patter of rain on pavement. Gallery lights, shimmering nights. "And no," I add. "I don't know what I'm ready for."

We sit in silence a while, listening to the air-conditioning, and my thoughts seem to cool, too. Except—there's something still itching at the back of my mind.

"Can I ask you something?" I say.

"Of course."

"On Tuesday, when that guy asked me about the Young Diverse Artists thing. Why didn't you want him to refer you, too?"

Ali sighs. She takes a moment to adjust her romper before answering. "I don't know. I didn't want them to look at my art through that lens. Like, here's Ali, future member of the Urban East Asian Diaspora exhibit that people don't go to because it's *unrelatable*."

I feel a twinge, thinking of the exhibit, but it's not as bad as it was before.

Ali bobs her shoulders. "But it's also . . . sometimes I don't really feel like that stuff is *for* me. It's not like I'm an immigrant. Our dad and Nai Nai went through all the upheaval, they're the ones who actually made sacrifices. All I did was grow up in Queens and get not even that good at Mandarin. No one in China would think of me as Chinese, I'd just be an American. And . . ." Ali's reddened eyes meet mine. "People aren't going to meet me, hear about my art, and ask me if it has to do with Eastern values, you know? So like, why should I get involved with a special program?"

I frown. "Yeah, but it's similar for me. My parents are—you know." I break off, embarrassment warming my face. "They have money. And it's not like I even know anything about being Chinese."

I tug my knees up to my chest, matching her posture. "I really thought our dad might be able to help with that. I mean, you saw me at Eight Tastes. I'm such a fucking tourist about the whole thing." I shake my head.

Ali smiles. "So I guess we're both fakers."

As we sit in the quiet hum of the fluorescents overhead, I realize that the envy I've felt toward Ali since my first sketch has finally dissolved. We both fit into two different worlds and into neither. We're the same colors marbled in different patterns.

If I belong anywhere, it's probably right here, next to her.

There's a squeak as Ali stands, her shoes slipping on the linoleum. "Come on," she says, sticking out a hand. Her voice is scratchy but determined as she helps me to my feet. "We've got work to do."

# Chapter 22

## ALI TAN

I walk over to one of the supply closets and fish out two enormous sets of shears. I hand one to Niko with a flourish.

"I have no idea what you want me to do with this," he says, "but I'm afraid. Are you asking me to do violence?"

I roll my eyes. "Only to this." I gesture at my showcase project, which is sitting where I left it, by my workstation.

"Are you sure?" he asks. "You've spent so much time on this." Neither of us mentions the prize. None of that feels like it matters anymore.

"It's not *mine*. It's just some attempt to be someone else. I'd rather turn in a blank canvas than this mess."

Because he's still hesitating, I take the shears and stab through the middle of the piece. The canvas stretches under the point of the blade, then finally gives way. With a big hole cut in the center of the pieces, it's easy to destroy the rest of it. I snip and snip, letting pieces of the canvas flutter to the ground.

"OK, that looks like fun," Niko admits, joining in. We cut and cut until there's nothing left but a littering of canvas scraps on the ground and an empty, square, wooden frame on the tabletop. I lift up the frame to smash it but hesitate. I kind of like the wooden frame. It's empty, full of possibility, the way I felt at the beginning of the summer. It reminds me that there's still plenty of possibility for me. Ogilvy might be over in a few days, but I'm never going to stop growing as an artist, or as a person.

And maybe it's too late for Grace to like me—but it's not too late to tell her how I feel. And for now, that feels like enough.

"I have to go," I tell Niko, and I run out of the room, the tile floor cold against my now-bare feet.

I run up to Grace's room and knock on the door. I'm not sure if she'll be there, but her voice comes, muffled, through the door. "Come in."

I open the door. Grace is lying on her bed, still dressed in her jump-suit from the dance, playing with her phone. She switches on her bedside lamp when I come in.

"Grace, I have a few things I want to tell you," I say. "If you want to hear them. But if you don't, I get that, too. I know I messed up."

She sits up slowly. "I'm listening."

I sit down on the edge of the other bed and take a deep breath. "The first thing is that I demolished my showcase piece. I feel so dumb that I ever thought that was a good idea."

"It's OK," Grace says, smiling. "You really shouldn't feel bad. People make mistakes. The important thing is that you get it. And you won't do it again." She pauses briefly, as if she's not sure whether she should say what she says next. "But did you really have to demolish it? You could have just turned it right-side-up again."

"It wasn't me," I say. "It was just me trying to copy a bunch of different ideas I had about what was cool. The only thing I liked was the fabric, and I'd already taken all of that off, anyway."

A smile twitches at the corner of her lips, and it gives me the courage to say the next part.

"I really like you," I admit. "I've never felt this way before. And . . . I want to know if you still like me."

"I *do* like you," she says. "But I just don't understand. Why would you try so hard to be something else?"

"I wanted Ogilvy to be a chance for me to reinvent myself," I say. "I wanted to be someone different from who I was at school."

"I don't care what you're like at school!" Grace exclaims. "You heard all about how much I hate *my* school."

"I know. But I feel so out of place here. Everyone here is cool and rich and, you know, white. I was worried people would treat me differently if they knew that I wasn't any of those things. I guess I just wanted a role model, and I took it too far."

"I don't think of you as Asian or anything," Grace says. "I just think of you as a person." This irritates me—*like being white is the only way to be a person?*—but I don't think Grace's intent is to be mean-spirited or exclusive. I think of LaTonya's class, and I think I might have the right vocabulary to explain what I want to say.

"I mean, I am a person," I say. We both laugh. "But also, I'm Chinese. My background isn't the only part of me, and I don't like when people focus only on that. But it is a part of me. An important part of me, just like how your family is important to you. Sometimes I feel like people want to focus only on the parts of me that are different, because it's interesting, but I don't want to do the opposite either. I don't want to pretend those parts of me don't exist. I tried that, and I didn't like it."

Her mouth drops open. "I'm so sorry!" she exclaims. "I didn't even—yes, I totally came across that way. I would *hate* it if someone made a really big deal out of me being gay. I know it's not exactly the same thing, but it's the best comparison I have."

I give her another awkward smile. She gets it, or she's trying to. "No, not quite the same thing," I say. "But it's a pretty good analogy."

"I'm really, really sorry. We learned all about microaggressions in an Interpersonal Dynamics class I took in eighth grade."

I shake my head to rid myself of the weirdness of having microaggressions on the syllabus and attending a class named Interpersonal Dynamics. Private schools are strange.

"It's fine," I laugh. "No one is born knowing the right things to say."

"So . . . are we good?" Grace asks.

"We're good."

She leans forward and reaches for my hand across the gap of the two beds. Her fingers interlace gently with mine, her skin cool and soft. Heat rises in my cheeks and I'm glad for the dim lighting in the room. This time, when she looks at me, I know she's really seeing me.

# Chapter 23

When I run my fingertips over my sketches, they pick up a fur of charcoal dust. I've been hanging out here for a while, listening to an indie-pop playlist and circling the workshop, watching everyone's pieces pass me by. Now I've returned to my own station, where my sketches are fanned around the canvas, the photo of Ali's suitcase in the middle.

I settle onto the stool and unpin the reference photos from my corkboard one by one. I imagine a world where we found him, and he sat us down for hours and told us his whole biography. I slide the photos into the dark space under my easel. The last years of his life will always be invisible, along with the shape of whatever family we could have been.

But after talking with Ali, that doesn't feel so painful. She's the one who guided me through New York, the one who translated signs and menus and bad news, the one who's already translated something about me to myself.

Seated at the workstation, I feel like the hours I've poured into these sketches have shown me something real about myself, too.

Suddenly, I remember my parents' delighted faces on that video call.

With a pang, I tug out my phone and tap through to my family's group text. **Call tomorrow morning???** my mom said not even 24 hours ago. **We miss you SO much Nicky!**

**I am working from home tomorrow.** That's my dad. **I'm available to video chat any time. Let us know. Dad**

Something softens in me. Then it's crumbling away completely. Because I know that when I get home and tell my parents this whole bizarre story, my mom will speak-whisper, "Oh, sweetie," and hustle over to where I'm sitting and cradle my head in her arms and kiss the top of my head. And that night, my dad will make my favorite pasta, the one with fresh tomatoes and zucchini and vegan sausage, and he'll take care to ask me what my plans are that week, because he knows that I tend to lock myself up when I'm feeling low. And one of them will take Justin and Anastasia aside and quietly tell them I'm having a tough day, and so Justin will say something over dinner about how he doesn't really want the PS5 tonight, so like, if I want it, it's all me; and Anastasia will put her favorite unicorn sprinkles on the ice cream I like for dessert, then suggest that I play soccer with her in the yard before the sun sets.

And suddenly I'm feeling this flood of homesickness beyond anything I've felt this whole summer, because I do belong there, with them. Of course I do. I can belong with my family even while being different. It seems so obvious now that I could have just told my parents how I was feeling: desperate to blend in, worried I never would.

But I don't feel that way anymore.

I think of Ali and me ensconced in the corner of Eight Tastes, slurping soup, and in the elevator at the MoMA, laughing. I remember my camp friends knowing immediately what I meant when I told them my worries about my looks. I even remember what I felt standing in front of my dad's piece, that his art understood something about me. Maybe I'll always ache for that mirror feeling of easy recognition.

But now I get what LaTonya was telling me about tributes. Try too hard to define yourself by other people, no matter who those people are, and you'll disappear. I do want to belong. But I don't want to vanish.

There's a gentle tap on the door behind me. When I turn, Nathalie is standing in the threshold. Her hair is cascading over her shoulders, carefully curled. She's wearing a black dress with one thin strap.

My heart misses a single beat. "Hey," I say.

"I thought you might be here." Nathalie winds between the workstations toward me. "Andrew told me what happened."

I sigh. "Of course he did."

"I thought he was joking." She pauses. "He wasn't joking, right?"

"You'd think so. But no."

Nathalie stops at the next workstation over. "I wanted to say I'm sorry about what happened, with Andrew." Her voice is low but even.

"None of that was your fault."

"Well, I could have prevented it if I'd just said earlier that I wanted to go to the dance alone."

I'm saying it before I can stop myself. "Did you?" I look over at her. "Want to go alone?"

A long pause. "I," she says, and suddenly her cheeks are reddening. "Well, um. Sure, I . . ."

I've never seen Nathalie flustered before. At first it's kind of sweet, but then her elbows draw in, and she begins to look uncomfortable.

"Sorry," I say. "I'm sorry." I scrub my hand through my hair, trying to force out the tension in my scalp. "I wouldn't ask. But I'm in a weird place right now, with the stuff with my dad, and—and Hailey and I broke up. So I'm in this place where I want to, just." I motion with my hand, trying to indicate getting things out in the open. Unable to get even that simple idea out in the open.

The fluorescent bulbs overhead seem to be humming a bit more loudly. There's a squeak as Nathalie settles onto a stool.

"No," she says quietly. "I didn't want to go alone."

When I look over at her again, she's tugging at the neckline of her dress. "So you guessed," she adds. "That, um, I like you."

"Kind of. I wasn't a hundred percent sure."

"Well, I didn't want you to know at all." She lets out a frustrated breath. "I was trying to be a normal friend, because I knew you were seeing someone, and I didn't want to make—and now you're—"

"Hey. It's OK. We didn't break up because of any of that."

She sneaks a look at me.

"Promise," I say. "It was for . . ." A painful laugh works out of my throat. "Way worse-feeling reasons. So."

The blush slowly fades from Nathalie's cheeks. She considers for a while before saying, more evenly, "I'm sorry. I hear long-distance is hard, and the timing is awful, with your dad."

"Thanks. Yeah, it's been a long night."

She nods. Then, setting her shoulders back, she stands.

"I don't know how I feel," I blurt out. It's just suddenly there, between us, and my face is burning. "About you. Everything's been a lot and . . . and I just . . ."

"Niko. Hey." Nathalie steps toward me with a concerned expression. "Stop. You don't have to know, OK? I don't want anything from you that you're not sure of, even an answer. Of course that's not going to be tonight."

When she says it, it seems so obvious. "OK," I murmur.

I let out a slow breath and close my eyes. "God. Back at home, I felt like I was so good at being Hailey's boyfriend. Every conversation, everything, I could figure out the right thing to say. But the past few weeks, I feel like I'm only getting things wrong, over and over." I wince. "Sorry. Even this. Like, it's weird to be telling you this. Right?"

Nathalie moves over to my workstation and pages through my charcoal sketches. "I'm not an authority here. But if you were always giving her what you thought was the 'right' answer, it sounds like you weren't leaving much room to express yourself."

She holds up one of my sketches. It's a cherry-sized piece of wax perched on top of a papier-mâché bulb. The bulb's shadow is a black slash across a flat surface. As she examines it, she says, "Life doesn't run off a script. It's not like we're all reciting lines. If you feel like you're getting things wrong . . . OK, maybe sometimes you might mess up and hurt someone, but maybe other times you're just starting to go off-script." Nathalie lets the sketch float back down to the table and smiles. "And if you're going off-script, it's because you're making choices for yourself. And you already know how I feel about that."

"Yeah, I think I'm remembering something about not being a frictionless surface?"

"Good memory." She indicates the sketches. "What are these, by the way?"

"Sculptures by my dad. Mine and Ali's. I was going to collage them into a portrait."

"*Was* going to?"

"Yeah, I don't know how I feel about it now." I chew the inside of my cheek, considering. Ali's suitcase as a subject might really have worked, but the choice of materials was selfish. I could scrap the sketches and go for a pastel or charcoal piece of her suitcase, but that seems too straightforward compared to the other showcases. A few steps away, someone has sculpted a freakishly lifelike miniature of a colonial house from a dozen different kinds of wood, sanded and stained to perfection. At the next station down, the fragments of a shattered glass sphere have been painstakingly rearranged and individually tinted, dangling from nearly invisible filaments.

Nathalie is frowning at my empty canvas. "I don't see why that shouldn't work. Self-portraiture can feel kind of indulgent if there's no reason for it, but I think the idea of you re-creating your own image out of these sketches is powerful."

"Oh, it wasn't going to be a portrait of—of . . ."

My voice falters and dies.

I look at the blank canvas. In my mind a new image bursts over it, sharper and more vivid than my last idea ever was. I remember Meng Tao's startled face when he met my eyes—*Christ, you look exactly like Bo*—and the way I looked at myself in the mirror when I was working on that first draft, Ali's face drifting near my shoulder in my imagination.

I look over at Nathalie with something like disbelief, gratitude suddenly burning through me.

A smile tugs at the corners of her lips. "Am I responsible for just committing you to a hundred more hours locked away in here this week?"

"Yeah. That's all you."

"Oops." She considers the spread of sketches. A pause. Then she says, "I'll leave you to it, then. Want me to bring you some punch?"

I consider it. Trying to figure out what *I* want, not just what I think I should say.

I meet her eyes. "You could stay and keep me company. Tell me about Postimpressionism or whatever."

A red tinge enters the curve of her cheeks. "Or whatever," she says, fully smiling. She has a crooked canine, top left. The single strap of her dress has a knot at her shoulder, and she adjusts it when she sees me looking.

Something about the fabric makes my wheels start turning again. "Help me with something first?"

"What is it?"

"Over here," I say, leading her back toward the door, toward Ali's workstation.

# Chapter 24

ALI·TAN

It's the last day of class and once again, I'm checking myself out in the full-length mirror. Grace opens the door to my room, sees me admiring my reflection, and rolls her eyes. "You're gonna miss breakfast, Narcissus," she teases.

"OK, OK!" I say. "Don't leave without me." I grab my backpack from where it sits by the door. I'm not wearing makeup today. Once I realized that I only liked the lipstick because it made me feel more like Brook, it kind of lost its appeal. Now it's sitting at the bottom of my trash can along with some eyeshadow.

This yellow dress, though, I really like. I twirl once, enjoying the feeling of the light cotton swishing against my skin. Then I reach for Grace's hand and we walk toward the cafeteria together. We sit with Niko and his friends at breakfast.

"What's everyone getting up to after Ogilvy?" Andrew asks us.

"Surfing," says Niko through a mouthful of eggs. "If I haven't completely forgotten how by then."

"I'm fairly confident your muscle memory will let you pick up where you left off," says Nathalie, deftly stealing a slice of bacon from Niko's tray. "I'm going to catch up on college applications—I'm way behind."

Niko and I make eye contact, both suppressing smiles.

"Tennis practice starts as soon as I get back," Jen says. "Practicing backhand in one-hundred-degree weather—try not to be too jealous!"

"My family's going camping upstate," says Grace. "Kinda close to the retreat, actually."

"I'm visiting my grandparents," says Jeremiah. "How about you, Ali?"

"Hanging out here," I say. "Quality time with my grandma. Eating. I have a lot of lost dumplings to make up for." I feel ready to go home, but not because I'm homesick. I feel like I've gotten so much here, and now I want to take it all back with me. I have a bunch of ideas for new projects, and I'm planning to spend the summer working on some of those.

Besides, I've felt awful about Nai Nai being alone after I broke the news to her about my dad's death. It felt wrong to tell her on the phone but even more wrong to keep it to myself for an entire week. I also didn't want to tell her during our final showcase, when there would be people around. She's a private person. *We* are private people. So I waited until I had a quiet moment alone in my room to call her. My fingers shook as I tapped my phone to dial her. *Is this the right way to do this?* I wondered.

"Nai Nai," I said, nervous. "I have to tell you something." It felt like our roles were reversed: like I was the adult, about to tell a child bad news for the first time. "I did what you always told me not to do. I went looking for my dad."

She was silent on the other end, but I heard the tiniest intake of breath. She could tell from my tone that my news wasn't going to be good.

"I found his most recent address in Manhattan," I said. It felt weird, to say "I," erasing Niko from the story. But two bombshells at once felt like too much, and this one was the urgent one. "He—he'd been in the city the whole time. But his neighbor was there. And she told me that he died."

A deep, deep silence on the other end of the phone. I'm not sure what I expected. I've never seen her cry. I barely even see her laugh. Her face is usually placid, with a smile she breaks out mostly for me.

"Thank you for telling me," she finally said. Her voice sounded controlled, rehearsed, the way it sounds when she's talking to authority figures like my teachers or when she's asking a stranger for help. It's inorganic, a practiced voice she puts on to hide her fear that she'll look foreign, weak, her fear of being judged. Now it was me she was afraid to look weak in front of. Strange as it seemed, I felt a flood of relief, glad I'd chosen this faceless way to tell her. All she had to control was her voice; she didn't have to worry about her facial expressions or tears.

"I wish I didn't have to," I said quietly.

"I know," she said, and this sounded more like her real voice.

We sat in silence on the phone for several minutes. I knew she didn't want to talk, but I wanted her to know I was there anyway. I heard creaking, running water, the banging of pots and pans. She was doing dishes. I heard the occasional sniff over the background noise, but pretended not to. At the thought of her crying, tears ran down my face, too. I muted myself when I had to blow my nose. The only thing worse for her than crying would be her tears making *me* cry. It was weird not being able to imagine how she looked, since I'd never seen her visibly upset before.

She finally broke the silence. "So, I see your big final project when I come into Manhattan next week?"

I gladly seized on this. "Yes! I think you'll like it a lot. And my friends will be excited to meet you."

"Silly," she tsked, and now I could picture her small smile returning to her face, skin crinkling around her eyes.

So even though I'm a little nervous about how Nai Nai will be in grief, now I have something to look forward to instead.

I kiss Grace goodbye outside the cafeteria, and Niko and I head off to Art and Heritage for the last time. Now that our showcase pieces are done, I'm not sure what we'll cover today. In the middle of the room is a table with a sculpture on it, a female figure made of scrap metal, about two feet high.

"That's hers," I whisper to Niko. "Obviously, she's more known for her paintings, but she's had a career as a sculptor, too."

"I know," he says.

"How?"

"You're not the only one who knows how to google their professors, Ali."

LaTonya walks to the center of the room and raises a hand. We all quiet down immediately, and I lift my pen to hover above my notebook, ready to take notes. She smiles and looks around at all of us before she begins.

"We've spent the last five weeks on a journey of exploration. How our heritage can help us create art. Today, I want to turn the tables a little and talk to you all about how *my* past, *my* heritage has influenced my work."

I put my pen down. Somehow, I feel like writing this down won't really capture what's important. I think I just need to listen and learn. I put the binder away and prop my chin on my hands, listening intently.

"Each of my sculptures represents something different to me, and a different aspect of what I consider my heritage." She gestures at the figure on the table. "This one represents my grandmother's grandmother. She was a Haitian woman who moved to the United States shortly after the Civil War. She raised my grandmother, who in turn raised me. I never met her, but I grew up hearing stories about her and how she kept her household running with discipline and love. I feel connected to her, like I carry her legacy with me.

"I hope in this class everyone has learned something about how our pasts can serve as a source of inspiration, looking beyond the obvious to find moments and truths that have shaped who we are as people. Maybe some of you more than others." Her eyes move around the class, landing on Niko and me as she says this last bit.

LaTonya knows everything now, of course. For Niko and me to get approval for our final showcase idea, we had to come clean to her last weekend. She's agreed to keep it under wraps until the showcase tomorrow, so that the news that we're siblings will still hit Ogilvy with a splash. But now that she, all our friends, and both of our families know, Niko and I aren't feeling the pressure of secrecy anymore.

At the end of class, we're all milling around, talking about our showcases and who's planning to come from each of our families.

"Ali, can I speak to you?" LaTonya calls, and I meet her at her desk.

"I know you're local," she says.

I nod.

"I also know that your school, while . . . *competitive*"—she says this word delicately, like it's deeply distasteful—"doesn't have the same kind of artistic resources that many of the local private schools have."

I shrug. It may be true, but now I think I can do great work without all the bells and whistles of Ogilvy. After all, I did before.

"We run evening and weekend programs here during the year, for high schoolers like you," LaTonya says. "There are scholarships available, for those who qualify. Normally, your . . . unconventional . . . showcase would make it a difficult sell to the committee, but I think a strong recommendation could tip the scales in your favor. Would you be interested?"

"Absolutely!" I say. "I'm not sure who I could get a recommendation from, but I'll think about it."

LaTonya laughs. "I was offering, Ali. I think you'd be a really strong fit for the program."

The next day, at 11:00 A.M. sharp, our professors open the door to the light-flooded Ogilvy foyer, and the crowd of people who have accumulated down the sidewalk begins to filter in. The parents beeline toward their kids' pieces, but others are drifting among the showcases like museumgoers, some making notes on their phones or small paper pads. Before, the foyer was hushed, with everyone in the program standing beside their showcase displays and trying not to look nervous. Now the glass walls ring with conversation.

I crane my neck to pick out our friends. Grace's six-foot-tall canvas is turned away from the brilliant sunlight so that the film playing over her flowers doesn't get washed out. Jeremiah's small city scenes have been framed and hung from the portrait wall at the back. Not far from Niko and me, Andrew's final six photos are displayed in groups of two, each pairing a photo in nature with a photo of the city. He makes a puddle in the gutter look as huge and beautiful as the lake upstate.

I look back at the frame standing between Niko and me and take a steadying breath.

"Wow, this is unusual," says a voice. A stranger has approached us, a woman with a chin-length bob and a high-necked linen dress. "That's the pair of you, isn't it?"

"Yes," I exclaim with a touch of relief. I'd been a little worried that nobody would be able to tell what our portrait was unless Niko and I explained.

The morning after the dance, Niko found me and brought me back to the workshop and showed me what he'd done. For a minute or two I just stood in front of his station, wordless before a five-foot-wide canvas he'd found somewhere in the Ogilvy supply room.

"Do you hate it?" he said. "I can get rid of this part, if you hate it."

He waved his hand over the section of the canvas where he'd provisionally pinned components of my old showcase drafts. The textiles I'd been piecing together for his portrait. Sketches I'd balled up and tossed into the discard pile at my workstation. The ruined shreds of the canvas we destroyed together. He'd also worked in some of the sketches he'd done of our dad's sculptures, and the receipt from Eight Tastes, and even a sliver of the Ogilvy brochure that read: *ost prestigious learning opportunity for artistically inclined high-scho*

Taken together, it was a canvas that showed our faces, both looking over our shoulders, both with ambiguous expressions, both with our features partially obscured.

"I don't hate it at all," I said. Actually, for the first time in a long time, I felt a spark of real excitement. Niko's work looked *good*. The scattered components already looked chaotic and artful instead of childish.

"But," I added, "it's messy. We need to come up with a unified approach."

His face broke into a smile. "All right. We've got a week. Direct me."

And so, over the course of the week, we worked together. I had the idea that we should use Niko's sketches of our dad's work as a black-and-white base for the canvas. Both visually and thematically, our dad's work would form a kind of skeleton for us, showing the bones of the self-portrait. After the shapes of our faces and features were complete, we glossed over those sketches in polyurethane, sealing our dad away.

Then, flowering out from the center of the canvas, we set colorful pieces of the lives we've lived. I created a kind of mosaic with textiles on my side of the canvas, combing out thread to form my hair. Other pieces of fabric, I wove together with colorful hand-drawings of my high school and Nai Nai's tailoring storefront. The drawings are like the ones I made at the lake upstate. They look like their subjects. But intertwined with the fabrics, they look stranger, more broken up, more complete.

My side looked soft, dense, and bright; Niko's glossy and dark. He tinted his paper components with watercolors, snipped glittering surfboard stickers to fit the curve of his ear, and mapped high-gloss photos of his life in California over one another, his friends' outstretched hands and his parents' shoes when they dressed up for Halloween.

You can see all this when you look close. But standing several feet away, like the woman with the bob, I guess it does come through. It's us. Our big picture.

"We're siblings, but we didn't grow up together," Niko is telling her. "So, the charcoal stuff we used as a base for both portraits, that has to do with our shared parent. Kind of showing how we started with the same material."

I find myself smiling. It's a description that's so Niko. Plainspoken, but honest. But when he gives me a pleading look, I take over easily. "We planned to start with unity, then slowly layer in disruption. So, the connection point between the two portraits is single-medium and visually neat, but as you approach the border of the canvas, each new medium represents an experience that's unique to one of us. We also liked how the confines of the canvas symbolize the fact that we're young, and we've only lived so much. There are going to be so many more directions to go in the future."

As the woman scribbles in her notebook, Niko leans over and says in a quiet, amused voice, "Yeah, definitely things 'we' liked and planned."

I whisper back, "It's what you put on the canvas, whether you can describe it or not."

"Siblings who didn't grow up together," says the woman, looking up from her notes. "So, you planned to meet here and create something jointly?"

Niko and I exchange a look and a bashful grin. Then we start to explain. The woman's eyes widen. Some curious members of the crowd drift over and start to listen. And soon enough, we're describing this summer to a group of people like the one that clustered around the photographer at that gallery.

As Niko answers a question about our dad's art, my eyes find four of the Ogilvy professors prowling through the crowd as a group. LaTonya, Abbott, Rosa, and Ziegler, discussing with their heads held close together. The judging panel.

I expect for my stomach to leap with nerves, but I feel only a small squeeze. Someday, I hope there'll be a place for me in the art world. But I already know what this piece is worth, ribbon or no ribbon.

Niko's and my station stays busy for a full hour, different groups of people attracted to see what the commotion is. We field rounds and rounds of questions—but we don't stop answering until noon, when Niko's eyes land on something in the next aisle, and his smile becomes fixed.

"What?" I say, but when I glance around, I see what's caught his attention right away.

Our dad's neighbor has moved through the Ogilvy foyer and stopped at the edge of the small crowd around our piece.

"Everyone," I say, "thank you so much for your interest. We're going to take a short break." And Niko unfurls the dark cloth over our canvas that draped it this morning.

Soon the crowd has dispersed. Everyone but our dad's neighbor. She's holding a paper bag in her arms.

When she approaches us, I greet her in Mandarin. "Hi, again."

"Good morning," she says in English, to both Niko and me, before switching back to Chinese. "I brought this for you. I remembered that the woman who owns our building still had something from your dad.

**310**

They were friends; she lives on the top floor. When I told her, she insisted that you should have it."

"What is it?" I ask, my throat tight.

She reaches into the paper bag and lifts out a wooden box. The wood is beautiful, sanded smooth and stained near black. "She said he was nearly finished with it."

My breath sticks in my throat. I look over at Niko. "It's our dad's. It's a piece he was working on."

She passes it carefully into my hands. "I have to go," she says, "but it's good that I found you."

I nod. "Thank you so much."

I glance at Niko, and he says, "Thank you" in such inflectionless Chinese that the woman lets out a little laugh. Just like that, she's scooting across the foyer and gone.

Niko and I exchange a look before he lifts off the box's lid.

We both gaze down into it, not speaking. I feel something pulse inside me. I was so excited to learn my dad had a piece in the MoMA, and so excited to see his evolution. But looking at the contents of this box, what I appreciate instead is the way that this piece is still recognizably my dad's. Just like with his college work, the weirdness of the found materials makes you look twice at every component, rethinking its source, rethinking how things fit together.

He kept what was wonderful about his early pieces. It's still him, even though you can see how his work has matured. As I look over at our showcase's canvas sprawl, I think it's the same thing I've done.

Then my eyes drift to the front door, and my hands tighten on the box. Coming through the door, small and upright, is Nai Nai. She catches my eye almost immediately, and I sprint to meet her before she can set eyes on Niko, earning displeased looks from the professors milling about.

I encase her in a huge hug and lead her outside the room quickly.

"Nai Nai," I say. "There's someone I need you to meet. I didn't tell you this on the phone, earlier. I wanted to tell you in person, so you could meet him."

Her eyes widen. "Not a boyfriend?"

"No, nothing like that," I say, and then I take a deep breath. "Nai Nai, it turns out Dad had another kid. A son. His name is Niko, and I met him here at Ogilvy." I steel myself for a reaction. I'm not sure whether this will be good, neutral, or bad news to her.

Her expression stays unreadable, for a moment. Then she smiles at me. "I am *very* excited to meet this boy," she says.

I slide my arm through hers and we walk together back into the showcase room.

"Hi," I say, oddly nervous. Ali never showed me a picture of our grandma, and she looks younger than I imagined. Her shiny gray-and-black hair is permed and clipped short. Her cheeks are freckled from the sun, and shallow wrinkles diagram her face, running from the corners of her nose to her softly rounded jaw, radiating from the corners of her eyes toward her hairline.

I'd feel rude for staring, but she's studying me, too. Eventually she nods and pats me on my upper arm. "It's true. You look like my son." With that, she turns to the canvas showing our collage. "Very bright, ah?" she says. When she smiles, her dark eyes twinkle. "You are both very talented."

"We get it from you," says Ali, and though Nai Nai scoffs and waves her hand as though swatting a fly, Ali seems to take that as an invitation and gives her a one-armed hug.

"Here, let me get you a chair," I say, hurrying over to a nearby table and pulling up a folding chair so she can sit.

*Nice*, Ali mouths. Then she adds something that might be, *Filial piety!*

"Niko, will you come for dinner tomorrow?" Nai Nai asks as she settles into the chair.

"Oh, that's a great idea," Ali gushes. "We can take pictures for your parents!"

I smile. I told my parents everything the day before yesterday, when Ali and I finally crossed the finish line on our showcase. Mostly, my parents seemed baffled that I hadn't kept them up-to-date every step of the way.

"We could have helped you," said my dad. "We could have told the camp people you needed to get signed out of evening activities every night! This is much more important."

"I can't believe you were dealing with this on your own, Niko," said my mom. "I would have flown right out there to be with you. Just flown right out there."

"I know. Maybe that's why I didn't . . ." I sighed. "I needed time to figure it out myself. It's just that I've felt kind of out of place lately."

Finally, I told them the weird feelings that had been accumulating the past couple of years. I explained my friends' jokes and my breakup with Hailey, and I even told them other stories that went back to elementary school: the times that other kids tugged at the corners of their eyes or asked why my parents picked me, assuming I was adopted.

"I don't want to seem like I'm blaming you," I said quickly, realizing how long I'd been going on and how negative I sounded. "You guys are great parents. I—"

"Niko," said my dad, "it's all right."

"We had no idea this was happening," said my mom. "Sweetheart, why didn't you tell us?"

I shrugged, then said quietly, "I guess I thought it'd upset you."

I'd been right about that, too. I could see the distress on my parents' faces.

"But we wouldn't have been upset with *you*," said Dad.

I shrugged again. It hadn't seemed like an important distinction at the time. Even as an elementary schooler, I'd understood innately that if I brought this stuff up to my parents, it would make them see me differently. Suddenly I'd be a kid who was a target at school, who was really not the same as every other kid. I'd no longer be their normal son with his normal life, who could be loved in normal ways.

Even sitting at my desk in front of the camera, I felt weirdly exposed, like I was revealing a side of me that my parents had never seen before.

"I just didn't want to turn into this thing you had to worry about," I said.

My mom seemed to be pulling herself together. "Well, from now on, no more of that, OK? We want to know about these things."

I nodded and sneaked a guilty look at the camera. "Could you also . . ." I took a deep breath. It was something Nathalie had suggested bringing up, but it felt so wrong to know what they'd poured into my childhood and ask them to change how they acted. "Could you maybe ease up on the stuff where you tell me I'm exactly like Justin and Anastasia? Because—I get it, I'm sure you see me that way. But they're never going to deal with any of this."

"Of course," Dad said right away, although Mom flinched. She'd mostly been the one making those kinds of reassurances. Dad's hand found Mom's arm and squeezed. "Maybe we could google some more about all this, too. Right, Ceels?"

My mom nodded. "Of course."

The call was subdued there for a little bit, but it got better. By the end, Mom was gasping with excitement over the idea of meeting Ali and Nai Nai—even pitched the idea of flying them out to Landry Beach for

Christmas. And after hanging up, I promised by text that I'd send them family photos.

Ali, Nai Nai, and I spend the next half hour or so getting into the rhythm of conversation. Nai Nai asks questions about how school is for me, about what I like to do, and about California. She seems enthusiastic about the beach and tells Ali and me a story about how when our dad was a kid, they all took a trip to Thailand. "The water was beautiful," she says, closing her eyes. "Your father spent hours collecting leaves on the beach. He liked the way they looked, he said."

Ali asks a few probing questions about our father, in a careful but hungry way that makes me certain these are things she's wanted to ask for years. Nai Nai answers, and slowly the picture of our father starts to take shape—our grandfather's steady but unglamorous work in manufacturing, our father's childhood dreams of leaving Shenyang. It leaves me wondering about her own life. She's still here. She's the one who sacrificed to support Ali, who raised Ali. I want to know her story.

Ali has dragged Andrew over to our display to photograph us. "Smile," Andrew says as he adjusts the phone, holding it as precisely as though it were a film camera. I smile, knowing that with him in charge, it'll be a perfect shot.

Andrew and I have spent the last week having some pretty deep roommate conversations. Last night, as we were lying awake after lights-out, he told me with a weird kind of pride that I was the first person he'd ever yelled at.

"Um, congrats," I said, grinning at the darkened ceiling.

"Thanks! I *do* get mad at stuff," he mused, "but I think usually I sort of go away with it and turn it into getting depressed. That's not great, right? Doesn't seem great. So I feel like it's good to practice being angry."

"Bro, our fight lasted like, twenty hours."

"OK, so next time we can schedule one that's like, two days. Sound good? And then I can work up to holding an actual grudge. Or living with a lifetime of resentment. Not at you! But like, at someone who deserves it."

I laughed, and Andrew shushed me. Abbott's footsteps were clicking down the hallway.

As much as Andrew clearly can't hold a grudge, I think a couple of things helped us get past the fight. For one, he actually *did* hook up with someone at Ogilvy. He didn't tell me this until a couple of days ago, but the night of the dance, he stayed until the very end and, around eleven, wound up making out with some first-year girl from Manhattan.

"What?" I practically shouted in the courtyard when he told me. "What the shit, Andrew! Why didn't you say?"

"Because." He made a face. "It was the worst experience I've ever had with my mouth. I had no idea tongues could move like that. Oh my God? I'm thinking of doing a photo series inspired by it, like, by photographing the earthworm birthing process."

Despite his descriptions only getting worse from there, there was a jaunty way he walked that made me pretty sure he didn't mind *that* much. Or at least, he didn't mind all the questions I asked.

The other factor that's probably helped keep things smooth with Andrew and me is the fact that Nathalie and I didn't jump right into something. Looking back at the first few weeks, I think some of what I'd been feeling toward Nathalie was appreciation for the parts of her that differ from Hailey. She was interested in my art, she took everything seriously, she asked me about my feelings, she cared about my questions about being half-Chinese. But I'm starting to realize that Hailey should have done some of those things—any girlfriend should have.

So I'm trying to tease things apart. Trying to figure out whether I really do like Nathalie or just this concept of a more equal relationship. It's hard to be sure, when I still sometimes wake up and think about the way Hailey touched me, or the secretive smile she used to give me.

But yesterday, for the first time since the upstate trip, Nathalie and I sat beside each other in Abstracting the Figure, our last class together. And when Abbott took the lights down and set the projector up, I was suddenly aware of her posture beside me and the hint of her perfume, like vanilla and oranges. I was measuring the distance, thinking how I could have reached out and touched her.

I look at her now, one row over, standing with hands clasped behind her back, a dark linen dress waterfalling down her frame. Her showcase looms over her: a series of abstracts painted onto eight planks of wood, each one eight feet tall, each one representing in a swirl of formless color one of Erik Erikson's eight stages of psychosocial development. She's answering an elderly woman's questions, but catches my eye and smiles. I feel something warm in my stomach and smile back, and for just a moment, I'm feeling the ways something like this could be wonderful. Not just because she'd listen to me or care about me, but simply because she's Nathalie: steady and brilliant, articulate and honest, intimidating and reasonable. Herself.

My phone brings me back to myself with a *ding*! My parents have reacted with emojis and exclamations to Andrew's photo of me, Ali, and

Nai Nai, and suddenly my curiosity expands. When I get back home, maybe I'll ask my parents more about their pasts, too. It's like I'm zooming out from the world, suddenly seeing trails that my family has left over continents and oceans, wanting to know how we all wound up here.

"Mrs. Tan," says a familiar slow, warm voice. I glance up from my phone to find the panel of professor judges approaching our showcase, LaTonya at the forefront. She's in a rippling blue blouse today, which matches the wrap she's wearing over her hair. "I'm LaTonya Sherman. It's wonderful to meet you. And it's been a pleasure to teach your grandchildren this year."

A smile tugs at my lips. My mom has this habit of reading out nice comments from teachers on report cards. Anastasia is always *a pleasure to teach*. I have never been a pleasure to teach, until now.

"Thank you," says Nai Nai. "Ali is very hard worker. I'm sure Niko is, too."

I grimace and open my mouth to correct her, but LaTonya says, "Yes, he's been one of the hardest-working students in the program this year." Her eyes play over the canvas, their mysterious twinkle brighter than ever. "We're all very proud of that work, and relieved that Niko didn't slip through the admissions office's cracks, as talent often can . . . I am exceptionally glad Arthur here felt so strongly about Niko's portfolio."

*Arthur?* I think, and when LaTonya indicates Professor Abbott, I can't help it. My mouth drops open.

For the first time in five weeks, I see a smile pulling at one corner of Professor Abbott's mouth. "Very good, Castadi," he says in that cold, disinterested voice, with a dismissive wave of his hand. "Carry on."

As the judging panel continues down the aisle to the next project, Ali starts laughing at my expression, and I get my face in order. I wonder for the first time if I could take more art classes outside of school. Probably not in Landry Beach, but maybe I could drive up to San Diego or something. Take a sculpture class, or an animation class—Professor Abbott's lectures on animation are still bouncing around in my mind.

Extra classes. For fun. I can already imagine someone at school making fun of me for coming back from camp as an actual nerdy Asian, but I'm surprised to find that the thought doesn't bother me.

"Nai Nai," says Ali, reaching below our display table, "we wanted to show you something."

"What's that?"

She withdraws the box that holds our dad's last project. I take the box from her, holding it steady while Ali works the heavy lid out of place.

Nai Nai's face slackens. Her breath catches in her throat, making the loose skin at her chin wobble.

The piece is a diorama, precisely detailed. It's a small, two-bedroom home set over a single floor—an apartment, I think. In the kitchen, pots are stacked on the stove, hand-carved from walnut shells. In one bedroom, a twin bed is covered with a scrap of cotton sheeting that's been colored with an ink pen so that its pinstripes look proportionally tiny. Minuscule shoes are lined by the door: seashells.

Holding the front door open is a woman with dark hair and an impeccably tailored dress, made from a small silken drawstring bag. There's no one on the other side, and the woman—cut from a delicate pink sponge—doesn't have facial features, but something about her posture looks welcoming to me. Somehow I know it's Nai Nai.

"His neighbor said he was working on it not long before he died," Ali says, her voice thin and shaky. "I don't know what he might have wanted to do with it, but . . ."

I offer the box to Nai Nai. She takes it and stands slowly, running one hand over the wood and down into the delicate scene within.

Then, gently, she sets the box on the table beside our showcase piece and gathers Ali and me into an embrace. She doesn't have to speak. I understand. Maybe he was planning to reconcile with his mother. Maybe he was just reminiscing. It's one more thing we'll never know, but what we have is enough.

# Chapter 26

I'm back in the apartment where I grew up, in the kitchen, and the room is full of the smell of frying garlic. Niko and Grace are here, too, having come back from Ogilvy with me and Nai Nai. A trickle of sweat runs down my forehead, despite the wide-open window behind me. Jessie and Elise insisted on coming over and meeting my "new camp friends," so now all five of us kids are packed around the table.

After the showcase finished yesterday, the final day passed in a rush. I packed hastily, needing two extra shopping bags to carry all my new purchases home. I congratulated Brook—she ended up winning the Alicia Barry Award, to no one's surprise.

"You really deserve it," I told her, and meant it. Things had been tense for the last week. I pretended that I didn't know that Grace turned down Brook, but I could still sense her hurt feelings, which she tried to hide by being extra know-it-all-y. Fortunately, she'll never know how close I came to submitting a rip-off of her idea. I cringe thinking about it, and feel a touch of relief to have left the intensity of Ogilvy behind, for now.

"This is my favorite smell in the entire world," I say, more for Niko and Grace's benefit.

"We *know*," Jessie says. "I honestly don't know how you didn't waste away all summer without this cooking. You're so spoiled."

"I realize that now, after five weeks of mystery meat," I say.

"It wasn't *that* bad," Niko says.

"Excuse me, it absolutely was that bad," says Grace.

"Truly, I suffered more than anyone else this summer, though," says Jessie. "I count on your Nai Nai for all my delicious meals, and I didn't get to go to art camp."

"It's not a camp," Niko and Grace say in unison, in a mocking tone.

I roll my eyes. Elise and Jessie look amused but don't even need to ask them to explain the joke: They can imagine that sentence perfectly well in my voice.

Nai Nai hurries back and forth to the stove with more and more dishes in hand, doling out hearty portions to everyone.

At long last, she sits down. Niko begins to pepper her with questions. She insisted on hosting Niko tonight, since he flies back to California tomorrow. He moved his flight specially to have an extra night in the city before heading back, and I'm so excited to show him my neighborhood.

"So when did you move to the US, Nai Nai?" he says. It's hilarious hearing him call her that, but there was no question of him calling her anything else.

"Thirty years ago," she says.

"And did you move straight here, or did you live somewhere else first?"

"Brooklyn first," she says. "Then Queens, after a couple years."

I didn't know that about her. I realize how much there is I don't know about her life before me. I never wanted to ask her before, because it was all tied up in the story of my dad, his leaving, and their estrangement. Now it feels like everything is out in the open, and there's so much I want to learn. And so much I want to tell her about myself and my life, too. I want to tell her everything about my summer at camp, what it was like chasing around the city looking for our dad's art, the struggle of being artistically blocked for the first time, and the roller coaster of falling for Grace. I haven't told Nai Nai who Grace is to me yet, but our bond has been tested this summer and proven to be strong. I feel like nothing can truly shake our family unit.

I look at Grace across the table. She seems perfectly at home with Jessie and Elise, asking them questions about their summers, making appropriately horrified faces when Jessie talks about her lab mice. Once I realized I was ready to tell Ah Mah, I didn't feel the need to hide Grace from my friends, either. When I texted them that I had a girlfriend at camp, they responded with a string of excited GIFs and insisted on meeting her as soon as possible.

After dinner, we go out for bubble tea and walk around, grateful for the slight breeze that cools our sweaty skin and brings all the familiar city smells back to me: the smell of frying oil from one of the food stands, a waft of hot garbage, a brief moment of exhaust from the bus pulling away.

I breathe in deep, glad to be home.

Grace hands her bubble tea to me and we swap.

"I'm gonna miss you," I say. "I can't believe you didn't invite me on your family's camping trip."

"Very funny," she says. "I wouldn't wish a week without showers on you. I know how you feel about that."

"Guilty as charged."

"You have plenty of time to meet them," she assures me. "You can come over for dinner as soon as we're back. They'll love you."

I squeeze her hand and am about to tell her how glad I am that we met, when I feel something hit the back of my head. I turn and see a tapioca pearl hit the ground with a splat.

Niko, Jessie, and Elise are all laughing, but it's obvious who the guilty culprit is because he's hiding behind the other two. I turn and chase him down the street.

"I'm gonna get you back!" I scream. "Just wait, I'm going to empty this whole thing on your head!"

I pursue him for half a block before it's obvious that my short legs will never close the gap, and he slows to let me catch up. Before I can make good on my threat to douse him in my bubble tea, he snatches it out of my hand and takes a sip.

"It's good," he says, and hands it back.

"Ugh, you've contaminated my perfectly delicious drink," I grumble, but he hands me his to try as well. I hold both cups in my hand, sipping out of each contentedly.

We walk in silence for a few minutes, then suddenly Niko looks at his watch. His spine straightens and he seems to grow two full inches as an idea hits him.

"It's only nine P.M.," he says.

"I, too, can tell time," I say, waiting for him to get to the point.

"It's not *that* late. What if we took Grace and your friends into Manhattan? To see our dad's piece?"

"Is that crazy?" Before he can answer, I say, "It's crazy. Let's do it!" I take a final slurp of my bubble tea and slam the container into the nearest trash can.

The five of us bundle onto the subway station as I hastily text Nai Nai that we'll be home late.

"I hope they like it as much as we do," Niko says anxiously under his breath, audible only to me over the roar of the subway.

"They'll love it," I say. "I know what you mean, though. It's weird when parts of your life collide. All you can do is hope that the things and people that mean the most to you will mean a lot to the people who care about you."

He squints at me. "You're not talking about art anymore, are you?"

"I'm talking about finding a new brother and bringing him home to meet my grandma, obviously," I say.

"*Our* grandma," he says lightly, rapping me on the head.

After we exit the subway, as we make our way through Chinatown toward Eight Tastes, I feel a thrill rise up and I, too, wonder what my friends will think of the piece. But we needn't have worried. When we stop in front of the restaurant's renovated façade, they're as entranced as we were, drawn in by the brightness, the variety in the textures. Grace reaches out and lightly runs a finger over one of the envelopes, then takes my hand in hers as we silently admire it.

"I like it," Jessie says, serious for once. "It reminds me of you. Is that weird?"

I blush. I'm pretty sure she's just trying to be nice.

"I'm sorry about your dad," Elise says, more quietly. "I wish it had turned out differently. This is so beautiful. I feel like he would have been proud of who you've become."

"Thanks, guys," I say, staring straight ahead and working very hard to keep my voice from cracking.

We stand in silence a little longer, and then Jessie reluctantly begins to head back to the subway, the others following. It's getting late.

Niko and I hang back, looking at the sculpture one last time together.

Tonight's been a converging of worlds; my art friends visiting my Chinese community; my new friends and old friends mingling effortlessly; my world and Niko's joining under our grandmother's roof. Our dad's piece feels like the last part of the puzzle, a last bit of me—of *us*—that's both old and new. He feels real to me now, more flawed than I'd imagined him, but more tangible. His story is part of my story—part of both of our stories—but it's only the beginning.

I lean forward and my nose and forehead brush the cool brick. I inhale, and for just one moment, I believe I detect clay and glue, the scent I remember of him. Then the fleeting memory gives way to the scent of sizzling garlic from the restaurant, and I become aware of shouts from the kitchen and chatter from the people at the tables inside. I remember our friends are waiting, and I step back, into the present. Niko puts one hand on my shoulder and puts his other hand flat against the wall, in a reverie of his own.

"I'm glad you brought me here," he says finally, turning to me.

I smile at him. "I'm glad to share it with you," I say, and I mean it wholeheartedly. "Come on, let's go home."

# Acknowledgments

First, we'd both like to thank our amazing team, who helped this book become a reality: Caryn, Anne, Erum, and Laura. Thanks also to our first reader, Merry. We owe you a bowl of wonton soup.

(From Rioghnach:) Thanks always to my friends and loved ones: Hunter, Noelle, Anne, Rose, & the O'Briens, Li An, Kshipra, Liam, Dyer, Chelsea, Sarah, Nina, Scott, Ben, Aaron, Lilith, Emma, Foss, and Piper. Many hugs to my friends in writing, Mackenzi, Bri, Justin, Janet, Traci, Emily, Elliot, and Becky. You are all five-star human beings. And lastly, thank you to Sam. I am also sorry about Niko's beagle, and it was my fault.

(From Siofra:) Thank you to my nearest and dearest for believing in me, and especially to my Chicago crew for getting me through long winters and short deadlines. Thanks most of all to Sam. I really am sorry about Niko's beagle. It wasn't my fault.

Finally, a huge thank-you from both of us to our family, especially Mom and Dad, for all your support over the years and ~~bad~~ great jokes.